SENTINEL
MAGE

THE
SENTINEL MAGE
EMILY GEE

SOLARIS

First published 2011 by Solaris
an imprint of Rebellion Publishing Ltd,
Riverside House, Osney Mead,
Oxford, OX1 0ES, UK

www.solarisbooks.com

UK ISBN: 978 1 907519 49 9

Map by Pye Parr

10 9 8 7 6 5 4 3 2

A CIP catalogue record for this book is available from the
British Library.

Designed & typeset by Rebellion Publishing

Printed in the UK

In memory of Katy,
who died January 7th 2010

And with deep thanks to M and M
for their hospitality and generosity.

CHAPTER ONE

JAUMÉ WAS IN his father's barn when the curse broke free of its dormancy on the easternmost rim of the Seven Kingdoms. As it burst into life, shadows settled like dark stains on every man, every woman, every child in the kingdoms. No one noticed; these were shadows only mages could see, and the Seven Kingdoms had purged itself of witchcraft centuries ago.

The curse began its slow, inevitable creep westward, passing through the fishing village of Girond. Grains of soil trembled as it passed, blades of grass quivered faintly, and the water in wells and creeks seemed to shiver for a moment. Girond's inhabitants knew nothing about magic and they couldn't see the shadows that lay over them. No one realized anything was wrong until it was too late.

Jaumé was playing in the loft. He burrowed deep in the straw, digging with his hands, wriggling and twisting, holding his breath, and then the straw parted between his scrabbling fingers and he looked down at his little sister, Rosa.

Rosa sat cross-legged in a patch of sunlight, singing. Jaumé gulped for breath and watched as she arranged the dolls in her lap. Four dolls, a family.

Da had carved them in the evenings while Rosa slept, and then he'd painted smiling faces on them and glued wool to their smooth wooden heads, and Mam had stitched clothes out of scraps of fabric.

Jaumé began to burrow backwards. It was harder this way—

The door swung open. It slapped lightly against the wall and stayed there, shivering on its hinges. Rosa stopped singing. "Da?"

Jaumé peered through the straw. He saw his father's curly brown hair and the scarred blacksmith's apron and—

Blood. Blood on the thick leather apron. Blood streaking his father's forearms. Blood staining his mouth and chin.

"Da?" Rosa said again, her voice thin and uncertain.

Da's lips curled back from his teeth. He reached down and grabbed Rosa by the hair and lifted her off the floor. The dolls tumbled to the ground.

Jaumé lay frozen in the straw. He couldn't breathe, couldn't utter a sound, couldn't move.

His sister began to scream, high-pitched.

The scream broke through Jaumé's immobility. He pushed backwards, bursting free of the straw, scrambling across the rough floorboards. Panic bubbled inside him. He pushed headfirst out the small window, tumbled down the shingle roof, and fell to the ground.

Rosa's scream stopped abruptly.

Jaumé stayed where he was for a moment, panting, sobbing, his face pressed into the dirt, and then he pushed to his feet and began to run, around the back of the barn, through the yard, scattering hens, up the shallow stone steps to the kitchen.

He barreled through the door. "Mam!" His voice was as shrill as Rosa's had been.

Mam lay on the floor with the clothes torn from her body. The kitchen stank of her blood.

Jaumé stood, gulping for breath. The wooden floorboards seemed to tilt beneath his feet. Silence filled his head, echoing, so loud it was almost deafening—

A flurry of squawks erupted from the yard.

Da's coming for me.

Jaumé ran through the kitchen, his bare feet slipping in Mam's blood, and into the front room. He shoved at the door, wrenching the latch open, and then he was outside, running so hard it felt as if his heart would burst.

It was only a quarter of a mile to Girond. He ran it blindly, panic blurring his vision. It wasn't until he reached the first house that he realized something was wrong.

The door hung slightly open, crooked on its hinges, and in the middle of the whitewashed planks of timber—a handprint in blood.

Jaumé shied off the road. He scrambled over the stone wall into Farmer Gabre's cornfield and pressed himself flat to the ground. For long minutes he heard nothing but his own heart beating. The sound filled his head, squeezing out everything else.

Gradually his heartbeat slowed. Other sounds returned. Birds sang. A dog barked. The corn plants rustled in the breeze. Everyday noises. And beneath them—

A woman screamed.

Jaumé rolled over. He looked up at the sky. It was the bright blue of early autumn. High overhead, seagulls wheeled and soared.

He inhaled, his breath catching in his throat like a sob, and then froze. Someone was running towards the village. A man, grunting with each step.

He knew it was Da.

The stone wall seemed to shrink, to become made of nothing. He waited for the footsteps to stop. For Da to find him.

The runner passed.

Jaumé lay for several minutes not daring to move, breathing shallowly, smelling dust, smelling wood smoke and the stink of curing fish, smelling the scent of Mam's blood. Then he rolled onto his belly and crawled deeper into the cornfield, burrowing as he'd burrowed in the straw, hiding.

JAUMÉ STAYED IN the cornfield until night fell, then he scrambled back over the stone wall. The village was burning. Flames leapt from the thatched roofs. Figures moved, silhouetted against the blazing houses. He heard yelps of laughter, like something from an animal's throat.

He ran away from Girond, barefoot and quiet, on the very edge of the road, pressed against the forest, heading west. Thirst burned in his throat, in his chest. The creek flowed on the other side of the road, but he dared not drink, dared not even get close to it.

Those who drink the water shall thirst for blood. They shall be as wild beasts.

The tales he'd heard all his life were true. The curse was real, and if he drank from the creek it would take him too.

CHAPTER TWO

THE DIPLOMATIC SEAL had brought them this far: into Osgaard's marble palace with an escort of armed guards, along echoing corridors where nobles stared openly and bondservants wearing the iron armbands of slavery cast cringing glances at them, into the throne room to stand before the king and his heir.

King Esger sat on his throne like a bull, thick-necked and massive with fat. Prince Jaegar sat beside him, bullish too. Both men had ash-blond hair and silver-gray eyes. Their expressions matched their coloring: cold.

Dareus had said they would walk out of the palace, that there'd be no need for bloodshed—but Innis knew he was wrong. The king's pale eyes, flat with hostility, told her that. Like everyone in the Seven Kingdoms he saw them as monsters, abominations from across the sea.

He wants us dead.

King Esger and his heir wore golden crowns. The crowns didn't rest on their heads; they were bound there, woven in place by their own long hair. Innis averted her gaze. The crowns seemed to grow from the king's head, from his son's, like misshapen antlers.

Guards flanked the throne, standing to attention. Their uniforms were gaudy—gold breastplates over scarlet tunics, loops of gold braiding—but the men were fighters, their arms corded with muscle. Sharp-edged swords hung at their sides.

Curse shadows shrouded the guards, a promise of coming death. The shadows lay on her, too, now that she'd set foot in the Seven Kingdoms. Innis saw them clearly—as if a veil of black cobwebs had been thrown over each person in the throne room—but the guards couldn't see them. They stared ahead, stony-faced. She'd caught one looking sideways at her as they'd walked through the corridors, the ceilings resonating with the sound of booted feet. The expression on his face had been easy to read: fear, revulsion. If not for the diplomatic seal, he'd have killed them without hesitation.

Innis counted the exits silently: the wide double doors at the far end and the smaller doors along the sides of the room, all decorated with gold leaf.

Six doors and a score of guards. *And four of us.*

Only the silver disk around Dareus's neck, stamped with the seals of kings half a world away, kept King Esger from ordering them dead. It seemed insubstantial protection, as puny as a child's wooden shield against a battle-axe.

Tapestries stitched with gold thread hung on the walls. Between them, gilded mirrors were suspended, so tall they reached nearly to the ceiling. Innis saw herself in one, elongated and twisted slightly to the right. Beside her were Cora and Petrus, and one pace in front, Dareus. The mirror didn't show the magic that was buried deep within them, the fire inside

Dareus and Cora, the animal forms within Petrus and herself—lion, wolf, hawk.

They stood silently, waiting. Innis tried to be still, tried to not shift her weight, but it was unnerving to be surrounded by so much hatred. *They'd behead us if they could, dismember us, burn us.* Her heart beat too fast. Magic was a low hum beneath her skin. She wanted to grab hold of it, to change her body into something less vulnerable.

Footsteps echoed in the throne room. A young man dressed in brown with a royal's long hair entered, and one pace behind him, a guard in scarlet and gold wearing the silver torque of a personal armsman.

Her nervousness intensified. *This is it. Don't make a mistake.*

For a brief moment she heard the voices in her head again, the councilors debating: *She's too young to be a Sentinel. Her inexperience will jeopardize the mission.* Innis pushed the voices aside. She drew a deep breath and measured the distance to the nearest guard, preparing herself for what might come.

"Father." The newcomer bowed. He was dressed plainly in a shirt and trews and huntsman's boots. He'd come from the practice ground, Innis guessed. Wrestling. A few grains of sawdust clung to his trews. He had no sword belted around his waist and wore no golden crown; instead his brown hair was tied simply at the nape of his neck.

King Esger turned his gaze to Dareus. "Prince Harkeld. As you requested."

The prince looked at Dareus, at the close-clipped gray beard and the plain traveler's clothes, at the diplomatic seal, heavy and silver around his neck, and then glanced briefly at the three of them, standing behind. "You wish to speak with me?"

"Yes."

The differences between the two princes were obvious: dark brown hair instead of ash-blond, hazel eyes instead of gray, sun-browned skin instead of pale. There was nothing bullish about Prince Harkeld, he was lighter on his feet, leaner, but he had the same strong jaw as his half-brother, the same strong nose and brow, the same strong, square hands.

"And you are?" the prince asked.

Dareus bowed. "We are from Rosny, sire. In the Allied Kingdoms."

"They're witches," King Esger said. "Come all the way across the ocean to speak with you."

Shock flared in Prince Harkeld's eyes. He stepped back a pace. His face twisted for a second—revulsion, fear—and then settled into an expression as hostile as his father's. He glanced at the diplomatic seal. His jaw tightened. "Then speak."

Dareus bowed again. "You've heard of the Ivek Curse, Prince Harkeld?"

"A peasants' tale." The prince's voice was curt, dismissive. "To frighten children."

"No tale, your highness." Dareus shook his head. "The curse spreads in water. In lakes and rivers, in town wells. Those who drink become monsters. Mothers eat their babies' flesh. Fathers violate their children and then slaughter them—"

"A peasants' tale," the prince said again. "If this is what you wish to talk to me about—"

"The curse has risen on Vaere's eastern coast," Dareus said. "Unless it's broken it will roll across the Seven Kingdoms like a tide. It will claim this continent. Every village and town."

The prince shrugged, his disbelief evident. "Why come to me?"

Innis glanced at King Esger. He was leaning forward slightly, his eyes on Prince Harkeld. The king's expression arrested her attention. The back of her neck prickled as tiny hairs stood on end. *He hates his son.*

"Because you are the only person who can break the curse."

Prince Harkeld laughed. "Your wits are addled, witch." He turned to the king. "Father, must I listen to this nonsense—"

King Esger silenced him with a flick of his hand. "Listen."

The prince turned back to face Dareus. Anger colored his cheeks.

"The curse can only be broken by someone of royal birth. A direct descendent of the house of Rutersvard."

"So? I'm hardly the only—"

"Someone who also has mage blood."

Fury flared on Prince Harkeld's face. He took a step towards Dareus. "How dare you—"

"Your mother's father was a mage," Dareus said.

Prince Harkeld halted. His face blanched white. Shock rustled through the throne room. The guards stirred. Prince Jaegar jerked back. Only the king sat unmoved.

Innis's magic spiraled closer to the surface. She braced herself for whatever came next.

Prince Harkeld swung round to face the king. "Father?"

Prince Jaegar's expression was exultant. He laughed aloud. "Witch blood!" He leaned forward, his expression hardening into hatred. "Get out of this palace—"

King Esger halted him with a raised hand. "No." The king wasn't looking at either of his sons, he was looking at Dareus. "Harkeld is useful. Isn't he, witch?"

Prince Harkeld swallowed. His face was pale.

"He's the only person who can break the Ivek curse," Dareus said.

"My son... or his blood?"

Foreboding gathered in Innis's chest, squeezing her lungs.

"His blood."

King Esger smiled. He sat back and folded his hands over his stomach. "Harkeld will do it."

The foreboding evaporated. Innis drew in a deep breath. Relief made her almost feel lightheaded. Dareus had been correct—they'd walk out of here. There'd be no bloodshed.

Dareus bowed. "Thank you, your highness."

"Once certain conditions have been met."

"Conditions?"

"Payment for my son's services. For his blood."

"Payment? Your highness, I have no—"

"Not from you," King Esger said. "From my fellow kings. They shall pay for Harkeld's blood."

Innis took a shallow breath. The foreboding was back, clenching in her chest.

"But your highness. I have no authority to negotiate—"

"That's what ambassadors are for," the king said.

"But your highness, there's no time—"

"There's plenty of time," King Esger said dismissively. "Where's the curse now? Vaere's east coast? More than a thousand leagues from here."

"People are already dying in Vaere." Dareus took a step towards the king.

One of the guards flanking the throne drew his sword.

Innis shifted her weight, standing on the balls of her feet. Her heart was beating fast, her magic close to the surface, tingling on her fingertips.

Dareus stood his ground. "Thousands will die if we wait, your highness. Tens of thousands."

"Then I'm certain the other kingdoms will be happy to meet my terms." King Esger turned his head to one side, dismissing them. "You may leave now."

Not without the prince. Innis took a deep breath, ready to move at Dareus's signal.

Prince Harkeld spoke. "Father."

King Esger looked at his younger son. Displeasure was evident on his face.

When Prince Harkeld had entered the throne room he'd had the arrogance of a king's son; he no longer did. Gone was the easy confidence, the pride. His skin was pale with shock, and beneath the shock was something that looked like fear.

You are right to be afraid, Innis told him silently. *You're one of us now, an abomination. They'd kill you if they could.*

Muscles worked in Prince Harkeld's throat as he swallowed. "Father, I must break the curse as soon as possible—"

"Be silent." It was a command, flat and final.

"But—"

"Or I shall have your tongue cut out."

Prince Harkeld closed his mouth. Innis saw on his face the realization that his father hated him.

"The curse will reach Osgaard," Dareus said into the silence.

The king shrugged. "Not for many months. And I have the means of stopping it before it does."

"But whole kingdoms will be emptied!"

King Esger smiled slightly, his cheeks pouching. "I'm aware of that."

There was a moment of stillness, of silence. Innis stared at the king. Disbelief grew inside her. No one could be that—

"You intend to use the curse to increase Osgaard's wealth?" Dareus asked. His voice was uninflected, without censure.

King Esger shrugged lightly. "It's my duty to expand Osgaard's territory." He lifted a hand from his belly, waved it in dismissal. "You may go now."

Dareus didn't move. "It will be the worst kind of butchery, your highness."

King Esger lost his smile. He straightened on his throne. "Get out of my palace."

Innis tensed. She took hold of her magic. Clarity expanded in her mind. She inhaled, feeling magic running under her skin, stinging—

"No, Father!" Prince Harkeld stepped forward. "Osgaard loses its honor if you do this. I won't allow it!"

"Allow?" King Esger laughed, a loud crack of sound. He leaned forward on the throne, hatred twisting his face. "You'll do as you're ordered! You are nothing here. Nothing!"

Prince Harkeld shook his head. "I refuse to wait."

Silence stretched in the throne room, tight and brittle, and then King Esger sat back in his throne. "If you disobey me, I'll place a traitor's bounty on your head."

Prince Harkeld stood his ground. "If you kill me, the curse can't be broken."

The king smiled, his lips stretching across his teeth. "I don't need you alive," he told his son. "I only need your blood."

"Prince Harkeld's hand must touch the anchor stones," Dareus said. "Or else the curse can't be broken."

King Esger glanced at him. "Yes. But Harkeld doesn't need be attached to his hands, does he? He doesn't even need to be alive."

Prince Jaegar stirred. Innis glanced at him. He was watching his half-brother. His mouth moved, as if he savored a sweet taste on his tongue.

"The choice is yours," the king said. "Your obedience—or I take your blood and your hands."

Prince Harkeld swallowed. He touched his hip, as if reaching for a sword—but he wore no sword belt.

Dareus glanced back over his shoulder. He raised his hand, a tiny gesture. *Now.*

Innis inhaled deeply. She let the magic rush through her body. "I choose honor," *she heard Prince Harkeld say.* "I'll have no part in your—"

She held the image of what she wanted to be firmly in her mind—a lioness—and changed. There was a dizzying second when she was neither one thing nor the other, when magic poured through her, stinging, a sensation close to pain, and then everything

*was solid and real again. Scent and sound rushed
at her: the sharp smell of fear, the hiss of swords
being drawn from gilded scabbards, the scrape of
hobnailed boots as the guards scrambled to protect
their king and his heir.*

*"Kill it!" Fear made King Esger's voice shrill. "Kill
the witch!"*

*A guard brandished his sword at her. The blade
was trembling.*

"Kill Harkeld!" King Esger cried. "Kill them all!"

*Prince Harkeld's personal armsman, the torque
gleaming silver at his throat, raised his sword, his
eyes on the prince.*

*Innis charged past the guard, bunching her
muscles, leaping. In her human form she would
have been too late; as a lion, she was swifter than the
armsman. She struck the man with her full weight,
propelling him backwards. He dropped his sword as
he fell. It spun across the floor and struck the wall
with a loud clang.*

Another lion roared. Innis glanced back. Petrus
stood with Dareus and Cora. He was a lion, silver-
maned and deep-chested. A dozen guards faced him,
swords drawn, protecting their king and his heir.
The rest faced her and Prince Harkeld. Eight men.
Her lion eyes saw their fear: the wide pupils, the
sweat, the rapid beating of their pulses.

"Guards, kill them!" King Esger screamed.

Men ran to obey, swords raised and fear in their
eyes. Innis crouched, ready to leap.

Petrus roared. He charged at the guards, scattering
them. Innis felt the hiss of fire magic over her pelt as
Dareus and Cora unleashed their magic. The guards'

tunics began to smolder. One of the tapestries on the wall burst into flames.

Petrus rounded on a guard, knocking him down, opening the man's cheek with razor-sharp claws. The smell of blood suddenly filled her nose.

Petrus turned to the next man. He roared again.

All the tapestries along one side of the throne room were alight. Flames swept towards the high, golden ceiling. The mirror frames burned, gilt melting from the wood. One crashed to the marble floor, spraying splinters of glass and burning wood across the throne room.

And above it all—lion's roar and crackling flame—was King Esger's voice: "Kill them! Kill Harkeld!"

Innis turned to Prince Harkeld. He stepped back, holding up a hand to ward her off.

I won't hurt you, she tried to tell him. *I'm here to protect you.* The sound was a grunt, almost a mew. The prince didn't understand it. He kept backing away. His foot caught on the clothes she'd worn. He glanced down and then sharply back at her. She saw the depth of his fear, of his revulsion.

Dareus ran past her. He took the prince by the elbow. "We must get out of here!"

Innis glanced at the throne. The guards' clothes were on fire. Breastplates clanged on the marble floor as they tore off their uniforms. Behind them was King Esger, livid, screaming.

Cora ran past, flames trickling from her fingertips. Petrus was suddenly alongside her, smelling of blood. He butted her shoulder, telling her to hurry.

Another mirror smashed to the floor. The roar of flames was loud. And louder than that was King

Esger's voice. "Kill Harkeld!" he shrieked. "Don't let him escape!"

CHAPTER THREE

HARKELD WRENCHED FREE of the witch's grip. "No. This way." The tall double doors would only lead them to the main corridor and more guards. He headed for one of the side doors at a run.

The gray-haired witch followed. Harkeld didn't look to see whether the others came. Grotesque perversions of human and animal. Better that they died in the throne room.

He wrenched the door open. The corridor was plain, low-ceilinged and unadorned. A bondservants' corridor.

Harkeld ran. The door slammed shut behind him. Footsteps echoed in the corridor—his and two others, boots slapping on the flagstones.

He focused on what was simple: a route out of the palace. The events of the throne room—the witch's revelation, his father's reaction, the magic— clamored in his head, so shocking, so huge, that he had to push them aside. *Don't think. Just run.*

The corridor branched. He turned left and ran down the stairs, taking the steps three at a time, then turned left again, pushing open the door at the end of the corridor. They were no longer in bondservants' territory. The walls were hung with tapestries. Windows looked out over manicured hedges and flower beds.

Harkeld slowed to a fast walk. In the distance a bell rang frantically. "There'll be guards here." He glanced back. Two witches followed him—the gray-haired man and a middle-aged woman. Behind them were a pair of long-legged hunting dogs, one silver-white, the other black.

Human beings in the form of dogs. *Monsters.* Harkeld jerked his gaze ahead again.

Three guards turned into the corridor, striding. Their eyes flicked to him and they halted, snapping to attention.

Harkeld halted too. To these men he was still a royal prince. "My father needs you in the throne room," he said, authority ringing in his voice. "Hurry!"

The guards obeyed without hesitation, breaking into a run, not stopping to ask where his personal armsman was or who the strangers following him were.

Harkeld began to walk again, almost jogging. "The gates will be sealed," he said, not looking back at the witches. "They'll have heard the bell. Our best chance is to go through the gardens." Ahead were double doors, embossed with gold. Harkeld pushed them open and stepped out onto a marble terrace. The sun was high overhead. He slowed, strolling.

"The outer wall?" the gray-haired witch asked, lengthening his stride until he was alongside Harkeld. For all his appearance of age, he was barely out of breath.

"It's less heavily guarded at the eastern corner."

They went down the steps into the garden. The paths were made of crushed pink and white marble. The tiny chips crunched beneath their feet. Above that small sound, the bell tolled urgently.

"I'll have the horses meet us there." The witch snapped his fingers. "Petrus!"

The silver-white hunting dog trotted up, ears pricked.

"Tell Gerit to meet us at the eastern corner. Hurry!"

The dog nodded.

"How heavily guarded is the outer wall?" the gray-haired witch asked.

"In the eastern corner, two men in each tower." Harkeld glanced back. The silver-white hunting dog was gone. A hawk rose in the sky, gaining height with every flap of its wings.

He jerked his gaze forward again. They were between the clipped hedges now, out of sight of all but the topmost windows of the palace. Harkeld lengthened his stride into a run. The witches followed.

The gardens stretched for more than a mile, a labyrinth of groves and flower beds and secluded, sunlit lawns. Harkeld took a route that avoided the courtyards where the ladies liked to sit and gossip, heading for the outer wall, running fast, listening for the sounds of pursuit behind them. The bell pealed loudly, but beneath that sound he heard nothing— no shouts, no baying hounds.

Ahead, the wall towered high. He could see the blocks of stone, could make out the steps leading up to the guard tower—

"Harkeld!"

He swung around, panting.

Behind them, where the path branched to a rose bower, stood his half-sister Brigitta and her armsman.

"Harkeld, what's happening?" Brigitta stepped forward. The sunlight caught her hair, making it gleam as brightly as the golden crown woven into it. She shone with youth, with beauty. "Why is the bell ringing?"

Her armsman stepped forward too, one pace behind her. He had the dark hawk-like features of an Esfaban islander. A silver torque gleamed at his throat.

The black hunting dog came forward to stand in front of Harkeld. It was panting, its tongue hanging from its mouth.

The armsman laid one hand on the hilt of his sword.

Brigitta stared at the dog and the two witches. Her brow creased. "Harkeld, where's your armsman? What are you doing?"

For half a second he considered lying, then rejected it. Britta deserved the truth. "I'm leaving."

Her eyes widened. "Leaving?"

"Now. Over the wall." Harkeld caught the armsman's gaze, held it. "Don't try to stop us," he told him.

The armsman hesitated, then raised his chin in a slight nod.

Brigitta stepped forward, ignoring the dog. "Take me with you."

"I can't, Britta."

Her hands clasped together, white-knuckled. "Please, Harkeld." He heard desperation in her voice. "You know what will happen to me if you go. Duke Rikard—"

"There's a bounty on my head." He glanced at the armsman again. Would the man attack? "That's why the bell"s ringing."

"I don't care! Take me with you. Please!"

The armsman stood, still and watchful. He made no attempt to move.

Harkeld looked at Brigitta. Tears were bright in her eyes. "I'm sorry. It's too dangerous." He stepped past the dog and pulled her into a hug. She was slender in his arms, fragile. He tightened his grip, hearing the strident peal of the bell, smelling the scent of roses. His half-sister, his friend. *I love you.* He bent his head and kissed her soft hair and said it aloud, so that she could hear, "I love you." The golden crown pressed against his cheek.

He lifted his head and looked at the armsman. "You keep her safe."

This time the man spoke. "I will."

Harkeld stepped away from Britta. He couldn't say goodbye; his throat was too tight. He was trying to protect her. Why did it feel as if he was abandoning her?

Because I am.

He turned and ran, paying no attention to the witches or the dog. He glanced back once. Brigitta stood in the middle of the path. Behind her was the armsman, watching.

The wall loomed ahead, cliff-like. It was easy to turn grief and guilt into rage, to take the stairs three at a time, to burst out onto the rampart, to take advantage of the two guards' hesitation when they recognized him. He took the closest man, bringing him down, slamming his head against the stone parapet.

The guard slumped, unconscious.

Harkeld pushed to his feet. The second guard lay on the floor. Standing over him were the two witches, man and woman. The black dog was gone. Two hawks soared above the guard tower.

Harkeld bent and removed the guard's sword belt, buckling it swiftly around his own hips. The familiar weight made him feel less vulnerable. Now he could defend himself.

The baying of a hound rose from the garden.

The wall was too high to jump from, too sheer to climb down, but the rope for hoisting the tower's flag, hastily cut, was long enough for their purposes. The female witch went first, a small, middle-aged woman with her sandy hair in a thick plait down her back.

Harkeld leaned over the battlement, watching. A mile away, to the right, was the town, its slate roofs gleaming in the afternoon sunlight. Ahead and to the left was the royal forest, a sea of trees. Between forest and wall was a furlong of cleared land. Horses galloped towards them from the town. "Yours?" he asked the gray-haired witch.

"Yes."

Harkeld followed the woman, landing jarringly on the hard-packed dirt at the base of the wall. He spun to face the riders. Five horses bore down on them, four riderless. Above swooped the hawks.

The gray-haired witch clambered down the rope. He jumped the last few feet, landing lightly in a crouch. "Take the bay."

Harkeld nodded, glancing up at the guard tower. He heard shouting. A guard peered down. The rope twitched.

The horses halted. "Quickly!" the gray-haired witch cried, thrusting reins at him. Above, a guard was already scrambling down the rope.

Harkeld grabbed the reins and swung up into the saddle. Out of the corner of his eye he saw the guard push away from the wall, swinging towards him.

The man's weight knocked him from the saddle as the bay surged forward. Harkeld struck the ground hard. He rolled, pushing up on one elbow. There was a ringing sound in his ears and no breath in his lungs. Dimly he heard the guard shout. Sunlight gleamed on an uplifted sword.

Harkeld raised an arm in defense. He had time for one thought—*I'm dead*—and for one emotion—astonishment—before a lioness barreled into the guard, knocking him off his feet.

The guard released his sword as he fell. The blade sliced past Harkeld's upraised hand and smacked into the dirt.

Harkeld lowered his arm. He coughed, tasting dirt and blood, and inhaled deeply. The guard screamed. The sound echoed in Harkeld's head. He blinked, trying to focus his eyes, and rose unsteadily to his knees. The smell of smoke was strong. He looked up. The rope was on fire, flames licking upwards. Above, on the parapet, a silver-maned lion roared.

The lioness suddenly pushed her face into his, her eyes golden. She turned her head and uttered a sound—part grunt, part roar—that sounded like a summons.

He raised his hand to push her away. Foul creature. Blood dripped from his fingers.

Harkeld shook his head to clear it. He turned his hand palm-up. For a second he stared dumbly, seeing red flesh and white bone. Blood spurted from the wound.

Someone gripped his collar and hauled him to his feet. Harkeld jerked away, almost stumbling, before he realized it was the gray-haired witch.

He stood, blinking, trying to get his eyes to focus fully as a man he'd never seen before, with a grizzled brown beard and bristling eyebrows, ripped off a shirtsleeve and tied it tightly about his wrist. The spurting blood slowed to a trickle. The man tore off his other sleeve and bound Harkeld's hand roughly.

"Mount!"

Harkeld did, clumsily, and sat swaying in the saddle, gripping the reins in his left hand.

They rode at a slow canter, the lioness loping alongside and a hawk flying overhead. By the time they reached the cool shade of the forest, the ringing in Harkeld's ears had lessened and his head had begun to clear. He looked back before the trees closed around them. A line of fire ran up the wall as the rope burned. Figures clustered on the battlement, and behind them were the gilded roofs and gleaming marble of the palace.

Home.

Not anymore.

He waited for an emotion—loss, rage—but all he felt was sheer and utter disbelief.

Movement drew his eye. Guards on horseback, at least a score of them, riding from the direction of the main gate with a pack of hounds streaming in front of them.

He dug his heels into the bay's flanks.

The lioness kept pace with him, but when he glanced back he saw that the other riders followed more slowly. Behind them, flames rose high. The forest was on fire.

Harkeld brought his horse to a halt. He twisted in his saddle. The flames spread as he watched, to the left and right, an impregnable wall of fire. And as the flames spread, so did his disbelief.

This isn't happening to me.

CHAPTER FOUR

THEY RODE THROUGH the royal forest for the rest of the afternoon. The witches followed no trail—huntsman's or deer's—that Harkeld could see, yet they rode without hesitation, pushing deeper into the coolness of the forest, beneath broad-boughed oaks and towering ash trees, through thickets of prickly yews.

Whenever they rested the horses in a walk, the gray-haired witch came up alongside him and unwound the bandage around his hand. The first time, Harkeld jerked his hand away.

"I need to heal it," the witch said.

"Magic?"

The man nodded.

Harkeld hesitated. Everything he knew about magic flooded into his mind. It was foul, filthy, a perversion of what was natural and right.

He looked down at his hand. The fingers almost severed from the palm. Instinct told him not to let the man touch him; self-preservation insisted he did.

Harkeld braced himself and held out his hand. He sat stiff and unwilling while the horses walked and the witch's fingers rested on his palm. The edges of the wound slowly drew closed; after the third healing session, the bones were no longer visible, after the fourth, the witch released the tourniquet. When no blood flowed, he gave a nod of satisfaction. "Can you move your fingers?"

Harkeld shook his head. Bitterness surged inside him. He was a cripple, a swordsman who couldn't wield a sword.

"Innis will finish the healing," the man said. "Tonight."

"Innis?"

The witch nodded at the lioness, pacing beside the horses.

THE WITCHES HAD a camp deep in the forest, beside a creek. Four tents and a campfire. Beneath the smell of wood smoke was the smell of stew.

A young, red-haired man tended the fire. He straightened at their approach and waved cheerfully. Harkeld eyed him. He had to be another witch; no human would travel willingly in such company.

The glade looked like a thousand others in the forest: trickling creek, oak and ash and rowan trees. Above the leafy canopy, dusk was settling into night. A glow from the burning forest lit the sky behind them. Harkeld dismounted. "The forest fire?" he asked the gray-haired witch.

'It won't come near us."

Harkeld drew back, remembering tales of witches using fire to subjugate and punish, to burn people alive.

The red-haired witch handed Harkeld a mug of cider and took the bay from him.

Harkeld drank, counting the witches and trying to stifle his fear. *Six witches.* More tales crowded into his head, tales of infanticide, of bestiality, of cannibalism. He forced himself to concentrate on the ordinariness of the scene: the tents, the pots hanging over the fire, the tartness and sweetness of the cider on his tongue. The red-haired witch whistled between his teeth as he unsaddled the horses.

"Let me see your hand."

He turned his head.

The girl from the throne room stood beside him. He recognized the black hair curling halfway down her back, the pale skin, the dark eyes.

She looked human; Harkeld knew she wasn't. She was a shapeshifter. Neither human nor animal, but a monstrous combination of both.

"Dareus says the tendons are severed." The girl had the same accent as the gray-haired witch: sibilant *s*, guttural *r*. "If you wish to use your fingers again, I must look at your hand."

She was dressed in a shirt and trews. Harkeld remembered the pile of clothes on the floor of the throne room, the shirt with its seams burst open, the ripped trews.

She'd been a lion, a hunting dog, a hawk. She'd been covered in fur and in feathers.

"The sooner it's done, the better it will heal," the girl said. She didn't look like any of the animals she'd been. She was long-legged and slender, like a gazelle.

Harkeld inhaled, bracing himself before holding out his bandaged hand.

The girl didn't touch it. "Let's sit by the fire." She turned away from him.

Harkeld followed, his legs stiff with reluctance. *She's a monster*, a voice whispered in his head. By not killing her, he was going against everything he'd been taught, against every principle of rightness and conscience.

A log had been placed alongside the fire. The girl sat. He could see her more clearly in the firelight. Freckles scattered her pale skin. Her eyes were dark gray.

Harkeld sat on the log, putting as much space between them as he could. He extended his hand towards the witch, looking at the fire, not her.

The girl unwrapped the bandage and dropped it on the ground. He felt her fingers on his skin, cool, turning his palm towards the fire, examining the wound. Harkeld's skin crawled beneath that light touch. It took all his willpower not to jerk his hand free. He clenched his jaw and stared at the flames.

He knew when she started. He felt it—a prickling sensation, neither hot nor cold. He was aware of every bone in his hand, every tendon, every nerve, every blood vessel.

Harkeld held himself utterly still, fighting the urge to snatch his hand from her grasp. He tried to concentrate on other things, on the stew pot and the steaming pot of water that hung alongside it, on the moths that darted close to the flames, on the witches rubbing down the horses, on the sound of the red-haired witch whistling.

Time seemed to stretch interminably. Each second was as long as a minute, each minute as long as an hour. Finally the girl released his hand. "Try to move your fingers."

Harkeld hesitated, then flexed his fingers.

They moved.

Relief surged through him, so intense that, for a moment, he couldn't breathe. He flexed his fingers again, clenched them into a fist, spread them wide. There was no pain, no stiffness.

The witch had given him back his hand, and twice today she'd saved his life. Monster or not, he owed her gratitude.

"Thank you," he said, glancing at her, seeing gray eyes and a fine-boned, gamine face.

"You're welcome."

Harkeld looked down at his palm. A scar ran across it from one side to the other, pink and fresh. His skin crawled where her fingers had touched, as if her filth had contaminated him.

He stood abruptly and headed for the creek. He had to wash the touch of her off his hand, had to wash *her* off.

THE GRAY-HAIRED WITCH told him his name while they ate—Dareus—and the names of the others: the woman, Cora, and the young male shapeshifter, Petrus, who'd both been at the palace. Bearded Gerit, who'd bound his hand at the palace wall. Red-haired Ebril. And the girl, Innis. Harkeld paid little attention. He didn't want to know the witches' names. They were monsters, not people. He ate without looking at any of them. When he was finished he put down his wooden bowl.

"Do you have any questions?" Dareus asked. "About your grandfather? About the curse?"

Harkeld looked at him across the campfire. "You have proof my grandfather was a witch?"

Dareus put down his own bowl and sat back. "Your mother's birth was carefully planned. We've been trying to get mage blood into royal lines for close to a century. Although you're the only—"

"It was deliberate?"

"Yes." The firelight cast deep shadows over the witch's face. His eyes were dark caves, his nose a bony ridge. "It was necessary to break the curse."

They'd mixed their filthy blood with his mother's line on purpose? Outrage held Harkeld rigid for a moment, then he pushed to his feet. "How *dare* you—"

"It had to be done," Dareus said. "Ivek was a mage. It was our responsibility to find a way to break the curse."

Me. I'm the way you've found. You bred me as a farmer breeds cattle.

He was aware of the other witches, dark shapes around the campfire, watching. "How long will it take to break?"

"Three or four months," Dareus said. "Maybe longer. The bounty on your head will make it difficult."

"Three months?" he said, appalled.

"The curse is anchored in more than one place," the witch said. "It's quite complex."

Three months. Harkeld shook his head. "I'm going to bed." He turned away from the campfire.

"Ebril will share your tent."

Harkeld turned around. "No," he said flatly. "I will not sleep in the same tent as—" *as a monster*

"—one of you." He'd rather sleep in a midden than alongside a witch, sharing the same space, breathing the same air.

"We must guard you," Dareus said. "There's a bounty on your head. Every man in Osgaard will be trying to kill you."

"I will *not* sleep in the same tent as a witch." Harkeld articulated each word carefully, cutting them off with his teeth.

"You have no choice, prince." The old man's voice was faintly apologetic.

Harkeld laid his hand on the hilt of his sword. "Try it, and you'll be one witch short."

There was silence for a moment, except for the faint crackle of the fire and a soft sigh from one of the horses.

"Very well," Dareus said finally, without inflection.

Harkeld nodded. He turned on his heel.

CHAPTER FIVE

"I DON'T LIKE him," Gerit said.

"We could kill him while he sleeps," Petrus suggested, his tone only half-joking. His pale hair gleamed like silver in the firelight. "And claim the bounty for ourselves."

Gerit grunted a laugh. "And the curse?"

"We only need his blood," Petrus said. "And his hands."

"He's afraid of us," Innis said, reaching for her mug. "He's afraid of magic. When I healed him, he fought it the whole time." She'd been aware of the prince's fear, aware of how much effort it had taken him to sit still, to let her heal him.

"Afraid?" Gerit said sourly. "Seems to me he hates us."

"Of course he does," Cora said. "Everyone in the Seven Kingdoms does. They think we're monsters." She flicked her plait over her shoulder and shrugged. "You know the stories they tell about us."

Dareus leaned forward and stirred the fire. "The prince needs a guard. We need to make sure he's never alone." He jabbed at the logs, making sparks rise into the sky. "That cursed bounty!"

"He needs a personal armsman," Cora said. "One who won't try to kill him."

Gerit exhaled through his nose, a sound that was almost a laugh.

Innis didn't laugh. She remembered the prince's armsman raising his sword, murderous determination on his face.

"He needs an armsman who's a mage," Dareus said. "And that's what we'll give him."

"One of us?" Ebril said. "But you heard what he said. He'll kill—"

Dareus shook his head. "We'll give him someone he doesn't know is a mage."

"But he's seen us all," Petrus protested.

"We'll give him a shapeshifter."

Ebril whistled between his teeth. "Take the shape of another human? That's forbidden."

"We're Sentinel mages. We can do whatever needs doing." Gerit leaned forward, his gaze on Dareus. The shadows accentuated the bristling eyebrows, the bristling beard. "But what I want to know is whether this prince is worth breaking a Primary Law for."

"For the sake of so many lives? Yes."

Gerit shrugged and sat back.

"Who'll do it?" Petrus asked. "Me or—"

"Innis," Dareus said. "She's the only one who can hold a shift long enough."

Innis's mouth fell open. *Me?* But the word remained unuttered on her tongue. All she could do was stare at Dareus. What he suggested was doubly forbidden: to take the form of another person; to change gender.

"She's too young for something that demanding!" Petrus said. "She's not yet twenty."

"Innis's strength as a shapeshifter is why she was chosen to join us," Dareus said. "Her age isn't an issue."

"It's too dangerous," Petrus persisted. "She'll lose her sense of self. She could go mad!"

"You and Gerit and Ebril can relieve her for a few hours each day," Dareus said. "So she may be herself." He looked across the campfire at her. "Innis?"

Innis wanted to say no. Petrus was right—it was a dangerous undertaking. She'd be living as another person. It would be easy to lose herself and go mad.

She looked at her hands. She'd sworn the oath of a Sentinel: to protect the innocent, to place the welfare of others ahead of her own. Tens of thousands of lives depended on Prince Harkeld. He was the single most important person in the Seven Kingdoms.

"I'll do it."

As soon as the words were out, she wanted to take them back. Dismay surged inside her.

"Are you certain you can do it, girl?"

She looked at Gerit.

"I don't question your ability to take male form, or to hold it—you're the strongest shapeshifter I've ever seen. What I want to know is, can you act like a man?" Gerit pinned her with his gaze, his eyes dark pits beneath shaggy eyebrows. "An armsman would be assertive, girl. He'd be confident." She heard the unspoken words: *And you're not.*

"I have faith in Innis," Dareus said.

Gerit ignored the comment. "Can you do it, girl?"

Can I? She glanced at Petrus. He was staring at her, a fierce frown on his face.

Innis studied him. She'd trained alongside Petrus for years. She knew him inside out—how he talked, how he ate, how he cleared his throat and spat when he thought she wasn't looking. *I'll pretend to be him.* She'd mimic his maleness, his easy confidence. She turned to Gerit. "Yes, I can do it."

"I hope you're right, girl," Gerit said. "Because if the prince suspects the truth, he's likely to kill you."

"He'll never know," Dareus said.

"But won't he notice we're a mage short?" Cora asked.

"Not if we're careful. He'll see Innis for a few hours each day; the rest of the time he'll think she's in animal form." Dareus scratched his jaw, his brow furrowed in thought. "Tomorrow I'll ride back to the port. Petrus, you come with me. The rest of you head for the mountains."

"The port?" Gerit said. "It that necessary?"

"The armsman will need his own horse and weapons, if he's to be believable."

Gerit grunted. "True."

"Innis, let the prince see you as a hawk, then come after me."

"And tonight?" Ebril asked. His red hair glinted in the firelight. "How do we guard the prince?"

"I could be a mouse," Innis said. "Or a—"

"Too dangerous," Gerit said. "The mood he's in, he finds a mouse in his tent he'll chop it into pieces."

"Tonight we"ll guard from the outside," Dareus said. He stood. Innis saw how tired he was. "Ebril, take the first watch. Gerit, the second."

Innis stayed seated while the others rose, as bowls and mugs were collected. She stared at the fire, at the leaping flames, at the bark curling up, shriveling, blackening as the logs burned. Taking the form of a man wasn't something to fear, she told herself. It was a *challenge*. A chance to prove that her advancement to Sentinel *hadn't* been a mistake.

"Innis?"

She glanced up. Petrus stood there.

He sat down alongside her, the log shifting slightly with his weight. "Are you certain you can do this? Because if you don't want to—"

"I have to. This is why they made me a Sentinel. For tasks like this." Fear tightened in her belly. "Petrus, will you watch me? You know me better than anyone else. You'll see if... if I start—"

"I won't let you go mad." His voice held utter conviction. He reached out and took one of her hands. "You're strong, Innis. If anyone can do it, it's you."

Innis smiled at him. "I'm glad you're here." He was her anchor, her friend, the closest thing she had to a brother.

"I'll always be here." Petrus's grip tightened. He had a swordsman's callused fingers. "You did well today, at the palace."

The praise made her flush. Innis touched the log lightly with her other hand. Her parents were buried in the soil an ocean away, but the All-Mother connected them—wood, soil, water. *Are you proud?* she asked. *I'm a Sentinel now, like you were.*

Petrus stood, pulling her to her feet. "Come on sleepyhead, bed time." He turned her towards the tents, giving her a little push. "Go. Sleep. You'll need all your strength tomorrow."

CHAPTER SIX

JAUMÉ WOKE TO rain on his face. For a moment he
lay blinking, and then memory flooded back: Rosa's
scream, the smell of Mam's blood. He sat up and
rubbed his face, knuckling his eyes, trying to push
the memory out of his head. But no matter how hard
he rubbed, he couldn't erase the memory of Rosa
swinging from Da's grip. He heard her scream above
the rain.

Rain.

Thirst kicked in. He lifted his face to the sky,
opening his mouth.

Once the gulping thirst had eased, Jaumé started
walking, staying in the fir forest, paralleling the
road. His pace was slow. Hunger cramped his belly.

Soon he'd reach Neuly, and in Neuly there'd be food.

But what if the curse had passed him while he
slept? What if Neuly's water was already poisoned?
What if—?

Jaumé froze as a man on horseback came around
a bend in the road ahead of him. He crouched low
behind a tree trunk, scarcely daring to breathe.

Horse and rider drew closer. The horse was
ambling, its hooves splashing in the puddles. The

man sat relaxed, the hood of his brown woolen cape pulled over his head.

Should I warn him?

Fear kept Jaumé hidden as horse and rider came abreast of him. What if the man was like Da? What if the curse had already taken him?

The traveler began to whistle despite the rain, a cheerful, jaunty tune.

It was the whistling that decided him. Jaumé stepped out from behind the tree. "Wait!"

The rider halted. He turned in his saddle, pushing the hood back. He had a farmer's face, tanned and weather-beaten, jovial.

"Girond has the curse," Jaumé said. "Don't go there."

The farmer laughed. "Away with you, boy. Find someone else to frighten."

"It's true."

The man shook his head. "The curse is a tale, boy."

"It's *true*," Jaumé insisted, an edge of desperation in his voice. "They're killing each other."

The farmer's face lost its joviality. For a long moment he did nothing but stare at Jaumé, then he hauled on the reins, turning his horse around. He dug his heels into its flanks.

The horse reared forward.

"Wait!" Jaumé shouted. He began to run. "Take me with you!"

But the farmer didn't slow down.

CHAPTER SEVEN

INNIS WOKE TO the gray light of predawn and the sound of birdsong. She washed her face in the creek and joined Cora and Gerit in the clearing beside the fire for the dawn exercises. Nervousness eddied in her belly. The precise flow of movements, the slow rhythm of stretches and lunges and blocks, the control she had over her body—flex of muscle, quietness of breathing—was calming. Dareus and Petrus joined them.

Innis went through the sequence three times before stopping. A feeling of quiet confidence had replaced the nervousness. *I can do this.* She washed her face in the creek again and turned back to the campsite.

Prince Harkeld stood beside his tent, watching Dareus and Petrus complete the exercises. His antipathy was clear to see. He looked as if he'd smelled something unpleasant; his lips flattened against his teeth, his nostrils slightly flared.

The prince turned his head and caught her looking at him. She read his opinion of her clearly in his eyes.

Innis flushed. She ducked her head and walked towards the fire and breakfast.

*   *   *

AFTER THE CAMPSITE was dismantled and the packhorses loaded, they split into two groups. Gerit jerked his thumb at the sky. "Get up there with Ebril, girl. Keep watch. Anyone follows us, I want to know."

Innis's heart kicked in her chest and sped up. This was it, the first step towards breaking a Primary Law. She went through the preparations mechanically: removing her boots, unbuttoning the top few buttons of her shirt. She focused on the form she wanted to take, took a deep breath, and changed. Magic surged through her, stinging beneath her skin. For a dizzying moment she was neither human nor bird, then everything became solid again. Her lungs expanded as she inhaled, her heart beat in her chest, blood flowed through her veins.

She stayed in the nest of her clothes for a few seconds, while the disorientation of viewing the world through different eyes eased, then shrugged free of the shirt. Her nervousness vanished as she spread her wings. Exhilaration caught her as she climbed swiftly upward. There was nothing but pleasure in the strong flex of her wings, in the speed of her ascent, in the utter freedom of flight.

The sky was stained with smoke from yesterday's fires. To the north, the forest stretched for miles before trailing into a patchwork of fields and villages. To the east was more forest, and mountains rising jaggedly in the distance. South, past a ragged fringe of forest and farmland, was the sea. Dimly, through the haze, she saw the curve of the horizon.

Ebril swooped towards her with a shrill cry of welcome. Like her, he'd chosen to be a hawk. His breast and the underside of his wings were a russet-brown. His eyes were ringed with yellow above the vicious curve of his beak. The shimmer of magic surrounded him, like sunlight sparkling on water.

Innis circled high above the campsite. She saw Prince Harkeld glance upward, saw the muscles contract alongside his mouth.

Gerit lifted his hand, a silent command. *Go.* Innis uttered a cry of farewell to Ebril. She dipped a wing, gliding east until she was out of sight of the campsite, then swung west. From this height, the forest was crisscrossed by strips of burned trees. The fires had clearly been laid by mages; there was nothing natural about those narrow, blackened strips, they were too straight, too discrete.

It didn't take her long to find Dareus and Petrus. She swooped down, landing on a branch.

"Take us as close to the port as you can," Dareus said. "And keep close watch. They'll be hunting us."

IT WAS LATE morning by the time they reached the edge of the forest. Dareus dismounted. He held out his arm.

Innis landed lightly, taking care not to grip too strongly with her talons.

"Is there anyone nearby?"

She shook her head.

"Good. Change back."

Petrus dismounted. He unstrapped a blanket from behind his saddle. Innis glided across to him.

She landed and shifted. There was a moment of disorientation and then she settled fully into herself: a human, not a bird.

Petrus handed her the blanket. Innis wrapped it around herself. The clarity of vision she'd had as a hawk was gone. Through the smoky haze, the port and the lower portions of the town were only dimly visible. She could no longer see the ships riding at anchor in the harbor.

"I've given some thought to the shape you'll shift into," Dareus said. "There are certain difficulties. You can't be from Osgaard or any of the Seven Kingdoms. Your accent marks you as not from here."

"Where, then?"

"Across the ocean," Dareus said. "The Allied Kingdoms."

"The prince isn't a fool," Petrus protested. "Everyone knows mages come from Rosny—"

"She'll not be from Rosny," Dareus said. "She'll be from the Groot Isles. She'll be Justen."

"Justen?" Petrus's surprise echoed her own.

"You both trained with him. You know how he speaks, how he acts. There's less chance that one of you will make a mistake." Dareus rubbed the furrows in his brow. "It's the best I can think of."

Petrus glanced at her. "Can you do it?"

"Ach," she said, the way Justen always did. "By the All-Mother, I think I can."

Petrus grunted, the sound was almost a laugh. "Ebril knows Justen," he said. "But I don't think Gerit does."

"He can learn from watching you."

"We'll need an amulet," Innis said. Justen always

touched his when he mentioned the All-Mother. "And one of those daggers with a decorated hilt."

"We'll need a lot of things," Dareus said. "But first, let's make sure you can both do the shift. I want an image you can both focus on. Petrus, you brought the parchment?"

Petrus had. He spread a sheet on the ground and anchored it with stones. "You draw," he said, handing Innis the stick of charcoal. "You're better than me."

Innis sat cross-legged and stared at the parchment, turning the charcoal over in her fingers, trying to see Justen's face on it. She began to sketch.

"Snub nose," Petrus said over her shoulder. "And his hair's down past his ears."

When she'd finished, Justen's face looked back at her from the parchment—square and plain, with a broad brow and wide mouth. A dependable face, an honest, good-humored face.

"Good," Dareus said. "Let's practice. Innis, you go first."

She stood, drawing the blanket tightly around herself, suddenly nervous. She was about to break one of the Primary Laws. "How tall is he?"

"Same as me," Petrus said.

"Use Petrus's body," Dareus said. "Petrus." It was an order.

Petrus began to strip. He kicked off his boots and shrugged out of his shirt.

Innis studied his bare chest as he unbuckled his belt. She'd seen Petrus naked dozens of times, hundreds, but this was the first time she'd ever looked at him properly: the broad shoulders, the muscled abdomen.

He wasn't as hairy as some of the other mages.

Petrus stepped out of his trews. He peeled off his underbreeches, not looking at her.

Innis averted her gaze. Shapeshifters were used to each other's nudity, but it was bad manners to stare.

"Copy Petrus," Dareus said. "But give Justen darker body hair."

Innis nodded. She brought her gaze back to Petrus. He was heavily muscled, his skin tanned golden and lightly dusted with white-blond hair. She studied his body—the strong throat, the broad ribcage, the dangling genitals.

Innis flushed slightly. She looked down at his feet, at the shape of his toes.

"Turn around," Dareus said.

Petrus did. Innis stared at the angles of his shoulder blades and line of his spine, his buttocks, his legs.

"Ready?" Dareus asked.

Innis nodded. "Yes."

Petrus turned around again. She looked at him one last time, gauging his height, and then glanced down at the sketch: square face, broad brow, curling hair. "Eye color?"

No one answered. She looked up.

"Make them brown," Dareus said.

Innis nodded. She took a deep breath and closed her eyes, building the image of what she wanted to be—*who* she wanted to be—in her mind.

Magic rippled under her skin. She opened her eyes, uncertain. It was easier than a shift had ever been before, swifter, less close to pain. "Did it work? Have I changed?" Her voice was wrong, too deep, not her own.

Both men were staring at her. "Hair's too dark," Petrus said, after a moment.

Dareus shook his head. "Looks fine to me." He gestured. "The blanket."

Innis let the blanket fall to the ground.

Both men stared at her again. Innis looked down at herself. She had hair on her chest, a penis. She almost took a step backwards, away from the wrongness of her body. She held herself still with willpower. *This is me.*

Dareus circled her slowly, frowning as he scrutinized her. He was shorter than her now. It was disorienting to be looking down at him, not up. Innis blinked, fighting a surge of dizziness.

Dareus turned to Petrus. "You try."

Petrus closed his eyes. His features blurred and rearranged themselves—nose, mouth, chin. His hair darkened, lengthening slightly.

Innis had watched mages shift before, but this time nausea twisted in her belly. She averted her gaze. When she looked back, Justen stood before her. A shimmer of magic lightly coated his skin and hair.

She stared at him. *Is that what I look like?*

Dareus walked around them both. "Perfect. You're identical."

Petrus touched his face, molding his jaw and cheekbones with his fingers. "That was easier than any shift I've ever done."

Dareus nodded. "Good."

Petrus lowered his hand. "Let me do it. Innis doesn't have to—"

"Innis is our strongest shifter."

"But—"

"The decision has been made." The note of authority, of finality, in Dareus's voice was unmistakable. "Innis will be the prince's armsman for the bulk of the time."

Innis bit her lip. She looked down at the ground and rubbed her big toe in the dirt. A toe that was too large, with a nail that wasn't her own.

She glanced up. Petrus was watching her. "Don't do that," he said, gesturing to her mouth. "Justen wouldn't do that."

Innis stopped biting her lip. She raised her chin.

"Better," Petrus said. He sighed and turned to Dareus. "What now?"

"Stay in that shape and head down to the town. We need clothes and weapons for Justen, and a Grooten amulet. And a horse."

Petrus nodded. He reached for his discarded clothes and began to dress.

"And me?" Innis asked.

"You need to learn to be comfortable in that body. We'll start with the dawn exercises."

Innis nodded. She inhaled, centering her energy, and began to move through the first sequence. She'd done these exercises every morning for years—the movements were so familiar she could do them in her sleep—but this time the proportions of her body were different. She almost overbalanced as she stepped into a low lunge. She steadied herself with one hand—a broad hand with thick, strong fingers—and watched Dareus give Petrus several gold coins.

"I'll be back as soon as I can," Petrus said.

"Be careful." Her voice was a baritone.

"I will."

* * *

THE SUN HAD slid past noon by the time Petrus returned, leading the horse he'd bought, a sturdy dun mare. Innis was part way through the third warrior sequence – advancing, blocking, kicking high. She stopped when she saw him. Her face was Justen's but the hand raised in greeting, the shy smile, was Innis's.

"How's it going?" Petrus asked, sliding from the saddle.

Innis glanced at Dareus.

"Very well," Dareus said.

A comment rose to his tongue. Petrus bit it back, and then made himself say it: "Justen wouldn't do that."

Her broad brow wrinkled. "What?"

"Let someone else answer for him."

"Oh." She flushed at the criticism.

Petrus turned and unstrapped a bundle from the dun mare's saddle. "Justen's clothes. And I've got a dagger and a sword. Both Grooten."

"Did you find an amulet?" she asked, taking the bundle.

"An amulet... and a keepsake from your sweetheart."

Her thick eyebrows rose. "Sweetheart?"

Petrus shrugged. "Sweetheart. Wife. Whatever you decide."

Innis crouched, opening the bundle, spreading the clothes on the cloak they were wrapped in: underbreeches, shirts, trews, a pair of boots. "Grooten," she said, fingering the black and white embroidery along the hem of the cloak.

"The boots are too. See here?" Like the cloak, the boots were well-worn, the embroidery faded but still recognizably Grooten.

"Well done," Dareus said. "And the weapons?"

Petrus unstrapped them. "Dagger," he said, handing it to Innis. "And a sword." The hilts of both sword and dagger were decorated with geometric Grooten designs.

Innis hefted the sword in her hand.

"It's heavier than you're used to," Petrus said. "The same weight as mine."

She nodded. "Where did you get all these?"

"Trader," he said. "A Grooten ship was in port last month. Some of the sailors bartered their belongings." For money to visit the local whores, the trader had said, but he didn't tell Innis that. Instead, he fished in his pocket. "Here. Your amulet." The disc was round and thin, a slice from a walrus tusk.

Dareus leaned close. "Excellent."

Petrus nodded. It wasn't a souvenir, shiny and new; the amulet had the patina of long wear, the ivory burnished to a creamy color.

Innis slipped the leather cord over her head. The amulet nestled just below the hollow of her collarbone. "What do you think?"

Petrus stared at her, unsettled. "That you look like Justen."

Innis grinned.

Petrus looked away. He thrust his hand into his pocket again. "Here. Your sweetheart."

The portrait was painted on a small piece of wood. The girl was flaxen-haired, pink-cheeked. The image was slightly worn, as if someone had touched the painted face often.

Innis took it. She turned it over, but there was nothing on the back. "Someone bartered this?"

Or was robbed. Petrus shrugged.

"Get dressed," Dareus told her. "Sparring with swords first, and then wrestling." He turned to Petrus. "Are you having any difficulty holding the shift?"

"No."

"Balance and co-ordination?"

"The same as when I'm me."

Dareus nodded. "Good. You may change back to yourself."

THEY'D SPARRED TOGETHER often, but usually Petrus tempered his blows, not striking with his full weight. This time, when he did that, Innis pushed forward, forcing him to retreat. Petrus gritted his teeth and began to defend himself more vigorously. Innis didn't pull back; she pressed her advantage, her lips pulled back from her teeth in a fierce grimace. She forced him to retreat another step.

"Stop thinking of her as Innis," he heard Dareus say. "Fight as if she's a man."

But she's not a man. Protectiveness surged inside him.

Her blade swiped at him, deflecting his blow, striking his upper arm. "Out!"

It was no gentle tap. Petrus bit back a yelp of pain.

Innis lowered her blade, her expression instantly contrite. "Did I hurt you? I'm sorry."

"You were holding back," Dareus told him.

"Next time I won't." Petrus said, massaging his upper arm.

"Well done, Innis." Dareus held out his hand for the Grooten sword. "Let's try wrestling now."

Petrus stripped off his shirt. The sword blade had left an angry red welt on his arm. Innis winced when she saw it. "I'm sorry," she said again, reaching out to touch him. "Does it hurt?"

"Don't," he said roughly. "You're behaving like a girl. Justen would laugh and tell me it served me right."

Innis flushed and lowered her hand.

Petrus balled up his shirt and tossed it aside. He kicked off his boots. "Wrestling. Best out of three."

He won the first bout easily. "You hesitated," he told Innis as he pinned her to the ground.

Dareus spoke behind them. "Don't be afraid of hurting Petrus."

Innis shrugged him off and pushed to her feet. "I'm not," she said, but her voice lacked conviction.

They circled each other, crouching slightly, their weight on the balls of their feet. Petrus saw Innis inhale, saw her muscles tense, saw her hesitate.

He took advantage of the hesitation, rushing her. They grappled, arms locked around each other.

"You're still holding back," he told her.

Innis grunted. "So are you." Her hip dipped as she threw him.

Petrus rolled and sprang to his feet. They circled again, panting. This time it was Innis who moved first, tackling low, her shoulder slamming into his ribs.

He let her weight propel them backwards and

twisted, bringing her to the ground. They rolled. He almost had her pinned—

Her knee caught Petrus hard beneath his breastbone. The air left his lungs. He doubled over on the ground.

"Petrus!" Her hand gripped his shoulder. "Petrus, are you all right?"

He squeezed his eyes shut and dragged air into his lungs. "Don't you dare apologize."

Innis was silent. After a moment the hand left his shoulder. When he opened his eyes, he saw her crouched alongside him. Her expression was anxious, the broad brow creased.

Petrus sat up, biting back a groan. He felt his ribs gingerly and then climbed to his feet. "Last bout."

Innis didn't move. "Are you sure you're up to it?"

"I don't break that easily."

Still she hesitated.

"If you hold back, we'll do it again," Petrus told her. "And again. And again."

He saw determination settle on her face. The square jaw firmed. "No holding back."

Innis kept her word. The bout was hard and fast, rough.

"Much better," Dareus said, as Petrus scrambled to his feet after being thrown.

They circled, panting heavily. Petrus wiped sweat from his brow. He and Innis were evenly matched. No, not evenly matched; they were *exactly* matched. They had the same training, knew the same moves— and Justen's body was modeled on his. They now had the same reach, the same strength, the same weight.

Petrus blew out a breath and started forward.

Innis met him halfway. For a moment they grappled, each trying to tip the other, then Petrus managed to hook his foot around her ankle.

They fell, twisting for dominance. His head hit the ground so hard that for a moment he saw stars. The hands grabbing him gentled. "Petrus?"

"Don't hold back," he panted, trying to catch Innis in a choke-hold.

Innis wrenched free of his grip. A strong arm hooked around his throat. The next moment, his face was being ground into the dirt and a crushing weight was on his back. "Do you yield?"

Petrus tried to shrug her off.

The arm tightened until he couldn't breathe. "Yield," he wheezed.

Innis laughed, an exultant sound, and released him.

Petrus pushed up to sit, grimacing, panting. He spat dirt from his mouth. "I hope you get the chance to do that to the prince."

"The prince?" Innis glanced at Dareus. "I won't, will I?"

Dareus shrugged. "Noblemen often wrestle with their armsmen."

"He certainly won't want to wrestle with any of us." Petrus heaved to his feet, stifling a groan.

"Well done, Innis," Dareus said. "That was excellent. Get dressed. We need to start back."

Petrus wiped dirt and sweat from his face. He walked across to where his shirt and boots lay.

Dareus followed him. "You were still holding back," he said in a low voice. "You could have won that bout."

Petrus glanced up sharply. Innis hadn't heard; she was pulling Justen's shirt over her head.

"She needed the confidence," he muttered, reaching for his boots.

"I'm aware of your feelings for her," Dareus said. "But you must treat her as a man. I won't have her fail because of you."

Petrus straightened. Dareus was shorter than him, leaner, but he carried the weight of decades as a Sentinel mage on his shoulders—judgments passed, punishments meted out. His authority was palpable.

"Yes, sir," he said.

Dareus gave a curt nod. "See that you do." He turned and spoke more loudly, so that Innis could hear. "From now on, you answer only to Justen."

CHAPTER EIGHT

IT WAS LATE afternoon when Jaumé reached Neuly. The village gates were shut. Armed men stood atop the wall.

He halted uncertainly at the fringe of the forest. Were the gates closed because the curse had reached the village?

He listened, straining his ears. No screams came from within the walls. He heard only the soft rain. Everything was quiet, peaceful.

Hunger forced him from the forest. He walked towards the gates, his gaze lifting to the men on the wall. Before he'd covered half the distance, one of them shouted: "Come no closer!"

Jaumé halted.

"Go away!" the man shouted.

"I don't have the curse," Jaumé called out. "I haven't drunk—"

"Be gone!" A stone struck the ground, spraying mud and water.

Jaumé stepped back a pace. "Please—"

This time the stone almost struck him. He stumbled backwards.

"Be gone!" the man cried again.

Jaumé swallowed. "But I don't have the curse."

The men on top of the wall made no reply. Their faces were grim.

"Please—" Jaumé's voice broke. "Please may I have some food?"

"We keep our food for our own. Now go!" Another stone accompanied the words.

Jaumé blinked back tears. He turned away from the village.

After half a mile, he came to a farm. Smoke rose from the chimney. Jaumé wiped his face. He walked down the path and knocked on the door. It swung open, revealing an empty kitchen. "Hello?"

No one answered him.

Jaumé stepped into the kitchen. A fire still smoldered in the hearth, but the larder had been hastily emptied. Spilled flour lay on the shelves and the floor. The storeroom was bare apart from a string of onions hanging in the farthest corner. It was full of smells— cheese, cured sausages—that made his mouth water.

He went outside, into the rain. The farmyard was eerily silent. The hen house was empty, and the pig pen. No dogs barked a warning at him.

The garden had been stripped—pumpkins cut from the vine, carrots pulled from the ground—but in a far corner Jaumé found a row of radishes that had been overlooked.

He squatted in the dirt, pulling up radishes and eating them.

When he was finished, he started walking again. West. Away.

CHAPTER NINE

DUSK HAD FALLEN by the time they reached the new campsite. Sometime during the afternoon they'd passed from the royal forest into the unbroken tract of woodland that stretched to Osgaard's eastern border. Nothing marked that boundary. The trees looked the same—oak and ash, rowan and yew. Innis saw no roads, no dwellings, nothing but trees and the occasional animal trail.

Petrus soared overhead, his pale-feathered breast tinted orange by the setting sun. The sky was hazy above the treetops, streaked with fiery bands of cloud.

"Are you having any difficulty holding the change?" Dareus asked.

Innis shook her head. The campsite was visible through the trees: tents, a fire, horses tethered. She glanced up, searching for Petrus, following him with her eyes for a moment. It was his easy confidence, his relaxed masculinity, that she needed to mimic. She took a deep breath, feeling her chest expand. *I'm him.*

"You have your story straight?"

"Yes."

"Good." Exhaustion was etched on Dareus's face, beneath the soot and sweat.

It had been a long afternoon. They'd pushed east through the forest as fast as they could, riding hard when possible, slowing all too often to avoid bands of soldiers and huntsmen. Twice they'd passed through walls of fire laid by Cora, Dareus holding the flames at bay as they forced the horses through. Once, hounds had caught their scent and Dareus had started a fire himself.

"Gerit and Ebril can practice shifting into Justen tonight," Dareus said. "Once the prince is asleep. By tomorrow they'll be able to swap with you."

Innis nodded.

"Remember, you'll need to keep each other informed of things the prince has said and done, things Justen would know."

"Yes."

People were visible ahead through the tree trunks: Cora, Ebril. Prince Harkeld. She heard the sound of Ebril whistling.

Innis watched as the prince walked across to the campfire, as he glanced up at the sky, at the two hawks—Petrus and Gerit—circling overhead, as he looked away.

"Remember, you're not a mage. React as if it's all new."

She nodded again.

"*Be* Justen."

HORSEMEN CAME THROUGH the trees. Two riders, three horses. Harkeld stayed where he was, watching the riders dismount. One was the leader of the witches, Dareus. The other was a stranger. Harkeld examined him suspiciously. He was a big man, young, with a fighter's lean-muscled build.

His new armsman.

Harkeld narrowed his eyes. Was the man a witch?

The newcomer surveyed the campsite. His face, beneath the light brown hair, was smeared with soot from the forest fires.

A hawk circled down to land. The newcomer turned his attention to it. Harkeld didn't. He watched the man's face, saw interest, curiosity. He didn't need to see the hawk to know when it changed; the newcomer's expression told him. The man blinked, his eyebrows rising, and rocked slightly on his feet as if he wanted to step backwards.

Perhaps not a witch.

"I'm starving," someone said. "Tell me that stew's ready."

Harkeld glanced sideways. The fair-haired witch stood where the hawk had been. He was naked.

The witch yawned. He walked across to the trio of horses and unstrapped a bundle from behind one of the saddles. Clothes.

Harkeld turned his attention back to the newcomer. The man was staring at him.

"Prince Harkeld," Dareus said. "I'd like you to meet your new armsman."

Harkeld crossed the clearing, eyeing the newcomer. *Can I trust you?*

He'd trusted his last armsman, Ralf—and Ralf had tried to kill him.

"What's your name?"

"Justen," the man said, and then, after a faint hesitation, "Highness."

"Sire," Harkeld said. Highness was for the rigid formality of the palace, for marble rooms with gilded ceilings, for clothes stitched with gold and silver thread.

The man nodded. "Sire."

They were of an equal height. Harkeld looked Justen up and down. He was a plain man, with a direct gaze. His clothing was well-worn, trews and shirt made of rough cotton, faded and fraying at the seams, dark with soot and sweat. The shirt was open at his throat, the sleeves rolled up to show brawny forearms. Swordsman's forearms. Above his sternum a pale disc was visible. "You're Grooten." *And down on your luck.*

"Yes, sire."

"How old are you?"

"Twenty-five."

"What are you doing in Osgaard?"

"Trying to get home."

The sun had set. The clearing was rapidly darkening. "Have you been an armsman before?"

"No, sire. But I know how to fight."

THEY ATE AROUND the fire. Harkeld chewed slowly, ignoring the witches. His gaze kept returning to Justen. *Can I trust you?* "Where's Innis?" he heard Dareus say.

"Sleeping. She'll take the second watch tonight."

When the meal was finished, Dareus stood. In the shadows cast by the fire his face was hawkish. "Justen will share your tent tonight."

And cut my throat as I sleep? Harkeld gulped the last mouthful of cider and put his mug down. He stood and looked at Justen. Tension vibrated inside him.

Justen put down his bowl and scrambled to his feet. "Sire?"

Harkeld turned on his heel and walked across to his tent.

Justen followed.

"See if you can find a candle."

"Yes, sire."

Harkeld crouched and crawled into the tent. He'd done no more than take off his boots before Justen was back.

"Here." Justen held the lit stub of a candle out to him.

Harkeld took it. In the candlelight the man's face seemed to flicker between menacing and harmless.

"Nice tent," Justen said, removing his boots. He had the same accent as the witches: throaty *r*, sibilant *s*. "Goat hair. Waterproof."

Harkeld twisted the candle into the ground. "How do you come to be in Osgaard?"

"My ship sailed without me," Justen said, placing his boots beside the entrance.

Harkeld glanced at him sharply. "You're a sailor?" The man didn't look like a sailor.

Justen shook his head. "Merchant's assistant." He frowned. "Was." He unbuckled his sword belt.

Harkeld tensed, watching the blunt fingers, the sword. "Why did the ship sail without you? Were you drunk?"

"No." Justen laid the sword belt aside. "The captain couldn't pay the port fees, so he pulled anchor and sailed half a day early. Me and a couple of sailors were left behind."

"When was this?"

"Last month."

Harkeld eyed the sword belt. "What have you been doing since then?"

"Trying to earn my fare home. But I don't belong to a guild, so no one will hire me."

"There's bondservice."

Justen snorted, a contemptuous sound. "In Groot, we call that slavery."

Harkeld sat back on his heels. He watched as Justen unrolled a blanket. It was threadbare. "You could claim the bounty. The weight of my head in gold."

Justen looked at him. "No, I couldn't."

"Why not?"

"Because I don't want to." Justen pulled his shirt over his head. The Grooten disc lay above his sternum, round and pale, like the moon.

"You're not tempted?"

"No." Justen wadded the shirt up and placed it on the ground as a pillow.

The simple matter-of-factness of the answer was more believable than a wordy protestation. Harkeld looked at Justen and believed him.

Even so, he slept with his sword in his hand. He woke at dawn to the sound of the man's breathing, deep and steady. He turned his head. He dimly saw Justen's face, slack in sleep. The Grooten sword lay between them, its blade naked.

Harkeld looked at it for a moment, and then released his grip on his own sword. He pushed aside his blanket and sat up, yawning.

Justen's eyes opened. For a moment he stared at Harkeld, his brow creased in bewilderment, then an expression almost of panic crossed his face and he sat abruptly, shoving the blanket aside. He looked down at his bare chest and reached for the amulet, gripping it. He inhaled a shuddering breath. After a moment he turned his head to look at Harkeld. "Sire."

"Are you all right?"

"I... I didn't know where I was."

Harkeld grunted and looked away. He knew where he was: in a nightmare. He reached for his boots and sword belt and crawled out of the tent. Dawn was breaking over the trees, as hazy and fiery as sunset had been. The red-headed witch was tending the campfire, whistling between his teeth. Two other witches were moving through slow exercises, stretching, warming up their muscles.

Harkeld watched for a moment, aware of how stiff he was.

The tent flap was pushed aside. Justen emerged hurriedly. His shirt was in one hand, his sword in the other. "You shouldn't be out here without me, sire."

Above them, a hawk uttered a shrill cry. Harkeld heard the sound of wings making a swift descent. "Do you wrestle?"

"Yes, sire," Justen said, shrugging into his shirt. Yesterday's soot and sweat stained it.

Harkeld stretched his arms above his head. "Shall we?"

"Now?" Justen paused in the act of pulling on one of his boots.

Harkeld shrugged. "Why not?" A short bout

before breakfast, to loosen their muscles—and give him the chance to get Justen's measure.

Justen looked past him. He frowned suddenly. "Something's wrong."

Harkeld swung around.

"Innis says there are soldiers less than two miles away!" Dareus hurried towards them. Above him, a hawk soared into the sky. "Their dogs have our scent."

Harkeld shoved on his boots. "Saddle our horses. I'll strike the tent."

Justen ran to obey.

THEY RODE HARD, following first one hawk and then another. Branches swiped at Harkeld as he galloped through the trees. He kept his eyes on Dareus, not bothering to look behind him. Justen rode at his back, and behind Justen, the witch Cora. At one point, he heard the high, excited barking of dogs from close behind—and then the crackle of flames as Cora set the forest on fire.

He caught occasional glimpses of the sun rising in a smoky sky. "We're going in circles," he said, when they rested the sweating horses in a walk.

"There are soldiers on three sides of us," Dareus said.

"Herding us?"

"Trying to cut us off before we reach the river."

They changed horses. There were four empty saddles, four witches flying in the form of birds. Harkeld rode a gray gelding, and when it tired, the bay again. One of the hawks landed when they were changing horses for a third time. Gerit.

"We'll be at the river soon," the witch said. "They've blocked all the fords. Can you swim?"

Harkeld wiped sweat from his face. "Yes."

"And you?"

"Yes," Justen said.

"Good." Gerit gave a short nod. "Follow me."

THE RIVER BANK, when they reached it, was a broad stretch of shingle, curving out of sight upstream. The river was half a furlong wide, flowing in slow, deep eddies. Oak trees clustered thickly on the far bank, their branches reaching out over water so dark it looked almost black. Smoke filled the sky above them, and the sound of hounds baying drifted on the wind.

A second hawk swooped down, becoming Petrus as it touched the ground. He pointed upstream. "Archers are coming!" A heartbeat later, a silver-maned lion stood on the shingle.

Justen drew his sword. "Go, sire!"

The lion began to lope along the bank. Harkeld reached for his sword.

Justen thumped his shoulder with a closed fist. "Go!" He swiped his sword blade against the gray's rump. "Cross the river!"

The gelding surged forward, its hooves sending up a spray of water. Harkeld hauled on the reins.

"Get across!" Cora was alongside him, her face fierce. "Before they come!"

Harkeld ignored her. Running away, leaving others to fight for him, was a coward's course.

"If you die—"

If I die, whole kingdoms will be emptied.

Harkeld clenched his jaw. He dug his heels into the gray's flanks. The horse surged forward again.

Cold water engulfed Harkeld's legs. Upstream, he heard the roar of the lion and the excited barking of hounds.

Cora was alongside him, the packhorses horses trailing behind. Harkeld glanced back. Justen was in the water, and Dareus. The lion and the barking hounds, the archers, were out of sight upstream. He looked ahead again, concentrating grimly on the far bank. It crept closer as the gray splashed and surged in the dark water.

The lion roared again. The sound reverberated loudly. Harkeld glanced back. The river bank was no longer empty. The lion stood there, facing a pack of hounds—and running along the shingle towards them were archers.

A hawk swooped low and fast over the water, screeching an alarm call.

"Sire, get off the horse!" Justen yelled. "They're aiming for you!"

The skin between his shoulder blades tightened, as if a target had been painted on his shirt. Harkeld kicked his feet out of the stirrups and shoved himself from the saddle. He plunged under the surface and came up gasping, surrounded by churning water and thrashing horses' legs.

"Swim, sire!"

Harkeld swam grimly, aware of the bulk of a packhorse behind him, shielding him. The river bank came nearer; branches hanging low over the water, dark shadows. Arrows plunged into the river ahead of him. One struck the bank, burying itself in the soil. Behind him a horse screamed.

The bank came closer. Around him horses surged out of the river. His own feet found the bottom. He ran, the water dragging at his legs, and scrambled up the bank surrounded by horses.

"Run, sire!" Justen cried behind him.

Harkeld ran. The forest seemed full of noise: shouted voices, the thunder of hooves. When he was deep among the trees, he stopped. Ahead of him, horses still galloped. He turned, gasping for breath, water streaming from his clothes.

Justen came crashing through the trees, still mounted. "Sire!"

"I'm fine." Harkeld braced his hands on his knees, panting. "You?"

Justen's hair was plastered to his head. "You need a horse."

"The gray—"

"The gray's dead. We're lucky it wasn't you."

CHAPTER TEN

IN THE AFTERNOON, Princess Brigitta visited her half-brothers in the nursery. The tension in the palace hadn't reached here. Outside the gilded door, people spoke in hushed voices and hurried about their business with downcast eyes; inside, were the smells of cinnamon and warm milk and a sense of safety.

She knelt at a low table, parchment spread before her. "There." Six-year-old Rutgar pointed with a grubby finger. "Draw a horse on top of the hill, Britta. Please!"

Britta dipped the goose feather in ink and obediently drew a horse. Beside her, Lukas squirmed excitedly. "And an axe, Britta!" he cried. "Give the woodcutter an axe, so he can fight the wolf!"

Britta drew an axe in the woodcutter's hand, with a sharp, curving blade. It made her think of Harkeld and the bounty on his head.

Run, Harkeld. Don't let them catch you.

"Where do you want the wolf?" she asked.

Rutgar leaned over the parchment, examining the scene she'd drawn. "There," he said, his fingertip leaving a smudge on the parchment. "Under the tree."

"No, no!" Lukas cried. "Not there! That's where the witch is going."

Witch. The word seemed to resonate in the room. Britta glanced at her armsman, standing beside the door. Did he hear it ringing in his head the way she did?

"I don't want a witch this time," Rutgar said.

Neither do I.

"Why not?" Lukas demanded of his older brother.

Rutgar glanced at her. Britta tried to read his face. Worry? Confusion? Fear?

"Because of Harkeld?" she asked.

He nodded.

Britta looked at the parchment, at the place where Lukas wanted her to draw the witch. *Harkeld, are you a witch?*

Of course he's not, she told herself for what seemed like the hundredth time.

"Are we witches too?" The words burst from Rutgar, full of anxiety.

Britta laid down the quill. "No, sweetheart," she said, reaching out to stroke the blond hair back from his face. "It was Harkeld's mother who had the witch blood, not your mother or mine."

"Or Jaegar's mother?" Rutgar persisted.

"Or Jaegar's mother."

"Harkeld's a witch," Lukas announced.

"No, love. He's not."

"But he *could* be," Rutgar said, the same mix of confusion and fear and worry on his face.

Yes, he could.

"Even if he is a witch, he's your brother and he would *never* hurt you." Britta said the words firmly and smiled at the little boy. "Don't be scared of Harkeld." *Be scared* **for** *him. Father has a bounty on his head.*

She picked up the quill again and dipped it in ink. "Now, where would you like the wolf?"

A knock on the door made her lift her head. Her armsman, Karel, opened the door. The mood of the palace seemed to leak into the nursery: edgy, fearful.

Britta heard low voices, then Karel stepped back and a bondservant entered the nursery.

"Princess." The man bowed low.

She recognized him: he served her father. *No. Not now.* Her hand quivered slightly and a drop of ink fell on the parchment.

Britta swallowed. "What is it?"

"The king demands your presence, princess."

Her throat tightened. For a moment she couldn't breathe. *What shall I do without Harkeld to help me?* She placed the quill carefully in its silver holder. "Inform my father that I shall be there shortly."

"Yes, highness." The man bowed again and scurried from the room.

Britta capped the ink pot.

"But you haven't finished," Rutgar protested.

"I'll come back tomorrow." She forced a smile to her lips. "I promise."

"You made a mistake," Lukas said, pointing.

Britta looked at the ink blot. "Never mind. We'll turn it into a rock."

She kissed both boys on the cheek, inhaling the scent of the cinnamon buns they'd eaten for lunch and the rosemary the nursemaids washed their hair with.

"May we start coloring it in?" Rutgar asked as her armsman opened the door for her.

"Of course." Britta smiled at them from the doorway. "But let the ink dry first."

She hurried back to her rooms. The sound of her armsman's stride echoed flatly in the marble corridors. Memory came, Harkeld's voice: *You need to understand who our father is, Britta. He's a dangerous man. I think he killed the boys' mother.*

Her maid was in the bedchamber, mending the hem of a gown. She glanced up as Britta entered.

"Yasma, my father wants to see me. I need a new overtunic. This one's creased."

Yasma scrambled to her feet. "Do you think—?"

"I don't know."

Britta unfastened her girdle and shrugged out of the wrinkled tunic while Yasma fetched a fresh one. A glance in the mirror told her that the silk undergown had survived the nursery unmarked by ink or grubby fingers.

Yasma returned with a sky-blue tunic in her arms. She lifted it over Britta's head and settled the fabric neatly over her shoulders, smoothing the long folds. The heavy silk was embroidered with gold thread.

Yasma fastened the girdle briskly. "Your hair."

Britta sat before the mirror.

"What do you think he wants?" the maid asked.

"I don't know."

Their eyes met in the mirror. *Probably Duke Rikard.* But neither of them said it aloud.

Britta watched as Yasma tidied her hair, catching up stray tendrils and weaving them back into place around the crown. Her eyes were drawn to the iron band of bondservice that gleamed dully on the girl's arm. "A few days before he left, Harkeld told me something about Queen Sigren."

"Yes?" Yasma said, her fingers moving deftly.

"He said that she argued with my father the night she died. About bondservice."

Yasma's fingers slowed.

"Sigren said that bondservice was barbaric and cruel, and it had to stop." Britta glanced at Yasma in the mirror, remembering the first time she'd seen the girl, remembering the mute misery on her face and the utter despair in her eyes. "Father said that Osgaard's economy couldn't survive without bondservants."

Yasma said nothing. She continued weaving strands of hair around the golden crown.

"Sigren disagreed. She said it's the greed of Osgaard's rulers that keeps the people so oppressed. She said that if we forwent our golden bathtubs, our gilded roof tiles, we wouldn't need to raise taxes again. We could free the bondservants." Britta stared at her reflection. Gold threads gleamed in the tunic she wore. The chair she sat on was gilded. The pins Yasma used to fasten the crown into her hair were set with precious stones. Even the mirror was gilt-framed.

"Father threw his goblet at Sigren and ordered her from the room. Harkeld said that was the last time he saw her. She died that night, in her bath tub." A golden bath tub.

Yasma said nothing.

"Harkeld said... her death was no accident."

Yasma met her eyes in the mirror. She lowered her hands and stepped back. "I've finished."

Britta swallowed. She stood and looked at herself in the mirror. A princess stared back at her, a delicate crown woven into her hair. Gold thread glinted on the sleeveless overtunic. A golden girdle circled her waist. The long-sleeved cream undergown with its flowing sleeves was made of silk, the fabric rich and shimmering.

Her face was as pale as the undergown, her lips colorless.

Father's a bully, Harkeld's voice said in her head. *Never let him see you're afraid of him.*

Britta pinched her cheeks and watched some color flow back into her face. "I must go," she said, turning away from the mirror. "Father hates to be kept waiting."

Yasma didn't curtsey. Instead, she reached out and clasped Britta's hand. "Be careful."

Britta returned the grip tightly, then she blew out a breath and strode into the parlor. Her armsman stood alongside the door, his feet the regulation twelve inches apart, his dark, hawk-like face expressionless.

He opened the door.

Britta marched through it. The armsman fell into step behind her.

She heard Harkeld's voice as she walked: *We will defy him over Rikard, but we must be careful.* A bondservant scurried ahead of them along the corridor, his head lowered submissively and an iron armband pinched around his upper arm.

They came to a flight of shallow steps. The bondservant scuttled down them and hurried out of sight. Britta followed more slowly, her hand skimming the balustrade. The marble was smooth and cool beneath her fingers.

We will present Father with a solution that satisfies his greed and his pride: marriage to Prince Tomas of Lundegaard.

At the foot of the stairs, Britta turned right. The armsman kept pace behind her, his hobnailed boots striking echoes from the marble floor.

Stand your ground, Harkeld had said. *We'll wear him down. It's a good match, better than what he's proposing.* And last week, before the arrival of the witches, their father had talked of sending Harkeld to Lundegaard to discuss the subject with King Magnas and Prince Tomas.

Britta turned another corner. Armsmen lined the corridor outside her father's apartments, standing to attention in their scarlet tunics and golden breastplates. She halted at the door to the king's antechamber. Dread fisted in her belly.

She looked back at her armsman, seeing curling black hair, dark eyes, brown skin. If she told him to take her back to her rooms, he would.

"Please knock, Karel."

KAREL FOLLOWED ONE step behind the princess. The antechamber, with its heavy scarlet hangings and gilded mirrors, was empty except for the armsmen positioned along the walls.

The door to the king's audience chamber opened. Prince Jaegar stepped through. "Ah, Britta." The prince scrutinized his half-sister and gave a nod, as if approving of her appearance. He opened the door more widely. "Don't keep him waiting."

Princess Brigitta crossed the room. Karel followed. "You aren't required," Prince Jaegar said without looking at him.

Karel halted.

"A word of advice, Britta. Don't cross him. He's looking for someone to punish. I wouldn't want it to be you." A smile glinted in the prince's eyes.

He's enjoying this.

"Thank you," Princess Brigitta said. She stepped past her half-brother. Karel watched as she surreptitiously pinched her cheeks, as she lifted her chin.

Be careful, he told her silently.

CHAPTER ELEVEN

HER FATHER SAT on his throne. He was as motionless as the armsmen standing around the walls. Only his eyes moved, watching her as she walked across the marble floor.

Britta halted at the foot of his dais. She sank into a low curtsey.

"Brigitta," her father said coldly. "What took you so long?" Jewels set in gold glittered on his fingers. Anger glittered in his eyes.

"Forgive me, Father." She straightened, biting her tongue to keep from babbling excuses. "I came as quickly as I was able."

The king looked her up and down. It was hard not to cringe beneath that scrutiny. With every second that passed, her chest tightened and her heart beat louder.

"I've had enough of this nonsense about your marriage." There was a harsh edge of anger in her father's voice. "Duke Rikard is my choice of husband for you. He's commander of my army. I see no reason why you should object to him!"

An image of the duke rose in her mind's eye: fleshy body, cruel mouth, face glistening with sweat. Britta's stomach clenched in a sick knot.

"Answer me," her father demanded. "Will you, or will you not, marry Rikard?"

Britta swallowed. *I'd sooner die than marry Rikard.* She looked at her father, saw the rage swelling his face, and knew with absolute certainty that Jaegar was correct: Father would punish her in Harkeld's stead, if she gave him the chance.

There was utter silence in the room. Britta heard her heart thudding in her chest. This wasn't a decision about her marriage; it was about her life.

When Princess Brigitta emerged from the king's audience chamber, her face was wax-like, pale and stiff. She didn't seem to see Karel when he stepped away from the wall.

He followed her back to her rooms. Yasma emerged hurriedly from the bedchamber. "Princess?"

"I wish to change."

Karel caught Yasma's eye. *Find out what happened.*

Yasma gave a tiny nod. She followed the princess into the bedchamber and shut the door. Ten minutes later, she emerged. Her face was sober.

Karel stopped pacing the parlor. "Well?"

"She's marrying Rikard."

"What?" He took an involuntary step backwards. *Not Rikard!*

"The king says it's a good match." Yasma pressed her hands to her temples. "He's commander of the King's Army. And a duke."

"He's a thug! With the manners of a hog scrambling for the best place at the feeding trough."

Yasma didn't appear to hear him. "Karel, do you

know anything about Queen Sigren's death?"

He blinked. "What about it?"

"Britta said... she said Prince Harkeld told her it wasn't an accident. He thought the king had Sigren killed."

Karel nodded. "I've heard that rumor."

"Do you think it's true?"

Karel hesitated, remembering Queen Sigren's death two and a half years ago, remembering the rumors rife in the palace—and remembering that the queen's armsmen had been quietly pensioned off with fat purses of gold in the wake of her death. He nodded again.

"So does Britta," Yasma said miserably. "So you see, she daren't disobey her father." She turned back towards the bedchamber.

"About Queen Sigren, you mustn't repeat–"

"I know."

Karel held the question between his teeth while Yasma walked away from him, and then had to ask: "When is the wedding?"

"In three days."

BRITTA SPENT THE afternoon in her garden. The things she normally delighted in—the scent of roses, the hum of bees gathering pollen—didn't lift her mood. She saw only the clouds in the sky, not the sunshine, heard only the discordant crunch of her shoes on the crushed marble paths, not the birdsong.

Her eyes kept turning to the high stone wall that ringed the palace grounds. With Karel guarding her, she'd never escape. His footsteps crunched behind her on the path even now. He watched her so intently it was impossible to imagine evading him.

I could kill myself.

Britta turned the thought over in her head. Would it be better to be dead than be pawed over by Rikard? To share his bed?

Better to be dead.

But if she killed herself, Yasma would lose her protection. The maid would go back to scrubbing floors and being bedded by any man who wanted her.

I can't do that to her.

In front of her a worm struggled to cross the path.

"Careful, Karel."

Her armsman halted. Britta bent and picked up the worm. She deposited it beneath a rose bush, where the soil was rich and damp.

I wish I wasn't a princess.

But then what would she be? A commoner, living in a dirt-floored house, wondering where her next meal was coming from, watching her children die of illness and hunger? Or perhaps she'd be a bondservant like Yasma, condemned to a life of slavery, being passed from man to man because of her pretty face, bound into servitude so that her children might be free.

Isn't that what I am? A bondservant, with no control over my own life, no say in who my body goes to?

Britta halted in front of her favorite rosebush. The petals were creamy white, glowing softly golden at their heart, the edges tipped with pink. She gently brushed a drop of water from one smooth petal.

No, her position was nothing like Yasma's. She was being given to one man, within the laws and protections of a marriage contract. And she wasn't twelve years old, as Yasma had been the first time a man had taken her. She was eighteen. A grown woman.

The petal was as soft as silk beneath her fingertips. Sweet scent drifted up.

Yasma survived. As will I.

CHAPTER TWELVE

THEY PUSHED EAST while smoke rose in the sky behind them. Harkeld rode a packhorse, a sturdy roan Cora had caught. Midway through the afternoon shapeshifters brought one of the packhorses, carrying food. They ate riding, chewing on nuts and strips of dried meat.

Several hours later they emerged from the cool shade of the forest into a grassy clearing beside a creek. Ebril was there, whistling between his teeth as he laid a ring of stones for a fire. Behind him, several horses grazed. Harkeld recognized the bay he'd ridden that morning.

Dareus dismounted stiffly, wearily. "Our pursuit?"

"South," Ebril said. "The fires confused them. They haven't found your trail yet."

Dareus grunted. He looked across the clearing. Shadows were lengthening along the ground. "The other horses?"

Ebril shook his head. "Two dead, one injured. Lame. We had to leave it."

They tended the horses as the sun sank behind a veil of smoke. Cora built a fire from fallen branches and lit it with a snap of her fingers. There were no tents; the packhorse carrying them had died at the river crossing.

Everything was wet—boots, saddles, clothing, blankets. Harkeld dried his sword with a handful of yellowing grass. He looked down at his belongings. They made a pitiful collection, spread out to dry.

Two days ago he'd been a prince, eating the finest food, sleeping on silken sheets. Today he was a fugitive, bare-footed and bare-chested, clad in damp trews, with nothing more than a wet blanket to sleep in tonight. *How did I fall so far, so fast?*

"We need to cut your hair, sire," Justen said. "The archers knew who to aim for."

Harkeld touched the tangled strands that hung down his back. His hair was the last thing tying him to his birthright, the last sign he was of royal blood.

He couldn't summon the energy to object, just nodded. "You have a razor?"

Justen shook his head. "Back on the ship. I've been getting shaved at the public baths. But Ebril or Petrus will have one."

"The witches won't have razors," Harkeld said. "We'll have to use your dagger."

"Why won't they have razors?"

"Because they grow feathers, not hair. They have to pluck themselves."

Justen stared at him for a moment, and then gave a shout of laughter. "By the All-Mother, you don't believe that, do you?"

Harkeld flushed. "It's true."

"Then how do you explain Gerit's beard? Innis's hair?" Justen asked, grinning widely.

"They're shapeshifters. They've made themselves look human."

"Ach, you don't truly believe that, do you, sire?" Justen's grin turned down at the corners. "That they grow feathers, not hair?"

"Of course. Everyone knows it's true."

Justen's grin vanished entirely. "What else does everyone know?"

"That witches mate with animals. That their women give birth to litters of kittens."

"Kittens?"

"And other things. Some witches have goats' eyes and walk on cloven hooves, others have the heads of dogs or asses, others—"

Justen snorted. "I've never heard such nonsense in my life." He paused, and then added, "Sire."

Harkeld stiffened. "It's true."

"We had a mage born in my village. He didn't have an ass's head or cloven hooves. He didn't grow feathers or fur. He was just like anyone else."

"He can't have been a witch then."

Justen grinned. "He's one, all right. When he's home, he sometimes turns into a sea eagle and goes out ahead of the fleet to find where the fish are running." His arms lifted, mimicking a bird's wings. "Must be marvelous to be able to fly."

Fly? With feathers sprouting from his skin? The thought made Harkeld's scalp prickle.

Justen lowered his arms. "Fredrik didn't even know he was a mage until he was tested."

"Tested?"

"All children in the Allied Kingdoms are tested, to see if any of them have magic. Mages come to Groot every few years." He shrugged. "They don't find many. Groot doesn't breed a lot of mages."

Harkeld flexed his hand, looking at the way skin moved over muscle and bone. An ordinary hand—and yet the blood that flowed beneath his skin was tainted. *Would the test show I am a witch?*

He clenched his hand into a fist. No. The blood was too diluted. He was no witch. He *refused* to be a witch. "What happens to them? The children?"

"They go to Rosny when they're old enough. To learn to use their magic."

They should be culled. Like deformed calves are culled from a herd.

"Fredrik has to shave, like you and me. He grows whiskers, not feathers." Justen indicated the witches with his hand: Cora stirring the stewpot, Ebril and Petrus spreading bedrolls and blankets to dry beside the fire, Dareus checking horses' legs. "That's the truth. Not asses' heads and cloven hooves. The truth is what you see with your own eyes, sire. Not what someone tells you."

Harkeld looked coldly at his armsman. "How dare you speak to me—"

But Justen didn't hear the reprimand; he was striding towards the fire. "Petrus, Ebril, do either of you have a razor?"

Both witches looked up.

"I need to cut the prince's hair. Makes him a target."

Ebril nodded. "Use mine."

Harkeld maintained a reproving silence while Justen cut his hair. The armsman didn't appear to notice. "There," he said cheerfully when it was done. "Now you look like the rest of us."

A commoner. Harkeld touched his hair. The strands were short, no longer than his thumb.

They ate around the fire. The girl, Innis, came out of the darkness and sat wrapped in a blanket. Harkeld half-expected to see her guzzle the food from her bowl like an animal, but she ate with a spoon, as neatly as any court lady.

He looked down at his stew. Would the witches bother to cook if he and Justen weren't with them? Or would they eat the raw flesh of slaughtered beasts, as the tales said they did, and rotting carrion and dead babies?

The truth is what you see with your own eyes.

Not always. Sometimes what you saw was what people *wanted* you to see.

Beside him, Justen scraped his wooden bowl clean with a spoon. "By the All-Mother, I needed that," he said, stifling a belch.

Gerit grunted his agreement.

Harkeld finished his stew. He put down the bowl and closed his eyes for a moment, remembering the arrows, the churning water, the screaming horses, and silently thanked the All-Mother that Britta hadn't been with them. If she had, she'd most likely be dead.

Emotion tightened his throat. He opened his eyes and looked up at the starless sky. *Be safe, Britta. Be safe, Rutgar. Be safe, Lukas. May the All-Mother watch over and protect you.*

An owl hooted softly in the forest. Or perhaps it was a witch.

Harkeld cleared his throat and stood. "I'm going to bed," he told Justen, ignoring the witches.

The bedrolls were still damp. The blankets were too.

After a few minutes, Justen joined him. He laid his sword between them, the blade bared. "Let's hope it doesn't rain tonight."

Harkeld grunted. He glanced towards the fire. The girl, Innis, was gone. As he watched, Petrus emerged from the darkness and sat.

He rolled on his side, putting his back to the fire, to the witches.

CHAPTER THIRTEEN

AT MIDNIGHT, KAREL handed Princess Brigitta's safety into the care of her second armsman, Torven, and went off duty. The corridors of the palace were still brightly lit. He descended the stairs to the armsmen's barracks, slung his sword belt over a peg in the antechamber, and joined the line of men waiting for food in the mess hall. The air was thick with the smell of mutton and leeks.

Karel took his plate and sat down at one of the long tables. He began to eat, paying no attention to the men sitting around him. The low ceiling echoed with a hundred different conversations.

"Island girls are such whores. They squeal loudly when you take them, but really they want to be rutted."

Karel chewed stolidly, letting the words pass over his head. They were aimed at him, bait for him to rise to if he was foolish enough.

They'll try to goad you, to break you. His uncle's words came back to him. *You must resist. You must prove that we are loyal and obedient. That we are worthy of freedom.*

He'd done more than that: he'd proven he was among the best. There wasn't one man in this hall he hadn't beaten in the training arena, either with his sword or his bare hands.

"... Princess Brigitta."

Karel's ears pricked at the words. He stopped chewing.

"Lucky whoreson. I wouldn't mind rutting her."

Karel forced himself to swallow. *Ignore them*, he told himself, but anger bunched in his muscles.

"I bet she squeals like a bondservant when Rikard ruts her," another man said, provoking laughter.

"I bet she likes it!" someone else said. "I bet she begs for more!"

Karel raised his eyes and gazed at the man, schooling his face into an expression of boredom. *Next time we're on the practice field, I'll have you.* He fixed the armsman in his memory and returned to his meal.

"The islander would know," a sly voice said to his right. "He's probably had her already."

Karel's grip tightened on his knife and fork. He reached for memory of his uncle's voice: *Your parents suffered in bondservice so that you might have this opportunity. Don't waste their sacrifice.* The words steadied him. The flare of anger died.

"Him!" someone exclaimed. "She'd never want an islander. Little better than animals, they are."

"I bet the islander dreams of her," the sly voice said again. "I bet he ruts her in his dreams."

Guffaws of laughter greeted this sally.

Karel glanced at the sly-voiced speaker, noting his face. *I'll have you, too.*

He ate the rest of his meal slowly, imagining what he'd do to the men. Break their elbows first, then their knees—

No, that was too elaborate. *Best make it simple. Best just rip off their heads and be done with it. They're not worth more.*

Karel chewed, enjoying the fantasy. When he'd finished the meal he pushed his plate aside and stood, paying no attention to the men around him. He collected his sword belt from the peg and went to bed.

CHAPTER FOURTEEN

IT STARTED RAINING during the night, soft rain that fell on her face, waking her. Innis pulled the blanket over her head and went back to sleep.

It was still raining at dawn. She woke, blinking, and stared up at the gray sky. *Who am I?* She groped at her throat and found the Grooten amulet, gripping it tightly. She was Justen.

Innis pushed aside the wet blanket and stood. Across the muddy clearing, Cora crouched at the dead fire, her plait hanging down her back. She snapped her fingers. The branches began to burn sluggishly.

No one did the morning exercises. They ate quickly, huddled around the fire, and loaded the packhorses. A russet-brown owl glided down, landing beside Dareus. It shook its feathers and changed into Ebril.

"Pursuit?" Dareus asked.

Ebril wiped rain from his face. "They're a good half day behind."

"And ahead of us?"

"Forest's full of them to the south. Keep going northeast and we should be fine." Ebril looked at the dying fire, at the loaded packhorses. "Is there any food left? Ah, bless you, Cora." He took the bowl of gruel Cora held out to him.

Ebril ate quickly, hunched in a wet blanket, while the horses were saddled.

"Mount," Dareus said.

Innis swung up into the saddle and adjusted the weight of Justen's sword more comfortably at her hip. She watched as Ebril changed into a hawk and spread his wings. Water trickled down the back of her neck. *I wish I had feathers today, instead of soggy clothes and boots that squelch.*

She tipped her head back, watching the hawk climb into the sky, and then glanced at the prince. His face was averted, tight-lipped.

They mate with animals, he'd said last night. *Their women give birth to kittens.*

Innis grimaced. How could he believe that?

As the day progressed the rain became heavier, drumming down. Her world narrowed to the water streaming from her hood, to the horse in front of her, to the drenched form of Prince Harkeld, wrapped in Ebril's spare cloak.

Finally they halted for the night beneath the outspread branches of a massive oak. Petrus glided down to land while they were unsaddling the horses. His feathers were dark with water, bedraggled.

Innis hefted her sodden saddle on one arm and walked towards the fire. Petrus intercepted her, wrapped in a blanket. His face was weary, his pale hair plastered to his skull. "Change into yourself," he said. "I'll be Justen for a couple of hours."

"But you've been a hawk all day—"

"And I'll be myself all night. You won't be."

It was the rain that made her hesitate, the *wetness* of everything. The thought of stripping out of wet clothes, of having to dress in them again later... Innis shook her head. "I'll be fine, Petrus. It's not a difficult form to maintain."

"Innis, *change*."

It was a nuisance peeling out of the trews, dragging off the clinging shirt, but once she'd shifted, she knew Petrus had been right. It felt odd to be herself. Her own body felt too small, too short, too... *wrong*.

Petrus handed her the blanket. "Anything I should know? Anything he's said?"

She shook her head.

"Go." He reached for one wet boot, grimacing as he forced his foot into it.

Innis walked back to the oak tree, hugging the blanket tightly around herself. She paused and looked at the horses, the smoldering fire, the prince.

She'd felt naked wrapped in just the blanket last night. Not because of the other mages; because of the prince.

"Thirsty?" Cora asked, glancing up from the pot she was stirring. "Like some cider?"

"Give me a minute."

Innis dressed in her own clothes, pulling them on over damp skin. The shirt and trews made her feel less exposed. *They mate with animals*, the prince had said, and last night she'd felt as if he was waiting for her to throw the blanket aside and run naked into the woods, to rut with the nearest beast she could find.

"Cider," Cora said, holding out a mug when she returned to the fire. "But no tents. I know which I'd prefer to have."

Innis sipped the cider. She watched as Petrus stepped into the firelight. Stubble was dark on his cheeks and throat. She touched her face with a fingertip. The skin felt too smooth.

This is me, Innis told herself, stroking her cheek. *This is who I am. A woman; not a man.* Yet her skin felt soft and hairless and wrong.

They ate a stew of dried meat, huddling with the horses beneath the shelter of the oak. Water dripped steadily from its boughs and fell with sharp hisses into the flames. Even with Cora's magic, the wood burned sluggishly.

Innis looked across the fire at Prince Harkeld. He was unrecognizable as the prince who'd walked into King Esger's throne room. He looked like the poorest of commoners, his clothes stained and torn, his hair roughly hacked short, his face dark with stubble and grime.

It wasn't just his appearance that was different, his manner was different, too. He'd walked into the throne room with his head held high, self-assured, confident, alert. A man used to being noticed, to being obeyed.

Innis studied him, frowning as she tried to identify what was different about Prince Harkeld. It wasn't that he was cowed or that the confidence was gone, it was more as if....

As if he'd closed himself off. *He holds himself apart from us.*

"More stew anyone?" Cora asked.

The prince glanced at her. His face momentarily hardened.

"Please," Petrus said, holding out his wooden bowl. "By the All-Mother, I'm starving!"

Innis looked down at her own stew. She stirred it with her spoon. *To him we're filthy, foul, loathsome.* She grimaced, remembering the prince's words. Humans mating with animals. Women giving birth to kittens.

How could he believe such things?

Because he knows nothing about who we really are.

Innis lifted her head. "Dareus? Justen wondered what a Sentinel mage is. I said you'd be able to explain it best." She glanced at Petrus. "Didn't I?"

Petrus paused with his spoon halfway to his mouth. He stared at her for a moment and then shrugged. "Yes."

"A Sentinel mage?" Dareus's eyebrows quirked slightly as he looked at her, then he put down his bowl and turned his attention to Petrus. "Sentinel mages make sure that the rules governing the use of magic are upheld."

Petrus glanced at her. "Er... rules?"

Innis gave him a tiny nod.

"There are certain dangers inherent in the use of magic. Take shapeshifting, for example. A mage who stays shifted for too long can identify too strongly with a body that's not human, become stuck there. It's a form of madness."

Petrus pulled a face. "Ach, that doesn't sound good."

"No. The rules are to prevent it happening." Dareus counted them off on his fingers. "No eating while in animal form. No sleeping. No copulation."

Innis glanced at the prince. He gave no sign that he was listening. He ate, not lifting his gaze from his bowl. *Listen*, she told him silently. *Hear the truth about us.*

"There are other rules," Dareus continued. "For example, shapeshifters are forbidden to make partial shifts—to become part one thing and part another— and they're absolutely forbidden to take the form of another human."

"Why?" Petrus asked.

"In the past there've been shapeshifters who abused their power. You've heard the tale of Ysaline?"

"The most beautiful woman in the world. Kings fought over her, nations fell..." Petrus paused. "She was a shapeshifter?"

Gerit spat into the fire. "Stupid bitch wanted to be a queen."

"Any power can corrupt," Dareus said. "Magic is no exception. It's our task as Sentinels to make sure it doesn't happen."

"And if it does?"

"We stop it." Dareus reached for his mug. "Magic is a responsibility. It's not something that makes you better than other people. In the past, there have been mages who failed to recognize that. These days, there are rules. There's *us*."

Innis glanced at the prince. Had he thought himself better than a commoner because of his royal blood? Had he seen his status in terms of power, or responsibility?

The prince looked up, as if he'd heard her silent question. His expression was closed, stony.

"If a mage abuses his power, we hunt him down and strip him of his magic. It's one of the tasks we're charged with. For that reason, only the most powerful mages may become Sentinels. Those who're extraordinarily adept in one of the disciplines."

"Disciplines?" Petrus asked.

"Shapeshifting. Fire magic. Healing. They're the most common."

Innis watched the prince. He ate his stew, giving no indication that he was listening.

"Most fire mages can do no more than this—" Dareus snapped his fingers. A flame flared at his fingertips for a second and then snuffed out. "Light a candle, start a cooking fire."

The prince glanced at Dareus's hand, and away.

"A strong mage can set fire to an object and control the spread of the flames," Dareus said. "As long as he's touching whatever he's set fire to."

Petrus nodded.

"But only the strongest mages—those able to *throw* fire and still control it—are capable of being Sentinels."

Petrus chewed and swallowed. "And shapeshifters? What about them?"

"Shapeshifters..." Dareus reached for his mug. "A lot of shapeshifters aren't capable of much. They can take one shape, perhaps hold it for half an hour. Some can't even do that."

Petrus nodded. Beside him, the prince had put down his bowl. He stared past Dareus, at the rain, but Innis thought he was listening.

"It's not an easy skill," Dareus said. "Every part of a shapeshifter's body changes—flesh and blood and bone. I'm not a shapeshifter myself, but I understand it's uncomfortable, even painful, to change shape."

Petrus nodded again.

Innis nodded too.

"Shapeshifters need to have a thorough understanding of anatomy. They have to know each animal inside *and* out before they can become it. Most never learn more than one or two shapes. To be a Sentinel, a mage has to be able take a dozen or more shapes, and they have to be able to hold each one for at least half a day." Dareus leaned forward. "You have to understand, Justen, being a shapeshifter isn't just about *taking* another shape, it's about having the strength to shift *back* into your own shape."

"Or you get trapped in a body that's not your own?"

"Yes." Dareus nodded. "And then you lose yourself, become an animal."

Innis repressed a shiver.

"That's why all mages are trained," Dareus said. "To prevent accidents like that happening."

Petrus grunted and nodded, as if this was all news to him. "So, Sentinels are strong mages?"

"Strong mages. Strong fighters. Each Sentinel must be able to defend himself not just with his magic, but with weapons—and his bare hands."

"Like an armsman," Petrus said, scraping his bowl clean and licking the spoon.

"Somewhat. We protect, we punish." Dareus paused. "Does that answer your question?"

Petrus glanced at her. His eyebrows lifted slightly. *Does it?*

Innis raised her chin, a tiny nod.

* * *

"WHAT WAS THAT about?" Petrus asked later as he stripped out of Justen's clothes.

"He thinks we mate with animals," Innis said, placing the amulet around her throat. Its weight felt familiar and right. "That we give birth to kittens and—"

"So?" Petrus said. "Everyone in the Seven Kingdoms thinks that."

"I want him to know the truth."

Petrus snorted. "He can hear it, but I doubt he'll believe it."

Innis pulled the shirt over her head. It was damp, and warm from Petrus's body. "He might."

"When hens grow teeth," Petrus said.

HARKELD WOKE FROM a nightmare in which he'd become a bird. Feathers sprouted from his head, from his chest, from his groin. Down grew on his face.

He sat up, gasping, his heart thudding in his chest. It was dawn.

"Sire?" Justen asked, slitting open his eyes. "Are you all right?"

Harkeld touched a fearful hand to his chin. The rasp of stubble was reassuring.

"Sire?"

"I'm fine," he said, pushing back his damp blanket and standing.

Nothing had changed overnight—the steady *drip drip drip* of water, the smell of wet soil, wet leaves, wet horses. "Still raining," Justen said, coming to stand beside him. He sighed. "Ach, it could be worse. Could be winter. Could be sleeting."

Harkeld grunted. He reached for his boots. The leather was cold, clammy.

Packing up camp took a matter of minutes; they rolled up the wet bedrolls and blankets, strapping them on the packhorses while Cora ladled gruel into wooden bowls.

A hawk landed while they ate. It shook itself and changed into Ebril. "They have our trail," he said, taking the blanket Dareus held out to him. "But they're still almost half a day behind. The rain's washed away a lot of our tracks and the dogs are having difficulty with the scent." He wrapped the blanket around himself and wiped his face with a corner.

"And ahead of us?"

"They're trying to cut us off, but we should be fine. We're further north than they think."

Cora handed him a bowl. Ebril began to spoon the gruel into his mouth, not bothering to sit.

"And the passes?" Dareus asked.

"They're blocking them," Ebril said, between mouthfuls. "But there are lots of passes, and only so many soldiers."

"And on the other side of the Graytooth range?" Cora asked. "In Lundegaard?"

Ebril shook his head. "No sign of activity."

"Choose a pass," Dareus told him. "We'll try to reach it tomorrow, before King Esger's men."

"And if they get there first?" Justen asked.

"Let's hope they don't. I'd like to avoid a fight. The risks are too great—"

Harkeld looked down at his bowl. He stabbed the gruel with his spoon. "Burn down the forest, if you're afraid of fighting," he muttered.

Beside him, Justen stirred slightly. "Can't you just raze the forest?" he asked. "Get rid of the soldiers that way?"

"Using magic to kill another human is forbidden. It's one of the Primary Laws."

"But the archers," Justen persisted. "Back at the river—"

"I burned their bows," Dareus said. "Not the men."

Harkeld glanced up. The witch could wield fire, but not kill with it?

"Cora and I have been laying narrow bands of fire. If the soldiers get too close, we'll do it again."

Beside him, Justen licked his spoon. "Does the rain make it harder?"

"Harder to start, easier to control. Fire wants to consume. The difficulty is always in holding it back." Dareus stood, stiffly.

Harkeld stabbed his gruel again with the spoon. His protectors weren't allowed to kill. *We won't make it out of Osgaard.*

CHAPTER FIFTEEN

"THE FINAL ITEM, highness, is the matter of your personal servants. Do you wish to take them with you into the duke's household?"

"My maid comes with me," Britta said, and watched as the palace secretary appended this to the end of the long list.

None of it felt real. The scratch of the quill as the man wrote, the words in black ink on the cream–colored parchment, were part of a dream. No, a nightmare. And it *was* real. Tomorrow she would become wife to Duke Rikard, Commander of the King's Army.

"And your armsmen?" the secretary asked. "The duke is most eager to provide you with men of his own."

Britta looked across the room, to where Karel stood at parade rest.

He was young, no more than twenty-five, at the beginning of his career. And he was one of the few Esfaban islanders who'd made it into service in the palace, the only islander who'd been assigned a royal charge. He'd want to climb higher, not to follow her into Duke Rikard's household. "I'll let you know."

"Very good, your highness."

The secretary gathered his things—ink pot and writing implements, the roll of parchment—and bowed and departed. Britta stayed at the table, watching the sunlight move slowly across the polished marquetry, highlighting flowers formed from golden oak and birds hovering on outspread wings of walnut and cherry.

"Princess? Britta?"

She looked up. Yasma stood there, her face anxious.

"Is everything all right?" the maid asked.

"Perfectly."

"Duke Rikard will be here shortly. Do you wish to change?"

No, I wish to run away. Britta stood. Her limbs seemed to creak stiffly. "A new tunic," she said.

SHE STARED AT the mirror as Yasma tidied her hair, winding the strands tightly around the golden crown. "Princess?" the little maid said hesitantly when she'd finished. "Britta?"

Britta blinked. Her face came into focus in the mirror. She turned and looked at Yasma. The girl was clearly an Esfaban islander. She had the dark skin and hawk-like face—winging eyebrows, high cheekbones, aquiline nose—but her features were delicately drawn. She wasn't pretty; she was beautiful.

Britta forced herself to smile. "The duke is allowing me to bring my personal servants into his household. I said that you'll come with me."

She saw Yasma swallow, saw the sudden sheen of tears in her maid's eyes. "Thank you."

Britta stood, turning away from the tears. "Do you think the armsmen will want to come?" she asked brightly.

"I think... Karel will wish to stay with you."

She glanced at the maid. "Truly?"

Yasma flushed and lowered her gaze. "Yes, princess. But ask him if you wish to be certain."

A week ago, that blush would have made her curious. Did Yasma and Karel have an understanding? Were they in love? Now, the weight of her own problems smothered any curiosity she might have.

PRINCESS BRIGITTA EMERGED from her bedchamber, dressed in an undergown of white silk and a long rose-pink tunic stitched with silver.

Karel glanced at her briefly, and then looked stolidly ahead as she crossed the chamber.

"Karel," she said, halting in front of him.

He transferred his gaze to her face. "Yes, princess?"

"Do you wish to accompany me to Duke Rikard's household? I had thought you'd prefer not to, but if I'm wrong—"

Not go with her? His heart kicked in his chest. "I wish to accompany you."

"Are you certain? The opportunities for advancement will be limited."

"I'm certain." In her service, Osgaard was bearable. *Without you, I would fill up with hatred.*

"Very well. I'll see that you're added to the

list." The princess glanced back over her shoulder. "Yasma, when the duke arrives, please tell him we're in the garden."

KAREL STOOD WITH his back to a hedge and tried to concentrate on his task: protecting the princess. He scanned the garden—flowerbeds, hedges—but his gaze kept returning to the rose-draped bower, to Duke Rikard and the princess seated on the cushioned bench.

He watched as Duke Rikard spoke to the princess, as she replied. Above them, the rose bower arched, dripping with blooms. Their scent drifted on the breeze.

The duke was eager to claim his rights to Princess Brigitta's body. His hand kept creeping across the cushions towards her, kept withdrawing. He didn't quite dare to touch her.

After tomorrow Rikard could touch her as much and as often as he wished.

Impotent rage rose inside him as he imagined the man rutting her. Karel discovered he was gripping his sword hilt tightly. With effort he uncurled his fingers and looked away.

DUKE RIKARD LEANED towards her. Sweat glistened on his cheeks. The expression in his eyes made panic spike sharply in her chest. Britta dug her fingernails into her palms to keep from scrambling backwards over the cushions. She was a princess, and she *wasn't* going to cringe from him like a helpless bondservant.

She lifted her chin. "I shall be bringing some of my servants with me," she said. "My personal maid, and at least one of my armsmen."

The duke stopped leaning towards her. "I'm perfectly capable of providing armsmen for you."

"I am aware of that. But I should like to bring Karel with me." She looked across to where he stood, the sunlight glinting on his black hair, on his golden breastplate.

The duke followed her gaze. "An islander." His voice held a sneer.

"Yes."

Her armsman stood at parade rest, his feet twelve inches apart, his shoulders back, his hand resting lightly on the hilt of his sword. He scanned the garden, his gaze resting on her for a moment, on Duke Rikard. His face was expressionless, but she'd learned during the past three years to read the tiny signs that told her what he was thinking. She knew when he was bored, when he was amused. Today he was neither amused nor bored. She saw a much darker emotion in his eyes as he looked at the duke, in the set of his mouth.

He hates Rikard.

For some reason, that knowledge made her feel safer. "Karel comes with me," Britta said firmly. "He has been an exemplary armsman."

CHAPTER SIXTEEN

RAIN FELL STEADILY. Mid-afternoon, the ground began to rise. The vegetation changed, oak giving way to low-boughed mountain beech. Wet leaves slapped Harkeld in the face as he rode.

"By the All-Mother," Justen muttered behind him. "I wish I could change into a bird and fly above these cursed trees."

Harkeld's skin prickled as he remembered the dream he'd woken from—feathers bristling from his chest, down growing on his face. *I don't.*

They halted for the night at an outcrop of rock. Gerit was waiting for them, drenched and naked. "It's not a cave," he said. "But it's the best shelter I can find."

Harkeld looked up at the slight overhang.

"It'll do," Dareus said.

Harkeld dismounted stiffly. Every item he wore was saturated. His muscles told him he'd been doing nothing but sit in a saddle for the last three days. He swung his arms, trying to work out the stiffness. "How about some wrestling?" he asked Justen.

The armsman blinked. "Now?"

"After we've seen to the horses."

Darkness fell while they unloaded the packhorses. Cora and Gerit set about making a meal. "Well?" Harkeld said, once the horses were hobbled.

"Er..." Justen glanced towards the fire. The witch, Petrus, walked into the circle of firelight, a blanket around his shoulders. "I don't want to hurt you, sire."

"A friendly bout," Harkeld said, stripping off his shirt.

Justen hesitated, and then shrugged. "All right." He pulled his shirt over his head and kicked off his boots.

They started slowly, testing each other's strength, each other's skill, grappling and breaking off, their feet scuffing up wet leaves. Harkeld saw an opening—*now*—and came in low, driving his shoulder into Justen's hip. The armsman grunted and sprawled backwards. Harkeld followed him. They wrestled, rolling, rising to their knees. He had his arm around Justen's throat—

Justen grabbed his elbow and drove his weight forwards, breaking the hold. He rolled free and sprang to his feet. His teeth glinted in the firelight as he grinned.

Harkeld stood. He wiped sweat and rain from his face. Justen's amulet caught the firelight as they circled. They came together again, forehead to forehead, gripping each other's arms. Harkeld tightened his hold on Justen's left arm and shifted his balance, preparing to bring the armsman down. *Got you.*

Justen twisted free, his skin slick with rain. He dropped to one knee. Harkeld's breath exhaled in a *whoosh* as his armsman's shoulder rammed into his stomach. Justen grabbed him behind the knees, heaved—

Harkeld found himself face down on the ground, gasping for breath.

Someone laughed. He thought it was Petrus.

Harkeld pushed himself up and spat leaf mold from his mouth.

"Did I hurt you, sire?"

Only my pride. "No." Harkeld climbed to his feet. He looked at his armsman with newfound respect. "Again."

They wrestled until the stew was cooked and it was too dark to see more than the pale blur of Justen's amulet. Harkeld walked back to the overhang and the fire, breathing heavily. He rolled his shoulders. The stiffness was gone.

"THAT WAS A good wrestling match," Petrus said as he changed clothes with Innis. "You nailed him a couple of times."

It was hard to tell in the dimness, but he thought Innis grinned. "I like being Justen."

Petrus paused, one leg in the wet trews. "Innis, you need to be careful."

"Don't worry," she said, wrapping herself in the blanket. "I know this is the shape I'm meant to be. It's just... you're lucky to be so strong." She handed him the amulet. "Can you ask about the curse tonight?"

"The Ivek Curse?" The disc of walrus ivory was warm in his hand. "What about it?"

"How much do you think he knows?"

Petrus shrugged. "Not a lot."

"So ask questions."

Petrus grunted. He put the amulet over his head. It rested below his collarbone, warm and smooth. "If he wants to know, he can ask himself. Surly son of a bitch."

"You'd be surly too, if you were him. He's lost everything. He's like a mage who's been stripped of his magic." She laid her hand on his arm. "Please, Petrus?"

Jealousy stabbed inside him. "Fancy him, do you?"

Innis removed her hand. "No. I feel sorry for him."

Petrus bit his tongue. *Fool.* He shrugged into the wet shirt. "Fine," he said. "I'll ask about the curse."

PETRUS PUSHED A lump of meat around his bowl. Beside him, Prince Harkeld ate silently, not looking at anyone. His face was dark with shadows, dark with stubble. His hostility was almost a tangible thing.

Petrus glanced at Innis. He scooped up a spoonful of stew. "Dareus, can you tell me about Ivck's Curse?"

"The curse? What about it?"

Petrus shrugged, chewing. "Everything. All I know is that it'll kill everyone in the Seven Kingdoms. And that he's the only one who can stop it." He pointed at Prince Harkeld with his spoon.

Dareus glanced at the prince. "Very well." He put down his bowl. Behind him, water dripped steadily from the edge of the overhang. "It started nearly three hundred years ago, when the rulers of the Thirteen Kingdoms decided to purge this continent of mages. There were thirteen kingdoms back then, not seven; Osgaard hadn't yet begun its expansion."

Petrus nodded.

"Hatred of mages had been growing for some time. Admittedly, a few were abusing their powers, but mostly it was just rumors."

"What sort of rumors?"

"Mages eating human flesh, procreating with animals—absolute nonsense, but you'll find that people here still believe such things today."

Petrus glanced at Prince Harkeld. He appeared to be paying no attention to Dareus.

"Some mages managed to flee across the ocean to the Allied Kingdoms," Dareus said, picking up his mug, "but most didn't. A lot of completely ordinary people were killed too, merely on the suspicion they had mage blood." He lowered the mug without drinking. "The killing of suspected mages is a practice that continues to this day. They have a saying here: the only good mage is one that's dead and burned."

Petrus grimaced, and then smoothed the expression from his face. Justen wasn't a mage; he'd hear those words with nothing more than mild interest.

"Witch," Gerit said. "The only good witch is one that's dead and burned." He scowled. "They call us witches here."

"The wife and children of a mage named Ivek were among the first to die," Dareus continued. "Ivek laid the curse as his revenge."

"What does it do?"

"It strips people of their humanity."

"What?" Petrus wrinkled his brow. "It makes them into animals?"

"Less than animals. They become maddened by blood lust. They"ll slaughter each other, just as Ivek's family was slaughtered."

Petrus tried to react as if the tale was new to him. "But... all this happened three hundred years ago. Why didn't the curse kill everyone then? Why now?"

"The curse was dormant while it gathered power. It's... as an analogy, imagine a pot of water over a fire. Ivek placed it there, but it's taken this long for the water to boil."

"And only Prince Harkeld can put out the fire?"

"Yes."

Petrus shoveled stew into his mouth and chewed, trying to think of another question. "How did the curse gather power?"

"Ivek anchored it with three stones. You've seen a map of the Seven Kingdoms? You know that it's roughly divided into three regions? North, east, west?"

He nodded.

"Ivek anchored the curse in each region. In the north, Ankeny. In the east, Sault. And here, in the west, Lundegaard, up on the Masse plateau. Each stone has been drawing power from the kingdom it's anchored in." Dareus laid his hand on the wet soil. "From the ground."

Petrus tried to look as if he didn't already know this. "Did Ivek know it would take three hundred years for the curse to gather enough power?"

"He thought it would take longer. We have some of his writings. He estimated four centuries."

Petrus lifted his eyebrows. "A slow revenge."

"He died knowing that everyone in the Seven Kingdoms—the Thirteen Kingdoms, then—would die, just as his family had." Dareus shrugged. "It didn't matter to him whether he witnessed it or not; he knew it would happen."

Gerit grunted. "He was mad."

No kidding. "How did he die?" Petrus asked.

"The soldiers caught him, in the end. Cut off his head and then burned him."

Petrus pushed the stew around his bowl. "And the curse is in Vaere now?"

"Yes. Ivek crafted it to rise in the east and pass across the kingdoms until it set in the west, like the sun."

"Only much slower," Gerit said, leaning forward to throw another branch on the fire. Sparks rose like a cloud of fireflies.

"How slow?"

"At the moment, about a league a day," Dareus said. "Three or so miles. We believe it'll move faster once it reaches the first anchor stone. Within a year, all the kingdoms will be infected."

"Infected?"

"The curse is waterborne. Drink one drop of infected water, and you'll go mad. And since everyone needs to drink, everyone will go mad."

Petrus looked up at the rain, falling steadily beyond the shelter of the overhang. "Water?"

"Rivers, lakes, wells. The curse is bound into the soil, so rain is safe until it reaches the ground. Then it becomes infected too."

"What about animals? Does it affect them?"

Dareus shook his head. "Only humans."

"So... how do we stop it?"

"Ivek crafted the anchor stones so they can be

destroyed. He called it his joke against the Thirteen Kingdoms."

"Joke? How's that a joke?"

"The anchor stones can only be destroyed by a royal prince or princess descended from the house of Rutersvard *and* a mage. Something Ivek knew was impossible."

"Sick son of a whore," Gerit muttered.

"Why a Rutersvard?"

"Because the purge was led by a Rutersvard."

Petrus chewed slowly, trying to think of something else he could ask. Something Prince Harkeld wouldn't know. "Can you lay curses?"

Dareus shook his head. "None of us can. The ability to cast curses is rare."

"Just as well," Gerit said.

"Casting a curse is a very personal thing," Dareus said. "It usually requires physical touch. It's... think of it as *un*-healing."

Petrus nodded.

"What Ivek did with the anchor stones is extraordinarily complex. He somehow managed to bind his curse to the land itself. We're still not certain exactly how he did it."

"So Ivek un-healed the Seven Kingdoms? Thirteen Kingdoms, I mean."

"Thirteen, Seven..." Dareus shrugged. "It means the same thing: the entire continent. Yes, that's exactly what Ivek did."

Petrus gestured at Prince Harkeld with his spoon. "And only he can undo it?"

"Only his blood. And his hand laid on the anchor stones."

"But... he doesn't have to be alive?

Dareus shook his head. "As far as we can tell, no."

"How much blood will it take? It won't kill him, will it?"

Dareus shook his head again. "No."

Petrus stirred his stew. What else could he ask? "If the prince has mage blood, is he a mage?"

"It's possible," Dareus said, with a shrug. "Prince Harkeld would have to undergo testing to know that. By breath and by blood."

"You should do it, sire," Petrus said.

Prince Harkeld glanced at him. He uttered the only word he'd spoken since sitting down to eat: "No."

"But don't you want to know? I would."

"I am not a witch."

It's mage, *you surly son of a whore.* Mage, *not witch.* Petrus shrugged.

"Can't know that," Gerit said. "Not unless you take the test."

Prince Harkeld ignored Gerit. He continued eating.

"If all the mages were killed, how does the prince have mage blood?" Petrus asked, his tone innocent.

Gerit uttered a snort of laughter, and changed it into a cough.

"For the past two hundred years Sentinels have been coming here in secret," Dareus said. "Monitoring the Rutersvard bloodline, looking for a child who could break the curse. When it became clear it wouldn't happen naturally, we decided to intervene."

"Intervene?"

"To introduce mage blood into the other royal houses in the hope that one of the children would marry a Rutersvard. We waited three generations for it to happen."

Prince Harkeld put down his bowl. His movements had the rigidity of rage.

"Why was marriage necessary?" Petrus asked. "Couldn't a bastard—"

"It was one of the first things we tried," Cora said.

Prince Harkeld turned his head to stare at her.

"Who was the bastard?" Petrus asked.

"A boy called Kiel. His father was a legitimate Rutersvard prince, his mother was a Sentinel mage. She'd been pretending to be a servant."

"What happened?"

"Kiel's blood and hand were tried on all three stones." Cora lifted her shoulders in a shrug. "It didn't work."

"The child has to be born in wedlock," Dareus said. "It has to be legitimately royal. Ivek worked it into the anchor stones."

Prince Harkeld stopped looking at Cora. He frowned down at his bowl.

"So why didn't you just ask a Rutersvard to marry a mage?"

"We tried that, when Kiel's blood didn't work," Dareus said. "One of the Sentinels approached the Rutersvards and explained the situation and—"

"They killed him." Gerit spat into the fire. The flames sizzled for a moment.

"They thought the curse was a tale. A century had passed since Ivek's death. A century with no signs of anything wrong." Dareus shrugged. "Do you know what they say here, when something's never going to happen?"

Petrus shook his head.

"They say it's as certain as Ivek's Curse."

Petrus grunted. "They won't be able to say that any more."

"No." Dareus rubbed his jaw. The close-cut beard rasped beneath his hand. "Where was I? Oh, yes. They killed the Sentinel. So for the next hundred years we watched and waited, until finally it was decided that we *had* to act. So we created an opportunity to break the curse."

"Prince Harkeld?"

Dareus nodded. "Once he was born, there was a lot of debate about what to do next. Should we steal the child and raise him in the Allied Kingdoms? Should we leave him where he was?"

Prince Harkeld lifted his head. He stared across the fire at Dareus.

"In the end, the Council ruled that we couldn't take away his birthright. Harkeld had been born a prince; he had the right to grow up a prince. The question then became, how to inform him of his destiny—and when."

Gerit snorted. "They debated that for nearly two decades."

"Finally it was decided to follow diplomatic channels. This was a chance to forge a relationship between the Seven Kingdoms and mages. A delegation was sent to Osgaard, to speak with King Esger. I was one of them."

"Weren't you afraid they'd kill you?"

Dareus shook his head. "We carried a diplomatic seal granted by the rulers of the Allied Kingdoms. It guaranteed us safe passage. King Esger took some convincing that we spoke the truth about the curse and his son's blood, but he took the news surprisingly well. Much better than we'd expected."

"When?" Prince Harkeld demanded. "When did you tell my father?"

"When you were eighteen."

The prince's mouth tightened. He turned his head away.

"Why didn't you speak to the prince, then?" Petrus asked.

"We asked to, but King Esger said Harkeld was too young, too immature. He requested more time and asked that we not approach the prince directly." Dareus shrugged. "We agreed. There was no urgency; we thought the curse would be dormant for decades."

"But weren't you worried about the prince's safety once you'd gone?"

Dareus shook his head. "Esger promised to protect his son. He swore an oath on the seal we carried. To break it would have been tantamount to a declaration of war against the Allied Kingdoms." He drained his mug and placed it on the ground. "We returned three years later, but the king declined to let us speak with Prince Harkeld. He said he was still too immature."

"We should have ignored the fat bastard," Gerit said. "Should have just gone in and—"

"We carried a diplomatic seal." There was an edge in Dareus's voice. "We were bound by oath to act with openness and honesty."

Gerit pushed to his feet, scowling. He stamped off into the darkness, his shoulders hunched against the rain.

"The curse took us by surprise, Justen," Cora spoke into the ensuing silence. Her voice was calm, matter-of-fact. "We thought we had plenty of time. Decades. King Esger's stalling didn't worry us overmuch."

"But then word came about the curse shadows," Dareus said. "And we knew we had to act immediately. Whether Esger agreed or not."

Petrus nodded, and then realized that the prince wouldn't know what a curse shadow was. "What's a curse shadow?"

"Anyone who's been cursed has one," Dareus told him. "It's like a shroud. Only trained mages can see them. There have been curse shadows across the Seven Kingdoms ever since Ivek laid his curse, but they've been extremely faint, almost impossible to see. In the weeks before the curse became active, they became noticeably darker."

"And now?"

"Now they're very dark."

Petrus looked across the campfire at Dareus, seeing the shadows cast by the firelight and the one cast by Ivek's curse, a dark and unwholesome stain. "Do I have an extra shadow?"

"We all do. Anyone who sets foot on this continent does."

"Until they leave," Cora said. "Or die."

"But... I'm not cursed, am I?"

"You're cursed, in as much as everyone in the Seven Kingdoms is cursed, but you won't go mad until you drink infected water. The curse shadow is... think of it as a promise of what's to come. If you stay in the Seven Kingdoms."

A shiver crept up Petrus's spine. "What happens when Ivek's Curse reaches the west coast?" he asked, placing his bowl to one side. "Will it spread across the ocean? Will it reach the Allied Kingdoms?"

"The scholars think not," Dareus said. "But the truth is that no one knows. There's a chance it will poison the whole world."

"So we'd better break it," Petrus said.

"Yes." Dareus turned his head and spoke directly to the prince, "Thank you for agreeing to come with us, Prince Harkeld. Things would be even more difficult if you hadn't."

"Would you have killed me?" the prince asked. "Taken my blood? My hands?"

"If necessary, yes."

The prince's lip curled contemptuously. "I thought you weren't allowed to kill."

"It's one of our Primary Laws," Dareus said. "But Sentinel mages have the authority to break those Laws, if the need is great enough."

The prince lost his sneer. His eyes narrowed slightly, as if he didn't know whether to believe Dareus or not.

IT WAS STILL raining in the morning. Harkeld pulled on his sodden boots and buckled the sword belt around his hips.

Justen held his shirt to his nose for a moment and grimaced, before shrugging into it. "Ach. I'm growing mold."

Harkeld grunted. "Me too." Everything smelled dank—his clothes, his hair, his skin.

Justen took a small cloth-wrapped object from his pocket and carefully unwrapped it. "The paint's coming off." His voice held a note of dismay.

Harkeld stepped closer to see what his armsman held. It was a tiny portrait painted on wood, smaller than the palm of his hand.

Justen held the painting out to him. "Doutzen. We're betrothed."

Harkeld took it carefully. The armsman was correct: in places the paint was peeling from the wet wood. Doutzen's face was untouched. She was a smiling, plump-cheeked girl.

"She's waiting for me," Justen said, pride in his voice.

"You'll have a happy marriage," Harkeld said, handing the portrait back. *If we survive.*

A HAWK LANDED while they ate breakfast. Petrus. "The pass is misty," he said. "Can't see an awful lot."

"Soldiers?" Dareus asked.

"Not that I can see. There are some on the next ridge, though."

"Keep an eye on them."

"Shall do. Is that bowl for me, Cora?"

"And on the other side?" Justen asked. "In Lundegaard. Have you seen any soldiers?"

The witch shook his head. He began to eat.

"Prince Harkeld?"

Harkeld glanced up.

"How well do you know King Magnas?" Cora asked.

"I lived in his court for two years when I was a boy."

"Why?" Justen asked.

"I was fostered," Harkeld told him. "It's common practice here among noble families."

"What's your opinion of King Magnas?" Cora said.

"I doubt he'll seek to stop us. He places higher value on human life than my father does."

"But isn't he related to King Esger?" A frown puckered her brow.

"By marriage," Harkeld said. "His daughter, Sigren, was my father's fourth wife. My half-brothers Rutgar and Lukas are King Magnas's grandsons."

Saying their names brought the boys' faces vividly to mind: Rutgar's gap-toothed grin, Lukas's dimples. His throat tightened.

"You don't think King Magnas's loyalty will be to Osgaard in this?"

"It could be." Harkeld stared down at his bowl. In the two years he'd been in Lundegaard's court, King Magnas had treated him no differently than his own sons, had even *called* him son.

Harkeld dug the spoon into the gruel, but didn't eat. He had witch blood. No man, king or commoner, would want him as a son now.

CHAPTER SEVENTEEN

KAREL WOKE AT dawn. The sound of the first bell drifted in from the courtyard. Two hours yet before he had to rise.

The bunks around him were occupied, the other armsmen still asleep. Daylight crept in through the half-open shutters. He stared up at the ceiling, seeing shadows, cracks, cobwebs.

Today she marries Duke Rikard.

Something clenched in his chest.

The first time he'd seen Princess Brigitta he'd taken one look at the golden hair, the sky-blue eyes, the rosebud mouth, and dismissed her as a pretty doll. Shallow. Spoiled. Worthless.

The scene spun in Karel's mind as he stared up at the ceiling: his first day as a royal armsman. He'd trained for that moment for five years—five years while they'd tried to break him and failed. Princess Brigitta had been his reward. He, an Esfaban islander, had been assigned a royal charge. He was one of the elite.

"Your new armsman, princess," his commanding officer had said, and the princess had looked at him and smiled politely.

You stupid fool, Karel told himself savagely, throwing back his blankets. There was no point in remembering these moments—the first time he'd seen her, the first time he'd realized who she was as a person. She was a princess and he was an armsman, an islander. He was wasting his time thinking of her.

Karel dressed quickly, quietly, and left the bunkroom. He had two hours until breakfast, three hours until he was due in the training arena. He could practice his archery, mend the hole in his second-best tunic, sharpen his dagger and sword.

He did none of those things; he sat on one of the long benches in the courtyard, in the morning sunshine, and polished his breastplate, his gilded scabbard and the buckles on his swordbelt, his greaves and wrist guards, the hilts of his dagger and sword. Today was Princess Brigitta's wedding day, and as her armsman he would honor her by looking the best he could.

Lastly, he polished the silver torque that said he was sworn to her, that he was hers.

The torque had shone this brightly on his first day as an armsman. Pride had stiffened his spine and triumph had swelled in his chest as he'd worn it, but the emotion he'd felt most deeply that day was hatred. Hatred for the country that had conquered his people. Hatred for the royal family of Rutersvard. Hatred for Osgaard.

Karel's hand slowed as he buffed the torque. Everything had been new that day, everything a surprise, the princess especially so.

Stop it!

Karel put aside the buffing cloth and fetched his bow and a quiver of arrows. Bowmen hadn't patrolled the walls surrounding Osgaard's palace for a century, not since King Harald had been assassinated by one of his own archers, but armsmen were still expected to practice—as long as the bows never left the training arena.

The targets stood on the far side of the arena, in shadow this early in the morning. Karel nocked the first arrow, drew back the bow string.

Pfft. The arrow buried itself in the straw-filled target.

His bow came from the islands. He'd used it as a boy, hunting birds, wild pigs, water rats, anything to put in their cooking pot. Usually, the smoothness of the wood beneath his hand brought memory of Esfaban—the sound of fishermen singing as they laid their nets, the warmth of rain on his skin, the smell of fermenting palm sap—but today the memory of his first day in Princess Brigitta's service intruded.

Pfft.

He'd followed the princess and her maid through the long marble corridors of the palace. The maid had been an islander like himself, but wearing the iron armband of a bondservant, walking one pace behind the princess, carrying her mistress's cloak.

Pfft.

He'd been watching the maid, not her mistress, as they'd entered the king's private atrium, a place of trickling water and lush ferns, marble statues and gold-embossed vases.

Pfft.

The cloak the maid carried had unfurled slightly, had fluttered and brushed a vase.

Thwack. Karel missed. The arrow smacked into

the stone wall behind the target and rebounded, broken.

He gritted his teeth and drew another arrow from the quiver.

Memory marched inexorably. He saw it in his mind's eye: the vase bursting as it struck the floor, sending fragments spinning across the marble flagstones. A piece shaped like a curving dagger had come to rest beside his right boot. The porcelain was so thin it was almost transparent, and the gold leaf on it had sparkled brightly in the sunlight.

Thwack. Another miss.

Karel lowered the bow and stalked across the dirt and sawdust of the training arena. Memory followed at his heels: the long moment of silence, the horror on the maid's face.

Karel jerked the arrows from the target. Two lay ruined on the ground. He picked them up, remembering the king striding across his atrium, his face livid with rage. "You stupid bitch!" he'd cried, striking the maid across the face. "That was priceless. *Priceless!*"

Karel turned and walked back across the arena. He nocked a fresh arrow, drew the bow—

"Have her flayed!" King Esger had bellowed, gesturing to one of his armsmen.

Thwack. The arrow missed the target.

Karel blew out a hissing breath. He nocked another arrow, but all he could see was Princess Brigitta stepping forward, her face as pale as her father's was flushed. He heard her voice clearly: "It was my fault, Father. I knocked it over. I'm sorry."

Thwack. He loosed the arrows quickly, trying to

block the flow of memory. *Thwack. Thwack.* And finally, *Pfft.* One hit the straw-filled target, piercing its heart.

Karel lowered the bow, remembering how the king had stared at his daughter, how his hand had clenched as if he thought of striking her, how he'd turned away. "Clean up this mess," he'd screamed at one of the servants.

They had stood in their tableau, unmoving, as a cowed bondservant swept up the shards of porcelain. The king's rage had vibrated in the atrium. Dust motes had spun in the sunlight, as if dancing to the sound of the trickling fountains. Beneath the sound of falling water had been the sound of the servant: the *shush* of the broom, the quiet *clink* of broken porcelain.

When the servant had finished, the king turned to his daughter. "You'll forfeit your horses for this."

Princess Brigitta had bowed her head. "Yes, Father."

Karel reached for another arrow, his lips pressed together. Blind, that's what he'd been. Blind. He'd looked at the princess and seen what he'd expected to see, not the truth. *Pfft.* The arrow struck the target, burying deep in the straw.

He nocked another arrow, drew back, loosed it. *Pfft.* Princess Brigitta had shown him who she was that first day, and she'd shown him a thousand times since. *Pfft.* He'd watched her lay sheets of parchment on the table by the window and teach Yasma to read and write—forbidden skills for a bondservant. *Pfft.* He'd watched her read aloud to her half-brothers, watched her spend hours drawing pictures for them to color in. *Pfft*. He'd watched her rescue worms and spiders, beetles and butterflies.

He'd watched—and he'd come to learn that it wasn't her face that made Princess Brigitta beautiful; it was her heart.

His hands clenched on the bow. *Duke Rikard will never see that.*

The third bell began to ring, chiming out across the training arena, across the palace. He heard the stir of movement in the barracks, the sound of voices.

Karel set down the bow. He strode across to the target. He laid out the day in his mind as he collected the arrows: breakfast and training, and then he'd scrub the sweat from his body, dress in a fresh tunic and the polished breastplate, and relieve Torven of his duty of the princess.

And then he'd watch her marry Duke Rikard.

CHAPTER EIGHTEEN

THE PATH BECAME steeper. The trees were stunted and gnarled. Harkeld didn't need to look at a map to know they were no longer in the foothills, but in the Graytooth Mountains proper. Mid-morning, they emerged into a landscape of rock: huge lichen-covered slabs, shattered boulders, scree. A ceiling of cloud hung above them, hiding the pass.

"By the All-Mother, I wish this rain would stop," Justen muttered behind him.

The footing was treacherous, the slabs slick with water, the rubble shifting and sliding beneath the horses' hooves.

"Dismount," Dareus said, after one of the packhorses lost its footing and slid several yards.

They led the horses after that; scrambling, sliding, climbing upward until the mist swirled clammily around them. Harkeld looked back the way they'd come. It was hazy, dreamlike, precipitous. He had the sensation that he stood on the edge of a cliff.

A hawk landed and shifted into Gerit.

Dareus grunted when he saw him. "If it gets any steeper than this—"

"It doesn't."

They kept climbing. The mist closed around them.

Gerit returned. "We can't see to fly."

Dareus paused, panting. "Behind us?"

"Behind us, we're fine. It's ahead that worries me."

"Wolves," Dareus said, wiping his face. "Or dogs. Use your noses."

"Ebril already is, but the mist and the rain..." Gerit shrugged. "It's hard to get a scent."

"Do your best."

Gerit nodded. His form wavered, shrank, solidified. A stocky wolf with a grizzled coat and yellow eyes stood beside Dareus.

They moved on. Harkeld's world narrowed to the slick, slippery rock beneath his feet, to the rain on his face, to the mist parting ahead of him and closing behind. He found he was gritting his teeth. *If this doesn't end soon—*

He slipped and fell jarringly to one knee.

Justen was at his shoulder. "Sire, are you all right?"

"Fine," Harkeld said, pushing to his feet. "This cursed mist. I feel like I'm going blind."

They scrambled up another hump of rock, slipping and sliding, the horses' hooves scraping gouges in the lichen. At the top, they paused. Rock curved away from them in all directions.

"Please tell me this is the pass," Justen said.

It was. They followed the wolf across the dome of rock. The mist retreated slightly and the rain eased until only a light drizzle fell.

The pass narrowed to a valley. A pool of water lay in a dip almost at its centre. They halted to eat, to let the horses drink. Gerit ate with them, not bothering to hide his nakedness with a blanket.

"I like Lundegaard already," Justen said, chewing on a strip of dried beef.

"We're not there yet, boy," Gerit said.

"How much further?"

Gerit shrugged. "An hour." He changed into a wolf, shook himself, and departed at a lope. Another wolf emerged from the billowing mist, a large male. The ruff of fur at its throat was pale, almost silvery.

"No sign of soldiers?" Cora asked once the wolf had shifted. It was the blond witch, Petrus.

Petrus shook his head. "Can't see any. It's practically impossible to smell anything." He reached for a handful of dried beef and froze as a wolf hurtled towards them out of the mist. Not Gerit; it was younger, leaner, a russet tint to its coat.

The wolf changed into Ebril. "Soldiers!" he cried. "Ten of them. Coming down the ridge."

They scrambled to their feet. "How far—?" But already Harkeld could see shapes running through the mist.

Justen stepped in front of him, thrusting him back, his sword drawn. "Sire! Mount!"

Run away? Harkeld hesitated.

Soldiers burst out of the mist a hundred yards distant. Seven swordsmen, three archers. His father's men, wearing the scarlet and gold of Osgaard. One of them uttered a shout. It echoed oddly, muffled by the mist.

"Ebril, get him out of here," Dareus snapped. "Go!"

Ebril shifted. The wolf stood in his place.

"Mount!" Justen yelled at him.

Harkeld swung up into the saddle. The blond witch was gone. In his place was a lion. It uttered a roar and charged at the soldiers.

Ebril began to run. Harkeld dug his heels into the horse's flanks and followed. He snatched a backwards glance as they plunged into the mist. It was like a scene from a dream—hazy, twisting out of clarity. He saw Dareus point at a soldier, saw flames burst into life on the man's tunic. He saw the lion leap at an archer, bringing him down. He saw Justen engage with a swordsman, heard the fierce *clang* of sword against sword, saw a second soldier rush at him, sword upraised.

They'll kill him.

Harkeld hauled on the reins, forcing the horse to turn. He drew his sword as he careened out of the mist, charging towards Justen, his mouth open, a shout in his throat.

An arrow sprouted from his horse's head.

The animal collapsed as if its legs had been cut from under it. Harkeld tumbled to the ground. His sword spun away across the slick rock. He rolled, scrambling to hands and knees. A soldier loomed above him, sword upraised—

A large wolf barreled into the soldier, knocking him sideways. Behind them, an archer's bow burst into flames.

Harkeld scrambled after his sword. He saw a blur of movement to his right—the archer had thrown aside his burning bow and drawn a dagger.

The hours of drilling took over. He rolled, his legs tangling with the archer's, bringing him down. The man grunted as he hit the ground. The dagger skittered across the stone.

They grappled, struggling for dominance.

His eyes caught a flash of movement: Justen

blocking a blow from one sword, twisting to fend off the second swordsman—

Harkeld smashed his forehead into the archer's face. He heard the crunch of bone as the man's nose broke. He gritted his teeth and did it again. Blood gushed across his face. The archer went limp.

He pushed the man off him, his eyes on his sword, and went sprawling as his boots slipped on the slick rock.

"Get up!" Dareus hauled him to his feet with one hand. The other he pointed at one of the swordsmen attacking Justen, his fingers outstretched and rigid. Flames burned at each fingertip.

Harkeld felt fire ignite inside him. It ran along his bones and burst out of his skin. The sensation lasted for a searing second, and was abruptly gone.

The soldier screamed as his clothes began to burn. He dropped the sword.

Harkeld wrenched free of Dareus's grip. "What the—"

"I told you to go!" Dareus said fiercely, pointing at the second swordsman. As he spoke, Justen swung his sword. The blade buried itself in the man's neck. A killing blow.

Harkeld bent and snatched up his own sword. He stepped past Dareus, taking in the fray with a glance. The silver-maned lion lay on the ground. Cora crouched beside it. He saw blood on its pale flank, an arrow jutting from its hip. Five soldiers were running—three of them naked apart from their boots—a wolf snapping at their heels. Four men lay unmoving on the ground. Another wolf hung from the arm of the last soldier standing. The man beat at the animal with his free hand, screaming.

Harkeld lowered the sword. He pushed back his sleeve, expecting to see singed hairs, singed skin. Nothing. His arm was fine, as if he hadn't felt the lick of flame, hadn't felt fire *inside* him.

He glanced up again. The last solder was following the others at a staggering run.

The wolf that had been hanging off the man's arm changed into Gerit. He spat and wiped the back of his hand across his mouth, smearing blood. He glared at Harkeld from beneath bushy eyebrows. "You shouldn't have come back."

Harkeld flushed, clenching his jaw. He knew Gerit was right. "I'm not used to running away."

"Get used to it," Gerit said, scowling at him. He hurried across to the lion, where Dareus now crouched beside Cora.

INNIS LOOKED AT the blood on her sword blade. Bile rose in her throat. *I killed a man.*

Someone strode towards her. "Are you all right?"

It was Prince Harkeld.

Remember you're Justen. Innis attempted a smile. "I'm fine." She couldn't bring herself to look at the man she'd killed. His legs were at the edge her vision. She focused on the prince. "You have blood on your face."

"So do you."

Innis scrubbed her cheek with her sleeve. Her hand was trembling, her arm, her whole body. *I killed someone. I have his blood on my face.* She tasted bile on her tongue and swallowed. *Behave like a man,* she told herself fiercely. Justen wouldn't fall to pieces; he'd take it in his stride. He'd be practical and pragmatic.

She turned to the soldier she'd killed and wiped the sword blade on his tunic. Practical. Pragmatic.

The smell of the man's blood filled her nose.

When she straightened, her head swam for a moment. Innis gritted her teeth and stopped herself from swaying, stopped herself from vomiting. She frowned at the prince. "What are you doing here?

"You were outnumbered," he said. "I thought they were going to kill you."

Innis sheathed the sword. It took two tries, her hands were trembling so much. "You shouldn't have come back, sire—" She focused on what was happening behind the prince: Dareus, Cora and Gerit crouched beside something on the ground. "Is someone hurt?"

"The lion."

"Petrus?" Her nausea vanished abruptly. She pushed past the prince and ran across to the others.

Petrus was no longer a lion. He lay naked on the ground, his face twisted in a grimace. Cora held a bloodstained cloth to his ribs.

Innis reached for him. "Let me—"

Dareus gripped her arm. "He's fine. We've stopped the bleeding." His voice held a warning. His gaze went past her to the prince.

The snapped-off shaft of an arrow lay on the ground. "The arrowhead?"

"In his hip. We'll leave it for now." Dareus released her arm. "Tonight Innis can heal him. Right now, we need to get into Lundegaard."

CHAPTER NINETEEN

THE MARRIAGE CEREMONY was performed in the Silver Hall, a room of white marble, cold silver, and glittering mirrors. Armsmen stood around the walls, their uniforms bold slashes of color.

The princess wore white and gold, the duke the scarlet and gold of Osgaard's army, with his plumed commander's helmet on his graying black hair. Karel glanced at the man once—the smug smile on his fleshy mouth, the bright, greedy eyes—and looked away.

The last royal marriage had been Prince Jaegar's, to a cowed little princess from Roubos. That ceremony had been held in the throne room, but the throne room still bore the marks of the witches' attack six days ago.

Prince Jaegar's annulment had been conducted with less fanfare, when the little princess proved unable to conceive. She"d been lucky to be barren; Osgaard's queens tended to be short-lived.

Karel's gaze settled on King Esger. Four dead wives. *How many of those deaths were at your hand?*

Queen Sigren's, without doubt.

Queen Agneta's—for the sin of producing one daughter and then five still-born babes—most likely.

Smothered in her sleep, if the tales he'd heard in the armsmen's hall were to be believed, while her daughter, Brigitta, slept in the next chamber.

Outside, the bell began to toll the hour. Karel counted the strokes: six.

The last echoes of the bell faded and the ceremony began. As the highest ranking male in the princess's family, the king spoke the words binding her to Duke Rikard. His voice rang flatly in the Silver Hall, echoing off the marble ceiling. A score of nobles were present, those whose blood-ties to either Princess Brigitta or the duke earned them places as witnesses.

Karel's gaze slid from King Esger to Prince Jaegar to Duke Rikard. Men of the same stamp, with the same brutal nature. Men of the same family, once this ceremony was over.

His hand flexed, clenched around his sword hilt, released.

Prince Jaegar stood at the king's right hand, as an heir should. A smile gleamed in his pale eyes, as if he enjoyed the prospect of his half-sister marrying the duke.

Your mother was likely killed, Karel told him silently. *Do you know that? Murdered in her sickbed, according to armsmen's gossip.*

Would the prince care, if he knew? Probably not. He'd have regarded his mother, Queen Hedrun, as a weak, complaining invalid, a hindrance, and disposed of her as Esger had done. He was his father's child: ambitious, cruel. In him the Rutersvard blood had bred truest.

King Esger's voice droned on. Karel studied him. The king's frame was heavy with flesh, the bones of his face hidden beneath a layer of fat, but there was nothing soft about him, nothing yielding. The slabs of fat looked as solid as muscle.

A ruthless man. A man who'd killed three of his wives. Only Harkeld's mother, Queen Elena, had died naturally, in childbirth, taking a second son with her.

Where were Prince Harkeld and the witches now?

Come back, with fire and lion-men, Karel pleaded silently. *Save her.*

But no commotion stirred the air, no gouts of fire, no beasts-that-were-men. King Esger finished reading the statement uniting the pair in marriage. He began listing the princess's dowry.

The bride and groom faced each other, their hands clasped, while the king read down the list. Princess Brigitta's face was bloodless. The muscles in her throat moved convulsively.

Karel watched her intently. Was she going to faint? Vomit? Have hysterics? *Do something*, he begged. *Stop this*. But even as he thought the words, he knew she couldn't. Not if she wished to live.

The king's voice droned on, listing the assets Princess Brigitta brought into the marriage. "And in her own right, my daughter shall retain the properties gifted her by her mother." With those words, the ceremony concluded.

IN THE BANQUET Hall, its marble ceiling painted with gold leaf, the nobles of the palace waited. A cheer rose up as the bridal couple entered.

Princess Brigitta flinched and stepped back, almost treading on Karel's boot. Duke Rikard raised their clasped hands high in a gesture of triumph, then strode into the hall, pulling her with him.

Karel followed, into the crush of nobles. The high ceiling trapped the sound of voices and laughter, trapped the heat of too many people pressed closely together, trapped the smells of perfume and perspiration.

Well-wishers swarmed around the bridal couple. Karel watched, sweating beneath the gleaming breastplate. The duke was enjoying the attention; the princess wasn't. Her eyes were wide. She looked like a wild animal, caged and on display in a busy marketplace. Unable to escape. Terrified.

He wanted to reach out and grip her hand, steady her, tell her *It's all right, I'm here, I won't let anything happen to you.*

Except that everything was not all right, and he was powerless to save her.

TABLES WERE LAID with crystal goblets and plates of beaten gold. Once everyone was seated, bondservants began serving. Karel stood behind the princess's chair and watched as the food was brought from the kitchens: whole boars glistening with fat, huge fish with gellid eyes, platters of tiny roasted quail, bowls of steamed and braised vegetables, loaves of bread, salvers piled with cakes and pastries, dishes of whipped cream sprinkled with sugar crystals and flower petals.

Princess Brigitta allowed the duke to load her plate with food and fill a goblet to the brim with wine. Karel watched as she cut a piece of pork, as she speared it with the tines of her fork, as she lifted it to her mouth, each movement careful and precise.

After a minute Princess Brigitta laid down the knife and fork. She didn't cut herself more food. Karel tilted his head slightly to one side, trying to see her face.

The princess was still chewing.

Karel watched as she reached for the brimming goblet of wine, as she withdrew her hand. He glanced around, catching a bondservant's eye. "A goblet of water for the princess," he said, beneath the discordant hum of voices, the *clink* of cutlery on the golden plates, the melodies of the fiddlers and pipe players.

The bondservant scurried to obey.

Princess Brigitta was still chewing when the servant returned. Her face, when the man presented the goblet, lit momentarily with relief. She took the goblet, lifted it to her lips, and swallowed.

For the rest of the meal she cut her food and pushed it around the plate, creating small piles, but she never lifted the fork to her mouth again. Beside her Duke Rikard ate and drank lavishly. His face was flushed, glistening with sweat, with triumph. He had a right to be triumphant; his years of loyalty to the king were well-rewarded this day.

The bells counted out the hours of the afternoon, and still the celebration continued, the voices of the assembled nobles ringing beneath the gilded ceiling, almost drowning out the musicians. Karel thought he heard a forced note to the cheer. Everyone was acting their part for the king.

King Esger sat at the head of the room, smiling

benevolently. *See, I am still strong*, he was saying. *I rise above last week's catastrophe*. But anger smoldered beneath the smiling mask. Witches had attacked him in his own palace. His son had dared to disobey him—and had escaped unscathed. He'd lost his chance to gain wealth and new territory for Osgaard.

Karel averted his gaze from the king. There should be exultation in his breast for the blow Osgaard had suffered; there wasn't. He couldn't rejoice, not when Princess Brigitta was bound in marriage to Duke Rikard.

He looked down at the crown woven into her shining hair, at the line of her neck and the delicate curves of her earlobes, at the pale, smooth skin. What Prince Harkeld had done was right—defying his father, vowing to end the curse—but also terribly wrong. *He should never have left you, princess.*

Prince Jaegar strolled across to speak in his half-sister's ear. It looked friendly—his hand on her shoulder—but his fingers whitened as he gripped her shoulder and his voice was cold: "I'd smile, if I were you."

After Jaegar had gone, Karel tilted his head to one side again. The princess was obeying her brother; a smile sat on her lips as she pushed her food around her plate.

"Your new home, princess," Duke Rikard said, with a flourishing bow.

Britta stepped through the open door. The duke followed. "The salon, as you see..." She scarcely heard a word he said, scarcely noticed the layout of the rooms: the large salon with windows looking east, the formal dining room, the study, the bedchamber. Her heart was beating too fast, too loudly. Knowledge of what must come next paralyzed her. *No. I can't do it. I can't!*

The tour ended at the bedchamber. "I shall leave you to refresh yourself, princess." Duke Rikard bowed and retreated. The door shut behind him.

Britta turned to Yasma. "I can't do it!" There was a high note of panic in her voice. "I can't!"

"Princess," Yasma said. "Britta... I have this for you." She placed an object in her hand, closed her fingers around it.

Cool. Hard.

Britta's panic receded slightly. She opened her hand. A flask of green glass lay on her palm.

She blinked, drew a breath, focused. "What's this?" She removed the tiny glass stopper. The liquid was dark, the smell bitter and faintly familiar. "Poppy juice?"

"Yes."

Britta closed her fist around the flask. *I can kill myself.* She inhaled a deep breath and looked at Yasma. "Thank you."

"It will help make it bearable."

"Bearable?"

Yasma nodded.

"Is this... what you used?"

"Only once," the girl said. "One of the other women gave it to me. It helped."

"And the other times?"

Yasma's face tightened. She looked away.

Britta looked down at the flask. She understood what Yasma had given her: not a way of escaping, but a way of enduring.

CHAPTER TWENTY

THE ARROW HAD gouged down Petrus's side, slicing through muscle and flesh, lodging just above his hip. Innis coaxed the arrowhead out while the others set up for the night—tending the horses, building a fire, hanging the blankets from low branches to dry. Above the trees, dusk gathered in the sky.

The arrowhead removed, she concentrated on repairing the wound. Petrus wasn't a strong healer, but he'd been able to hold the bleeding off while they rode down from the pass, going from barren rock to sparse trees to thick forest, from mist and drizzle to sunlight streaming through the canopy of leaves. He was exhausted now. She was aware of how weak he was, aware of the dull edge of his pain as she closed the wound, knitting muscles and flesh, hiding the white gleam of his ribs.

His pain eased as she worked, his tension lessening in tiny increments. When the deeper layers were healed and only the skin remained, he exhaled a sigh. "Thank you, Innis."

She smiled at him.

Twilight shadowed his face. "Dareus said you killed one of the soldiers."

Her smile faded. "Yes."

"Are you all right?"

"I'm fine," Innis said firmly, and began sealing the edges of skin together. Darkness had fallen by the time she finished. She smoothed her hand down the line of the scar, feeling with her magic. His body felt healthy, whole. "There." She sat back on her heels. "Finished."

Petrus pushed himself up on one elbow. He felt his ribs. "Thank you."

"You're welcome." She stood and held out her hand to him.

He let her pull him to his feet, but didn't release her hand. "Innis, that soldier you killed, he would have killed you."

"I know."

"You did what you had to do." His grip tightened on her hand. "You did well."

Innis had a flash of memory: her sword burying itself in the soldier's neck, the jolt as it struck bone, the spray of blood as she wrenched the blade free. She pushed the memory aside, swallowing nausea.

"We all did well." She turned her gaze towards the fire. "The prince is still alive."

Petrus grunted. He released her hand.

"He came back," she said, watching as the prince sat down alongside Justen. "Prince Harkeld. Did Dareus tell you?"

"What's the point of us protecting him if he—"

"He came back to help us."

"Brave," Petrus said. "But not smart."

She stared at Justen, trying to tell if he was Ebril or Gerit. She couldn't. Her gaze returned to the prince. "Do you think he's a mage?"

"I hope not. An arrogant mage is a dangerous mage."

Innis turned her head and stared at Petrus. "You think he's arrogant?"

"You don't?"

"He treats Justen like a comrade, not a servant."

"Well, he treats the rest of us like we're lepers." He turned away from her and rummaged in his saddlebag, pulling out trews, underbreeches, a shirt.

Innis looked down at the ground. She dug the toe of her boot into the dirt. Petrus was right. "Things will be better now we're in Lundegaard," she said, but her tone didn't sound as certain as she'd meant it to be.

"They can hardly be worse," Petrus said, pulling the shirt over his head.

"Pursuit?" Dareus asked the following morning when the hawks came back from scouting.

Harkeld looked up from tying his bootlaces.

"Twenty men spent the night at the pass," Ebril said. "They set off into Lundegaard at dawn, leaving their uniforms behind."

Gerit snorted. "Civilians now, are they?"

"And in Lundegaard?" Dareus asked.

Petrus answered, accepting a bowl of gruel from Cora. "A lot of activity. I saw half a dozen patrols on the roads, and two in the forest." He shrugged. "It may be normal."

"It's not," Harkeld said. "That number of patrols means they're looking for something. Us, at a guess."

There was a moment's silence. "We don't know their intent," Cora said. "It might not be hostile."

Harkeld stood. He reached for his sword belt. "I can't believe King Magnas would seek to hinder us. Not if he knows what we're doing."

Gerit grunted. "*If* he knows what we're doing."

"If King Esger told him you were a traitor," Dareus said. "And asked for his assistance in killing you... Would King Magnas ask why? Would he doubt your father's word?"

Harkeld buckled the sword belt around his hips. "I think so." *I hope so.* "He's a sensible man, a calm man. I never saw him act in haste or anger."

"So you think the patrols are there to aid us?" Justen said.

"Yes."

"Does anyone care to risk it?" Dareus asked.

There was silence.

CHAPTER TWENTY-ONE

As COMMANDER OF the King's Army, Duke Rikard had a large suite of rooms in the northern wing of the palace. Karel patrolled them, learning their dimensions, noting the doors and the windows: the antechamber, the large salon with its ostentatious furnishings, the formal dining room with seating for a score of guests, the duke's study, with its locked door into the salon. And the bedchamber.

The bedchamber was sumptuously decorated. Karel averted his gaze from the wide bed, with its silver and midnight-blue hangings and the rumpled sheets. Anger burned in his chest, or maybe it was despair.

On one side of the bedchamber were a second door into the duke's study and the door to his dressing room and bathing chamber. From the bathing chamber another door accessed a bondservants' corridor, so the man who attended the duke could slip in and out.He'd been informed yesterday by the duke's senior armsman that he was strictly forbidden to enter the duke's private rooms. "The duke is *our* charge, not yours." Karel had ignored the man's hostility, the attempt to put him in his place.

On the other side of the bedchamber was the door

to the princess's dressing room and bathing chamber. The bondservants' corridor could be accessed from these, too, but Yasma wouldn't be making the trek to the bondservants' dormitories each night; an alcove in the dressing room had been prepared for her to sleep in. And on the princess's orders, no armsman was allowed to enter that room.

"Stupid idea," the senior armsman had grumbled. "Pampering a bondservant like that!"

Karel had ignored that, too. He knew what the man was really complaining about: Yasma's unavailability.

The door to the bathing chamber and dressing room was firmly closed this morning. Yasma and the princess were behind it.

Karel took his post in the salon. The room was cluttered with rugs, wall hangings, tables. Contempt curled his lip as he examined the furnishings. His eyes lighted on a tapestry stitched with gold and silver thread, on a mirror framed in mother-of-pearl and ebony, on a cluster of gilded vases on a table. Individually, many of the pieces were beautiful. Collectively, the salon was gaudy, tasteless. *Look at me!* Duke Rikard was saying. *See what an exalted position I hold in Osgaard's hierarchy.*

And now the duke had a new item for his collection: Princess Brigitta.

A door opened in the bedchamber.

Karel snapped to attention; shoulders back, head lifted, eyes staring directly ahead.

Princess Brigitta emerged from the bedchamber. She wore a lose robe of pale blue silk. Her hair was tied at the nape of her neck in a simple knot.

The princess didn't appear to notice him. She

walked across the salon and sat on a low, long settle underneath one of the windows. Her movements were slow, lacking in their usual grace. She gazed out of the window as if she were daydreaming.

Karel concentrated on doing his duty—scanning the salon, listening to Yasma move in the bedchamber— but his gaze kept returning to Princess Brigitta. Her calmness, her languor, was puzzling. No, it was more than puzzling; it was disturbing.

Above her head a bee batted against the window panes in a vain attempt to get out. He waited for the princess to notice, to open the window for it. In the bedchamber he heard Yasma putting fresh sheets on the bed, plumping the pillows.

Karel's unease grew with each passing minute. Finally he wrenched his gaze away from the princess.

On the wall across from him were gilt-framed maps tracing Osgaard's growth during the past two centuries. His eyes skipped from map to map, noting each subsumed kingdom: Horst in the south, Karnveld and Lomaly to the west, Brindesan and Meren in the north, and above them, a chain of islands stretching up towards the equator: Esfaban. King Esger was the only ruler who'd failed to add to Osgaard's territory in seven generations. *I hope that hurts, you whoreson of a king.*

His gaze lingered on the Esfaban islands. On the map they looked like a string of beads. His memory supplied the details: the lap of waves on beaches of white sand, palm fronds rustling in the breeze, the heavy, warm rains, the chorus of frog song at night.

Home. A surge of longing ambushed him, so intense that his throat closed.

Karel looked away from the maps. The bee still buzzed futilely above Princess Brigitta's head. Her pose was unchanged—relaxed, dreamy, *wrong*.

Finally, after the bee had been batting at the window for nearly half an hour, Karel forced himself to move. His hobnailed boots sank into the rugs as he crossed the room. "Princess?"

Princess Brigitta turned her head and looked up at him. No, not at him, she seemed to look *through* him. Her eyes were slightly unfocussed, her pupils dilated. "Yes, armsman?"

"Would you like me to let the bee out?"

Her gaze turned to the window, and then away. "Oh, yes." Her tone was vague, uninterested, as if she didn't care about such things.

Karel frowned. "Are you all right, princess?"

"Perfectly," she said. The word was slightly slurred.

Was she drunk? Drugged? Karel opened the window and let the bee out, then glanced down at her face. Princess Brigitta's eyes were half-closed. She appeared to be dozing.

He walked back across the thickly piled rugs and took a post beside the door to the antechamber. From this vantage point he could see into the bedchamber: a slice of marble floor, the tasseled edge of a rug, one corner of the bed with its midnight-blue and silver counterpane.

Outside, the sun was high in the sky. The echoes of the sixth bell drifted faintly. He heard the sound of a door opening, closing, the clatter of boots on marble. The door from the antechamber swung open. Duke Rikard strode into the salon, followed by his armsman. "Stay out there," the duke said.

The armsman retreated into the antechamber and closed the door.

Duke Rikard's gaze turned to Karel. His lips compressed as if he wished to order him into the antechamber too.

Karel stared stolidly past the duke's shoulder. *I take orders only from my mistress.*

The duke turned away from him. His gaze lighted on the princess, seated on the settle with her eyes closed and sunlight gilding her hair. "My dear princess."

Princess Brigitta didn't flinch, didn't stiffen. She lifted her eyelids and watched him approach, her expression dreamy.

"You were asleep when I left this morning." The duke took both her hands and kissed them. "Are you well?"

"Perfectly."

Duke Rikard didn't appear to hear the faint slur, the way she dropped the *t* from the word. He cupped her chin in one hand and looked down at her. "You're not wearing your crown."

The princess blinked slowly. "No."

"I want you to wear it, always."

She nodded, but Karel doubted she'd fully heard the words.

"Come." The duke took Princess Brigitta's hand and pulled her to her feet. "I'd like us to spend some time together."

"Time?"

"Yes," the duke said, as he led her towards the bedchamber. He had the smile of a glutton about to indulge in a feast. "I'd like to spend time with my new wife."

You'd like to rut her, you mean.

The princess didn't demur. Her manner was acquiescent, her expression distant.

The door to the bedchamber closed behind them, and then opened again to expel Yasma. Rikard's voice followed the maid, containing a hiss of anger. "I want her to wear the crown every day. From the moment she rises."

"Yes, master," Yasma said, abasing herself.

The door closed again with a loud *snick*.

KAREL FOUND HIMSELF unable to look at Yasma. Knowledge of what was happening in the bedchamber churned inside him.

Let me kill him. His hand gripped the hilt of the sword so hard the ridges of metal dug into his skin. The duke's last words echoed, sharp-edged, in his mind: *I want her to wear the crown always.*

Always. Even when he was rutting her. *Especially* when he was rutting her.

Karel wanted to upend the lacquered tables, to smash the gilded vases against the wall, to shred the tapestries with his sword.

No, better to destroy the man, to castrate him, to cut off his head.

An image flowered in his mind, glorious: the duke's head spinning as it tumbled, spraying blood, the man's body falling heavily, striking the floor—

Movement caught his attention: Yasma, crossing to the settle where the princess had sat.

Karel strode after the maid, crushing the soft rugs beneath his hobnailed boots. "What's wrong with her? What did he give her?"

"Nothing," Yasma said, busily straightening the cushions.

"He drugged her!"

"No."

Karel's anger erupted. He took hold of the maid's elbow, swinging her around to face him. "She's been drugged!"

"The duke didn't give her anything." Yasma twisted her arm, trying to free herself. "I did. It was her choice."

"What was her choice?"

"Poppy juice."

Karel released Yasma's elbow. He stared at her, aghast. "But the danger—!"

"He's raping her," Yasma said flatly. "Would you rather she knew what he was doing, or that she went into it with her mind numbed?"

Karel shook his head. "It's too dangerous!"

"You've never been raped." Yasma turned away from him. "You don't know what it's like."

Karel looked down at her bent head. "My mother was a bondservant. She was raped."

"If she'd been able to take poppy juice, she would have." Yasma's movements were almost fierce as she straightened the cushions. "Believe me."

"It's too dangerous," Karel said again, but his voice lacked conviction.

Yasma swung around to face him. "You're a man! You will *never* know what it's like!"

Karel was silent. *You're right: I don't know.* He'd seen misery on women's faces, seen despair, seen fatalism. *I can't even begin to imagine how it must feel to be that helpless.*

He reached for her, putting his arms around her. "I'm sorry, Yasma."

Yasma stood rigid for a moment, and then her head bowed. She let him pull her close, let her forehead rest against his chest, against the polished Osgaardan breastplate.

"Did I hurt you?" Karel asked, stroking her hair. "I'm sorry. I didn't mean to."

"No."

He stood in the sunlight, holding her, trying not to think about what was happening in the bedchamber. *I hate this place. I hate what it does to people.*

Outside, the sky was the pale blue of eggshells. Karel stared at it, wishing he was seeing that blue sky from somewhere else. *I could take them away. The princess and Yasma.* They could look at that sky from somewhere safe. Somewhere that wasn't Osgaard.

But the course of his life was set, as was Princess Brigitta's, as was Yasma's. There was no escape.

"I know how you feel about her," Yasma said in a low voice. "I love her too."

Karel opened his mouth to protest—*I don't love her*—and then closed it again.

"I'm just trying to make it easier for her."

Yasma at least had done something. All he'd done was watch.

"How did you pay for it?"

"I took one of her coins." Yasma's head lifted. She met his eyes. "It wasn't stealing. It was for her, not me."

Perhaps it hadn't been stealing, but it was perilously close to it. "Shall I give you some money? So you don't need to use hers?"

He saw relief on her face. "Yes. Please."

There was nothing else he could do to help Princess Brigitta, but there was one thing he could do for Yasma, a protection he could offer. "After two more years' service, I can take a wife," Karel said. "If you like... we can marry. I'm certain the princess will give permission."

Yasma stiffened in his arms.

"I promise I wouldn't touch you," Karel said hastily. "I promise, you'd be quite safe."

No, that was wrong. She'd never be completely safe; not even the princess's protection could give her that. If Duke Rikard should decide to rut his wife's bondservant, Yasma would have to submit.

"Unless there's someone else you'd prefer?"

He felt her shudder. "No. No one."

The shudder turned his thoughts to the bedchamber, to Princess Brigitta and the duke. Anger rose inside him again. He barely heard Yasma say, "Thank you. That would be very kind of you, Karel."

He forced his attention back to her. "How many years service have you left?"

"Thirteen."

She'd only completed seven years, less than half her service.

"How old were you when you came?"

"Ten."

The youngest a bondservant could be. Her family must have been desperate, to send her so young. His arm tightened around Yasma's shoulders.

"I hate it here," she said fiercely, bowing her head against his breastplate again.

Karel looked out the window at the white marble

of the palace, the glittering gilded roofs, the clipped hedges and flowering rosebushes and lush green curve of a lawn. A façade of beauty, with ugliness beneath. "Yes," he said. "So do I." He gently stroked her soft black hair. His mother had been this young once, this helpless, trapped in a nightmare, earning her family's freedom through her own slavery.

An idea crystalized in his mind. "Yasma... do you know of a way to stop her becoming pregnant?"

"What?"

"If the princess proves barren, Duke Rikard might annul the marriage."

Yasma lifted her head and stared at him for a moment, her lips slightly parted, then she closed her mouth. Determination firmed her face. "Dung-root juice. If she drinks it, she won't conceive."

"Do you think she'll agree?"

Yasma gave a single, emphatic nod. "I'm certain of it!"

CHAPTER TWENTY-TWO

THEY RODE NORTH, keeping to the forested foothills of the Graytooth Mountains, avoiding the patrols. Harkeld didn't argue with the decision; the roads may have been faster, but the forest felt safer.

They maintained a hard pace, not stopping until dark, rousing before dawn. The forest looked no different on this side of the range: a mix of oak and ash, the odd yew tree or rowan. They ran out of cider, and then dried meat and vegetables for the stew. The men pursuing them neither gained nor lost ground; they stayed half a day behind.

On the fourth evening they halted beside a creek. Gerit waited for them. At his feet lay a doe. Its throat had been ripped out.

Gerit butchered the doe while they set up camp. Cora roasted the flesh in the fire. The smell rose in the air, making Harkeld's mouth water. He turned his back and walked down to the creek, crouching and cupping his hands, washing his face. Above, the sky was clear, scattered with stars.

"Ach, that meat smells good," Justen commented, joining him.

"I won't be eating it."

Justen turned to look at him. "Why not?"

"Gerit killed it."

"So?"

"He killed it with his *teeth*. Not a knife. Not a bow and arrow. He killed it *with his teeth*."

Justen shrugged. "However it died, I plan on eating it."

Harkeld shook his head, unable to understand the armsman's pragmatism. He dried his face on his shirt and walked back to the fire. The girl, Innis, was talking to Cora, her hair ink-black in the firelight. "A mug?" he asked.

Cora handed him one.

He filled it at the creek and sat on the bank. The smell of roasting meat hung over the small clearing. His mind was sickened, but his stomach growled hungrily. Harkeld sipped his water.

"Here." Justen handed him a wooden bowl filled with chunks of meat.

Harkeld put the bowl down. "No, thank you."

"It's haunch."

Haunch. Nowhere near where Gerit's wolf teeth had been. Harkeld looked at the meat. The smell wafted up. His mouth watered and his stomach growled again.

Justen sat beside him and began to eat hungrily.

Harkeld's stomach tightened in a painful cramp. He swallowed a mouthful of water. After a minute, he put down the mug and picked up the bowl. The smell was mouthwatering.

Just one piece.

The flavor invaded his mouth. His mind told him to spit it out; his stomach told him to hurry up and swallow.

"'S good, isn't it?" Justen said with his mouth full.

It was better than good; it was delicious. Harkeld ate as hungrily as his armsman, and licked his fingers once he'd finished.

They turned in early. Harkeld wrapped himself in his blanket and stared at the sky, at the stars. The meat sat queasily in his belly.

They'd been running for ten days, pushing the horses, pushing themselves, and yet the first anchor stone still seemed impossibly distant, three hundred leagues away on the Masse plateau.

We'll never get there.

A full moon rose above the tree tops, almost as bright on his face as the sun. Harkeld pulled the blanket over his head.

EBRIL ROUSED THEM several hours after midnight. "They've been riding by moonlight! They're less than an hour away!"

Harkeld thrust aside his blanket. He flung on his shirt and crammed his feet into his boots.

"They must've broken camp not long after nightfall," Ebril said. "It's my fault! I didn't think—"

Harkeld buckled the sword belt, his fingers clumsy with haste.

"They've never done it before!" Ebril's voice rose at the end, almost in a wail.

THE REST OF the night passed in a blur of shadows and moonlight. The darkness seemed to magnify every noise they made, until Harkeld thought they sounded like an army crashing through the forest. When dawn broke, Gerit flew down and joined them.

"Where are they?" Dareus asked.

"About a league behind."

They didn't stop for breakfast. They plunged onwards through the forest, while the sun climbed in the sky. Mid-morning, they came to a break in the trees, where the rubble of a landslide had carved a path down the hillside.

They were low in the foothills. Lundegaard lay spread at their feet: the undulations of hill and valley, the neat patchwork of crops and orchards, the lines of dusty roads, the clusters of farmhouses and villages. In the distance was a hump-backed shape that Harkeld recognized: King Magnas's castle atop its mount.

It was so familiar that for a moment something hurt in his chest. He'd lived in that castle, had hunted in these foothills with King Magnas's sons. The curse had been a fable, his blood had been pure.

Harkeld's hand clenched on the reins. He looked away from the peaceful farmland and distant hump of the castle. To the north, bluffs split the forest. Trees hugged the base of the cliffs for several miles, and then tapered away. "We need to be lower. If we stay up here, we'll end up on top of the cliffs. We won't be able to get down for days."

Dareus glanced at him sharply. "Days? Are you certain?"

"The bluffs run unbroken for more than a hundred leagues."

"But if we go down, we'll lose the forest," Justen protested.

Dareus waved down the hawk that circled above them. It landed and became the witch Petrus. Naked, the scar on the witch's side was clearly visible. It snaked its way down his ribs, pink against the tan of his skin. "Can you see any patrols?"

"On every road. They're stopping everyone."

"Looking for us?"

"I'd say so."

Dareus looked at the bluffs, at the farmland. "If we stay above the cliffs we'll have cover, but no escape should they catch us. If we go down—"

"We should go down," Cora said.

Everyone looked at her.

"We don't know Lundegaard's soldiers want to kill us." Her voice was calm, matter-of-fact. "We *know* Osgaard's do."

Dareus thought for a moment and then nodded. "Very well. We go down."

THEY ZIGZAGGED SWIFTLY down through the forest, crossing the face of the landslip once, and then a second time, and a third. On their fourth time across, Harkeld heard a faint shout. He looked up. High above them were men on horseback.

As he watched, a tiny object launched into the sky, an arrow, looking no larger than a seamstress's needle. It arced downwards, striking the ground halfway between their two parties, disappearing into the rubble of boulders and shattered trees.

They plunged into the forest again. The next time they crossed the landslide he saw how close they were to the bottom. One more traverse and they'd be on level ground.

A hawk swooped low, screeching a warning. Harkeld looked uphill. He saw their pursuers, high above them. He squinted. What were they doing? Laboring at something—

Above them, a boulder broke loose. A second boulder followed it. A third. He heard Justen curse. "Ride, sire!"

It was impossible to turn the horses, impossible to go back. There was only forwards, urging the horses faster than was safe, scrambling over boulders, over tree trunks, following Dareus and Cora, aware of the hillside in motion above them; boulders leaping and bounding, gathering speed as they tumbled.

His horse stumbled and went down. "Sire!" Justen shouted behind him.

The horse struggled to rise. Harkeld heaved himself out of the saddle and began to run.

Fifty yards. Twenty. Dareus and Cora reached the forest. There was a roar like thunder in his ears. Behind him he heard a horse scream.

Harkeld hauled himself over the last boulder, the last splintered tree trunk, and burst into the safety of the forest. His horse charged past him, followed by Justen's, riderless, staggering drunkenly.

Harkeld swung around. "Justen!" Relief lurched in his chest. His armsman was behind him.

He reached out and gripped Justen's arm. He saw the armsman's mouth move, but couldn't hear the words beneath the roar of the landslide. Dust billowed like smoke around them.

* * *

NONE OF THE packhorses made it. Justen's horse had a broken fetlock. "We'll have to kill it," Dareus said.

"Innis can heal it," Justen said.

"There's no time." The rumble of the landslide had died apart from the occasional clatter of falling rock. Shouts came from above them on the hillside.

"But that leaves us with only three horses," Justen protested.

"I'll be a horse."

Harkeld jerked his head around. Gerit stood beside Cora. His figure blurred, expanded... a brown horse stood where he'd been. It tossed its head and snorted.

Harkeld took an involuntary step backwards. "I'm not riding that."

"I will," Cora said. "I'm the lightest."

He helped remove the saddle from Justen's horse, then held the animal's head and spoke soothingly to it as Dareus drew his sword. The horse's death was neither quick nor easy. Dareus was grim-faced when it was over. Blood soaked the ground.

They mounted. The last stretch of forest sped past—branches whipping at Harkeld's face, roots snagging at the horses' hooves. Finally they burst from the trees.

The horses slowed, their flanks heaving.

Ahead were fields bounded by drystone walls.

Harkeld glanced back at the forest, at the gash of the landslide. He saw movement through the settling dust: men scrambling down the rubble only a hundred yard above them.

"Archers," he said, urging his horse forward. "Behind us."

The first field was planted with corn. They pushed through the plants, snapping stems, leaving a wide path in their wake. Harkeld snatched another glance behind them. The men were nearly at the bottom of the hill. *They'll never catch us, not on foot.*

A hawk swooped down, changing into a man as it landed. Petrus. The corn came up nearly to his shoulder. "There are a couple of patrols headed for you. They saw the landslide."

"How many men?" Dareus asked.

"A dozen in each."

"Stay close," Dareus said. "We may need you."

The blond witch nodded. He became a hawk again and swept up into the sky.

Beside him, Justen said, "I hope you're right about King Magnas."

"So do I." Magic suddenly seemed a puny weapon. What good was a burning field if they were surrounded by patrols? What good were a couple of lions against dozens of men?

The first patrol came into sight a minute later, cantering through the cornfield, armed and wearing the forest green of Lundegaard's army.

Dareus halted. "Cora, get down. Gerit may need to change."

Cora dismounted. The corn tips rustled in the breeze above her head. She flicked her plait back over her shoulder and stood squarely, her feet apart, her hands at her sides, ready. Above, two hawks hovered.

The patrol slowed from canter to walk—the horses pushing through the waving stalks of corn— and halted a dozen yards distant. Harkeld scanned the faces. His gaze halted on the soldier wearing the officer's badge of rank.

"The officer is King Magnas's youngest son," he said quietly.

Beside him, Justen loosened his sword in its scabbard. "Is that good or bad?"

"We're friends," Harkeld said, and then corrected himself: *We were friends.* The witch's blood running in his veins must change that.

The officer nudged his horse forward a few paces. "Harkeld. We've been looking for you."

Harkeld dipped his head in greeting. "Tomas."

"My father wishes to offer Lundegaard's assistance in your cause."

Dareus nudged his own horse forward, placing himself between Harkeld and Prince Tomas. "And what does King Magnas know of our cause?" There was no belligerence in his tone, no hostility, merely polite curiosity.

"The Ivek curse."

"A fable," Dareus said, with a casual, dismissive wave of his hand.

"Not according to the reports coming out of Vaere." Tomas regarded the witch steadily. "You need not fear us. We seek only to help."

The horse that was Gerit snorted.

Harkeld turned his head at the rumble of hooves. A second patrol came into view, cantering through the corn. Twelve more men. He was aware of Justen stiffening alongside him.

"We understand there's a bounty on Harkeld's head," Tomas said.

Dareus shrugged. His posture was relaxed, one

hand holding the reins, the other resting on his thigh, but tiny flames burned at the end of each fingertip. He was ready to fight.

"My father has issued a proclamation. Any man who attempts to harm Harkeld will forfeit his livestock, his holdings, and his life."

The second patrol slowed to a walk.

"A dreadful punishment," Dareus said, politely. "Tell me, why should we believe—"

The two hawks swooped low above their heads, shrieking. One plummeted down to land. It was Ebril.

Prince Tomas's mount shied. There was a scrape of steel as the soldiers drew their swords.

"Archers!" Ebril shouted, pointing back the way they'd come. In the blink of an eye he became a lion, another blink and he was gone, charging back through the cornfield.

"Sire!" Justen cried. "Get—"

Something struck Harkeld's shoulder blade. The impact almost knocked him off his horse. Justen grabbed him, steadying him in the saddle. "Sire!"

Harkeld clung to the reins with one hand. His left shoulder, his arm, were numb. He dimly heard Tomas shouting, heard the thunder of hooves as the patrol followed Ebril at a gallop.

Dareus was at his side. "Get him off the horse!"

He slid awkwardly from the saddle, staggering when his feet hit the ground. "What—" The numbness spread to his chest. There was something wrong with his heartbeat. Someone grabbed him as his knees buckled.

"Sire!"

Faces loomed in his vision. Justen's. Tomas's.

"What—" His vision grayed at the edges. He tried to make his tongue form words—*What happened?*—but everything went black.

CHAPTER TWENTY-THREE

JAUMÉ WASN'T THE only one heading west any more.
There were other people on the road. They passed
him on horseback and in wagons, grim-faced and
urgent. He learned to step to the side of the road
when he heard the sound of hooves. He learned not
to ask for food.

The rumble of wheels came from behind him.
"Out of the way, boy!" A stone shied at him.

Jaumé scurried aside.

A wagon passed him, drawn by oxen. On the
driver's bench were a man and a woman, two
children. The woman clutched the children tightly
to her. She turned her head and looked at him as
they passed.

The wagon was piled with belongings, with food.
Jaumé watched it disappear around the next bend.
Hunger gnawed in his belly. The apples he'd stolen
from an orchard yesterday were gone, eaten.

Two miles further on was a village. It was about
the size of Girond, twenty or thirty cottages with
whitewashed walls and thatched roofs, built around
a cobbled market square with a well at its centre.

The village was silent, empty.

Jaumé explored cautiously. He saw hens pecking between the cobblestones in the marketplace, a slinking dog. The windows of the empty cottages seemed to stare at him. He knew the curse wasn't here, knew it was miles behind him, days behind him, and yet hair pricked on the nape of his neck. He shivered.

Like Girond, the village had an inn. It had been looted. The door swung open in the breeze, banging against the whitewashed wall. Jaumé hurried past.

He chose a cottage at random, peering in the windows. Only his face looked back at him.

His stomach rumbled, loud in the silence. Jaumé took a deep breath and cautiously opened the cottage door.

He checked the kitchen first. The larder had been hastily emptied. Dried beans rolled beneath his feet. A sack of flour lay where it had been dropped, split open, and a layer of flour coated the floor.

Whoever had emptied the larder hadn't been thorough. Hanging in the darkest corner was half a leg of cured ham.

Jaumé scrambled up on a shelf and unhooked the ham. His mouth watered as he jumped down, his feet sending up a puff of flour. He bit into the ham, sinking his teeth into salty, stringy flesh, and hurried out into the kitchen, chewing.

It was no longer empty. A man stood between him and the open door.

Jaumé halted, his mouth full, the ham clutched to his chest.

The man wore muddy boots and had a rucksack slung over his shoulder. A week's worth of stubble covered the lower half of his face. A forager, like himself.

The man's gaze fastened on the leg of ham. His expression became sharp, intent. "Give it to me," he said.

Jaumé shook his head and shrank back, tightening his grip on the ham.

The man reached into his pocket. He pulled out a knife. "Give me the ham."

Terror locked Jaumé's muscles. He didn't move as the man walked towards him, couldn't move. He stared at the knife, too afraid to chew, too afraid to swallow, almost too afraid to breathe.

The man jerked the ham from his grasp. "Get out of here, boy."

His muscles unlocked. Jaumé ran for the door, stumbling over the step, his mouth still full of half-chewed ham. Once the village was out of sight he fell to his knees and spat out the ham, gagging, gulping for breath.

When he'd stopped shaking, he picked the ham out of the dirt and ate it.

CLOUDS GATHERED IN the sky as the afternoon progressed. It began to drizzle. Jaumé trudged through the mud, shivering, huddling to the side of the road whenever wagons and horse riders passed.

In the early evening, he came to a lane leading to a farmhouse. No smoke came from the chimney. To one side of the house, sheets were pegged to a washing line. Two of them dragged on the ground, muddy.

*　　*　　*

JAUMÉ HESITATED, AND then walked cautiously down the rutted lane. No dogs barked warning at him, no one answered his knock on the kitchen door.

He pushed it open and entered warily. The kitchen was empty, the ashes in the fireplace cold. He tiptoed into the larder. His feet left wet, muddy prints on the floor. The shelves were bare apart from a scattering of peppercorns and cloves.

Outside, a basin of muddy water and potato peelings sat beside the kitchen doorstep. Jaumé crouched on the step and groped in the water, catching a handful of peelings. He chewed them, fishing in the water for more. His fingers touched something sharp, something cold.

Jaumé stopped chewing. He tipped the water out of the basin. In the bottom, amid the peelings, lay a knife.

He picked it up and wiped it carefully on his shirt and put it in his pocket.

IN THE HENHOUSE, Jaumé found five eggs. He ate them, sucking the contents greedily from the shells. Next, he looked in the shadowy barn. He could see where the farm wagon had stood, where the horses had been stabled.

He found an empty waterskin hanging on a peg, and a thin blanket that smelled of horses. He took them both, filling the waterskin at the well. And then he set off west again, the blanket wrapped around his shoulders, the waterskin slung over one arm, the knife in his pocket.

CHAPTER TWENTY-FOUR

THE LAST TIME Innis had healed the prince she'd felt his loathing of her, like something crawling under her skin. This time he was unconscious. The healing was much easier.

As she repaired the broken shoulder blade and rib, the damage to his heart, she began to get a sense of who Prince Harkeld was. Without the revulsion and fear dominating his emotions, other aspects of him were discernable. On one level, he felt a lot like Petrus: a sense of youthfulness, maleness, vitality. But beneath those were other things. Her hands lay on his back. She felt the warmth of his skin, the movement of his body with each inhalation, each exhalation, but she was also aware of other things: confidence, stubbornness, determination, pride, honor.

Mixed with those things, tainting everything, was a turmoil of confusion and fear, a bitter edge of hatred, the sharpness of panic, a sense of helplessness, and grief.

What had she said to Petrus? *He's like a mage who's been stripped of his magic.*

She'd been wrong. What had happened to Prince Harkeld was worse than that. He hadn't lost one thing he valued; he'd lost it all—his home and family, his birthright. Everything. And he'd lost it through no fault of his own.

Innis realized she was stroking his shoulder blade lightly with her thumb, trying to give comfort. She stilled the movement.

She looked up as the door opened. Petrus entered. Behind him, guarding the doorway, was one of King Magnas's personal guardsmen. A russet-brown hound lay alongside the man. Ebril.

Petrus closed the door. He was dressed in fresh clothes. His face was clean-shaven. "How is he?"

"I'm almost finished." Innis stood and stretched. "Will you help me turn him over?"

They eased the prince onto his back. His skin was as tanned as Petrus's, the dusting of hair on his chest dark brown instead of golden.

Innis pulled the sheet up to his chin. "Where's Dareus?"

"Talking to the king. With Cora and Gerit."

She nodded and smothered a yawn, looking down at the prince. His face was dark with stubble, the muscles slack in sleep. A curse shadow lay over him, but she barely noticed it. She'd grown used to the sight of them draped over everyone. "I don't know how to shave." Innis touched a finger to the prince's cheek, felt the rasp of whiskers. "Will you teach me?"

"Yes, later." Petrus took hold of her arm and tried to shepherd her towards the door. "Let me finish healing him. Go and bathe. Rest."

She shook her head. "It's fine, Petrus."

"But—"

"I want to do it." She pulled her arm free.

Petrus's face tightened momentarily. "Very well."

Innis watched as he left the room. Was Petrus angry with her? She shrugged wearily and turned back to the bed.

It was a bed worthy of a prince, with posts carved from dark wood and a heavy canopy of green velvet. The room was worthy of a prince, too—the deep fireplace, the branching candelabra, the windows with tiny, diamond-shaped panes. Tapestries hung on the walls. Hunting scenes: boars with spears bristling from their backs, stags brought down by hunting dogs, birds tumbling from the sky, pierced by arrows.

Innis averted her gaze. She sat in the chair beside the bed and turned the sheet back slightly.

She laid a hand on Prince Harkeld's shoulder. There wasn't much left to heal. Bruising, some swelling. She closed her eyes and let the magic flow down her fingers, let it flow inside him, along veins and arteries, along nerves, through muscle and bone. The sense of who he was expanded around her again. Honor. Pride. Determination.

Innis worked methodically, seeking areas of damage, repairing them: the bruising around his shoulder blade, the swelling in the tissues surrounding the fresh scar. She checked that no other ribs were cracked, letting her magic feel its way along each bone, and examined his heart one last time. It beat steadily.

Innis opened her eyes. She yawned. *A bath*, she thought, rubbing her face. To scrub the dirt of the past week off her skin, to wash it out of her hair. And then she'd change back into Justen.

She yawned again and rested her forehead on the edge of the bed for a moment.

＊　　＊　　＊

FINGERTIPS TRAILED LIGHTLY *across his shoulder, eliciting a shiver of pleasure. Harkeld blinked his eyes open. The fingers stroked over his skin again, feather-light, tracing a path along his collarbone, down his chest.*

He captured the hand—a woman's hand, slender and fine-boned—and turned his head. The room was too dark to see her face.

The woman didn't pull away. She bent over him. He felt the soft brush of her hair against his cheek, the soft touch of her mouth on his shoulder. Her lips parted, her tongue tasted his skin.

Desire shivered through him. He made a sound in his throat.

She lifted her head and drew back. Her hand slid from his grip.

"No." Harkeld pushed up until he was sitting. "Don't go."

She stilled.

Harkeld reached for her, drawing her towards him, cupping his hands around her face and dipping his head to kiss her. Her lips were soft, sweet. "Don't go," he whispered against her mouth.

Her lips clung to his. She leaned into him. She was naked. He felt the silken warmth of her skin against his, the softness of her breasts, the taut crests of her nipples.

Arousal flowered inside him, hot and urgent. He gathered her to him, hungrily tasting her mouth, her cheek, her throat. "Don't go," he said again, fiercely.

"Are you certain?" Her voice was low, the accent familiar: a soft burr.

Harkeld drew back slightly. The room was lighter now, as if dawn broke outside the windows. He saw the woman's face, pale, dark-eyed.

HARKELD WOKE ABRUPTLY. He blinked, trying to bring the room into focus. Tapestries. Light streaming in through diamond-paned windows.

He turned his head. The witch, Innis, sat in a chair alongside him. She was asleep, her forehead resting on the edge of the bed. Her hand lay on his arm.

Harkeld jerked away from her, sitting up in the bed. Memory returned: an arrow thudding into his back, Justen holding him up in the saddle.

He felt his left shoulder blade cautiously. His fingertips found the ridge of a scar.

Harkeld shrugged his shoulder, expecting stiffness, tenderness, but there was none. He glanced at the witch. She'd healed him while he slept.

She'd healed him—and he'd dreamed of her while she did it. He flinched from the memory of her fingers sliding across his skin, memory of her mouth on his shoulder, her tongue tasting him, flinched from the memory of his response.

He'd *kissed* her. A witch.

How could I have dreamt such a thing?

He pushed aside the sheet and scrambled out the other side of the wide bed. His bare feet sank into a thick rug.

Harkeld frowned at the tapestries, at the four-poster bed with its dark green canopy, at the embroidered coverlet folded at the foot of the bed. The room was richly furnished—and utterly unfamiliar.

He strode across to the window. The view was one he'd seen a thousand times: battlements, steeply sloping slate roofs. He was in King Magnas's castle.

Below the castle were the tiled roofs and cobbled streets of the town, and beyond the town was the broad silver curve of the river Fors.

Harkeld relaxed, and then tensed again as he looked down at himself. He was naked.

He glanced around the room. No clothes were evident.

The witch sighed and stirred slightly.

Harkeld hastily pulled the coverlet from the bed. He wrapped it around himself and retreated to the window.

The witch lifted her head. She blinked, and saw the empty bed. "Prince Harkeld?" She pushed to her feet.

"Here."

She turned towards the window, clutching the bed with one hand. The alarm smoothed from her face when she saw him. "You're awake." She flushed. "I mean... How are you feeling?"

"Perfectly well," Harkeld said, with stiff politeness. "Thank you for healing me."

Her flush deepened. She bit her lip and glanced down at the floor.

"Where's Justen?"

"I think... I think he's bathing." The hesitancy in her voice, her shyness, had nothing to do with the woman in his dreams. "Would you like me to fetch him for you?"

"Yes, please."

His eyes followed her as she crossed the room. She was too slender for his taste, her hair too dark, her manner too diffident. *I don't find her attractive*, he told himself firmly. *Not at all*.

The witch hesitated at the door and looked back at him. "You're quite safe. There's a guard, one of the king's most trusted men. And Ebril, too."

He nodded.

She bit her lip and opened the door. He had a glimpse of a corridor and the burly back of a guardsman before the door closed behind her.

DRESSED, AND WITH Justen beside him, Harkeld went in search of King Magnas. One guard walked in front of them, another at their heels; even so, he found himself tensing at each doorway, at each branch in the corridor. His injury was healed, but memory remained: the thud of the arrow striking his back, the swiftly spreading numbness.

I should be dead.

King Magnas was in the smaller of his audience chambers, with two of his sons and Dareus. They stood around a table spread with maps.

Prince Tomas looked up as the door opened. "Harkeld!" He dropped the map he was holding. "Should you be out of bed?"

Harkeld shrugged. "I'm fine."

"But you had an arrow—"

"The witches healed me. I don't have a scratch on me."

Tomas came across the chamber, grinning. To Harkeld's astonishment, he hugged him, clapping him on the back, as if they were brothers. "You scared the crap out of me. I thought you were dead."

"I... uh..."

King Magnas followed his youngest son. "My dear boy," he said, embracing Harkeld. "I'm so glad to see you."

Harkeld swallowed. *Don't you know I have witch blood in me?*

The king released him and stepped back. His face was the same as Harkeld remembered: the broad brow, the deep-set eyes, the good-humored mouth. The lines creasing the king's face were slightly deeper, the hair grayer, but otherwise he was unchanged. A man one could trust.

King Magnas's eldest son, Erik, came towards him with his hand outstretched. "How are you?" he asked. "Tomas tells us you almost died." He had the same broad forehead as his father, the same direct gaze, the same fair coloring.

Harkeld returned Erik's handclasp. *Why are you being so welcoming? I have witch blood.* He almost opened his mouth, almost said the words aloud, and then he understood. King Magnas and his sons didn't like him; they *needed* him.

Harkeld cleared his throat. "I'm fine."

"Have you eaten?" King Magnas opened his hand, indicating the food on a side table: platters of meat, loaves of bread, cheeses, fruit.

"Yes, thank you, sir."

"Then join us. We're planning your journey up onto the Masse plateau." The king took his arm and led him across to the table with the maps.

"King Magnas has generously agreed to outfit us," Dareus said, looking up. "Horses, weapons, supplies."

Harkeld nodded, and accepted the goblet of wine Erik poured for him.

"And we'll provide an escort of fifty armed men as far as the escarpment," Tomas said. "It's the plateau that's the problem." He pulled one of the maps forward. "See? That's where you're headed. The ruined city of Ner. A good ten days' journey into the desert."

"It's barren country," the king said. "There's some water, but whether there'll be enough for so many men, so many horses…"

"A smaller party would be better," Prince Erik said. "But that would leave you without much protection."

Harkeld stepped closer to the table. Pushed to one side was a map of the northern hemisphere, showing the Allied Kingdoms. His eyes skipped over the Groot Isles, where Justen came from, Piestany, Lirac, and Rosny, home of the witches—

He looked away. "Will I need protection in Masse? It's Lundegaardan territory. My father's men will scarcely dare to—"

"You should take no chances," the king said. "Some of Esger's men may reach the plateau."

"And there are others who may decide to claim the bounty on your head." Tomas walked across to the platters of food and chose an apple. "Bandits. Mercenaries. Fithian assassins."

Fithian assassins? The skin on Harkeld's back tightened.

"Or a farmer," Justen put in. "Or a peasant. Anyone poor enough, or greedy enough."

Prince Tomas turned to look at him.

"The weight of a man's head in gold is a powerful incentive to commit murder."

"Thrice the weight of Harkeld's head," Tomas said.

Thrice? Harkeld met Justen's eyes briefly. The armsman grimaced.

"But even so, who'd be so foolish?" Tomas said, buffing the apple on his sleeve. "The curse—"

"The curse can still be broken if Prince Harkeld's dead, sire," Justen said. "All they need is his blood and his hands."

Harkeld looked down at his wine. It was as dark as blood. His father's voice rose in his ears: *Your obedience—or I take your blood and your hands.*

Harkeld placed the goblet on the table. He clasped his hands behind his back.

"You'll take all fifty men," the king said. "It will slow you down, but—"

Dareus shook his head. "Your highness, we have two more anchor stones after Masse. Speed is of the essence."

"Thirty then," Tomas said, and sank his teeth into the apple.

Dareus shook his head again. "Ten."

THEY ARGUED OVER the size of the escort for another hour, settling at last on fifty men until they reached the escarpment, and thereafter, twenty. The table was littered with maps and crumbs. King Magnas pushed away his goblet. "When do you wish to leave?" His manner towards Dareus was courteous, but Harkeld knew him well enough to see the revulsion behind the king's politeness.

"Ideally, tomorrow," Dareus said. "Although I realize that won't be possible."

"We need at least two days," Erik said.

"Very well." King Magnas nodded and pushed back his chair. "Two days."

"Who'll lead our men?" Tomas leaned across the table, his blue eyes alight with eagerness.

"Me," Erik said.

"No, me," said Tomas.

King Magnas looked at his sons.

"Not the heir," Dareus said. "It's too dangerous."

The king thought for a moment, and then nodded. "Tomas, then."

Tomas caught Harkeld's eye and grinned. "It'll be like old times!"

THE WITCH DEPARTED. The atmosphere in the room lightened, as if an oppressive presence had been removed. King Magnas refilled their goblets. "How are my grandsons?" he asked Harkeld, wedging the stopper into the wine flagon.

"They were in excellent health, sir, when I saw them last."

"My allying Lundegaard with your cause... do you think it will have consequences for them?"

Tomas paused, reaching for a piece of cheese. Erik looked up sharply from his perusal of a map.

By the All-Mother, I hadn't thought of that. Harkeld's fingers clenched around the goblet. "After Jaegar, they're my father's heirs. He won't harm them." He said the words with certainty, trying to believe them. "He loves them, sir."

King Magnas nodded. He picked up his own goblet, but didn't drink. Worry furrowed his face.

Harkeld glanced down at his wine, at the reflections shimmering on the surface, and then back at the king. *Should I tell him Sigren died at my father's hand?*

No. Not now. It would only make King Magnas more anxious about the boys' safety.

The king smiled. Harkeld saw how much effort it took. "How are they? It's been a long time since I saw them."

He forced himself to match the king's smile. "Lukas wants to be a woodcutter. I gave him an axe, a blunt little thing, and he drags it wherever he goes. His nursemaid complains that he even sleeps with it." There was an ache in Harkeld's chest; it had to do with memory of the boys—Lukas's dimples, Rutgar's mischievous grin. "And Rutgar is mad about horses. He has a pony of his own, but he likes nothing better than coming up on my blood bay with me."

Liked, he reminded himself. There'd be no more rides on that blood bay, Rutgar's face glowing with delight.

Harkeld cleared his throat. "Rutgar and I have... had an arrangement. For each tooth he lost, we went for a gallop outside the palace walls. So far he claims to have lost twenty-three teeth. Once he lost four in one week." He made himself chuckle. "The All-Mother alone knows where he's getting them from."

Tomas snorted, and King Magnas's smile became more relaxed.

*   *   *

As DUSK FELL, Harkeld walked on the battlements with Tomas, Justen one step behind, and behind Justen, two of the king's guards. Harkeld glanced sideways at Tomas, seeing the fair hair, the good-humored face. *You would have been a good husband to Britta.*

In his mind's eye, he saw Britta as he'd seen her last— sunlight on her hair, tears in her eyes, desperation in her voice. His chest tightened with guilt.

He'd done what he had to. Britta wouldn't have survived the flight to Lundegaard; he barely had. Better that she was alive and betrothed to Duke Rikard, than dead.

I'm sorry, Britta.

Harkeld forced his thoughts back to the journey that lay ahead. Ten years ago, he and Tomas had been as close as brothers. They'd wrestled and practiced sword-fighting, had hunted side by side, had played pranks together. With Tomas's older brother, Kristof, they'd explored the disused dungeons beneath the castle and—memorably—been lost in the warren of cells and passageways for a day and half the night. "You shouldn't come with us, Tomas. It's too dangerous." *It's not a game, like the dungeons. No one will come to rescue us.*

Tomas shrugged. "It's you they'll be trying to kill," he said flippantly. "Not me."

Harkeld halted. "If you die, your father will never forgive me."

Tomas turned to face him. Behind him, the sky was shading into darkness. A breeze drifted up, making the torches flare in their brackets, bringing with it the scent of wood smoke and meals cooking, the faint sound of laughter. "And if *you* die, he'll never forgive *me*."

"Tomas..." He looked away from that grin. "I have witch blood in me."

"Not a lot."

"A quarter. I'm a quarter witch." Fear clenched in his chest. *What if I'm a shapeshifter? What if there are feathers, bristles and scales waiting to burst from my skin?*

"Are you a witch?" The smile was gone from Tomas's voice. He sounded wary.

Harkeld looked at him. "No."

Tomas shrugged. "Then don't worry about it."

Harkeld laughed, a flat sound. "I wish my father had said that." He dragged a hand through his hair. Short hair. *I'm no longer a prince.* Bitterness surged through him. He resumed walking. "Fifty men? That's very generous of your father."

"How do we know we can trust them all?" Justen asked, behind them.

"They'll be hand-picked," Tomas said.

"But even so, all it takes is one man—"

"The soldier who attempts to kill Harkeld won't live more than a few minutes himself. There'll be forty-nine other men trying to kill him. And me." They passed a flaming torch. Tomas's eyes reflected the firelight for a moment. "And what use is gold to a dead man?"

Harkeld glanced at the two guards behind them. Justen's words echoed in his ears: *All it takes is one man.* He found himself wishing he had one of the witches guarding him instead. He hated the witches, but he trusted them not to kill him. He returned to one of Tomas's earlier comments. "Fithian assassins? You weren't serious, were you?"

"Why not? They kill for money, and there's a hefty bounty on your head."

"But there aren't any Fithians in Lundegaard, surely?"

Tomas shrugged. "They're like cockroaches. Turn up everywhere."

To the west, the last of the light crept from the sky; to the east, stars were faintly visible. Ahead, to the north, was the Masse plateau and the first of the stones anchoring Ivek's curse. *Will I survive this?* "I'm glad you're coming," he told Tomas.

"Wouldn't miss it for the world!"

I would. I'd give anything not to be here, not to be me. Harkeld shoved the self-pity aside. "How far will you come?"

"As far as you like."

Harkeld's spirits lifted slightly. *All the way to Sault, then.* "Where's Kristof?"

"Down at the Hook. Refugees are arriving from Vaere."

"Refugees?"

"More every day," Tomas said. "We're setting up camps. Father wanted one of us down there to make sure there's some kind of order." He sighed. "The All-Mother herself only knows what we'll do with them all."

"Bondservice?" Justen asked, his voice neutral.

Harkeld glanced back at him. The armsman's face was as expressionless as his voice, his condemnation carefully hidden. "Lundegaard doesn't have bondservants," he told him. As a boy, he'd once tried to defend the practice of bondservice. As an adult, he couldn't. A kingdom didn't need bondservants in order to flourish; Lundegaard proved that past any doubt. "King Magnas rules quite differently from my father."

And King Magnas gave his three sons command in Lundegaard's army, gave them the opportunity to acquire leadership skills, to show their mettle.

Harkeld compressed his lips, remembering the times he'd begged his father for a command in the army, however small, remembering the times he'd pleaded for an opportunity to do something more useful than practicing his wrestling skills and exercising his horses.

Be patient, his father had said. *I have greater things in mind for you.*

Now he knew what his father had meant.

Harkeld bit back a sour laugh. He'd wanted to be useful; he'd got his wish. The fate of the Seven Kingdoms rested on his shoulders. How much more *useful* could a man be?

"Come back to my rooms for a drink," Tomas said. "There's someone I'd like you to meet."

"Who?"

Tomas winked.

INNIS SHIFTED HER weight. She eyed the woman across the chamber from her. *Lady*, she corrected herself. The *lady* across the chamber from her. The *lady* who had all the subtlety of a tavern wench as she flirted with Prince Harkeld. She averted her gaze from the woman's full, pouting lips and lush bosom, and scanned the room.

Tomas was a prince, and yet his apartments had little of the lavish opulence she'd expected. The fabrics were rich, the furniture handsome, the tapestries on the walls exquisitely stitched, but there was none of the ostentatious display of wealth she'd seen in Osgaard's palace. *No bondservants either*, she reminded herself. Lundegaard might share a border with Osgaard, but their royal families lived by different philosophies.

Her eyes catalogued the room's occupants: the impassive guard at the door; Prince Tomas, lounging in a heavy oak armchair by the fireplace, one foot swinging, a tankard of mead in his hand; Prince Harkeld, his mead forgotten on the table, his attention on the lady seated alongside him on the settle; and Lady Lenora, widow of a baron, leaning forward as she spoke, laying her hand on the prince's arm, glancing up at him from beneath her lashes. The way she sat, her back slightly arched, thrust her full breasts into prominence.

Innis snorted under her breath. *Practically shoving them in his face*. She looked away. When she glanced back, Lady Lenora's hand had moved. It now rested on Prince Harkeld's thigh. The prince didn't appear to mind the lady's lack of subtlety. He was smiling.

Memory flooded through her of the dream she'd woken from. She'd touched the prince far more boldly than Lady Lenora was now doing. She'd stroked her fingers over his bare skin, had dipped her head and actually *tasted* his skin.

Embarrassment heated her cheeks. Innis thrust the memory firmly aside and tried to look as impassive as the guardsman.

Across the room, Prince Harkeld laughed. He looked like a stranger, not the man she'd traveled with these past eleven days. It wasn't just the cleanly-shaven jaw and the fresh clothes. Gone was the grim set of his mouth, the closed expression.

An attractive man, now that he was smiling. He had a strong face, a strong body.

Innis watched as Prince Harkeld laughed again, as he leaned forward and whispered in the lady's ear.

The lady blushed, giggled, and whispered a reply. Her smile was coy, the glint in her eyes triumphant.

Prince Harkeld rose to his feet, offering his hand to Lady Lenora. "If you'll excuse us, Tomas?"

Prince Tomas grinned. "Of course."

Innis tried to be as impassive as the guardsman by the door and not let her disapproval show.

They traversed two corridors and climbed a winding flight of stone stairs to reach Prince Harkeld's bedchamber, a procession led by one of King Magnas's guards.

Another guard stood at the door to the bedchamber. Beside him lay a large, russet-brown hound. Ebril. The prince looked back over his shoulder. "I shan't need you tonight, Justen."

Innis hesitated. There was a trestle bed set up inside, so Justen could guard the prince while he slept. How would Justen react? With a protest? With a grin like Prince Tomas? She settled on a wooden, "Yes, sire."

She waited while the guards opened the door, while they checked the chamber, while Prince Harkeld and his lady—*his whore*—entered and the door closed behind them, then she turned and went in search of the other mages.

They'd been allocated a suite—three bedchambers opening off a central room furnished with chairs and an oak table. Petrus and Gerit sat by the fire, drinking mead and playing cards. They looked up as she entered. "He's found himself a whore," Innis said, shutting the door with a snap.

Gerit grunted. "Lucky him."

"He sent me away, but..." She struggled to put her fears into words. "Shouldn't one of us be with him? Just in case."

"Isn't Ebril there?"

"Outside the door. No one's inside, guarding him."

Petrus laid down his cards. "You think she'll try to kill him?"

"No." Innis shook her head. "I don't know. She's... I don't trust her. One of us should be in there with him." She felt herself blush. "I'd do it myself, but—"

"I'll do it," Petrus said, pushing back his chair.

"Thank you." She bit her lip, and then remembered that Justen didn't do that. "Once she's gone, I'll take over."

"I will," Gerit said, shuffling the cards. "That was serious healing you did today, girl. You should sleep as yourself tonight."

Petrus nodded. He began to strip.

The shutters had been closed for the night. Innis unfastened one and pushed open the window. It was pitch black outside. Far below the distant lights of villages sparkled on the plains. When she turned back, Petrus had shifted. A snowy-white owl stood in the middle of the room. It spread its wings.

She stepped aside. The owl swept past her, the draft from its wings ruffling her hair.

Innis remained at the window after the owl had gone, staring out into the darkness. She was a Sentinel. She should be able to do what Petrus was doing: keep Prince Harkeld safe while he bedded Lady Lenora.

So why wasn't she?

Innis rubbed a finger over the window sill— Justen's finger, broad and blunt—feeling the grain of the wood. It was more than the invasion of privacy that made her balk. *If I wasn't a virgin, would I be so afraid of watching?*

In not doing this, she was letting everyone down. Including herself.

Her hand on the wooden sill connected her with the All-Mother, with soil, rock and water, with her parents, buried on the other side of the ocean. She tried to recall their faces, but the eight years had blurred them too much. She could imagine their quiet disappointment, though, through the palm of her hand.

Innis pushed away from the window. *Next time the prince takes a woman into his bed, I'll guard him myself.*

PETRUS FLEW AROUND to the prince's bedchamber. Predictably, the windows were shut and the shutters closed. He found an open window two levels down and changed into a cat. A minute later he was in the corridor outside Prince Harkeld's room. A guard stood with his back to the door, as far away from Ebril as he could be.

Petrus retreated around the corner and shifted into the shape of a lizard.

Stupid son of a whore, he grumbled to himself as he hurried along the corridor. *Thinking with his cock, not his brain.*

The guard didn't see him. Ebril did. The hound's tail wagged faintly, not drawing the guard's attention.

Petrus nodded to him, and darted through the crack beneath the door. The furniture in the bedchamber loomed as large as mountains: oak table, armchairs, the trestle bed for Justen. A fire was lit in the wide hearth—a towering bonfire—and candles burned in the sconces.

Petrus began to climb the wall, working his way towards the four-poster bed. The velvet canopy cast deep shadows, but the candlelight let him see the bed's occupants once he was above the mantelpiece. When he saw the woman, her blonde hair spilling across the pillows, he understood why the prince hadn't resisted. Lush mouth, lush breasts.

Lucky whoreson.

Petrus took up a position on the mantelpiece and watched.

CHAPTER TWENTY-FIVE

PERHAPS IT WAS because he'd almost died today, but Harkeld was hungry for sex. He couldn't get enough of Lenora's mouth, the delicious softness of her body. She was like a siren from sailors' tales: the full lips, the ripe breasts, the rich curves of waist and hip.

And she had a siren's skill at kissing, a siren's skill at touching him, at drawing pleasure from his body. He trembled as she cupped his testicles in her hand, biting back a groan as she explored with light, teasing fingers.

"You're everything I hoped you'd be, prince," she murmured.

And you're even more. More beautiful, more bold, more skillful.

He didn't say the words aloud. He couldn't talk with her caressing him like that, could barely think.

Harkeld reached for her. He wanted to bury himself in her ripe body, to lose himself in pleasure.

"No." Lenora released him. She drew back, her smile coy, teasing. "Not yet."

Harkeld dragged air into his lungs. Arousal burned inside him, urgent, insistent.

Lenora stroked herself, letting her fingers trail down the slope of one breast, circling the rosy nipple. "Touch me," she whispered, looking at him from beneath her lashes.

That, he could do.

He did more than touch; he devoured. The softness of her skin, her feminine scent, were intoxicating. Heat and urgency swelled inside him until he felt that he would burst from it.

Lenora arched against him. "Take me."

He needed no second urging.

INNIS WOKE THE next morning as herself, not Justen. For a moment she didn't know who she was, where she was—then everything settled into place around her. She pushed the coverlet aside. The other bed in the room was empty; Cora was gone.

She found Cora and Dareus in the main chamber, talking over the remains of breakfast. "What time is it? The prince! I should go to him—"

"Gerit is Justen this morning," Dareus said.

"But—"

"This morning you'll be yourself." It was an order. "You've spent too much time in a shape that's not your own."

Innis bit her lip. *But I like being Justen.* And then she realized how dangerous such thoughts were. It was the way to madness.

"Sit," Cora said. She pushed a basket of pastries across the table. "Eat. I recommend the nut ones."

INNIS DID THE dawn exercises first. She hadn't done them since she'd become Justen. Her limbs felt stiff and slightly awkward, uncoordinated. She went through the sequence four times—the stretches, the lunges, the retreats—before she was satisfied with her body's response. Then she sat and ate breakfast. Cora was right; the nut pastries were delicious.

Petrus entered the chamber, yawning. He did the dawn exercises and joined her at the table. "Morning." He reached for a pastry, broke it in two, and began to eat.

"How did it go last night?"

"Fine," Petrus said, not looking at her.

Innis glanced at Dareus and Cora. A map was spread between them. They were deep in conversation.

She leaned towards Petrus. "I'm sorry about last night," she said in a low voice.

Petrus stopped chewing. His eyebrows rose. She saw his confusion.

"Next time, I'll watch the prince myself. I promise."

Petrus choked and began to cough. When he'd caught his breath he said, "No."

"Why not?"

"Because..."

Because I'm a virgin. Innis looked down at the table. She pushed a crumb with one finger. "Next time I'm doing it."

"You're too young."

She looked up. "Not too young to be a Sentinel."

"Theoretically, you are." He reached for another pastry. "Age limit for a Sentinel's twenty-four, that I recall."

"But I *am* a Sentinel, and I should be doing everything you do!"

"Not that."

Innis felt herself flush. "Why not? I'm not a child. I'll be twenty soon."

"Because Gerit and Ebril and I can do it, that's why."

She studied his face while he ate. Petrus wasn't a virgin, hadn't been for several years. *Were you afraid the first time you did it?* She bit her lip, bit back the question. Of course he'd been afraid. Any mage— any mage with *sense*—was afraid the first time. So many things could go wrong.

But she was nearly twenty now. Old enough— despite the rules—to be a Sentinel. Old enough to have control over her magic, old enough to have sex and not unwittingly harm either herself or her bed partner.

If I wasn't a Sentinel...

If she wasn't a Sentinel, she'd be at home in Rosny, preparing to start her apprentice Journeys. And when the time was judged right—this year, next year—someone would be chosen to teach her how to control her magic during sex.

There was no one here who could do that. Dareus was too old, Ebril too young, too inexperienced, and Gerit... She repressed a grimace. No, not Gerit.

Which left Petrus.

Like Ebril, he was newly a Sentinel, too young to take the role of teacher. But even if he was older...

Innis studied his face: the white-blond hair falling over his brow, the long nose, the mobile mouth.

Memory came: for a moment she was twelve years old again, standing in the doorway of a classroom, trying to find the courage to step inside. Students sat in rows. One by one they turned their heads, until they were all staring at her. *This is Innis*, the Master said, his hand on her shoulder, urging her into the room. *She'll be in your class from now on.* She wanted to shrink into a corner, wanted to run home, except there was no home any more and her parents were dead. And then Petrus caught her eye and winked.

"What?" Petrus said, his mouth full.

Innis shook her head. "Nothing." She looked down at the table, pushed the crumb again with her finger. Since that first day at the Academy, Petrus had been like a brother. Sharing his bed would be...

She pulled a face. No, not Petrus.

Unbidden, an image of Prince Harkeld slid into her mind. As he'd been in the dream, naked, reaching for her. She pushed it firmly away. When she got back to Rosny, once the curse was broken, there'd be time enough for that aspect of her training.

AFTER LUNCH, WHEN she was back in Justen's shape, back in her place at Prince Harkeld's side, they went down to the training ground. Gerit trotted at their heels, a grizzled brown mastiff, and behind him were two of King Magnas's guards.

"Ready?" the prince asked, stripping off his shirt.

The training ground was a courtyard of packed dirt covered with sawdust. They weren't the only people there—half a dozen men wrestled or practiced their sword play. Stone walls rose on all four sides. Innis glanced up, scanning the windows that overlooked them. The eastern wall had an open gallery. It was empty, but even so... She laid her hand on her sword hilt, and released it as she saw a creamy-white dove circle down and land on the parapet. The faint shimmer surrounding the bird told her it was a shapeshifter; the color told her it was Petrus.

Innis unbuckled the sword belt and dropped it on the ground. Her shirt and boots followed. "Ready."

They wrestled for half an hour, until they were sweating, panting.

"Who's winning?"

Innis looked up from pinning Prince Harkeld on the ground. She saw fair hair and a grinning face. Prince Tomas. She released her hold and stood. "Sire."

Prince Harkeld raised himself on one elbow. "We're even."

"Looks like you lost that bout." Tomas's grin widened.

"I did," Prince Harkeld said, wincing as he pushed himself up from the dirt. "But I won the one before that."

"Not sure I believe you. Looks to me like your armsman had you whipped." Tomas was teasing; his tone took the insult out of the words.

Innis grinned, and wiped sweat and dirt from her face. Justen's body made wrestling much more fun. It wasn't merely that she was stronger; she had more weight behind her, more leverage. She felt a dangerous flicker of exultation for a shape that wasn't her own—and hastily quashed it.

"Grown soft, have you?" Tomas peeled off his embroidered vest and tossed it on the ground behind him.

Prince Harkeld narrowed his eyes. "Soft?"

Tomas shrugged, still grinning. "Flabby, weak..." He pulled his shirt over his head.

Innis swallowed a grin. Prince Harkeld was as hard, as muscled, as the guards who protected him.

"Flabby?"

Tomas kicked off his boots. "Uh huh. Flabby."

"Then I wonder you care to fight me."

Tomas shrugged. "For old times' sake. Unless... are you sure you're not too tired?" His tone was mock-solicitous.

Prince Harkeld flexed his hands and bared his teeth in a grin. "Try me."

Innis heard a murmur of feminine voices and glanced behind her. The gallery was no longer empty. A handful of noblewomen clustered there.

The pale dove sat on the parapet, watching too.

Innis turned her attention to the princes. There was nothing elegant about their wrestling, nothing restrained; it was rough, almost brutal.

Prince Harkeld won the first bout, emphatically. "Flabby?" he said. "Soft?"

"Soft as a girl," Tomas said, as he lay gasping on the dirt.

The prince grunted, and hauled Tomas to his feet. "Then what does that make you?"

The next bout was over almost before it had started. Tomas took Prince Harkeld down so fast, so hard, that Innis winced. "Soft," Tomas said, panting. "See?"

The prince spat sawdust from his mouth and pushed to his feet. "I'll show you soft."

Innis picked up her discarded shirt and walked across to the water butt beneath the gallery. She cupped her hands and drank, then washed the sweat and dirt from her face, her arms, her torso.

Behind her, someone grunted as they hit the ground. She turned and watched the princes grapple, rolling in the dirt, muscles straining as they each sought to overpower the other. The way they wrestled, they way they teased each other, had the familiarity of an old friendship.

I'm glad Tomas is coming with us. Prince Harkeld needs a friend.

She watched as Prince Harkeld pinned Tomas, as he laughed in triumph and then sat back on his heels, grinning. *This is who he used to be. Before we came and his life fell apart.*

"I enjoy watching wrestling. It's so animal."

Innis jerked her head around. A lady stood beside her, wearing a gown cut low across her bosom to show creamy skin and a magnificent cleavage.

"I watched you wrestle." Lenora looked up at her from beneath curling eyelashes. "You're very skilled."

"Thank you."

"What's your name, armsman?"

"Uh... Justen. Ma'am."

Lenora laid a hand on her arm. "You're very strong." Her fingertips stroked lightly. "Very well-muscled."

Innis blinked. Was Lenora *flirting* with Justen?

"I like well-muscled men. They have more stamina." Lenora smiled up at her. "I'm sure your master would spare you for an hour, Justen."

Innis jerked her arm free of those stroking fingers. "No, thank you."

The lady didn't lose her smile. "No?" She touched the neckline of her bodice. Her fingertips followed the curve of fabric until it reached its lowest point, then wandered up, over the lace trim, to rest against her skin and the deep valley of her cleavage.

"No." Innis stepped back a pace, flustered. She hauled the shirt roughly over her head. It clung to her wet skin.

The lady's eyes fastened on her chest—on Justen's chest, its ridges of muscles clearly delineated by the damp fabric. "You'd enjoy it," she said in a low, purring voice, her finger skimming lightly over the curve of one full breast. "I'd see to that."

Innis flushed, and stepped back another pace. She crossed her arms and grabbed the first words she could think of: "I have no interest in my master's whores."

Lenora's mouth opened in a gasp. There was a second of stunned silence, then: "I beg your pardon, armsman?"

Innis bit her tongue. She didn't repeat the words.

Color rose in Lenora's cheeks. "How *dare* you speak to me like that, armsman! I'm a baroness!" She turned and stalked from the training ground, the hem of her gown swirling angrily about her ankles.

Innis screwed her face up in a grimace. *Fool*, she told herself. *Next time a woman flirts with you, don't panic.* Justen would never be so insulting, whatever the provocation.

She glanced around. No one had witnessed the exchange; Prince Harkeld and Prince Tomas were still wrestling, the ladies in the gallery were still watching, as were the guards. Even the hound, Gerit, had his attention on the two princes.

A creamy-white dove swooped down to perch on the edge of the water butt. It cocked its head, looking at her with one bright eye, and made a chuckling sound.

Innis felt herself flush. How much had Petrus seen? "Go away," she whispered.

The dove fluffed its feathers flirtatiously and sidled closer.

Her face grew hotter. "Go away!" she hissed, flapping her hand.

Petrus made the chuckling sound again, then, to her relief, he spread his wings and flew away. Innis turned her attention to the wrestlers. They were on the ground, straining for dominance, grunting, grimacing.

Animal, Lady Lenora had said, and that was precisely what the princes looked like: animals.

PETRUS CIRCLED UP from the training ground, skimmed over the slate roofs of the castle, and swooped down into the next courtyard. Lenora was crossing it. The angry flounce of her hips, the flush of color in her cheeks, drew his eyes. He remembered the things he'd seen her do last night. *If it was me who was Justen, I wouldn't have said no.* He circled slowly, letting himself imagine what could have been.

A nobleman swept Lenora an admiring bow. She halted.

Petrus circled idly, watching as she preened, as she tossed her blonde hair, as she laughed. The man's glance was openly appreciative.

Lenora placed her hand on the nobleman's arm.

Petrus flew lower for a closer look. The man had swarthy skin and dark hair.

Lenora tossed her hair again. She raised her other hand and placed it casually on her bodice and let her fingers trail around the neckline of her gown until they rested at her cleavage, as she'd done with Innis.

Petrus saw the nobleman swallow.

Lenora smiled. She leaned close and whispered something in the nobleman's ear.

The man swallowed again. He didn't jerk back, as Innis had done. He placed his hand over Lenora's where it lay on his arm.

Petrus watched as they crossed the stone-flagged courtyard, Lenora's expression triumphant, the nobleman's dazed, as if he couldn't quite believe his good fortune. He flapped his wings crossly, climbing out of the courtyard. *That could have been me!*

He spent the next half hour irritably patrolling the castle, looking in the courtyards, in the stables, in windows, checking for anything sinister—

Petrus hurriedly circled back. Was that...?

Yes. Lenora and the swarthy nobleman. Glimpsed through a diamond-paned window.

Petrus landed on the window sill and glared at the nobleman. *Thrice-cursed son of a whore!* Those could have been his own hands exploring Lenora's lush body, his own teeth nipping her breasts—

Nipping?

Lenora didn't appear to mind the nobleman's roughness. She was urging him on, biting him, raking her nails down his back. He saw her lips form words: *harder, rougher, faster.*

Petrus backed away from the window. A reflection in one of the panes caught his eye. With a squawk, he launched himself backwards. Feathers puffed in the air as something struck him. He plummeted several yards before his wings caught the updraft.

His heart beat quickly as he clawed his way up through the air until he was level with the window. A black and white cat glared at him from the sill, lashing its tail.

Petrus flew swiftly away from Lenora's window, his heart pounding. Slate roofs flashed beneath his wings. *Idiot! You just about got yourself eaten by a cat!*

CHAPTER TWENTY-SIX

AFTER THEY'D WRESTLED, Harkeld went with Tomas to the men's bathing chamber, rinsing off the dirt and sweat before retiring to the steam room, with guards outside the door. He slouched on one of the benches, his eyes closed.

A hand on his shoulder jerked him awake some time later. "Asleep, old man? Lenora too much for you last night?"

Too much? No, she'd been just what he needed.

Harkeld grunted and pushed himself up from the bench.

A plunge in a cool bathing pool woke him fully. He toweled himself dry, and realized that Lenora was just what he needed again.

Justen brought him clean clothing. "I'll pay Lenora a visit," Harkeld told Tomas as he dressed. "See if she wants company."

Tomas grinned. "Company?"

Behind Tomas, he saw Justen frown.

"What? You're planning on helping her with her needlework?" Tomas teased. "Help sort the threads, perhaps?"

"I'm perfectly happy to help her with... a number

of things," Harkeld said, pulling on his boots.

Tomas laughed. "I bet you are."

Justen didn't laugh. In fact, his armsman's expression was clearly disapproving.

Harkeld felt a flicker of irritation. *A prudish armsman is just what I need.* "I won't be needing you," he said, turning away from Justen.

"But, sire—"

"You're dismissed for the rest of the afternoon."

PETRUS WAS IN the stables, choosing a horse for the journey into Masse. A piebald mare had taken his fancy. He ran his hand down the horse's flank and then crouched to examine its hocks.

He heard footsteps behind him "He's gone to visit Lady Lenora." The voice was Justen's. "I've been dismissed for the rest of the afternoon."

Petrus grunted. "I'll take this one," he said to the groom, straightening.

The man nodded, not meeting his eyes. He tugged the horse's bridle, urging it back towards its stall, clearly anxious to put as much distance between himself and a witch as he could.

Petrus sighed. *At least the mare won't care what I am.* He looked at Innis. "Lenora?"

Her mouth twisted, an expression of disgust. "What does he see in her?"

"If you really were a man, you'd know," Petrus said, grinning. He regretted the words as soon as he'd uttered them. "I mean—"

"I know what you mean." Innis turned away. "I'll guard him this time—"

"No," Petrus said, more sharply than he'd intended. He grabbed Innis's arm. "I'll do it. You choose a horse."

"I can do it."

Petrus lowered his voice. "Innis, what I meant was... sometimes a man needs to scratch an itch. And Lenora is—"

Innis pulled her arm free. "You don't need to explain. I understand."

I don't think you do. Petrus blew out a breath. "Stay," he said. "Choose a horse. I'll watch the prince."

He strode across the straw-strewn floor, heading for the vaulted doorway and daylight. At the threshold he glanced back, at Justen, at Innis. *I'd rather have you than Lenora.*

A flight of stone steps led up to his right. He began to climb them two at a time.

LENORA WELCOMED HIM with a blush and a smile. "Prince Harkeld," she said, holding out her hand to him. "What an unexpected pleasure."

"The pleasure is mine." Harkeld turned her hand over and placed a lingering kiss on her palm. Arousal and anticipation hummed inside him. He glanced around the parlor, seeing tapestries, candlesticks, a delicate fire screen. "What a charming room."

"Thank you." Lenora looked up at him through her lashes. "Would you like to see the other rooms?"

The bedchamber, yes. "If it pleases you."

Laughter danced in her eyes. "It does, Prince Harkeld."

The first room she showed him was a workroom, with a loom set up beside the window. Harkeld made appropriate noises of appreciation. The second room was the bedchamber. He tried to drag his eyes from the bed, to examine the other furnishings, to comment on them. "Nice, er... tapestries," he managed. "Very colorful."

"Thank you, Prince Harkeld," Lenora said demurely.

"And the... er, candlesticks are very... elegant."

"Thank you." A dimple quivered in her cheek. "And the bed, Prince Harkeld?"

The bed was wide, with a rose-colored coverlet and a pile of soft pillows. It invited, beckoned, promised. Harkeld swallowed. His arousal pressed against his trews. "The bed is very..." His mouth was dry, his mind blank. He couldn't think of words; all he could think of was stretching out on that rose-pink coverlet, of undressing Lenora, of burying himself in her.

She laughed softly. Her hand was on his arm, drawing him closer to the bed, to bliss.

It went swiftly after that. He didn't have to speak, didn't have to concentrate on anything except kissing her, unlacing her gown, stripping off his own clothes. He lay alongside her on the bed, naked skin to naked skin, and began exploring her with his mouth, with his hands. She was so deliciously soft, so warm, so...

"What the—?" The ripe curve of one breast was marred by a fresh bite mark. "I didn't do that."

She smiled languorously and reached for him. "Do what?"

Harkeld pushed her hand away. He stared at her, panting slightly, striving for clarity. "That."

It wasn't the only bite mark. He could see other places where teeth had nipped her soft skin, could see the beginnings of bruises where someone had gripped her arms. His arousal began to fade. The signs of someone else's lust on Lenora's body made her seem tawdry, soiled. He drew back. "You've been with someone else today."

Lenora's smile faded. She covered the mark on her breast with a hand. "I... Does it matter?"

Yes, it mattered. Had she bathed since then? Was he laying his kisses on top of another man's sweat, another man's spilled seed?

Lenora reached for him, tried to kiss him again. Harkeld pulled away. Had she pleasured that other man intimately, taken his organ in her mouth?

Probably, given her willingness to do that for him last night.

He looked at her ripe body. Lust clenched inside him, a base, animal emotion. He still wanted her, but not to kiss, not to taste intimately. He wanted her like a whore, not a lover.

Why did you have to spoil it?

Lenora must have read his thoughts on his face. She reached for the coverlet, hiding herself from his gaze.

That's that, then, Harkeld thought sourly. The moment had clearly passed.

He got off the bed and reached for his clothes.

"Prince Harkeld... it wasn't what you think."

He pulled on the underbreeches and trews, hiding his arousal. Curse it. Now he'd have to find a willing maidservant to slake his lust on. He shrugged into his shirt.

"It wasn't my fault. I didn't want to. He forced himself on me."

Harkeld froze. "What?"

Lenora wiped her eyes with the edge of the coverlet. "He forced himself on me."

Rage swept through him. "Who?"

She sniffed and shook her head.

"Lenora..." Harkeld took control of his rage, softened his voice. "Tell me who did this to you." *And I will rip his balls off and shove them down his throat.*

"It was your armsman."

Harkeld stared at her, his mouth open. "Justen?" He shook his head. "No. Impossible. He's been with me all day..." *Except when I was in the steam room.* In a flash, he understood. It hadn't been disapproval he'd seen on Justen's face; it had been fear. "After the wrestling," he said grimly. "That's when he came."

"He said... he wanted to try his master's whore for himself."

The rage flared inside him, so hot, so intense, that for a moment he was blind and deaf. *His master's whore.* Harkeld blinked, shook his head to clear it. "Why didn't you tell me—"

"He said he'd hurt me if I told anyone." Lenora dabbed her eyes.

"He did, did he?" Harkeld pulled on his boots with angry haste. *Thrice-cursed son of a witch. I'll kill him.* His hands shook with fury as he buckled his sword belt.

*   *   *

THIS TIME, PETRUS took the shape of a cat. But when he leapt down onto the stone window sill and peered in through one of the diamond-shaped panes, there were no lovers entwined in the bed. He watched as Prince Harkeld strode from the bedchamber.

That was quick.

The lady seemed satisfied, though. Her smile was smug.

Petrus shrugged, leapt lightly up onto the guttering, and padded back across the slate roof.

CHAPTER TWENTY-SEVEN

INNIS STEPPED OUT from the stables and the smell of hay and manure. She pushed Justen's short hair back from her brow. Above her, the castle rose in tiers—roofs, battlements, walls of gray stone—to its pinnacle, a squat tower from which the blue and gold flag of Lundegaard flew. She began the climb back to the upper levels, up a flight of stone steps that hugged the first buttress, then across a courtyard. She glanced up. High above, a face peered down at her from a parapet. From this distance, it almost looked like Prince Harkeld.

The next staircase ducked under a stone archway and climbed inside the outer wall of the castle, twisting and turning, rising steeply. The stairwell was dim; the torches in their iron brackets were unlit. The only light came from arrow slits.

Innis paused to catch her breath halfway up. An arrow slit gave her a narrow view north, towards Masse. She stared out. Cliffs and desert awaited them in the north, but all she could see was farmland, a neat patchwork of fields.

"There you are."

She turned her head, blinking. After the bright sunlight, the stairwell was as dark as night. "Sire?"

"I've been looking for you." Prince Harkeld's voice was grim.

"Do you want—?" Something slammed into her face. She fell, clutching for the wall, smacking her head against stone, and landed jarringly on the steps.

Innis shook her head, tasting blood. Was the prince being attacked? She pushed dizzily to her feet, groping for the wall, reaching for Justen's sword. "Sire—"

Someone kicked her in the chest. She went backwards, rolling, tumbling, bouncing down the steps, sliding at last to a halt, dazed and winded. Breath came after an endless moment, and with it, pain, blossoming inside her.

Footsteps rang on the stairs, coming towards her. Innis pushed up on an elbow. A shadowy figure loomed over her.

Someone hauled her to her feet, hands fisted in her shirt. She groped for her sword, struggling to see. Where were the guards? Where was Gerit?

"You son of a witch!" The voice was the prince's, fierce. "Thought you could get away with it, did you? *Did you?*" He slammed her against the wall.

"Wha—?"

She never finished the word. Prince Harkeld's hands were at her throat, gripping so tightly she couldn't breathe. "I'm going to make sure you can never rut a woman again." His voice was thick with rage.

Her brain barely had time to register the words before his knee took her hard in the groin. The agony was acute. If she'd had breath, she would have screamed. The prince released his grip on her throat. Her legs buckled and she collapsed.

Through the haze of pain she heard Prince Harkeld draw his sword.

Innis tried to breathe, to speak. "Sire..."

"Get up."

She couldn't move, could only lie gasping at his feet. Behind him, the staircase stretched upward, empty.

"Get up!" His hand fisted in her hair, hauling her upright. He thrust her against the wall and uttered a harsh laugh. "Not so brave now, are you, armsman?"

She couldn't see the prince's face, but she saw the gleam of his sword. *Shift!* she screamed to herself. *Become a lion.* But her magic was buried beneath pain, beneath dizziness.

"Nothing to say, armsman?"

Innis lurched backwards, aware of space yawning behind her. The stairwell. This time she didn't try to catch herself, she simply fell.

Time fractured, became disjointed—the steps tossed her, walls slammed into her. Finally she came to a thudding halt, sprawled face-down on a landing.

Innis blinked, trying to focus her eyes. Everything spun on its axis, tilting, lurching drunkenly. She saw shadows, the angles of steps rising into darkness. She squeezed her eyes shut. Somewhere, a dog was barking.

She gasped to breathe, but instead of air, came blood. Footsteps rang behind her in the stairwell. *He's going to kill me.* But she hadn't the strength to open her eyes again, let alone push to her feet.

She lay with her cheek pressed to the gritty floor, tasting blood. Pain swelled inside her, expanding until she couldn't think.

The stairwell echoed with barking, with shouts, with the clatter of boots. Even with her eyes closed the world spun around her.

Vaguely, she heard the deep barking of a dog, felt the touch of a wet nose against her cheek. *Gerit?* But she had no strength to open her eyes.

The dog stopped barking. Gerit's voice rose in a bellow, filling the stairwell.

Innis shut everything out and tried to reach for her magic. Too many bones broken, too much bleeding. She was choking on blood, drowning in it.

CHAPTER TWENTY-EIGHT

PETRUS SAT, HOLDING Innis's hand with both of his, pouring his magic into her. There was so much damage—he was aware of the grating edges of broken bones, aware of blood leaking inside her body. He tightened his grip and directed his attention to her right lung, to sealing the puncture wound. The broken ribs he'd mend later. Right now he needed her to *breathe*.

Dareus cradled Innis's head in his hands, a look of utter concentration on his face. The others stood around the bed—Cora, Gerit, Ebril, Prince Harkeld. "He got what he deserved," the prince said, his voice tight with anger. "Forcing himself on Lenora."

"It wasn't Justen," Petrus said, not bothering to look at him. "Justen refused her."

Prince Harkeld uttered a disbelieving laugh.

"It was a nobleman," Petrus said, looking up. "A man with black hair."

"You think I'd believe the word of a witch over the word of a lady?"

Rage flared inside him. He pushed to his feet. "You whoreson—"

"Sit down, Petrus." Dareus's voice was flat, hard.

Petrus clenched his jaw. Rage vibrated inside him. He sat slowly and took hold of Innis's hand again. "It was a black-haired nobleman. He was rough, but your precious Lenora enjoyed it. She wanted more."

Prince Harkeld's mouth twisted into a sneer. "And you know this how?"

"I was patrolling as a bird."

The prince turned away from the bed. "Justen raped her. And now he's been punished." He strode to the door and jerked it open. "Don't bother healing him. He's not my armsman any more."

The door shut loudly.

"Ebril, stay with him," Dareus said, not looking up from his task. "And you too, Gerit."

Gerit grumbled under his breath as he shifted. Cora opened the door and let them out, hound and pigeon. "And me?" she asked Dareus.

Dareus didn't answer for a long moment. Finally he said, "Petrus, what did you see?"

Petrus told them, while he held Innis's hand and focused on the gash in her lung, laboriously coaxing the edges of the wound closed. There was silence when he'd finished.

"How rough was he?" Cora asked.

"I saw him bite her."

Cora glanced at Dareus. "You want me to find him?"

"Is it worth it?" Petrus asked. "We don't need Justen any more, do we? Innis can be herself." *If she survives this. If she ever wakes up and can change herself back.*

"I want him to have an armsman we trust implicitly."

"One of King Magnas's men."

"Let's decide that once Innis is healed. For now... Cora, see if you can find this nobleman."

Cora nodded. "I'll do my best." The door shut quietly behind her.

Petrus looked down at Justen, at Innis. The punctured lung was mended—after a fashion. He had nowhere near Innis's strength at healing, or her finesse. She was breathing more easily now, but there were so many injuries, damage that was beyond his abilities to heal. He felt despair. "We need her to wake up. I'm not a strong enough healer. Neither of us is."

"She'll wake."

Will she? Petrus tightened his grip on her hand and drew on his healing magic again, focusing his attention on the blood leaking from her spleen. *Come on, Innis*, he told her silently. *Wake up.*

HARKELD GLARED OUT over the parapet of the topmost tower. *I should have ripped off his balls.* If that witch Gerit hadn't interfered—

"Harkeld."

He turned his head. Three people stood behind him. Tomas, the witch Cora, and a man he'd never seen before. A nobleman, by his dress.

"There's a matter that needs to be dealt with," Tomas said, his face, for once, quite serious.

"What?"

"Lenora's claim that your armsman forced himself upon her."

Harkeld stiffened. "It's not a claim. I saw the bruises." He transferred his gaze to the witch. What was she trying to do? Twist the truth? Confuse Tomas with her lies?

"Your armsman didn't visit Lenora this afternoon. Count Viktor did."

"Who?" Harkeld focused on the stranger, seeing him clearly for the first time: a stocky young man with black hair. His eyes narrowed. "You were with her?"

The man swallowed. "She invited me to spend some time with her."

"Invited?" Harkeld shook his head. "Someone took her by force."

Alarm widened the nobleman's eyes. "No, I didn't force—"

Harkeld took a step towards the man. "She had *bruises*. Bite marks!"

The nobleman shrank back. "She wanted it like that. Like an animal, she said. She asked me to bite her. She... she bit me." He flushed. "I only did what she asked." He glanced at Tomas, his eyes pleading. "I wanted to please her. I wanted her to invite me again."

Harkeld shook his head. "Why would she say that Justen—" He stopped, remembering the blond witch's words. Justen had refused Lenora's invitation.

"Why don't we ask Lenora?" Tomas said.

Harkeld hesitated. He looked at the witch. Was this some sly magic she was working? Weaving lies into truth?

"Lenora shares her favors with a number of men," Tomas said. "Sometimes she does like it rough."

Harkeld glanced sharply at him.

Tomas shrugged. "You're not the only prince who's enjoyed her bed."

Harkeld turned his back to Tomas and stared at the horizon. The sun was sinking towards the mountains. Had Lenora lied to him?

No.

But he was no longer utterly convinced. "Very well. Let's ask her."

THEY TRAILED DOWN stairs and along corridors— himself and Tomas, Count Viktor, the witch, the guards and the russet-brown hound. Harkeld's thoughts ran in tight circles. If Lenora had been lying—

He recoiled from that possibility. It didn't bear thinking about. She *had* to have told the truth, because otherwise...

His hands clenched.

At the door to Lenora's suite, Harkeld inhaled a deep breath. Beside him, the nobleman swallowed audibly.

One of the guards knocked. After a moment, a maid opened the door. She curtseyed low when she saw Prince Tomas.

"Is your mistress in?" Tomas asked.

The maid's eyes flicked anxiously from one face to another. "Of course, sire. Please come in. I'll fetch her."

She scurried across the parlor, but the door to the bedchamber opened before she reached it. Lenora emerged. "Olga, who is it?" She looked past the maid and smiled warmly. "Prince Tomas." And then her gaze went to Harkeld, to Count Viktor. Her expression froze.

He didn't need to hear Lenora speak; guilt was written on her face.

Harkeld turned and pushed his way through the people crowding the doorway.

He retraced the route they'd taken, up what seemed like a thousand stairs, until he burst out onto the top of the highest tower.

Two guards followed him, panting.

Go away! he wanted to shout at them. *I need to be alone.*

He turned his back to them, to the witch-dog that followed at their heels, and strode to the parapet. He stared out across Lundegaard, his hands gripping the stone.

The sun sank behind the Graytooth Mountains. The sky darkened, from pale lavender to indigo to a deep blue-black. And still he stood there.

Footsteps approached. Harkeld heard the heavy breathing of someone who'd climbed a lot of stairs. He didn't look around. *Leave me alone.*

"Harkeld?"

The voice was familiar. Tomas.

His friend came to stand alongside him. They stood in silence for several minutes, looking out at the darkness, at the lights flickering below on the plains.

"Did she say why?" Harkeld asked finally.

"She had a lot of excuses." Tomas turned and leaned against the parapet. "She felt insulted. She's not used to being turned down."

Of course she's not. Not with that face, that body.

Harkeld closed his eyes. "I almost killed Justen."

Tomas said nothing for a moment, and then: "The witches will heal him."

That's not the point.

Harkeld pushed away from the parapet.

Tomas followed. "Where are you going?"

NOTHING HAD CHANGED in the bedchamber. Justen lay motionless on the bed, Dareus cradling his head, Petrus clasping one hand. Harkeld halted in the doorway and stared at his armsman's face—eyes blackened and swollen shut, nose broken, mouth bloodied.

I did that.

Harkeld closed the door quietly behind him, shutting out Tomas and the guards. "Will he be all right?"

"It's too soon to tell," Dareus said.

"But... you healed me. The arrow—"

"That was one injury. This is many. And the head injury is serious."

Harkeld advanced into the room. He looked down at his armsman. Sharp emotions swelled in his chest: grief, guilt. "Lenora lied. Justen didn't harm her."

Petrus glanced at him. His hair was silver in the candlelight. His eyes glittered with hatred. "I told you that."

"I know," Harkeld said. "I apologize."

The witch's mouth tightened, his lips thinning. "Tell that to Justen."

"I shall."

Harkeld stared down at his armsman. Justen was ominously still. He looked dead. "Where's Innis? Isn't she your best healer? Justen needs her—"

"She's resting," Dareus said. "The healing is difficult. Draining. We're taking it in turns." He looked old, weary, lines deeply engraved on his face.

Harkeld glanced at Petrus. He looked exhausted too; the shadows beneath his eyes were as dark as bruises. Stubble glinted palely on his jaw. He looked back at Dareus. "Is there anything I can do to help?" he asked.

Petrus uttered a sound that was too harsh to be a laugh. "It's a bit late for that!"

"Petrus," Dareus said quietly.

The witch closed his mouth. His lips thinned again. He looked back down at Justen.

"Thank you, Prince Harkeld," Dareus said. "But there's nothing you can do."

Harkeld nodded. He stared down at the armsman, his throat tight. "If you think of any way I can help... please tell me."

He turned away from the bed and let himself quietly out of the room.

CHAPTER TWENTY-NINE

KAREL CHEWED HIS dinner slowly. Around him, men ate, talked, laughed. "I hear he makes her wear the crown when he tups her," he heard someone say, beneath the din of half a hundred conversations.

Every muscle in his body froze. *What?*

"He ruts her breakfast, lunch, and dinner," someone else said. "Can't keep away from her."

"Do you think she's any good?"

Someone sniggered. "The duke certainly thinks so."

Karel's fingers tightened around his knife and fork. He stared down at his plate, at the slabs of coarse sausage, the mashed turnip, the potatoes. *How can you laugh about such a thing?*

But these were the same men who rutted bondservants, whether they were willing or not, who raped casually.

"You'd know, wouldn't you, islander?" An elbow dug him in the ribs. "Is she any good?"

Someone leaned across the table. "Does the duke leave the door open? Let you watch?"

Anger flared inside him, so intense that for a moment he couldn't breathe. *Don't let them bait you, boy.* His uncle's voice rang in his ears. *They'll try to make you fail. Don't allow them to.*

Karel swallowed his rage. He fixed a bored expression on his face, lifted his head, and glanced at the men looking at him. *I will kill you if I get the chance.* He committed their faces to memory and resumed eating.

"Stupid son of a whore," he heard one of them mutter.

Karel cut a piece of sausage, lifted it to his mouth, chewed slowly. He'd spent years ignoring crude jibes, cruel taunts. They'd said worse things about his mother, about the island bondswomen they rutted each night. Why, now, did anger threaten to overwhelm him?

Don't let them provoke you, he told himself. He had too much to lose: his own freedom, his family's. *Ignore them.*

CHAPTER THIRTY

Pain. That was the first thing Innis was aware of. Her head felt as though it was splitting in two. Every bone in her body hurt, every muscle hurt. Someone groaned. She thought it might be herself.

"Innis? Can you hear me?"

The voice was faint, faraway, familiar. She tried to see who it was, but her eyes wouldn't open.

"Innis?"

She tried again to raise her eyelids. Only one of them opened. She saw a sliver of light.

"She's awake!"

Her vision was blurry. She blinked, and a shadowy room lit by candlelight came into focus.

"Innis!" Someone leaned over her. She saw white-blond hair, green eyes. Petrus. "Innis, stay awake! We need your help."

She tried to speak, to ask him what was wrong, tried to keep her eyes open, but it was impossible.

The next time Innis woke, it was daylight. She blinked heavy eyelids. A room swam into hazy focus: diamond-paned windows, stone walls, tapestries.

"Innis?" The voice was quiet, coming from behind her. Hands cradled her skull.

"Dareus?" It was a hoarse whisper. The voice didn't sound like her own.

"Yes."

There was magic flowing from those hands. She recognized the touch of it: healing magic, weak and faint. "What happened?"

"You had an accident. We need you to help us."

She blinked again, and tried to remember. Stairs?

"Try to heal yourself, Innis."

Obediently she reached for her magic. It came to her sluggishly.

She closed her eyes again and tried to sense what healing was needed. Pain swamped her.

"Start with your head," Dareus told her.

Innis tried to concentrate past the pain. She could feel what Dareus had done—mended fractures in her skull, repaired blood vessels—but there was still extensive swelling, extensive bruising.

She set to work, methodically repairing the damage. It was painstaking, tiring, but gradually the ache in her head eased. Pain stopped thudding against her temples. It no longer felt as if her skull were splitting open.

The hands cradling her head let go. "Innis, I have to sleep." She heard exhaustion in Dareus's voice. "Petrus will continue with you."

"Petrus?" She turned her head on the pillow, looking for him.

Dareus moved into her line of sight. He looked far older than she remembered, his face drawn. "He's asleep in the next room. I'll send him in."

She watched as he crossed to the door and opened it, his movements stiff, slow, then closed her eyes and began to explore the injuries in her body. Broken arm and wrist, ribs—

She heard the door open again, heard quick footsteps. "Innis!"

Innis opened her eyes.

Petrus stood over her. "You're awake!" She heard relief in his voice, saw it on his face. His hand reached to gently touch her cheek. "I've been so worried."

She smiled at him.

Petrus cleared his throat. He drew up a chair and sat alongside her. "I've repaired your lung," he said briskly, taking hold of her hand, wrapping his fingers tightly around hers. "And your spleen and the damaged kidney. But you may want to check them—I'm not as good a healer as you. I thought I'd do the big bones next, in your legs, but we can do the ribs first if you prefer."

Her legs? She hadn't reached that far in her exploration of the injuries. Innis sent her awareness further down her body: abdomen, pelvis, groin—

Panic spiked inside her. "This isn't my body!"

"It's Justen's," Petrus said soothingly. "Don't worry; you can shift back into yourself once we've dealt with the broken bones."

Justen?

Memory flooded her mind: Climbing stone stairs with a Grooten sword belted at her hip. The clatter of boots. Voices shouting. Blood mingling with each breath she took.

"Legs or ribs?" Petrus asked.

They worked together through the morning,

mending the bones one by one. By mid-afternoon Innis was well enough to sit up and eat soup with a spoon. Dareus joined them and the healing went even more swiftly after that.

Towards dusk, Cora entered the bedchamber. "How are you?"

"I'm ready to change back to myself." There were still bruises, still cuts and scrapes, but nothing that could harm her as her body shifted—no jagged edges of bone, no damaged organs.

"The prince wants to see you."

Petrus stiffened.

"He'd like to apologize," Cora said. "If you're well enough to see him."

"Apologize?" Petrus muttered. "Stupid whoreson should do more than apologize. He almost *killed*—"

"Petrus." There was an edge to Dareus's voice.

Petrus closed his mouth.

"Apologize for what?" Innis asked.

"He did this to you," Petrus said.

"What? I thought I fell down some stairs."

"You did. Because he pushed you."

She opened her mouth to ask why, but could only stare at him.

Petrus answered her unspoken question. "His precious whore told him you'd raped her."

"Lenora?" Innis blinked, and then frowned. "She told him that? Why?"

"You don't remember?"

She shook her head.

"She asked you to tup her, and you turned her down."

"Me?" Her voice squeaked. "Lenora wanted to do that... with *me*?"

"With Justen. Yes."

"Will you see the prince?" Cora asked again.

"Uh..." Innis tried to order her scrambled thoughts. *Lenora wanted to have sex with me?* An absurd urge to laugh filled her throat. "Yes."

Cora nodded and left the room.

Innis raised a hand to tidy her hair, felt the shortness of the locks, and remembered she was Justen. Justen wouldn't care what he looked like for the prince. *Only a girl would.* She lowered her hand.

Lenora had invited Justen to tup her?

She wished she could remember the moment. *Did I laugh in her face? Is that why she said I'd raped her?*

The door opened again. Prince Harkeld stepped into the room. He looked even grimmer than he usually did. Tight furrows bracketed his mouth. "Justen."

"Sire."

The prince walked into the middle of the bedchamber and halted. "Justen, I wish to apologize for what I did to you. It was unforgivable."

Petrus muttered something, too low for her to hear the words.

"I don't remember it, sire," Innis said.

"You want to know what happened? I attacked you—almost killed you." She saw bitterness on Prince Harkeld's face, heard it in his voice. There was something dark in his eyes: self-hatred. "I should have given you a chance to speak, but instead I—"

"Lenora said I'd raped her."

The furrows bracketing his mouth became deeper. He nodded.

Innis settled back on the pillows. "Seems to me you did the right thing, sire."

Petrus jerked his head around to glare at her.

The prince blinked. "What?"

If I was raped, I hope someone would punish my attacker the way you punished me. Innis rephrased the words: "If my sweetheart, Doutzen, said she'd been raped, I'd have done exactly what you did."

"I..." Prince Harkeld blinked again, and then his expression hardened. "I should have given you a chance to speak."

"You were angry." She glanced at Petrus. He was still glaring at her. She transferred her gaze back to the prince. "You made a mistake."

A baffled frown creased Prince Harkeld's brow. "You forgive me?"

Innis thought about the words, and then nodded. "Yes, sire."

The prince swallowed. "Thank you." For a moment he was silent, then he asked: "Will you continue to be my armsman?"

Petrus stiffened.

"You still want Justen as your armsman?" Dareus's voice was neutral.

"Of course." Prince Harkeld flushed. "That is... if he's willing."

"Yes," Innis said. "I am."

The prince's face relaxed slightly. Not a smile, but not as grim as it had been. "Thank you."

Petrus opened his mouth.

"Justen needs to rest now," Dareus said firmly. He spoke to the prince, but his eyes were on Petrus. "There's still some healing to be done before we leave tomorrow."

Petrus closed his mouth, glowering.

"Of course," Prince Harkeld said. He turned to Dareus. "Thank you for healing Justen." His gaze shifted to Petrus. "Thank you."

Dareus nodded acknowledgement of his thanks. After a moment, Petrus did too, a stiff movement of his head.

The prince glanced at her. "I shall see you tomorrow, Justen." He hesitated and then said again, "Thank you."

"What do you think you're doing?" Petrus demanded once the prince had gone. "He doesn't need you any more! He can have one of King Magnas's men."

"He'll be safer with a mage," Dareus said.

"Not Innis," Petrus said, pushing to his feet. "Not after this!"

"I'm a Sentinel," Innis said. "It's my duty to protect him."

Petrus swung around to face her. "You don't have to prove yourself—"

"I'm not. I'm trying to keep him alive."

His jaw clenched. He crossed the room with angry strides, wrenched the door open, and was gone.

Dareus sighed. "Ignore him, Innis. He's tired."

She nodded, her eyes on the door. It wasn't like Petrus to lose his temper. "He doesn't like the prince."

"No." Dareus rubbed his face wearily. "Come, let's finish this. Would you like to shift back to yourself first?"

GERIT CAME TO visit her when the shutters had been closed for the night. Innis sat up in the bed, playing

cards with Petrus. "I'm sorry, girl," Gerit said. He
had a tankard of mead in one hand.

"For what?"

Petrus laid down the last of his cards. "You win."

"For not stopping him." Gerit scowled and pulled
up a chair. "He was too fast for us. Took off like a
ruddy hare. The guardsmen lost sight of him and ran
the wrong way—" He gestured with his tankard.
"I followed my nose, but there was this door, see?
Couldn't open the cursed thing with my paws." He
made a sound of disgust. "So I shifted and opened
it and there was a serving maid on the other side."

Petrus grunted. The sound was almost, but not
quite, a laugh.

"What did she do?" Innis asked.

"Screamed loud enough to wake the dead and
threw her tray at me." Gerit grimaced.

Innis laughed. "What happened then?"

"I shifted back into a dog and followed the prince,
barking my head off. The guards caught up in the
end." Gerit's grin faded. "We were half a minute
behind him. A minute at the most."

"He did all that to me in a minute?" Her respect
for the prince's fighting skills rose.

"I think the stairs did most of it."

Petrus had stopped smiling. His expression was
grim. He picked up the cards they'd played.

"I don't remember," Innis said.

"Just as well." Gerit heaved himself out of the
chair. He stood for a moment scowling at her. "If he
tries anything like that again, I'll wring his neck for
him. Stupid whoreson."

He's not stupid. Innis bit her tongue, holding back

the words, and watched Gerit leave. He didn't like the prince any more than Petrus.

HARKELD DINED WITH the king and his sons. He would rather have dined alone; his mood was black. After the meal, King Magnas pushed back his chair and walked across to a chest beneath the shuttered windows. The wood was dark with age and bound with thick bands of iron. "Harkeld?"

"Sir?" He laid down his napkin.

"Come here, son. I have something for you."

Harkeld glanced at Tomas.

His friend winked. "Have a look."

Harkeld stood and walked over to the king.

King Magnas took a long item wrapped in heavy cloth from the chest, closed the lid, and laid the object on it. "For you."

Harkeld stepped closer. He folded back the fabric, revealing a sword. "Sir?"

"Something better than that piece of scrap metal you're lugging around."

Harkeld glanced at the sword strapped to his hip. It was plain, serviceable—a common soldier's sword.

The sword lying on the chest wasn't a common soldier's sword. Harkeld picked it up reverently. The blade was tempered steel, double-edged. A groove ran down its length. On either side a delicate pattern was engraved into the steel: flames.

The workmanship was extraordinary, not just the blade, but the delicately-ridged grip, the guard that flared back from the tang like a flame.

The engraving on the blade, the elaborate guard,

couldn't disguise what the sword was: a weapon crafted for killing. It was light in his hand, perfectly balanced. Deadly.

A king's sword. Or at the very least, a prince's. He glanced at King Magnas. "I can't—"

"Of course you can, son. You need a good weapon." The king opened the chest again. "Here's the scabbard. And a sword belt and baldric."

They were as beautifully wrought as the sword, the leather supple and intricately stitched.

Harkeld removed the sword belt he was wearing. He buckled the new one around his hips and slid the sword into its scabbard. The weight felt good. No, it felt perfect. "Sir, I can't thank you enough—"

"Nonsense," King Magnas said. "We're the ones who must thank you. Our lives rest in your hands."

Harkeld glanced across the room at Tomas and Erik. The two brothers sat talking. "Sir, are you certain you wish Tomas to accompany me? The danger—"

"He's able to take care of himself," King Magnas's smile was proud as he looked at his sons.

"But if Tomas should die—"

The king turned to him. "If he dies, he dies in a good cause." He held Harkeld's eyes. "That's the best that can be said of any man."

The words resonated quietly. Harkeld heard the truth in them.

King Magnas closed and latched the chest. "Your father has banished you."

"Yes." Harkeld looked down at the sword hilt, ran his thumb over it. *All my father wants of me is my blood. And my hands.*

"When this is over, you're welcome to make your home in Lundegaard."

Harkeld glanced at him swiftly. "But... I have witch blood."

King Magnas studied his face, a slow and thoughtful assessment. "Are you a witch?"

Something in the king's manner, in his voice, reminded Harkeld of Dareus. He blinked, disconcerted. King Magnas was a man he respected, whereas Dareus was merely a witch. He focused on the question and shook his head. "No," he said. "I'm not."

The king smiled. "Then I hope you'll think of Lundegaard as your home."

Harkeld's throat tightened painfully. He swallowed. "Thank you, sir, but..." *I have to tell him.* He took a deep breath. "About Sigren's death. I don't think it was an accident. I think my father had her killed."

King Magnas nodded. "Yes. I know."

"You know?" Harkeld stared at him. "But... how?"

Erik and Tomas had stopped talking. They watched from across the chamber.

"We have friends in Osgaard who tell us things. From them we heard... details about Sigren's death." Grief for his eldest child momentarily shadowed the king's face. "And the truth about your banishment."

"Oh," Harkeld said.

"What happened to Sigren doesn't affect my offer. Lundegaard may be your home, if you wish."

"But she died at my father's hand—"

"You are not your father. You've proven that, son, beyond any doubt."

Harkeld's throat tightened again. "Thank you, sir."

* * *

"WE LEAVE AT dawn tomorrow." Dareus placed his plate to one side and leaned his elbows on the table. "I've sent a message back to Rosny, asking for more Sentinels to join us in Ankeny. Fire mages, shapeshifters, healers."

Gerit nodded. "Good."

They sat around the oak table, Dareus and Cora and Gerit, and himself. Ebril was in the shape of a hound, guarding the prince. Innis was asleep.

"I want Innis to ride as herself tomorrow," Dareus said. "I'll assess her at the end of the day. If I think she's strong enough, she can be Justen overnight. If not, one of you will have to do it."

Gerit drained his tankard and placed it on the table with a thump. "Sounds good."

"I'd like you to take turns being Justen tomorrow." He looked at Gerit, and then Petrus. "But your attitude concerns me, both of you."

Petrus felt himself flush. "My attitude?"

"Your antagonism towards the prince."

Petrus moved uncomfortably in his chair, excuses crowding his tongue—*It's not my fault. It's the prince's!* He glanced at Cora. Her expression was grave.

"You may only be Justen if you can keep your hostility under control. Both of you."

Across from him, Gerit shifted his weight. "But the stupid whoreson—"

"I don't care what your opinion of him is. Right now, Prince Harkeld is the single most important person in the Seven Kingdoms. Lives past counting depend on him."

Gerit dropped his gaze.

"Justen is our best way of protecting him. A Sentinel at his side. But that depends on Prince Harkeld *wanting* to have him as his armsman. He has to trust Justen. He has to like him."

Petrus looked away from those fierce eyes. He stared down at his mead.

"I will not have you jeopardizing our mission. Either of you. Regardless of what you think of Prince Harkeld, you'll treat him the way Innis does. The way *Justen* does. Or I won't allow you to be Justen. Is that understood?"

Shame was hot on Petrus's face. He looked up and met Dareus's eyes. "Yes."

Dareus transferred his gaze to Gerit. "And you?"

"Yes," Gerit said gruffly.

"Good. Then you may take turns being Justen tomorrow." Dareus pushed back his chair and stood. "I suggest we all have an early night. Tomorrow will be a long day."

CHAPTER THIRTY-ONE

BRITTA LAY WITH her eyes closed. She let herself float upwards. The duke didn't seem to notice that she was no longer sharing his bed, that she had slipped free.

She drifted near the ceiling, as light as a leaf floating on water. The person Duke Rikard was grunting over, whose legs he was spreading, wasn't her. She was serene up here, where nothing could touch her.

WHEN BRITTA WOKE, she was alone. Even though he was gone, Duke Rikard's scent still seemed to smother her. She could smell his sweat, the musk of his arousal. It was ingrained in the sheets, ingrained in her skin.

Her throat closed. She couldn't breathe.

She thrust herself out of the bed, tangling in the sheets, landing on hands and knees, her chest heaving.

"Britta!" Someone knelt with her. Hands touched her lightly. She flinched before she realized they weren't the duke's—soft, small, gentle. "Are you all right?" It was Yasma's voice.

Britta squeezed her eyes shut, gasping to breathe.

"Princess?"

Her breathing steadied. Britta opened her eyes, allowing Yasma to help her stand. She turned her gaze from the bed, from the rumpled sheets and tumbled pillows, refusing to think about what those things meant. "What's the time?"

"The third bell has just rung, princess."

"I need to wash." *I need to scrub him off me.*

"I have a bath ready for you."

She allowed Yasma to slip an arm around her waist and guide her towards the bathing chamber. Her thoughts moved as slowly as her feet. Third bell. The duke usually returned at the fifth bell, at noon. Tightness grew in her throat again, in her chest. She halted.

"Princess?"

"The poppy juice. I'll take it now."

"So early, princess? You've only just woken."

Early, yes, but what if the duke came early too? What if he came back at the fourth bell, today, instead of the fifth? "Now," Britta said, making it an order.

Yasma hesitated. She shook her head. "Britta, I—"

"You have some? Tell me you have some!" Her voice held a note of panic.

Yasma bowed her head. "I have some. I'll prepare it while you bathe."

YASMA BROUGHT THE poppy juice while Britta scrubbed away Duke Rikard's scent. Was her skin thinner now from all the scrubbing she'd done, every day, with bristles and soap?

His smell washed away, but not the bruises that marked his ownership of her. They were stamped on her skin.

"Princess." The maid knelt beside the bathtub, a small goblet in each hand. She held out one.

Britta dropped the brush. She took the goblet with shaking fingers, lifted it to her mouth, gulped.

The dark juice tasted bitter. It tasted like serenity.

The duke seemed to recede as she handed the goblet back to Yasma. Her breath didn't hitch any more, nor did her fingers shake.

She drank the dung-root juice next. The liquid was pale and cloudy, with a fennel-like taste and sulfurous smell. It didn't give her serenity; it gave her hope. *No children*, she whispered in her mind as she swallowed, a silent prayer to the All-Mother.

Britta handed the goblet back. "Thank you." She picked up the brush and resumed scrubbing.

CHAPTER THIRTY-TWO

It was an eight-day journey to the cliffs that thrust up to the Masse plateau. They rode with their escort surrounding them: ten men in close formation protecting the prince, the remaining forty scouring the countryside around them.

Innis traveled as herself the first day. The castle atop its mount grew slowly smaller behind them. By noon, it looked like the humped back of a turtle crouching on the plains. By nightfall, it was the size of a peach stone. To the west, the bluffs kept them company, rearing up from the plains, thickly crowned by forest and with the Graytooth Mountains running in ridges behind.

They camped for the night in a hay field that had recently been harvested. Dareus gave her permission to become Justen again. Innis ate her dinner seated alongside the princes. The murmur of men's voices drifted on the breeze, punctuated by the occasional clink of metal or snort from a horse.

"Which is my tent?" Prince Harkeld asked once they'd finished eating.

Innis looked around, seeing a small city of tents and campfires within the drystone walls of the field.

Tomas pushed to his feet. "I'll show you."

Innis followed the princes. Dried hay stalks crunched beneath her boots.

"Here." Tomas halted. "This one's yours. Bedrolls and blankets are inside."

"Sentries?" Innis asked.

"Five," Tomas said. "Four tasked with the camp, one guarding this tent."

A SOLDIER'S BRASS lantern hung from the tent pole, a candle stub flickering inside. The huge shadows it cast made the small space seem doubly cramped. Prince Harkeld removed his boots and sword belt silently. Abruptly he said: "Thank you for choosing to come. After what I did—"

"Forget it, sire. The fault was Lady Lenora's, not yours." Innis shrugged out of her jerkin. The leather was new, supple and—best of all—didn't smell of mold. The shirt was new too, made from sturdy cotton. Folded, it made a nice pillow. "I'd have done the same as you. In fact, I'd probably have castrated me."

Prince Harkeld uttered a sound that was too harsh to be a laugh. "I was going to. Gerit stopped me."

"Oh." Innis unsheathed her sword and laid it alongside her bedroll.

Prince Harkeld removed his jerkin and shirt. His clothes were as crisp and new as her own. Nothing marked them as belonging to a prince. Should an attacker penetrate their defenses, he'd not know which of them to aim for.

The prince bunched his shirt into a pillow and asked abruptly, "Why did you refuse her?"

Innis lay down. She folded her arms beneath her head and stared up at the ceiling of the tent. *Yes, why? What would Justen answer?* Two moths danced in the candlelight, batting their wings against the lantern. "Because I've uttered my betrothal oath. I gave my word of honor I'd be faithful to Doutzen."

Prince Harkeld frowned. "Honor," he said, sliding a dagger beneath the balled-up shirt. It was one of Tomas's, the hilt stamped with Lundegaard's crest. "Yes, I understand."

Innis lay awake for some time after the prince had fallen asleep, listening to his steady breathing. Honor was paramount to him—she'd felt that clearly when she'd healed him. If she reached out and touched him now, if she let her healing magic flow into him, what would the magic tell her? Did Prince Harkeld feel that in believing Lenora, in taking vengeance on Justen, he'd lost some part of his honor?

She half-reached towards him—then tucked her hand inside the blanket and turned her back to the prince. Sensing his emotions while healing him was one thing; deliberately attempting to read them was something else entirely.

She'd crossed many lines in the past two weeks; she wouldn't cross this one.

THEY BROKE CAMP just after dawn. Innis swung up onto Justen's horse. She settled the new baldric more comfortably across her chest. The hilt of the Grooten sword protruded above her shoulder, easy to grasp. The sword and dagger and the amulet at her throat were the only Grooten items she owned now—and the peeling portrait of the unknown lady. Everything else had been discarded at the castle, the clothes too filthy and moldy to launder. Even her boots were new, soldier's boots, as sturdily crafted as the baldric.

They rode hard. Farmers paused in their fields to watch them and villagers stared wide-eyed as they passed with a clatter of iron-shod hooves on cobblestones. The soldiers reported no problems, but when they halted at dusk, a hawk circled down to land. Gerit. "A dozen men in the forest above the bluffs," he said, pulling on his clothes. "A day or so ahead of us."

Prince Harkeld looked at him swiftly. "My father's men?"

Gerit shrugged. "At a guess. They're not wearing uniforms, but they ride like soldiers."

Innis looked west. The bluffs were pale, crowned with dark forest, and the sky a dusky pink.

"If they're above the bluffs, we can't reach them," Tomas said. "Not until we get to Masse."

Dareus pulled his lower lip thoughtfully, and then turned to Gerit. "Tomorrow, try to get close enough to hear their conversation."

GERIT LEFT NOT long after dawn. Innis watched until he was a speck in the sky, then turned her attention to saddling Justen's horse. The bustle of the camp surrounded her: the jingle of harnesses, the hum of conversation, the nicker and *harrumph* of packhorses being loaded.

They rode as they'd done the previous two days: fast. Morning ripened into afternoon. Innis gazed around with interest. The cows in the fields were dun-colored, not black and white, the cottages were roofed with slate instead of thatching, but other than that Lundegaard looked no different from any of the Allied Kingdoms she'd seen—neatly-fenced fields, copses of trees, villages with market squares.

Prince Harkeld rode silently beside her, sunk in his thoughts. Above, a hawk swooped and soared. Innis shaded her eyes. A faint shimmer surrounded the bird. Its breast and underwings were cream-colored. Petrus. Justen would be blind to both those clues, so she said: "I wonder if that's Gerit?"

Prince Harkeld glanced up and shook his head. "It's the blond one. Petrus."

Innis blinked. "How do you know?"

"They all look different."

She frowned, her surprise unfeigned. "Different how?"

"The blond one is always paler, like his hair." The prince glanced skyward, at the circling hawk. "Ebril is always a bit reddish, whether he's a dog or a wolf or a bird. The other one, Gerit, is brown, and he looks older."

"Older?"

Prince Harkeld shrugged. "Thicker in the body. A little gray."

Innis stared at him. He was far more observant than she'd given him credit for. "And the girl?"

"Don't see her often." His brow furrowed. "Strange, that. Where is she all day?"

Innis cleared her throat. "Perhaps she looks like one of the others when she's shifted. Like Ebril."

Prince Harkeld shook his head. "She'll be darker. Like her hair."

Innis looked away, disturbed. The prince had noticed something few non-mages did—that shapeshifters kept some part of their coloring when they took animal forms. To change form was difficult enough; to change one's appearance within that form took much more effort. "Perhaps she's scouting ahead?"

The prince shrugged. "Perhaps."

Innis chewed her lip. If he could tell them apart, what else could he see? The shimmer of a shifted mage? "Are you sure that's a mage?" she asked, pointing at Petrus circling above them. "It could just be an ordinary hawk."

"Maybe."

Above them, Petrus uttered a faint cry and wheeled west. She shaded her eyes again and squinted up at the sky. A second hawk flew towards them, a faint glimmer of magic surrounding it. Gerit.

THEY HALTED LONG enough for Gerit to dress and swing up onto his horse. "They're definitely soldiers," he told them as they rode. "And they're on the look-out for mages. The archers fired at me."

"What!" Dareus swiveled in his saddle to stare at Gerit.

"Missed by a mile. I took care not to show myself after that." He snorted, a contemptuous sound. "Stupid sons of whores are shooting at anything that moves."

"Did you get close enough to hear anything?"

Gerit nodded. "The leader is a Captain Anselm."

"I know him," Prince Harkeld said. "An ambitious man."

"He's looking to claim the bounty on your head," Gerit said.

"He won't," Prince Tomas said confidently. "Even if he arrives in Masse before us."

"There's another party ahead of them," Gerit said. "Anselm's following their tracks."

"Soldiers?"

Gerit nodded. "Anselm's trying to catch up, but from what I gather, they're two days ahead. I had a quick look but couldn't see them."

This time Prince Tomas was silent.

CHAPTER THIRTY-THREE

KAREL STOOD ACROSS from the rose bower. The princess hadn't walked the crushed marble paths today, hadn't walked them for a week. She sat on the cushions, half-dozing, while bees hummed busily among the roses.

He paced another circuit of the garden, turning his head to keep her in sight. Her hair, binding the crown to her head, had lost its shining luster, her face had lost its bloom. She was fading, every day a little more listless, a little paler, a little thinner.

It's the poppy juice, he thought grimly. *She has to stop taking it.*

And what if she did stop? What then? Did she have the strength to survive her marriage to Rikard without it?

Karel looked away. He knew the answer.

The duke must have noticed the change in his wife, but he didn't appear to care. *As long as he has a princess to rut, he's happy.*

Ahead of him, a beetle struggled on its back among the pink and white chips of marble. Princess Brigitta would kneel and save it; Duke Rikard would grind it beneath the heel of his boot.

No, that was wrong. These days the princess wouldn't even notice the beetle's plight.

Karel bent and picked up the beetle. He placed it on leaf mold beneath a flowering rose bush, as Princess Brigitta would have done, and resumed his circuit, his boots crunching on the path. The daydream filled his head again, as it did more and more often these days: the weight of his sword in his hands, the flex of his muscles as he swung it, Duke Rikard's head spinning, spraying blood.

He would never do it. Could never do it. Everything his parents had slaved for during their bondservice would be forfeit. Not just his own freedom, but everyone in his family: the sisters he'd left behind, his aunts and uncles, his cousins.

It was the only way he had of saving the princess. And he could never take it.

"SHE HAS TO stop drinking the poppy juice!" Karel said. Outside, the sky was darkening and the tenth bell was ringing. "She's barely aware of anything that happens these days!"

"But how can I refuse it to her?" Yasma asked, wringing her hands.

The door to the bedchamber was closed. The duke had finished his day's duties and was rutting his wife before dinner, as was his habit. In a few minutes the light would fade from the sky and Duke Rikard would emerge from the bedchamber, his face flushed and smug.

The daydream blossomed in Karel's mind again: hefting the sword, swinging it, sending the man's head spinning across the room. He imagined blood spattering across the rugs, the walls, the ceiling.

When Duke Rikard emerged, the princess would remain in bed, lost in poppy-induced dreams. The duke would dine alone, and then return to her, closing the door again.

"She needs it," Yasma said. "Don't you see?"

Yes, he did see. But he also saw what the poppy juice was doing to her. "It's destroying her. You must reduce the dose."

"But she keeps asking for more!" Yasma cried. "How can I refuse her? She saved me!"

Karel took her hands to stop their twisting.

"I was scrubbing floors," Yasma said, tears in her voice. "One of the armsmen had just come off duty and he... he— And she saw me, Karel. She *saw* me."

"Yes, but Yasma—"

"She didn't have to stop," Yasma said. "She didn't have to take me as her maid. She could have walked past."

"No, she couldn't. It's not in her nature."

Yasma sniffed, and nodded.

"Yasma, if she dies, what will happen to you? You'd go back to scrubbing floors. Without her protection..."

Yasma's face was pinched, miserable. "I owe it to her."

"Reduce the dose," Karel said. "You must give her less. Otherwise you'll kill her."

"But—"

"Reduce it, Yasma. And get her to eat more."

Yasma ducked her head and nodded.

"Is she drinking the dung-root juice?"

"Yes."

He squeezed her hands and then released them. "Good."

The bedchamber door began to open. Yasma scurried over to one of the settles and began rearranging the cushions. Karel stepped back so that his shoulders were against the wall. He lifted his chin and stared stolidly across the salon.

Duke Rikard strolled into the room. His face was as flushed and smug as Karel had imagined. "You," he said to Yasma. "Go to the kitchen. I'm hungry."

Karel's hand flexed near the hilt of his sword. He saw blood in his mind's eye, a head spinning.

CHAPTER THIRTY-FOUR

"Prince Harkeld knows who we are when we're in animal form," Innis told Dareus that evening, while they ate dinner. She pitched her voice low; the prince sat with Tomas on the other side of the fire. Ebril sat beside Prince Harkeld, in Justen's shape. "He can tell us apart by our color."

Gerit grunted, a dismissive sound.

"Are you certain?" Dareus asked, frowning.

Innis nodded. "And he knows I'm not one of the hawks we've been seeing."

Silence greeted these words. A log shifted in the fire with a small cascade of sparks.

"We could change color," Petrus suggested. "For a short time each day."

Dareus thought for a moment and then shook his head. "It's a hard shift. It'd take too much energy; you're already stretched."

"Then let Innis be an animal for a few hours each day," Petrus said. "And we'll be Justen. Justen's an easy shift."

Dareus considered this, and then nodded. "We'll do that. We can't have him suspecting Innis is Justen."

"Can he see the shimmer?" Cora asked.

They all looked across the fire, to where Justen—
Ebril—sat with the princes. The shimmer was faint
around Justen, but quite clear, beneath the dark
shadow of Ivek's curse.

"I don't think so."

"A mage would be able to," Cora said.

"Untrained?" Dareus shook his head. "He'd have
to know it's there to see it."

"Is he a mage?" Gerit asked.

Dareus shrugged. "His grandfather was a Sentinel.
That's strong blood."

Innis studied the prince, seeing the shadow of
the curse lying over his face, seeing tiredness and
stubble. "I doubt he'd agree to the test."

Gerit snorted.

"An untrained mage is dangerous," Cora pointed
out. "He could harm someone. Harm himself."

"*If* he's a mage." Petrus's tone made it clear he
didn't think so. "He's what? Twenty-four? It would
have shown by now."

"Perhaps," said Dareus.

Innis scraped her bowl clean. *Or perhaps not.*

SHE SLEPT AS Justen alongside the prince. In the
morning, while she was tying her bootlaces outside
the tent, Dareus wandered casually over. "Have a
big breakfast," he said in a low voice. "I want you
to be a bird all day."

"All day?" Innis glanced across the smoldering
campfire at the prince. "But—"

"Find that second group of soldiers. We need to
know what we're up against. And Innis—be careful.

Remember what Gerit said: they're shooting at anything that moves."

Innis nodded.

She ate a big breakfast, then ducked back into the tent. A brown field mouse sat on her bedroll. It lifted its head and scratched vigorously under its chin. It wasn't pale enough to be Petrus or gingery enough to be Ebril. Which meant it was Gerit.

Innis stripped quickly and shifted, also taking the form of a mouse. She scurried to the tent flap and peeked out. Dawn flushed the sky. Her ears pricked at rustling sounds behind her. She glanced back. Gerit was dressing in Justen's clothes.

She slipped outside. Smells assaulted her: the odors of food and horse manure and many different humans. Innis scampered across to Cora's tent, taking cover behind tufts of grass. The tent was as large as a palace, looming up beyond the reaches of her vision.

Inside, she shifted into a hawk. Magic flowed through her, tingling. The tent seemed to shrink in size around her, becoming no larger than a house. Innis pushed out under the flap and flew up to the tent ridge, where she sat for several minutes watching the bustle of the camp. When she was certain Prince Harkeld had seen her, she spread her wings and swept up into the sky.

She hadn't been a bird for two weeks. The exhilaration, the pure joy of flying, caught her like an updraft. She circled upwards. Soldiers scurried like ants below her. Her eyes picked out Dareus, Prince Tomas in his forest green uniform with the officer's badge on his shoulder, Prince Harkeld and Justen—and then she swung westward, heading for the bluffs and the forest.

*   *   *

THE SUN WAS well above the horizon by the time Innis flew over the first party of men. They wore the trews and jerkins of commoners, but their weapons, their mounts and equipment, were clearly military.

Ahead, in the distance, her hawk's eyes saw the escarpment that marked the edge of the Masse plateau. The high cliffs shone palely in the sunlight.

For several hours Innis flew north. It was close to noon by the time she found the second party: fourteen men on horseback. Their lack of uniforms didn't disguise what they were: a disciplined troop of trained men.

Innis followed them for more than an hour, soaring on the air currents over the forest, careful to stay out of sight of the archers. Finally, the men halted at a creek to water the horses and to eat. She glided down to perch on a branch, then shifted into the shape of a forest robin and flitted cautiously through the tree trunks until she was close enough to hear their conversation.

"WHY DID YOU send the girl?" Tomas asked Dareus, when they halted for lunch. "Surely the men are stronger fliers. Faster."

"They are," Dareus said. "But they can't hold a shift all day. Innis can."

Harkeld glanced at the witch, surprised.

"You mean... she's stronger than them?" Tomas asked.

"Quite significantly so," Dareus said. "The others can hold a shift for half a day, perhaps a whole day if they're pressed. Innis..." He shrugged. "We haven't found her limits yet."

Harkeld bit into an apple and chewed thoughtfully. The girl didn't look powerful. She was slender and shy, ordinary. "Her magic is unprecedented?"

"Not unprecedented, just extremely rare. There are strong fire mages, too. Perhaps once in a century. Mages who can set stone alight. Your grandfather was one."

Harkeld stopped chewing. He rose abruptly to his feet and strode away, pushing through the soldiers and horses that surrounded them. Rage trembled inside him. *We made you*, the witch had been telling him. *You are one of us.*

He spat out the mouthful of half-chewed apple. It lay on the ground, glistening in the sunlight.

The witches may have made him, but he wasn't one of them, would never be one of them. There was no fire inside him, no scales and feathers. He was a human, not a monster.

ONCE THE SOLDIERS had mounted and moved off through the trees, Innis glided down to the ground and shifted into her own shape. She drank from the creek, thirstily.

Back in the shape of a hawk, she spread her wings and climbed above the treetops, looking north to where the bluffs and forest met the Masse escarpment. To her hawk's eyes, the towering cliffs seemed very close.

Innis veered south, flying back the way she'd come, uneasy. Within the next day, the men below her would reach the Masse plateau. And in a few more days, the second party would be there too. Twenty-six men. Swordsmen, archers.

It was close to dusk by the time she reached Prince Harkeld and his escort. She circled slowly down. Beneath her soldiers hurried to pitch tents, to build fires, to tend horses. She picked out Cora, with her long plait of hair, Dareus—

Innis shied in the air as another hawk swooped down alongside her. Petrus, his pale breast feathers gleaming in the last rays of sunlight. *Don't do that!* she told him, as her heart beat far too fast. It came out as a harsh squawk. *You scared me.*

Petrus uttered a sound that was suspiciously like a laugh. He veered away from her in a steep dive and then soared upward again, his manner playful.

Ordinarily, Innis would have chased him; today she was far too hungry. She spiraled down.

THE WITCH, INNIS, joined them when she was fully clothed. She pushed her black curling hair back from her face.

"Did you find them?" Dareus asked, handing her a mug.

"Yes."

Dareus gave the girl a handful of nuts, which she ate while she talked. Harkeld listened in silence, his eyes on her face.

"Captain Ditmer," Dareus said when she'd finished. "Do you know him, Prince Harkeld?"

"He commands one of my father's elite squadrons. They're not ordinary soldiers. They have a reputation for ruthlessness, for brutality."

Gerit grunted.

"Fourteen men," Tomas said. "And they'll reach Masse ahead of us?"

"Yes," the girl said. "Tomorrow."

"How far behind them are the others?" Cora asked.

"At a guess, two days."

"So, within three days, they'll all be there. Twenty-six of them."

The girl nodded.

"We're only taking twenty men up." Tomas's brow furrowed. "If Ditmer and Anselm join together and attack us at the top of the cliff—"

"We don't know that's what they're planning," Cora said. "Remember, they don't know where we are. For all they know, we're already in Masse. They may head directly for the anchor stone."

"Yes, but we're only taking twenty men up—"

"We can take more, if need be," Dareus said. "But let's not decide that until we reach the cliffs. By then we should have an idea of their intentions."

Tomas nodded. He looked at the girl. "Will you fly again and watch them?"

"Innis, or one of the others," Dareus said. "Don't worry, prince. They won't surprise us."

IT TOOK ANOTHER four days to reach the escarpment. The witch, Innis, flew twice more to watch the Osgaardan soldiers. The first time, she reported that Captain Ditmer's men had gained the desert plateau; the second time, that Ditmer's men weren't stopping, but were striking into the heart of Masse, and that Captain Anselm had reached the desert and was following Ditmer's route.

"They're not going to attack us on the escarpment," Tomas said, relief audible in his voice. "If they'd held the top, it would have been almost impossible to get past them." He turned to Dareus. "How many men should we take up?"

"As few as possible. We need to travel fast."

"There are twenty-six of them—"

"In two separate parties." Dareus examined the cliffs thrusting up from the plains, less than a day away, and then turned to the girl. "Can we reach Anselm before he joins with Ditmer?"

She frowned for a moment, as if she was calculating distances in her head, and then nodded. "Yes."

"Are you certain?" Tomas asked.

"I'll show you on the map."

They unrolled the map and crouched over it. The girl pointed, showing them where Ditmer was, where Anselm was. Harkeld stared down at the parchment, measuring the distances, trying to convert those markings in ink into landscapes—the blank section where her finger rested was barren desert, the wriggling line was a river, the drawing of a broken tower was the ruined city of Ner, where the first anchor stone lay.

When the girl stopped speaking, there was silence. Tomas glanced at the witch, Dareus. "Well?"

"We take twenty men," Dareus said. "That gives us speed and mobility, and we'll still outnumber each party."

CHAPTER THIRTY-FIVE

BRITTA WAS FLOATING near the ceiling. It was safe up here, peaceful—

She woke suddenly, squinting against lamplight shining across her face, and found that she was lying in bed, not floating near the ceiling at all. Duke Rikard's bed, where she was smothered by silk sheets and the scent of him.

The feeling of peace, of safety, vanished abruptly. Memory tried to push into her mind: the duke touching her, his weight on top of her—

No, don't remember.

The rumble of Duke Rikard's voice came to her ears. He was in his study. The door was open several inches, lamplight shining through on her face. She heard him speak, heard another familiar voice reply: her father's.

Hatred stabbed in her chest, brief, fierce. *I hate you, Father.*

Britta turned away from the light, away from the sound of voices. She curled up on her side, hugging her arms, and squeezed her eyes shut, trying to float back up to the ceiling, where everything was safe and peaceful.

Her body became light. She began to drift upwards—

The sound of those hated voices pulled her back down. Her father said something, Duke Rikard replied. She heard the rumble of Jaegar's voice.

Britta opened her eyes again. *Go away.*

Her father laughed.

Britta pushed back the sheet and stood unsteadily. The floor dipped and swayed beneath her feet. She held on to the bed, let go and lurched across to the wall. Her legs were boneless. Suddenly she was on her knees. Had she fallen?

Britta leaned her head against the wall. The ceiling seemed very close. She was floating again, drifting a few feet off the floor.

"...Lundegaard."

"Ours for the taking," Jaegar said. "They're fools, to allow so many refugees in!"

The open door, the band of lamplight, the voices, were just beyond the reach of Britta's fingers. If she could just shut the door—

"How many men do we have there now?" her father asked.

"Three squadrons, sire."

"Then we should be able to move within the month," Jaegar said.

"Yes."

"Excellent," her father said. "Excellent."

She heard the *clink* of glass against glass, the gurgle of liquid being poured.

"A toast!" Duke Rikard said, more loudly. "To the invasion of Lundegaard!"

Britta blinked. *What?* her brain asked sluggishly.

"...utmost secrecy," the king said.

"Of course, sire."

Her mind groped for what had alarmed her, something the duke had just said, but it swam out of reach.

Movement came from within the study, the rustle of papers, the sound of chairs being pushed back.

Fear pricked in her chest. *I mustn't let him find me here.*

Britta pushed clumsily to her feet, lurched across to the bed, fell onto it. Fumbling, she pulled the sheet over her. Voices murmured in the study, too faint now to hear the words. She heard footsteps, heard the door open from the study into the salon. Jaegar and her father were leaving.

Britta squeezed her eyes shut and tried to float up to the ceiling before Duke Rikard could come back to his bed.

BRITTA WOKE SLOWLY. The shutters were open. Outside, the sun shone.

She lay drowsily, staring at the blue sky with unfocussed eyes. Her body felt heavy, not her own.

As time passed, more awareness slowly came. The smell of Duke Rikard's sweat and his seed, the faint tightness where his saliva had dried on her skin, the damp stickiness between her legs.

Panic tightened in her chest. She pushed up to sitting.

"Britta, you're awake."

Her gaze fastened on Yasma's familiar face. "I must wash," she said, stumbling out of the bed.

"I have a bath ready." Yasma slipped an arm around her waist, steadying her.

"And the juices?"

"Those, too."

BRITTA SCRUBBED HER skin. Steam curled up from the bathwater, along with the scent of sandalwood. Bubbles drifted, disappeared. Light and shadow danced along the rim of the tub with each movement she made.

A golden bath tub.

Queen Sigren had died in a golden bath tub.

Her hand faltered, scrubbing. A memory came faintly, hazily. Something about Lundegaard. Something she'd heard recently.

"The poppy juice, princess."

Britta laid down the scrubbing brush.

Voices twisted in her head. Harkeld's: *Not everywhere is like this, Britta. Some kingdoms don't have bondservants. Lundegaard doesn't.* Duke Rikard's: *I want you to wear the crown always.* Jaegar's: *Ours for the taking.*

Britta took the goblet Yasma held out. Bath water dripped from her fingers. *A toast!* The voice was the duke's. She paused with the cool rim of the goblet pressed to her lips and tried to grasp the memory, but it slid away from her.

Britta lowered the goblet. "I think I'll wait a few minutes." She handed the poppy juice back to Yasma. "Where's the dung root?"

Yasma gave it to her. Britta gulped it down, tasting fennel, smelling sulfur. *A toast!*

A toast to what?

*   *   *

WHEN SHE WAS dressed, Britta walked back into the bedchamber and stood there, trying to remember. Something had happened last night. Something important. Something she had to remember.

She closed her eyes, groping for memory...

She had woken. She had woken and there'd been lamplight in the study, voices.

Britta opened her eyes. She walked across to the door to the study. It was shut.

Memory returned, swimming out of the haze that cloaked her mind.

She'd got up to close the door, to shut off the voices and the light. She'd knelt, there, on the floor, and heard... what?

Ours for the taking.

A toast!

Britta tried the door. It swung open on silent hinges.

The study was dark.

Britta hesitated on the threshold for a moment, and then walked across and opened the shutters. Light entered the room, glinting off wall hangings stitched with gold and silver thread, off gilded vases, off gilt-framed mirrors.

Britta turned and faced the desk. Jaegar and her father had been here last night, talking with Duke Rikard. Why? Why not in daylight in the audience chamber?

More memory came. Her father's voice: *Utmost secrecy...*

Three glasses sat on the desk. She recalled the clink of glass, the gurgle of liquid being poured. *A toast! To the invasion of Lundegaard!*

For a moment Britta stood frozen, then she shook her head. Osgaard had no reason to invade Lundegaard. The poppy juice was muddling things in her head. She turned back to the windows and closed the shutters.

But as she walked across to the door, another memory came. A clear memory, from when she was a child. Her father, his face red, bellowing, striking the table with his fist, making the cutlery jump and the goblets wobble. *Osgaard WILL expand under my rule!*

Britta halted in the doorway. Faintly, she heard the third bell ring.

"Princess?" Yasma said, emerging from the dressing room. "Would you like the poppy juice now?"

Yes. But the words that came from her mouth were, "No. There's something I need to check."

Yasma's face showed her puzzlement.

"Here, in the study."

The maid's eyes widened. "Britta... no, you mustn't! If the duke should find you—"

"It's important, Yasma. I shan't be long. If my—" her throat choked on the word *husband*. "If the duke should return early... if you should hear him..."

"I'll warn you."

"Thank you," Britta said, and then she turned and went back into the study and opened the shutters again.

THE DUKE'S DESK was bare apart from an oil lamp, three empty glasses, and a quill with a blunted, ink-stained tip. The drawers held more quills, ink of various shades in glass flasks, and rolls of sealing wax, all jumbled together with no care for the fragility of the flasks or the quills. Amid the clutter were no secret plans, no maps with invasion routes marked out in red ink.

Britta closed the last drawer. *See, you imagined it. There's nothing worthy of alarm here.*

She walked over to the ebony and mother-of-pearl table beneath the window, on which a pile of maps lay. Their edges were curling, creased, smudged with fingerprints. She flicked through them swiftly. They depicted Osgaard and the other kingdoms that made up the Seven.

No, not all of them.

She went through the maps again: Osgaard, Vaere, Sault, Ankeny, Roubos, the Urel Archipelago.

All of the kingdoms—apart from Lundegaard.

So where were Lundegaard's maps?

Britta turned away from the table. A tall cabinet stood alongside the door to the salon. She walked across and opened it.

Here was the duke's liquor—spirits and wines crammed together in no apparent order. Bottles of all sizes and shapes crowded the shelves, some tall and fluted, others smooth and squat. She saw clear glass, red glass, blue glass decorated with gold leaf, glass as green as the sea. The liquids they held shimmered in the sunlight, some the color of blood, some as clear as water, and all shades of brown and gold.

In the cupboard below were cut crystal glasses with golden rims, like the three on the desk. Britta closed the doors and turned to face the room again. Only one place remained to look: a chest crafted of maplewood and pressed gold, to one side of the desk.

She walked to the chest and lifted the lid. Sheets of blank parchment met her eyes, lying every which way, as if they'd been hastily bundled in.

See? she told herself, rummaging through the sheets. *There's nothing here—*

Beneath the parchment were maps of Lundegaard.

BRITTA SLOWLY UNPACKED the chest. The sheets of parchment were creased, in some places torn. A quill lay among them, and a roll of sealing wax. It was as if Duke Rikard had swept everything off his desk, to hastily conceal the chest's contents.

She laid the items out on the floor: maps of Lundegaard, several annotated with arrows and scrawled comments; lists of the squadrons that comprised Osgaard's army, also annotated; notes on scraps of paper; and a document, page after closely-written page, with comments jotted in the margins.

Britta read it, skimming quickly. When she'd finished, she sat staring at the final page. The words blurred, black ink on white parchment, the loops and twists of letters. *No. It can't be true.*

How long she sat, she didn't know. The tolling of the fourth bell brought her back to an awareness of where she was. Hastily, she piled everything back into the chest and closed the lid. She scrambled to her feet. For a moment the room spun around her and she had to grip the edge of the desk to stop herself falling, then everything steadied again.

Britta pushed away from the desk and crossed to the open door. At the threshold, she turned and looked back at the study. Had she left any sign of her presence?

The shutters were open.

She half-ran back across the room and hastily closed them. The study became dark. The bedchamber, glimpsed through the open door, was light and bright and safe, a sanctuary. Britta hurried towards it.

Her fear receded slightly as she stepped into the sunlit bedchamber, as she closed the door.

Yasma looked up from mending a tunic. Her face broke into a relieved smile. "Everything is all right, princess?"

No. I have to decide what to do. "Yes," Britta said. And then, "The poppy juice? Where is it?"

Yasma put aside the tunic and stood. "Here." She held out the goblet.

Britta looked at the dark liquid. *I should keep a clear head.* But the duke would be here soon, wanting to bed her. A fist seemed to tighten in her chest. She gulped a mouthful of poppy juice, tasting its bitterness on the back of her tongue. *Not enough,* a voice whispered in her head. *Not nearly enough.*

Britta took another sip, then she thrust the half-full goblet at Yasma. "Take it!"

In the afternoon, Britta visited her garden. She sat on the cushions in the rose bower and tried to decide what to do, while her armsman patrolled the paths. Her eyelids kept drooping shut. Thoughts went around and around in her head, slow and disorganized.

How can Father stoop to such a plan? So despicable, so utterly without honor!

She knew the answer: Because he was driven to expand Osgaard's borders, as his forefathers had done for the past six generations. He refused to be the first to fail.

And following on the heels of that thought: *What should I do?*

Drowsily, Britta tried to list her options. Easiest, would be to ignore what she knew. *But if I do that, then the dishonor will be mine, too.*

What else could she do? Who could she tell? Harkeld was gone, and there was no one else she trusted enough.

She could tell the ambassador from Lundegaard.

Britta pondered that for several minutes, while the armsman paced and the bees hummed among the roses in the bower.

Yes, the ambassador from Lundegaard. He was the logical person to tell. *But if I do that, I'll be a traitor. I'll be betraying my country.*

Should she be patriotic? Or honorable?

Shouldn't the two be the same?

Britta drifted asleep in the sunshine, pondering that question.

CHAPTER THIRTY-SIX

THEY REACHED THE base of the escarpment midway through the afternoon. Harkeld tilted his head back and stared up. The cliffs leaned over him, bulging outwards, sheer and impossibly high. "There's a way up?"

"Couple of ways," Tomas said. "But only one suitable for horses."

Clouds drifted in the sky. Their movement made it look as if the cliffs were toppling slowly forward. Harkeld looked away, blinking against dizziness. "Do we start today?"

Tomas shook his head. "Tomorrow."

"How high is it?" Justen asked.

"More than a mile."

The escarpment looked like the edge of the world, extending east and west as far as Harkeld could see. The sandstone was cream-colored at its base, shading up into pink and red as it reached towards the sky.

"Do we ride up?" Justen asked.

"Walk." Tomas grinned. "Good exercise."

*   *   *

THEY SPENT THE rest of the afternoon in preparation. Tomas divided their escort in two—the twenty men who would continue into Masse, and those who'd return the way they had come—and gave orders to his second-in-command. Supplies were split, packhorses chosen for the climb up the cliff, weapons sharpened, firewood collected to take with them, waterskins filled.

Finally Tomas declared them ready. "Now all we have to do is climb the cursed thing."

Harkeld grunted and turned away. It wasn't the climb he dreaded; it was what awaited him in Masse. The trek across the desert plateau. The first anchor stone.

They dined early, before the sun had sunk from the sky. A hawk spiraled down, landing in front of one of the tents. Gerit.

The witch dressed and joined them at the campfire.

"What's it like up top?" Tomas asked.

"Empty," Gerit said, filling a bowl with stew.

"Anselm's men—"

"Still heading inland."

"What about water?" Tomas asked. "Did you see the river?"

"Wouldn't call it a river."

"But there was water?" Tomas persisted.

"A trickle," Gerit said, shoveling food into his mouth. "Enough for us."

"Good." Tomas nodded. "We'll get an early start tomorrow."

"How early?" Justen asked.

"Two hours before dawn," Tomas said. "Otherwise we won't be at the top before dark."

CHAPTER THIRTY-SEVEN

IN THE MORNING, once she'd scrubbed the duke from her skin, Britta dressed. Yasma brought two goblets on a tray.

Britta drank the dung root juice, but put the second goblet aside. She took a deep breath. "Yasma, I must speak with you about something."

"Yes?"

She glanced at the door into the salon. It was closed. Even so, she lowered her voice "You know that Lundegaard is taking in refugees from Vaere?"

Yasma nodded.

"The boats are landing at the Hook, in southern Lundegaard. Near the goldfields." Britta looked down at her tunic and picked at a loose thread, wound it around her fingertip. "Not all the refugees are genuine. So far three squadrons of our soldiers have slipped in. One hundred and fifty men. Another squadron is due to depart this week." She glanced up at Yasma. "Once enough men are in place, they'll take the goldfields. And once the goldfields are secure, my father has promise of a fleet of Sarkosian mercenaries. With our army and navy, and the mercenaries, Lundegaard doesn't stand a chance."

Yasma's lips were half-parted, her expression aghast.

Britta took a deep breath. "I want to stop them. And the only way I can think of is to inform the ambassador from Lundegaard."

"But—" Yasma broke off, swallowed. "Britta, your father will kill you!"

"If he finds out, yes." She looked down at the thread wound around her fingertip. "I hope he won't. That's where I need your help."

"How?"

Britta unwound the thread. She walked around the foot of the bed and opened the door to the study. The shutters were open this morning. *I must remember that when I leave.* "First, I must copy the plans and the maps. Will you keep watch for me?"

Yasma nodded. Her hands twisted in a nervous, wringing movement.

"Does anyone else ever come in here? Rickard's bondservant?"

"He never comes past the dressing room."

"Good." Britta rubbed her brow. "I must contact the ambassador without being observed. My head's too slow, Yasma. I can't think of a way. If you can think of one, I should be very grateful."

The girl nodded again. Her eyes were wide and frightened.

WHEN THE FOURTH bell rang, Britta began clearing away the parchment. She moved slowly, carefully, capping the ink flask, wiping the ink from the quill she'd used, gathering together the sheets of paper.

Her fingers weren't as deft as they'd once been. If she fumbled, if she dropped something, spilled ink—

She paused, gathered calmness around her again, and continued placing the items back where she had found them. Then she picked up the pages she'd copied. She counted them: five. *Too slow.* But if she wrote any faster, the words had a way of turning into unreadable scrawls.

Britta took one last look around the study, satisfying herself that no sign of her presence remained, then backed out of the room and closed the door behind her.

Yasma looked up from her mending. Relief was bright in her eyes. "You've finished?"

"For today," Britta said.

The next question was where to hide the pages she'd copied? Somewhere Yasma wouldn't be implicated if they were found. *But she must be implicated. She's my maid; how could I do this without her knowledge?*

It was a sobering realization. It wasn't merely her own life she risked with this. She'd turned Yasma into a traitor too.

THE ONLY TWO hiding places Britta could think of were among her clothes in the dressing room, or under the mattress of the big bed. Neither seemed particularly safe. She chose the bed, shoving the pages under the mattress. She liked the irony of it: the duke sleeping on top of documents that would destroy his planned invasion.

"Princess," Yasma said, behind her. "I've thought

of a way to pass the information to the ambassador."

Britta rose and brushed the creases from her long tunic. "Yes?"

"You give it to his wife."

"How?"

"I thought... a garden party. To celebrate your marriage. You can invite the highest ranking ladies of the court, and the ambassadors' wives."

Britta nodded.

"You'll give them each a gift, a token." Yasma handed her the goblet containing the poppy juice.

"And to the ambassador's wife, I give the papers."

"Yes."

Britta swallowed half the poppy juice. She hesitated, and gave the goblet to Yasma. She had to clench her hands to keep from snatching it back.

"What do you think?" Yasma asked.

Britta dragged her attention away from the poppy juice. "I think it'll serve very well."

CHAPTER THIRTY-EIGHT

JAUMÉ FOUND THE horse when he was picking apples in an orchard. It came across the grass to investigate the intruder in its domain. He gave it an apple and looked it over. The horse was a dappled gray gelding, wiry, no longer young.

He glanced at the farmhouse visible behind the apple trees. No smoke came from the chimney. *It's empty. There's no one there.*

But he didn't go to check. He filled his blanket with apples, slung it over his shoulder, and led the horse up the rutted lane to the road.

Jaumé glanced again at the farmhouse, at the smokeless chimney, and clambered up on the horse's back. *It's not stealing. They left him behind. They don't want him.*

But he didn't quite believe it. Somehow he knew that if he walked up to the house and knocked on the door, there'd be someone inside. Someone who wanted the gray gelding.

Even so, he touched his heels to the horse's flanks. Obediently, it trotted westward, along the muddy road.

Jaumé fisted his hands in the gray mane and looked ahead. Guilt rode him, as he rode the horse. *Thief.*

CHAPTER THIRTY-NINE

By NOON THEY were halfway up the escarpment. Harkeld paused, panting. Sweat dripped from his chin and stuck his shirt to his back. He wiped his face with a damp sleeve. A glance downward made his stomach lurch. The fields of Lundegaard, spread far below, seemed to beckon. It was all too easy to imagine plummeting down. He pressed closer to the rockface. Ahead, the path zigzagged upward, following the folds of the cliff, narrow and steep, littered with loose rock. Bands of pink streaked the sandstone.

Harkeld unstoppered his waterskin and gulped a mouthful of lukewarm water. Behind and ahead, horses and men labored up the path.

Movement above caught his eye: a hawk gliding on the air currents. Its breast feathers were pale, silvery. Petrus.

Harkeld found himself envying the witch.

Envy a witch? *Next, I'll be wanting to be one.*

He set the stopper firmly back in the mouth of the waterskin, angry with himself, and began to climb again.

*   *   *

They reached the top as the wisps of a golden sunset were spreading across the sky.

"Thank the All-Mother," Justen said.

Harkeld nodded. His throat was dry; he'd drained his waterskin a good hour ago. He stared around him. He'd expected a flat plain of sand; instead a choppy sea of sandstone—cream, pink, red and every shade in between—stretched as far as he could see. The Masse desert. "There's a river?" he asked Tomas. Now that they'd stopped climbing, his legs were trembling.

"About half a mile that way," Tomas said, with a nod north. "We'll camp there."

"Good." His clothes stuck to him, drenched with sweat, but his throat was so dry it hurt. A headache hammered behind his eyes.

THEY REACHED THE River Ner as dusk fell. The river bed was wide, clogged with massive boulders, and apparently dry. "There's water here?"

"Follow Petrus," someone said behind him.

Harkeld looked over his shoulder. Dareus rode there, his face weary.

A snowy-white owl glided out of the deepening dusk. They followed, the horses picking their way carefully between the boulders.

The water, when they found it, was a thin rivulet. Harkeld dismounted, biting back a grunt of pain; the muscles in his legs had stiffened during the short ride.

The horses drank first, and then the men. He gulped thirstily, then cupped his hands and splashed water over his face. The headache still sat behind his eyes, but the urgent thirst was gone. Harkeld sat back on his heels and wiped his face. Around him were the dark shapes of men and horses, and a jumble of boulders.

So this is Masse.

HARKELD SLEPT LIKE one dead, rousing to sunlight on his face and the sound of voices. He pushed up on an elbow, seeing soldiers, horses, rock. They'd been too weary to pitch the tents last night.

The rock stretched in all directions: rounded boulders, craggy hillocks, ridges striped with bands of pink and red.

Beside him, Justen pushed back his blanket and sat up. He yawned widely. "Morning, sire."

Several people clustered around a small fire—soldiers, two of the witches. The smell of frying ham suddenly assaulted Harkeld's nose. His stomach growled loudly, telling him it was hungry. He thrust aside the blanket and stood. The muscles in his calves and thighs protested.

Justen groaned as he stood. "Ach, my legs." He hobbled a few steps. "I feel like an old man."

Harkeld grunted a laugh.

The smell of food was mouthwatering, but Harkeld washed his face first, clambering stiffly over the boulders and crouching to dip his hands in the thin trickle of water. Back at the fire, chewing salty fried ham, he examined the map of Masse with Tomas and the witches.

"We'll follow the river," Tomas said. On the map it traced a snaking course north and east. Two thirds of the way along its route a ruined tower marked the ancient city of Ner, abandoned centuries ago when the Massen Empire had fallen.

Ner, where the first anchor stone awaited him.

"Where's Captain Anselm?" Tomas asked.

"There." Gerit pointed to a stretch of waterless plateau on the map. "Following Ditmer's tracks. He's headed for the river, which he should reach here." He planted his forefinger on the parchment. "Some time tomorrow afternoon."

"And Ditmer? Where's he?"

Gerit's finger shifted north-east several inches.

"We need to eliminate Anselm before he catches up with Captain Ditmer," Dareus said.

Tomas tapped the map. "Anselm will reach the river here?" He glanced at Gerit.

Gerit nodded, chewing.

"Then let's meet him there."

THEY RODE HARD, that day and the next. It was like riding over a frozen sea of stone. Some ancient force—wind, rain—had scoured the rock into waves and troughs. Late in the afternoon of the second day, Petrus spiraled down from the sky. "They're less than a league away," he said, once he'd shifted.

Innis was aware of the weight of the sword strapped to her back. Her mind supplied her with a flash of memory: the sickening crunch of bones beneath her blade, the spray of blood. She took a deep breath and exhaled slowly. *I can do this.*

"Any scouts?" Tomas asked.

Petrus shook his head. "They're hurrying. At a guess, they're close to running out of water."

Tomas nodded. "Let's do it, then."

Dareus spoke: "Prince Harkeld won't fight."

The prince's head jerked around. He opened his mouth to protest.

"Your men outnumber them," Dareus told Tomas. "He's not needed."

Tomas met his gaze for a moment, and then nodded.

Innis felt a surge of relief. Prince Harkeld clearly didn't share the feeling. His mouth closed in a grim line. His horse shifted restlessly, as if his hands had tightened on the reins.

"You may have Cora," Dareus said. "She's a fire mage. And the shapeshifters."

DAREUS BECKONED HER aside while Tomas spoke with his soldiers. "I want Ebril to be Justen," he said in a low voice. "You be a hawk. Watch. Don't become involved unless it's necessary."

"But can't Ebril—"

"It'll be a useful experience for you."

Watching men kill each other? Innis bit her lip. She nodded.

"Observe their tactics," Dareus said. He beckoned to Ebril. "Go. shift."

Innis glanced at Prince Harkeld. He was listening to Tomas, his expression dour. The differences between the two princes had never been more obvious—one in soldier's uniform, giving orders to his men; the other in civilian's clothes, forced to watch.

Innis hurried behind one of the waves of rock. Ebril joined her. She stripped quickly, thrusting the clothes at him.

She shifted into the shape of a hawk, magic stinging along her bones, and flew back to the others, landing on a bundle of firewood lashed to one of the packhorses. Ebril returned and took his place alongside Prince Harkeld. The soldiers were checking their weapons, readying themselves for battle. "Let's go," Tomas said. He turned to Petrus. "You'll lead us?"

Petrus nodded. He became a hawk again, flapping up into the sky. He circled once, then set off westward, flying low. The soldiers and Cora followed him. The clatter of hooves and jingle of harnesses was loud in the empty landscape of rock. Innis glanced at Prince Harkeld. His mouth was tight as he watched the men leave, his jaw grim.

She spread her wings and launched herself into the air.

CHAPTER FORTY

KAREL CAUGHT YASMA as she exited the bedchamber. "What's going on?" he asked in a low voice.

The little maid avoided his eyes. "I don't know what you mean."

"I'm not a fool, Yasma. Something's happening."

"She's taking less poppy juice. That's all."

Karel shook his head. It was more than that. The princess was more alert, yes, but her manner had changed too. She seemed purposeful. And that scared him. *She's up to something.* "What's going on?" he asked again. "Tell me, Yasma. Please."

She looked up and met his eyes. "I'm sorry. I can't."

Karel stared down at her. She was afraid. He saw it in her face. "Is it dangerous?"

Yasma bit her lip. She nodded.

Fear blossomed in his chest. "She's not planning to run away?" If she was, what would he do? Help her, and sentence his family to bondservice again? Betray her?

"No, not that. Karel..." Yasma laid her hand briefly on his arm. "If you knew what it was, you'd agree with what she's doing."

"*Tell* me!"

She shook her head. "I'm sorry, I can't. I gave her my word."

Karel clenched his hands, frustrated, helpless. He glanced at the door to the bedchamber. To question the princess, to demand answers, would mean his dismissal. "Yasma—"

"Trust her, Karel."

"I do trust her!" Frustration made his voice harsh. "But how can I keep her safe if I don't know what she's up to!"

Yasma flinched. He'd frightened her.

Karel unclenched his hands. "I'm sorry, Yasma. I just..." He rubbed his brow with hard fingers. *I want to keep her safe.* He sighed. "If she gets into trouble, if either of you needs help... I'm here."

Yasma smiled at him, sudden and sweet. "I know."

CHAPTER FORTY-ONE

HARKELD WATCHED THE soldiers ride from sight. The sound of hooves lingered briefly after they'd gone. He lifted his gaze to the hawks. The girl was smaller than the others, darker. In a few moments, the shapeshifters were out of sight too.

Dareus mounted. "Let's find a good campsite."

Find a campsite? While Tomas and his men were riding into battle? *Women's work*. Harkeld bit back the words. It took conscious effort to not take out his frustration on his horse, not to jerk at the reins or dig his heels into its flanks.

They followed the river for a mile and then halted. "What do you think, Prince Harkeld?" Dareus asked courteously.

He glanced around. Rocks. "Fine," he said, and dismounted.

They tended to the horses and laid wood for a fire. Harkeld kept glancing westward. Was that the clang of swords he heard? The hoarse shouts of fighting men?

He stood still for a moment, his ears straining, but heard only Justen whistling between his teeth as he worked.

Harkeld looked at the closest ridge. Its crest curled like a wave. Perhaps from the top he might see something. "I'm going for a walk."

Dareus looked up sharply, and then nodded. "Justen," he said. "Go with him. Make sure he doesn't get too close to the fighting."

Justen glanced at Harkeld. He grinned, and rolled his eyes.

INNIS CIRCLED AS Tomas set his ambush in a narrow, winding gully. The archers crouched behind the cover of the ridges on either side, hidden. Swordsmen on horseback waited just out of sight, around a bend.

She watched as Captain Anselm's party trotted closer, watched as the Lundegaardan archers raised their bows. A cry of warning hovered on her narrow hawk's tongue. Anselm's soldiers were enemies, but they were also *men*.

The archers loosed their arrows, swiftly nocked again, fired a second time. Chaos erupted in the gully. Tomas and his swordsmen surged forward, shouts bellowing from their throats.

They looked like dolls, small figures poking toy swords at each other—but they weren't dolls, it wasn't a game. Those tiny, glinting sticks were real swords, shearing through real flesh and bone. Maiming. Killing.

Innis looked away.

A useful experience, Dareus had called it.

Innis circled. She watched the archers poised with their bows drawn. She watched Cora on the southern ridge, crouching, her plait dangling down her back, ready to use her magic if needed. She watched Petrus and Gerit hovering low over the battle. She didn't watch the slaughter, the deaths of the outnumbered men. She heard it, though—heard the ringing as sword blades clashed, heard the shouts and screams.

One man turned his horse and spurred it back up the gully. Tomas's archers loosed arrows at him. The arrows missed, smacking into the gully walls, shattering against the stone. Gerit swooped low, following the man.

I hope he escapes.

Innis dipped her right wing, turning away, ashamed with herself for having such a thought. The fleeing soldier was the enemy. He'd come to Masse to kill Prince Harkeld.

Movement near the river caught her eye. Prince Harkeld and Justen stood on one of the curling ridges. The prince shaded his eyes and looked towards the battle.

Innis circled, measuring the distance from the gully to Prince Harkeld. Almost half a mile. He was safe. She glanced down. Few of Anselm's soldiers were still standing. Four swordsmen fought desperately, and two archers crouched behind the cover of a dead horse.

She circled away, unable to watch.

"I CAN'T SEE a thing," Harkeld said, frustrated. The sounds of fighting reached his ears, faint, barely audible: the clash of swords, shouts.

He could see two witches hovering over the battle in the shape of hawks—a small, dark speck that would be the girl and, lower down, a larger speck that must be one of the males.

An arrow speared into the sky, tiny and swift. Harkeld frowned. "Is someone firing at the witches?"

"What?" Justen pushed forward to see. "Where?"

Another arrow stabbed into the sky, arcing upwards. Harkeld squinted, trying to follow its course. The smaller speck tumbled, caught itself, and began to glide steeply downward.

He heard Justen catch his breath. "Did it hit him?"

"Her," Harkeld said, beginning to run. "I think that's the girl."

They scrambled down into the next gully, then up another sandstone crest. Harkeld kept his eyes on the hawk as he ran. It was heading for the river in a lopsided glide. He heard Justen panting at his heels. The hawk was near enough now to see the dark plumage, to see the arrow piercing its wing.

They plunged down into another gully and scrambled up the next ridge. The sky was empty.

"Where is she?" Justen gasped, trying to catch his breath.

"Somewhere close. You go that way." Harkeld pointed. "I'll go this." He ran, following the ridge as it curved, scrambling down into the next gully. He wasn't sure why he cared about the witch. Perhaps because she'd saved his life. Because he owed her.

Justen scrambled down behind him.

"I told you to go the other way!"

"My first duty is to guard you," Justen said, panting. "Sire, we're too close to the fighting—"

Harkeld clambered up the crest of the next ridge. "There she is!" A hawk flapped awkwardly on the mottled sandstone, an arrow jutting from one wing.

His boots scraped on stone as he slid down into the gully. He lost sight of the hawk for a moment behind a jumble of boulders. When he rounded them, running, the witch had shifted into her own shape. She crouched with her head bent. He saw loose black curls hanging down like a curtain, hiding her face, saw the slender line of her bare back, saw the arrow impaled bloodily through her upper arm.

The witch heard their footfalls. She glanced up— white face, dark eyes, pain—and then abruptly shifted. A small black hound crouched on the sandstone, an arrow piercing its front leg.

Relief swept through him. A hound was much easier to deal with than a naked woman. Harkeld slowed his steps and crouched, reaching for her. The hound whimpered and drew its lips back in a half-hearted snarl. "Don't be silly," he told it. "I'm helping you."

He examined the injury carefully, Justen looking over his shoulder. "It's a clean wound," Harkeld said, sitting back on his heels. "It hasn't struck bone."

Justen blew out a breath. "Thank the All-Mother."

A pale-breasted hawk arrowed down from the sky, landed, and shifted into Petrus. "Innis!" he cried. "What happened to her?"

"Arrow wound," Harkeld said. "She'll be fine." He lifted the hound in his arms and stood. She flinched and whimpered again, but didn't try to snarl this time.

"Let me see!" The witch pushed Justen aside. He touched the hound gently, stroking his hand over her head and neck, and leaned close, examining the wound.

"The battle?" Harkeld asked.

"Over," Petrus said. He stroked the hound's head again, a tender gesture.

"Are there any injured?" Justen asked.

"I didn't stay to check—" Petrus glanced up, and flushed faintly. "I'd best get back."

Harkeld nodded. He shifted the hound slightly in his arms, not watching as Petrus became a hawk again. He heard the sound of wings flapping up into the sky. "Can you find the way back to the river?" he asked his armsman.

Justen nodded. "Shall I carry her, sire?"

"She's not heavy."

It wasn't until he was following Justen down the gully that Harkeld realized what the armsman had meant: *Shall I carry her because she's a witch?*

He almost missed a step, almost stumbled. The creature he held in his arms was a shapeshifter, a monstrosity, something both human and animal. But the hound—the witch—didn't seem monstrous at this moment. She rested quietly in his arms. Harkeld was aware of her heart beating beneath his hand, her rapid, shallow breathing, her warmth. *She trusts me.*

The thought alarmed him—not because she shouldn't trust him, but because she *could*. A few weeks ago, if she'd been pointed out to him as a witch, he would have killed her without hesitation; now he was trying to help her.

Because I owe her, he reminded himself, clambering after Justen up the sloping side of the trough.

But that wasn't the reason, and deep inside himself he knew it.

They reached the crest. Justen pointed. "The river's there."

Harkeld followed his armsman along the ridgeline, carefully holding the injured hound. Disquiet filled him. When had he stopped thinking of the witches as purely monsters? When had they started to become almost human to him?

THREE OF TOMAS'S swordsmen bore injuries, none of them serious. Petrus stopped the bleeding, his attention not wholly on his healing. "There," he told the last man. "That'll do until we get to the camp."

The soldier spoke his thanks awkwardly, hurriedly, and backed away. *As if I'm a leper.* But Petrus's rancor was half-hearted; his thoughts were on Innis.

A stir among soldiers made him turn his head. He saw men hastily stepping aside, hauling on their horses' reins. A lion came trotting through the parted men. Gerit. Blood streaked his flank.

"Is that your blood?" Petrus asked.

The lion shook his head. He sat down with a grunt and yawned widely, showing sharp, white teeth.

Petrus glanced up at the sky. "I'll see you back at camp. Innis has been hurt. An arrow."

The lion's eyes widened with alarm. He surged to his feet.

"It's not serious," Petrus said. "She'll be fine." But even so, he wanted to be with her. "Will you guide them back?"

The lion nodded.

Petrus shifted, leaping into the air almost before he'd fully changed. He flapped swiftly upward, leaving behind the aftermath of the battle—the stench of blood, the sprawled bodies, the riderless horses.

"IT WAS MY fault," Innis said. "I wasn't watching the fighting." She sat cross-legged on her bedroll, wrapped in a blanket.

"May I see?"

She turned back the blanket, showing Petrus her upper arm. "See? It's fine."

Petrus touched her arm, his fingers lightly resting on the fresh scar. She felt his healing magic flow gently as he examined the injury. "Did Dareus heal you?" he asked.

"No, I did. It wasn't a difficult wound."

Petrus released her arm. "A better job than I could do."

Innis shook her head. She studied his face. He looked the same as he always did: the steady gaze, the smile lines creasing the corners of his eyes, the mouth that laughed easily.

Petrus hadn't turned away from the battle. He'd watched, he'd seen the arrows coming and avoided them. *As I should have done.*

Outside the tent she heard the clatter of hooves on stone, heard the murmur of voices—Tomas and his soldiers returning. Innis looked down at the blanket. She picked at a thread. "I couldn't bear to see them kill each other. That's why I wasn't looking. Why I didn't see the arrows."

Petrus reached for her hand, his fingers wrapping comfortingly around hers. "Dareus shouldn't have asked you to watch."

"Yes, he should. I'm a Sentinel. I should be able to—"

"To watch people die and not care?" His grip on her hand tightened. "That's not what being a Sentinel is about."

"No, but—"

"I found it hard too, Innis."

She looked at him. "You still watched."

Petrus grimaced. "Yes."

The campsite was busy now. Through the open flap of the tent she saw a string of weary horses pass by. Captain Anselm's packhorses, with the captain's supplies loaded on their backs. Two soldiers strode past. Their voices were loud, boisterous. *Because they survived.*

"Did any of Tomas's men die?"

Petrus shook his head. "Three sword wounds. I patched them up." His tone changed, became neutral. "Did the prince carry you all the way back?"

Innis nodded.

"That was... good of him." The words were grudging, as if he found them difficult to utter.

"Yes."

Petrus released her hand. "I'd better help Dareus finish the healing. My patches were pretty rough."

"I can help—"

"No. They're not serious. You rest." Petrus paused in the opening, crouching, and looked back at her. "I think Dareus was wrong. He shouldn't have sent you."

"Why not? He sent you."

"Yes, but—"

"Because I'm not a man? Cora's not a man either."

"Cora's older. You're too young to see such things."

Too young. She'd heard that so many times in the past few months. "You think I shouldn't be a Sentinel?"

Petrus hesitated.

He does. Innis drew the blanket more tightly around her. Something clenched miserably in her chest. Petrus was one of those who'd thought her appointment a mistake.

"I don't know what I think," Petrus said. "Except that I want you to be safe. And being a Sentinel isn't safe." He sighed. "I'd better go."

Innis nodded.

She lay down and stared at the ceiling of the tent. Petrus was right: being a Sentinel wasn't safe. She of all people knew that. Her parents had been Sentinels; her parents had died.

Innis rubbed her arm, tracing the scar. *This was my own fault.* She should have been watching the fighting. She should have remembered that Anselm's men had fired at Gerit when he was a hawk.

Neither of her parents would have made such a mistake.

Her lips tightened. *I let them down.*

THE SCENERY CHANGED the next day. They left the choppy sea of rock behind as they followed the River Ner—and Captain Ditmer—further into Masse. The river carved itself a canyon, with high walls of red sandstone. Massive boulders lay tossed and tumbled by ancient floodwaters.

Picking their way around a boulder the size of a cottage, they found hoof prints in a sheltered patch of sand. "Captain Ditmer," Tomas said.

Harkeld nodded, seeing Ditmer's face in his mind's eye: square, flat-cheeked, brutal.

Late in the afternoon of the second day, the landscape changed again. The river swung east. On the southern bank of the River Ner, the sandstone cliffs still reared up, pock-marked with caves and hollows; north of the river, a plain of rock and sand stretched into a hazy distance. The sand was as red as the rock, huge drifts of it, rippled by the wind. It was surprisingly beautiful.

They rode until dusk, towering cliffs to their right, a sea of red dunes to their left. As sunset stained the sky, the color of the dunes deepened until they were almost blood-red. The last of the daylight drained away. The dunes shaded slowly from red to purple, and then faded into the gloom of night.

Rather than pitch tents, they camped in one of the caves that honeycombed the cliffs. A snowy-white owl flapped out of the darkness while they were eating. A few minutes later the witch, Petrus, joined them at the fire.

"How far ahead is Captain Ditmer?" Tomas asked. "Are we gaining on him?"

Petrus nodded. "He's about a day and a half ahead now." He took the bowl of stew Dareus handed him.

Tomas grinned. In the firelight he looked predatory, almost wolfish. "Good," he said. "We'll catch him before Ner."

CHAPTER FORTY-TWO

IT HAD TAKEN Britta four mornings to copy the invasion plans and another to copy the scrawled notes from the squadron lists and the assorted scraps of paper. Now, only the maps remained, five of them. "I need bigger sheets of parchment," she told Yasma. She rubbed her forehead, trying to get her brain to work more clearly. Three days until the garden party, three days in which to copy the maps. *Think*. There had to be some way of obtaining large sheets of parchment without arousing suspicion.

"Your brothers?" the maid suggested.

Britta lowered her hand. "What would I do without you, Yasma?"

IT WAS A question she asked herself again that afternoon, as she prepared to visit her half-brothers. She sat on a stool, cloaked in serenity. Yasma tidied her hair, winding strands of hair around the golden crown, anchoring it tightly again. Britta watched the maid's agile, brown fingers. For the past four years she'd been the girl's protector; now their roles were reversed.

"All the acceptances have come in," Yasma said.

"Twenty-three."

"The ambassador's wife...?"

"She's coming," Yasma reached for a jeweled pin and slipped it deftly into place. "The menu's gone to the palace kitchen and the musicians are engaged in your name."

Britta surveyed the litter of pins, brushes and combs on the gilded table top. The only things keeping her anchored in reality were Yasma—and the invasion plans. She couldn't think beyond the garden party, beyond giving the plans to the ambassador's wife.

I should stop taking the poppy juice altogether.

Her serenity faltered. The scent of the duke's bed filled her nose: sweat, semen. The smell made panic clench in her chest as memories spilled over one another—

No, don't remember.

Britta exhaled a shaky breath and tried to gather the serenity around herself again.

"All that's left are the gift baskets," Yasma said. "I'll start lining them with silk this afternoon."

Britta nodded. She imagined the bitter taste of poppy juice on her tongue. The tension in her body trickled away.

BRITTA WALKED SERENELY along the marble corridors. At the gilded door to the nursery, she halted. Karel stepped forward and opened it.

The boys were playing soldiers, their squadrons spread out across the floor. "Britta!" Rutgar scrambled up and launched himself at her, his arms wrapping around her waist. For a moment she felt the armsman's hand against her shoulder blade, steadying her, and then she found her balance again.

"Britta!" a shriller voice cried: Lukas.

Britta bent and hugged the children, kissing each of them, smelling milk and cinnamon and rosemary; the scent of childhood, of safety.

Lukas clung to her. "I thought you'd gone away, like Harkeld."

Her serenity vanished. In its place was guilt. "No, sweetheart. I've... I've been busy."

Rutgar tugged on her arm. "We finished coloring the last picture you drew for us," he said eagerly. "Do you want to see it?"

BRITTA SPENT THE next hour admiring the pictures the boys had drawn since she'd last visited, exclaiming over lopsided wolves and soldiers with crooked swords and horses that were an improbable shade of yellow. "You're getting very good," she said at last, shuffling the sheets of parchment together.

"But we're not as good as you," Rutgar said solemnly. "Will you draw something new for us?"

"Not today, sweetheart."

His face fell.

"But I'll take some parchment with me and draw something for you. I'll bring it with me next time I come."

Rutgar's face lit up. "With horses!"

"And woodcutters with axes," Lukas said. "And wolves!"

"With all of that!" Britta said, laughing. "I promise."

She took a dozen large sheets of parchment, rolling them carefully. Guilt was heavy in her chest. *You're using them.*

But the boys' mother had been from Lundegaard, and if they knew what she was doing, if they were old enough to understand—

She looked at the children, fair-haired like Queen Sigren. *You'd be glad that you'd helped me, if you knew.*

"Promise you'll come again?" Rutgar"s expression was anxious.

He'd never asked that of her before. *I left them too long.* The guilt became heavier. "I promise." Britta hugged them both, very tightly.

KAREL STOOD AT his post in the salon. The princess was dozing in her bedchamber, Yasma was sewing at the long table in the dining room, and outside the afternoon was slowly ripening towards evening. They were all waiting for the duke to return.

Tension built in him with each minute that passed. Karel tried to shake it off. He made himself release his grip on the sword hilt, made himself pace the length of the salon and back.

The door to the dining room was open. After his third traverse of the salon, Karel walked across to it and looked in. The long, polished table was strewn with baskets and lengths of silk.

Yasma glanced up, pausing in mid-stitch. "The duke?"

"Not here yet."

Karel walked over to the table. There were twenty-three baskets, prettily woven from reeds. Yasma had lined sixteen of them with silk of differing colors: crimson, sky blue, leaf green, yellow. Inside each completed basket lay a gilt-edged card.

Karel looked at the cards. *Lady Agata, Lady Fridetha. Lady Sofia.* "This is your handwriting."

Yasma laid down the needle and thread, alarm on her face. "How can you tell?" She reached for a card.

Karel shrugged. The letters were identical to the princess's—the slant of each *t*, the loop of each *g*— but to his eyes, the writing wasn't hers. He picked up one of the cards and examined it. "I think... you're more careful than she is."

"I'll have to write them out again," Yasma said, anxiety furrowing her brow. "I'm not free. I'm not meant to be able to read or write—"

Karel kicked himself mentally. "Don't write them out again," he said. "It looks just like her writing."

"But you noticed—"

"Only because I know you can write. No one else does." He laid down the card. "Why is she having this party?"

Yasma looked away. She picked up the needle again. "Because it's fitting. She's a new bride."

There was more to it than that. Karel surveyed the items on the table—baskets, silk, thread, scissors, gilt-edged cards. This had something to do with the secret purpose that was driving the princess. *There's something here I'm missing.*

"Yasma, please tell me what's going on."

She bit her lip and glanced up at him. "I'm sorry, Karel."

He stared at the little maid. *I could bully you, force it from you.* And then he sighed and went back to pacing the salon.

CHAPTER FORTY-THREE

Ahead, the fir trees pulled back from the road. There was a sunny patch of grass, a brook.

Jaumé nudged the old gray gelding towards the brook. Others had halted here before him—the grass was flattened and muddy.

He and the horse drank from the brook, then Jaumé sat in the sun and ate two of the pears he'd scavenged yesterday. Juice dribbled down his chin. He wiped it away with the back of his hand.

The sunshine made everything seem brighter. He had a knife, a waterskin, a blanket, and a horse, and one pear and three apples left to eat. The curse was falling further behind him. If he just followed the other people on the road, he'd find somewhere safe.

The sunshine and the sound of running water, the sound of the gelding cropping grass, almost lulled him to sleep. Jaumé pushed to his feet and filled the waterskin at the brook. It was too early to stop. They could travel a few more miles before night fell.

When he turned back to the horse, someone else was standing in the glade. A man with a shaggy red beard and mud-stained clothes.

"This your horse, boy?"

Jaumé nodded, hugging the waterskin to his chest. "I'm taking it."

Jaumé dropped the waterskin. He fumbled in his pocket for the knife, pulling it out. "No."

The man grinned. "What you going to do with that thing, boy?"

Jaumé gripped the knife more tightly. His heart thudded in his chest. "Go away."

The man took a fistful of the gelding's mane. "Come on, horse."

Jaumé gulped a deep breath and ran at the man, holding the knife out in front of him. Sunlight glinted off the blade.

The man watched him coming, still grinning. He released his grip on the horse's mane and swung his arm. His fist struck Jaumé in the face.

For a moment, everything went black—and then Jaumé was blinking up at sunlight. The taste of blood filled his mouth. He pushed up on one elbow.

The man glanced back at him from astride the old gray gelding. "Thanks for the horse."

JAUMÉ TRUDGED ALONG the road, clutching the waterskin, the blanket, the knife. His nose still bled sluggishly. Tears leaked from his eyes.

The rumble of wagon wheels came from behind him. He stepped to one side and hunched his shoulders.

The family in the wagon stared at him as they drove past—a man, his wife, two young boys.

The wagon halted. The man looked back. He had a bald head and a long, curling black beard. "Had some trouble, did you, son?"

Jaumé nodded and wiped his nose, smearing blood on his sleeve.

"How old are you?"

"Eight," he said.

"Alone?"

Jaumé nodded again.

The man looked at him a moment longer, and then jerked his head. "Get in. We'll give you a ride to the top of the pass."

CHAPTER FORTY-FOUR

THEY SLEPT WRAPPED in blankets and woke to a chilly dawn. Innis huddled in her cloak, eating breakfast as the sky shaded from palest gray to a delicate eggshell blue. They rode following the river, hugging the base of the cliffs, with the desert on their left. As the sun rose higher and the blue of the sky deepened, a northerly wind picked up. Innis no longer needed the hood of Justen's cloak pulled over her head for warmth, but for protection from wind-blown sand.

"What are those things?" Prince Harkeld asked when they halted for a lunch of hardbread, cheese and peppery smoked sausages. He pointed at the cliff.

Innis blinked, not seeing anything but sandstone and a few scraggly thorn bushes.

Tomas glanced at the cliff. "A granary."

"A granary? Here?"

Innis chewed, squinting at the sandstone. The cliffs were pock-marked with holes and caves, but nothing resembling a granary—

And then, as if a veil had suddenly been drawn back from her eyes, she saw them: cavities that had been bricked up. Both the bricks and the crumbling mortar were the same color as the sandstone.

"This used to be fields," Tomas said, with a sweeping gesture at the desert. "When the grain was harvested, they stored it in caves and bricked them up."

Innis shook her head. It was impossible to imagine the sand dunes covered in grass and the river running high, filling its banks. "Fields?"

Tomas nodded.

"What happened, sire?"

Tomas shrugged. "The grass died, the trees died, the river dried up."

"When?"

"More than a thousand years ago."

"Magic?" Prince Harkeld asked. "A curse?"

"What else could it be?"

Innis chewed on a piece of sausage. She studied the cliffs, the sand dunes. She couldn't see any signs of an ancient curse.

"It was natural," Dareus said. He sat across from them. "A drought."

"But the tales say—"

"Do you believe every story you hear?"

Tomas closed his mouth. His expression was mulish. Innis read his thoughts clearly on his face: *You think I'd trust the word of a witch?*

As the afternoon progressed, wind began to gust off the desert. With it, came swirling clouds of red sand. When they finally halted for the night, Harkeld slid wearily from his horse. Sand grains were gritty in his eyes, in his mouth. He unslung his waterskin and drained it, gulping the lukewarm water greedily.

They sat around two small campfires and ate a stringy stew made from dried fish. Sand crunched between Harkeld's teeth as he chewed. "How far ahead is Ditmer now?" Tomas asked the shapeshifters. He put his bowl to one side and unrolled the map.

"He was setting up camp... there." Ebril pointed with his spoon. "Where the river enters the canyon again."

"We've gained on him, then."

Harkeld leaned forward to look at the map. The distance they'd covered seemed tiny. "How many days to Ner?"

"A week or so. We'll catch up with Ditmer before then." Tomas traced the river's course on the map with one finger. "Somewhere here," he said, tapping. "In the canyon. Horrible place."

Harkeld glanced at him. "Horrible? Why?"

"You'll understand once we get there." Tomas surged to his feet, half-drawing his sword as one of the soldiers around the second campfire shouted.

Harkeld stopped chewing. The soldiers were stamping at an object in the sand.

"Scorpions." Tomas sheathed his sword and sat again. "They like fires. The heat, the light. It draws them." But his manner wasn't as nonchalant as his words; he glanced uneasily at the ground before picking up his bowl.

"Are they poisonous?" Harkeld asked.

"They won't kill you," Tomas said. "But for a day or so you'll wish they had."

"Painful?"

"Very."

Harkeld half-choked on a mouthful of stew as shouts rose from the soldiers again. There was a note of pain in one of the voices.

"Someone's been stung." The girl, Innis, put down her bowl and hurried across to the other fire. Dareus and Tomas followed her.

After a moment, Harkeld rose and followed them.

Innis crouched beside the stricken man. The sting was on the soldier's calf; his face was twisted into a grimace of pain.

The girl laid her hand over the puncture wound. She closed her eyes for a long moment, an expression of concentration on her face.

"Well?" Dareus asked, crouching alongside her.

Innis opened her eyes. "It's a strong poison, but not deadly."

"Can you heal him?" Tomas asked.

She glanced up. "I can't draw out the poison, if that's what you're asking. But I can alleviate some of the symptoms."

"Poison's difficult for us," Dareus told Tomas. "It's much easier to fix a broken bone or repair torn tissue." He reached for one of the soldier's hands, turned it palm up, and laid his own hand on it. "To remove poison from the bloodstream requires us to clean each drop of blood—a task that would take many mages many days."

The soldier was shivering. Sweat stood out on his face.

"Will he be well enough to travel tomorrow?" Tomas asked.

"We'll do our best."

At Tomas's order, they extinguished the campfires,

smothering them with sand and then retrieving the precious, half-charred wood.

Without the firelight to coax them in, no more scorpions came scuttling over the sand dunes. Even so, Harkeld slept fitfully, jerking awake several times to the sound of the witches working on the soldier— the low murmur of their voices, the man groaning.

By morning, the soldier was well enough to travel—after a fashion. He lurched and stumbled towards his horse, blinking as if his vision were blurred. Despite the chilly dawn, a sheen of sweat covered his face.

Dareus rode beside the soldier, easing the cramps that periodically racked him. "How long does it take a man to recover?" Harkeld asked Tomas.

"Three or four days before they can even stand upright."

Harkeld glanced at the soldier riding hunched over on his horse, at Dareus alongside, his hand resting on the man's arm.

"We're lucky we've got the witches with us," Tomas said. He pulled a face and laughed. "Never thought I'd hear myself say that!"

CHAPTER FORTY-FIVE

THERE WERE TWO maps left to copy. Britta used red ink to mark the arrows, as the duke had done. The fourth bell was ringing by the time she finished the last one. She laid down the quill and flexed her fingers.

"Britta?" Yasma appeared in the doorway to the bedchamber.

Terror froze her in the chair. Her heart seemed to stop beating. "He's here?"

"No." Yasma shook her head. "But the fourth bell has rung. You need to stop."

Britta pressed her hands to her face for a brief moment. Her fingers were trembling. "I've finished." She picked up the maps and thrust them at Yasma. "Here, hide them."

THE DUKE EMERGED from the bedchamber, flushed and smug. Karel stared stolidly at the opposite wall and imagined drawing his sword. He listened to the duke's footsteps come closer. His fingers flexed, touched the sword hilt. *Here, when you're this close, I'd take your head.*

Once the duke had departed, Yasma went into the bedchamber. Nearly an hour passed before she emerged again.

"How is she?" Karel asked. It was a stupid question. *How do you think she is? The duke's just spent an hour rutting her.* The daydream blossomed in his mind again, so vivid he could almost smell the duke's blood.

"Sleeping," Yasma said.

The afternoon passed slowly. Yasma was busy in the dining room, lining baskets with silk. Karel watched a band of sunlight slowly move, sliding along a wall, making silver threads glint in a tapestry, then inching across the floor, where the thickly piled rugs came alive with color. He paced the salon, and then looked into the dining room. Baskets were lined up on the long table. Inside them, crystal vases lay on beds of silk. One vase stood on the table, a delicate fluted shape. Yasma was bent over a basket lined with moss green silk, sewing. He thought he heard the crackle of parchment. "What are you doing?"

Yasma started so violently that her elbow thumped the table. The vase teetered. Karel strode across and steadied it before it could fall. He had a flash of memory: the king's atrium, a gilded vase smashing.

Perhaps Yasma had the same memory. Her face was pale, her eyes wide with fear. "I was just... The lining was crooked. I'm re-sewing it." She thrust the vase on top of the moss green silk and stood, her movements jerky and flustered.

"Are you all right?" Karel asked.

"Yes," Yasma said, but she still looked pale. "You

startled me, is all." She rubbed her elbow. "What time is it? I should check on her." She hurried across to the door.

Karel eyed the moss green basket. The silk lining looked thicker than the others. He reached out to touch it.

"Karel." Yasma's voice was sharp. "Don't touch them."

Karel looked over his shoulder.

Yasma stood in the doorway, anxious, edgy. "The vases are fragile. You might break one."

I don't think that's what you're afraid of. "They look nice," Karel said mildly. And then he followed Yasma back into the salon.

ONCE YASMA WAS closeted with the princess, Karel went back to the dining room. He studied the long table. Twenty-three baskets were lined up on the polished wood. Delicate crystal vases nestled on beds of crimson and yellow, leaf green and sky blue. Only one basket was lined with moss green.

He walked over to the basket with the moss green silk. The needle and thread still dangled from it. Karel carefully picked up the vase and placed it on the table. He fingered the lining, heard the rustle of parchment beneath the silk.

A gilt-edged card lay on the table. *Lady Pirnilla*, he read. The wife of Lundegaard's ambassador.

Karel sat in the seat Yasma had vacated. He slid the needle from the thread, undid half a dozen stitches, and lifted up one corner of the lining. Sheets of parchment lay folded underneath the silk.

Karel pulled the sheets out and laid them on the table. Pages of writing, folded maps. *What's going on here?*

He opened one of the maps. It showed the border between Osgaard and Lundegaard. Red arrows were drawn on it. Understanding flared inside him. For a moment he couldn't breathe, could only stare, then he reached for the top sheet of writing and began to read swiftly. It was a letter, written in the princess's hand, more scrawled than usual, but with the fluidity Yasma's writing lacked.

Karel skimmed it quickly. *Osgaardan soldiers*, she'd written. *Guise of refugees*. And further down the page, *Take the goldfields*, and *Sarkosian mercenaries*.

The princess finished simply: *I enclose copies of the maps and plans. Please believe that every word is true.*

She had signed the letter: *A friend*.

Karel refolded the map and replaced everything in the basket. He understood Yasma's fear now. The maps, the pages of writing, were proof of treason. To be found with them would mean death.

He rethreaded the needle, his fingers clumsy with haste. If the duke returned now, if the pages were discovered—

With the lining stitched back the way Yasma had left it and the vase lying snugly in the basket again, he felt only marginally safer. Fear sat beneath his breastbone as he hurried back into the salon and took his position alongside the door.

If you knew what she was doing, you'd approve, Yasma had said.

Karel shook his head. He didn't want to see Lundegaard conquered, he truly didn't, but—

Cold sweat broke out on his skin at thought of what would happen if Princess Brigitta's treason was discovered. She was walking an extremely dangerous path. One misstep could kill her. And Yasma.

Karel closed his eyes. *All-Mother*, he prayed. *Keep her safe. Please.*

CHAPTER FORTY-SIX

THEY FOLLOWED THE river all day, red desert to the north, red cliffs to the south. Harkeld found his mood almost cheerful. Partly it was the scenery—the stark, barren beauty of sand and rock—partly it was the company: Tomas on his right, joking as he rode; Justen, laconic and dependable on his left. He could forget the witches riding behind, forget the curse, forget the bounty on his head—forget that his life had fallen apart, as the crumbling stones that sealed the granaries in the cliffs were falling apart.

At dusk they reached a place where the River Ner entered a wide canyon. "We'll camp here," Tomas said.

Men began to dismount. The soldier who'd been stung by the scorpion stumbled and fell to his knees. His skin was pallid, slick with sweat.

Tomas scrambled from his horse to help him. "Is he getting worse?"

Dareus shook his head. "The poison's nearly out of his system." He knelt on the soldier's other side, gripping the man's hand. "By tomorrow he should be fine."

Tomas grunted. He stood and raised his voice in an order: "Dig pits for the fires tonight. We don't want to attract any more scorpions."

Harkeld dismounted and examined the canyon. It looked no different to the canyon they'd ridden through a couple of days ago, the high red sandstone walls pockmarked with caves. "Why did you say it's a horrible place?"

"I'll let you discover that for yourself. I want to see your expression when you first, uh... experience it."

"Experience what?"

But Tomas only shook his head.

Harkeld studied the canyon again. It didn't look sinister. "You're being childish," he told his friend.

"Merely continuing a long tradition. No one told *me* the canyon's secret, the first time I came up here." Tomas laughed, a sound that echoed off the sandstone cliffs. "I was so frightened I almost wet myself."

Harkeld glanced at him sharply. "It's that scary?"

Tomas grinned. "You'll see."

THEY ROSE IN the chilly half-light of predawn, entering the canyon as daylight began to creep across the sea of sand, washing it with color. Gray stone became lilac, then pink, and then blazing red. Harkeld examined the canyon as they rode. The cliffs on either side rose several hundred feet, honeycombed with holes.

Terrifying? The canyon looked utterly ordinary, the sandy floor littered with chunks of stone, the high walls banded with shades of red. The sandstone was bisected by ravines little wider than cracks, too steep and narrow for man or beast to climb, and burrowed with cavities. All of the lower ones were bricked up.

"Lot of granaries here," Justen remarked, after they'd been riding for several hours. "Wouldn't have thought they'd have been able to grow so much grain in a canyon. Too narrow."

"They're not granaries," Tomas told him. "They're tombs."

Justen's eyebrows climbed up his forehead. "Tombs?"

"The Massens didn't burn their dead, or bury them. They walled them up in caves. " Tomas gestured at the sandstone cliffs. "This canyon is where they buried their warriors. To guard the route to the city."

"Guard it?" Justen asked. "How?"

"Their spirits are said to linger." Tomas looked sideways at him, a sly gleam in his eyes. "They dislike intruders."

"Linger?"

Harkeld snorted. "Haunt." Was this what Tomas hoped to scare him with? "I don't believe in ghosts."

Tomas smiled slightly. "Of course not."

They rode for several minutes in silence, apart from the sound of horses' hooves muffled by the sand. Harkeld's gaze kept straying to the base of the cliffs, to the blocked-up caves, the tombs. There were dozens. Hundreds, if you counted those they'd already passed. Thousands, if you counted those that lay ahead.

"I confess, I find the notion that the caves are filled with corpses slightly disturbing," Justen said.

So do I. "What do you do in Groot?" Harkeld asked his armsman. "With your dead?"

"Uh..." Justen blinked. "We give them to the sea."

Harkeld nodded. It seemed a fitting conclusion for men who lived surrounded by the ocean. "We bury ours," he said, trying to ignore the tombs. "But further east, in Ankeny, they burn them."

"They bury them in Rosny, too," Justen said.

"The sea?" Tomas said, turning in his saddle to look at the armsman. "How?"

"The fleet goes out to where the current is strongest." Justen touched his hand to his chest, where the ivory amulet lay beneath his clothes. "And the body is placed in the water."

Harkeld understood the gesture: A Grooten carried his amulet to his grave. His mind turned back to the witches. "They bury their dead in Rosny? They should burn them."

Justen glanced at him. "Why?"

To get rid of them. So they can't contaminate the soil.

As the sun rose in the sky, so too did the wind rise, gusting in puffs from the direction of the desert, swirling sand and dust in little eddies along the canyon floor. They halted at noon for a hasty lunch. Harkeld ate mechanically, barely tasting his food.

A sound tugged faintly at the edge of his hearing. He stopped chewing and lifted his head, listening. He heard the mutter of voices, heard one of the horses snort, heard someone snap a round of hardbread in half. Other than those sounds, there was silence. Not even the wind blew.

Harkeld shook his head and resumed chewing.

Wind gusted in from the desert again, ruffling his hair, creating a small flurry of sand. A sound came with it, a whispering moan. Harkeld looked up sharply. "What's that?"

"What?" Justen asked.

"Can't you hear it?"

Justen shook his head and bit into his hardbread with a crunching sound.

The wind blew more strongly and the whisper became louder, rising to a wail that made the hairs on the back of Harkeld's neck stand on end.

Justen froze, his mouth full of cheese and hardbread.

"That," Harkeld said, reaching for his sword.

"Ghosts," Tomas said.

"Nonsense!" Harkeld stood, drawing his sword, trying to face the sound, but it surrounded them—ahead, behind, above—riding on the wind.

"Ghosts," Tomas said again, and continued eating.

None of the soldiers seemed alarmed. The horses were more perturbed, stamping nervously, rolling their eyes. Harkeld tightened his grip on the sword. "I don't believe in ghosts." His tongue spoke the words, but his mind was telling him otherwise. Terror prickled over his skin. The wailing was inhuman, terrifying. No living person could make that sound.

"I told you," Tomas said, raising his voice to be heard above the wail. "The warriors were buried here to protect the city. To scare intruders away. They can't touch us, so there's nothing to worry about."

Harkeld glanced at Justen. Why wasn't his armsman on his feet, sword in hand?

Justen was grinning.

Harkeld blinked. He looked around sharply.

The soldiers were grinning too. And the witches.

Tomas wasn't grinning. His face was perfectly straight, but his eyes brimmed with laughter.

"You son of a whore." Harkeld loosened his tense grip on the sword. "It's not ghosts." He swung around to his armsman. "What is it?" he demanded, pointing the tip of his sword at Justen.

"As I understand it, the wailing comes from holes bored in the cliffs," the armsman said. "The wind produces sounds as it blows through them, like pipes."

"Son of a whore," Harkeld muttered again. He sheathed his sword.

Tomas gave a shout of laughter, startling the frightened horses further. One of the soldiers made a choking sound, and hastily smothered it.

Harkeld sat. "You could have warned me."

Justen's expression was sheepish. "Prince Tomas asked me not to."

"Your face—" Tomas said, and began to laugh helplessly.

CHAPTER FORTY-SEVEN

WHEN KAREL CAME on duty at noon, the princess's garden was bustling with activity. Gilt and marble tables stood on the smooth oval of grass, set with cutlery, crystal goblets, and plates with golden rims that gleamed in the sunshine.

Bondservants brought sweetmeats and pastries from the palace kitchen, while musicians set up their harps in the rose bower.

The princess was already dressed in one of her finest tunics, a sky blue silk embroidered with gold thread. Karel saw at a glance that she hadn't drunk any poppy juice that morning. She stood in the middle of the lawn, directing the servants. "There," she said to a woman carrying a deep silver bowl of fruit punch. "On that table." And to three men bearing gilded chairs : "Over there."

The twenty-three reed baskets were on a table to one side of the rose bower, with the crystal vases now nestling amid freshly cut flowers. Yasma hovered over them, rearranging the flowers, guarding the basket with the moss green silk.

Karel took up position where he could watch the princess. Tension sat in his shoulders. With every minute that passed, Princess Brigitta came closer to her act of treason, closer to the possibility of being caught, of being sentenced to death. *Stop her!* a voice inside him urged. And yet, he couldn't, because what she was doing was right.

If Princess Brigitta was frightened, it didn't show. She was paler and thinner than she'd been before she married the duke, but there was purpose on her face and her eyes were clear.

Footsteps crunched on one of the paths. Karel turned his head and watched as Duke Rikard approached, preceded by three bondservants carrying gilded chairs and followed by his armsman.

The duke halted at the edge of the lawn and watched his wife for a moment. His gaze was greedy, possessive.

Not today, Karel told the duke silently. *Can't you see she's busy?*

The duke apparently could not. He strode across the grass towards his wife.

The princess's voice faltered when she saw him. She shrank back slightly. Karel saw her lips move, *I'm too busy,* but she said it with fear, not authority.

The duke took her arm.

Karel reached out and tipped over a goblet. It fell with a *clang*, scattering cutlery.

"Oh, dear!" the princess cried. She pulled free of Duke Rikard's grip. "Excuse me, but I can't come."

"Let the servants—"

"My guests will be here soon," she said, backing away from him.

The duke's face tightened in displeasure.

Princess Brigitta turned her back to him and hurried across the grass. Her fingers trembled as she picked up the fallen goblet and straightened the cutlery.

Duke Rikard turned away and strode back towards the palace. His armsman followed. Their boots made sharp crunching sounds on the path.

"He's gone," Karel said in a low voice.

The princess glanced at him. Her eyes were the blue of the sky, the blue of her tunic. "Thank you," she whispered, and then she straightened her shoulders and turned back to directing the servants.

When the sixth bell tolled, the guests began arriving with their armsmen. Princess Brigitta greeted the ladies, accepting their gifts graciously. Yasma took each present and placed it on the table beside the baskets of flowers. Karel saw jeweled combs and gold-backed mirrors, mother-of-pearl brooches and delicate glass vials of perfume.

The armsmen arrayed themselves around the garden, their faces blank. The air filled with the sound of ladies' voices, the *clink* of cutlery, the tinkle of harps playing.

Princess Brigitta stood out among her guests, her hair gleaming as golden as the crown woven into it. Karel watched as she spoke with various ladies, as she handed out her gift baskets. It seemed to him that a sword hung over her head, waiting to fall.

And then came the moment he'd been dreading: she picked up the basket lined with moss green silk and walked across to the wife of Lundegaard's ambassador.

*   *   *

"LADY PIRNILLA," BRITTA said. "Thank you for being my guest today."

The woman turned from the rose bush she'd been admiring and sank into a curtsey. "The pleasure is mine, princess." She was a regal woman, with brown hair and cool gray eyes.

"A gift," Britta said, holding out the reed basket. "As a token of my gratitude."

The ambassador's wife took the basket. "How lovely!" she exclaimed politely. "Such an exquisite vase! Such beautiful flowers! Are they from your garden?"

Britta looked at the woman. *Can I trust you?* She took a deep breath. "Lady Pirnilla, the gift is more than you realize." She had the sensation that she was leaping from a cliff. "I beg that you not allow anyone else to touch it."

The woman looked at her sharply.

Britta lowered her voice. "Beneath the silk lining is some information for your husband. It's imperative that you give it to him as soon as possible—and in the strictest privacy."

Lady Pirnilla glanced around the garden, smiling. "What kind of information?"

"Information that's vital to Lundegaard's future. It must be given to your king."

The woman's gaze came back to her. Gray eyes regarded her steadily.

"I must beg that neither you nor your husband reveal that I'm the source of your information."

The ambassador's wife lifted a flower to her nose and sniffed. "And if my king should ask?"

Britta bit her lip. She looked at Yasma, standing

beside the rose bower. The maid's eyes were fixed on her, anxious. She returned her gaze to the ambassador's wife. "Your king, but no one else. Else my life will be forfeit." *And that of my maid.*

Lady Pirnilla regarded her steadily again, and then nodded. "You have my word, princess."

Britta inhaled a deep breath. *It's done.* "Thank you." She glanced at the armsmen lined up around the garden, at the chattering ladies, at the musicians plucking their harp strings, and then she turned away from the ambassador's wife and went to fetch another basket.

CHAPTER FORTY-EIGHT

THE WAILING ACCOMPANIED them for the rest of the afternoon, rising and falling with the wind. Even though he knew it wasn't the voices of the dead, even though he'd seen some of the bored holes that the wind whistled through, the ghost-like sound made Harkeld's skin crawl.

The witch, Gerit, flew back as the sun set, landing beside one of the fires. Harkeld looked away. The other shapeshifters hid their changes—or at the very least, didn't try to draw attention to themselves; Gerit seemed to derive perverse pleasure in the hastily averted heads, the mutterings of shock and distaste. *He delights in disgusting us*, he thought sourly.

"Ditmer's only three or so leagues ahead of us," Gerit said once he'd dragged on his clothes.

"Three leagues?" Tomas looked at him, startled.

Gerit grunted, a sound Harkeld took to mean *yes*, and hunkered down at the firepit, holding out his hands to the flames. "He's pushed his horses too hard, stupid whoreson. Several of 'em are lame."

"Three leagues," Tomas repeated thoughtfully. He fetched the map and spread it on the ground. "We'll catch up with him tomorrow."

"We have the advantage of numbers," his sergeant said, a lean man with sun-browned skin creased like leather.

"Yes." Tomas grinned, his teeth gleaming in the firelight. "This is a battle Ditmer won't win."

THEY WENT WITHOUT tents again; sleeping on the sand was easier, quicker. It was also colder. Harkeld wrapped himself in two blankets and lay down alongside his armsman. Despite his physical tiredness, sleep took a long time to come. His dreams were uneasy.

"Hold him down."

Harkeld jerked awake. Someone pinned him to the ground, a heavy weight on his back. He smelled sawdust and dirt: the training arena.

"His right hand." The voice was Jaegar's.

Harkeld bucked and struggled, trying to break free. The weight on his back became heavier, almost crushing. He could scarcely breathe. Hard fingers gripped his right wrist, extending his arm. He heard the sleek sound of a sword blade sliding from its scabbard.

"Hold him still."

Panic kicked in Harkeld's chest, and with the panic was the sensation of flames igniting inside him. Fire crackled through his veins and danced over his skin, lighting up the arena. He saw Jaegar's face, saw the crown woven into his hair, saw the upraised sword—

Harkeld jerked awake, a shout in his throat and a feeling of fire in his blood. His heart galloped in his chest, kicking against his ribs.

"Nightmare?" a woman asked alongside him.

Harkeld took a deep, shuddering breath. He turned his head.

Fingers lightly touched his cheek, stroking. "It was just a dream."

"I know." He rolled on his side, reaching for her, drawing her close.

Slender arms came around his neck.

For several minutes he just held her, while the thunderous pace of his pulse slowed and the sensation of fire running through him faded. Then he bent his head and found her mouth. It opened to him shyly.

The kiss was slow, thorough. Heat began to rise in him again. Not flames, this time, but arousal. Harkeld slid his hands down the smoothness of her back and pressed her more closely to him—the softness of her breasts and belly, the tickling curls at her groin. Heat flushed sharply under his skin—and with it, urgency. He nudged her legs apart with his knee. This was what he needed: the warmth and softness of a woman, the uncomplicated pleasure of sex.

She broke their kiss and drew back slightly. "Harkeld... I've never done this before."

He knew that voice. With the recognition came an image of her face: gray eyes, black hair, pale skin.

HARKELD JERKED AWAKE. He stared up at a starry sky. Night air was cold on his face. A body was pressed against his side: Justen. He heard his armsman's slow breathing.

Tell me I didn't just dream that.

He scrubbed his face with a hand, squeezing his eyes shut, trying to erase the dream from his mind—the witch's mouth opening for his kiss, her body pressing so softly and warmly against him. He'd been about to bed her, to bury himself in her. His body still wanted to. Arousal thrummed in his blood.

Not a witch. Never a witch.

Harkeld opened his eyes and stared up at the glittering stars. There was no wind, no wailing coming from the sandstone, no—

He stiffened. What was that?

Harkeld held his breath, listening. He heard the sound of men breathing in their sleep, the soft crunch of sand as the sentries paced, and then at the edge of his hearing... a faint scream?

He pushed up on one elbow. One of the sentries heard the movement. Starlight glinted on the man's cheek as he turned his head. "Sire?"

"Did you hear that?" Harkeld asked in a low voice.

"Hear what?"

He didn't answer, just listened, his ears straining. The faint sound came again. "That," he said. "Screaming."

"It's just the wind, sire."

The sentry was right—he *knew* that—but his subconscious told him there was danger out there, that something prowled in the darkness, that the distant screams came from a man's throat, not wind blowing through holes bored in rock.

Next I'll be believing in ghosts.

Harkeld shook his head angrily and lay back down. He pulled the blankets tightly around himself and shut his eyes.

* * *

THEY SET OFF before dawn. No one said anything, but Innis was aware of a change in the soldiers' mood. They loaded the packhorses with efficiency, but there was an edge of suppressed excitement as they worked, a quiet, grim eagerness. Captain Ditmer's party was less than ten miles ahead. Today they'd engage him and his men in battle.

And kill them.

She set her jaw and mounted, bringing her horse alongside Prince Harkeld's.

The canyon seemed particularly gray this morning, the pre-dawn light leaching the sandstone of all color. Even when the sky above their heads had lightened to a pale blue, the grayness persisted. Shadows seemed to cling to them all, man and beast.

The first puff of a dry breeze blew along the canyon from the desert. In its wake came a wail from the cliffs. Innis repressed a shiver and looked around her. Dawn was past, and yet shadows still shrouded the canyon—

The moment of insight was sharp. *Fool, they're not ordinary shadows*. It was the curse she was seeing, lying over them all, cloaking face and form more heavily than it had before.

Innis dropped back slightly from her place beside Prince Harkeld and caught Dareus's eye. A moment later he cantered up alongside her. "Do you see them?" she asked in a low voice. "The curse shadows? They're darker."

Dareus glanced around. His eyes narrowed.

Innis touched her heels to her horse's flanks,

coming abreast of Prince Harkeld again. The wailing rose around them, and with it, her uneasiness.

"We must halt!" Dareus called out.

Prince Tomas reined his horse, slowing it. "What?"

"The curse," Dareus said tersely. "Something's happening."

Tomas shouted a command. His voice echoed off the walls, blending with another keening wail.

The soldiers ahead of them halted.

Prince Tomas swung around to face Dareus. "What do you mean, happening?"

"The curse," Dareus said. "Something's changed."

"Changed? How?"

"I don't know." Dareus dismounted.

"What are you doing?" Prince Tomas demanded.

"Checking the water."

Innis jumped down from her horse and followed with the princes. They scrambled over the boulders of the dry riverbed after Dareus.

"You think the curse is in the water here?" Prince Tomas asked, his voice slightly higher than normal.

"It shouldn't be. Not yet." Dareus reached the trickling river. "Ivek created the curse to rise in the east and pass across the land until it set in the west, like the sun."

Tomas nodded. "That's what the stories say."

Dareus dropped down on one knee and scooped water in his cupped hands.

They crowded close—the princes, Gerit and Cora, herself—and watched as Dareus looked intently at the water. He raised it to his face, almost as if he smelled it.

"Well?" Prince Tomas asked. "Is it cursed?"

Dareus shook his head. "No. The water's fine." He opened his hands, letting the water splash to the ground, and turned his head, still crouched on one knee, scanning the canyon. "But something has changed. And not for the better."

"You're certain about the water?"

"Yes." Dareus stood, his face set in a frown.

"Perhaps the curse lies heavily here because we're nearing one of the anchor stones," Innis said.

"Perhaps. But I don't like it. It's... dangerous."

Innis followed his gaze, seeing the dark veil of the curse resting heavily on them all.

"It's not right," Dareus muttered under his breath.

Movement caught her eye: a hawk arrowing downward. Petrus, from its pale breast.

The hawk swept low over the dry riverbed, alighted on a boulder, and changed form. Petrus stood there, his face grim. "Ditmer's soldiers are all dead."

"Dead!" exclaimed Prince Tomas. "How—"

"I don't know," Petrus said. "There was fighting, but I don't think they were killed by men."

"Why not?" Cora asked. In contrast to Prince Tomas, her voice was calm.

"They've been torn to pieces."

Wailing whispered in the air around them, lifting the hairs on the nape of Innis's neck. "Wild animals?"

Gerit snorted. "Here?"

"Could it be the curse?" Prince Harkeld asked.

"I don't see how," Dareus said, beginning the scrambling journey back over the boulders to where the horses waited.

*   *   *

THEY RODE WARILY, the soldiers drawing close around them. Innis was aware of the weight of the sword strapped to her back, the snug fit of the baldric across her chest. Foreboding grew inside her—the stark barrenness of the canyon, the wailing that filled the dry air, the dark curse shadows, the tombs honeycombing the cliffs—all seemed filled with menace.

"Horses!"

The shouted word brought her head around. One of the soldiers was pointing ahead.

There were indeed horses, in a tight, nervous cluster on the other side of the stony riverbed.

They slowed to a trot. "Ditmer's," Tomas said as they came closer. "Do you think?"

Innis nodded silently.

They halted. The horses stared at them uneasily, jostling each other.

"Do we take them with us?" a soldier asked.

Innis glanced back at the long train of horses behind them—their own packhorses, and Captain Anselm's captured horses. "They'll die if we don't." There was water here for the beasts, but no food.

"We'll take them if we find supplies for them," Tomas said. "Ditmer's camp must be nearby."

They cantered again. The beat of hooves echoed back at them from the sandstone. The canyon swung east, the cliffs pulling back as it widened.

Tomas reined in his horse. "What the—"

Innis followed his gaze. The tombs lining the base of the cliffs had been broken open. Dark holes gaped in the stonework.

The damage looked fresh. The little piles of rubble hadn't been dispersed by the wind.

Gerit pushed his horse forward. "It wasn't like this a few days ago."

"Did Ditmer's men loot the tombs?" Prince Harkeld asked.

Gerit shrugged. "Not that I saw."

"They were fools if they did," Tomas said. "There's no treasure in these tombs. Everyone knows that."

Innis glimpsed what looked like a pile of dead leaves and bleached sticks inside the tomb nearest her. She averted her gaze.

A hundred yards further on, a wolf sat beside a stunted thorn bush. It shifted into Ebril as they approached.

"As far as I can tell, no one other than Ditmer and his men were here last night," he said, shading his eyes against the sun as he looked up at them. "The only human scents here belong to the dead."

"Animals?" one of the soldiers asked.

Ebril shook his head. "Only their horses."

"What do you smell?" Dareus asked.

"Ditmer's men. His horses. And the bodies from the tombs."

"From the tombs?" Tomas said. "Why would you smell them?"

"See for yourself." Ebril gestured behind him.

Tomas dismounted and strode in the direction Ebril pointed. Prince Harkeld followed.

Innis hastily slid from her horse, hurrying to keep up with the princes, the long sword in its scabbard slapping against her back. Behind her she heard the crunch of booted feet on stony ground as others followed.

The ground rose slightly in a low hump, and on the other side—

Innis halted alongside the two princes. She blinked, and for a moment was unable to take in what she saw. It was beyond comprehension, beyond what was possible. *Not real. This isn't real.*

Bodies lay strewn on the ground. Not one of them was whole. Limbs were scattered like children's toys. She saw legs and arms, a headless torso resting against a lump of red sandstone, and then she caught the stench of death—the heavy, coppery smell of blood, the smell of urine, of excrement, the smell of intestines torn open and exposed to the air.

Someone to her left began to retch. The smell of bile joined the others—a stomach-turning medley.

Innis swallowed and clenched her jaw. Her gaze jerked from one item to the next: a boot with someone's foot still in it; an outflung arm, its hand loosely curled around the hilt of a sword; a head staring at her from beside a thorn bush, eyes dusted with gritty red sand.

She looked away, towards the broken tombs, but even there, the slaughter continued: body parts were strewn across the churned-up sand.

"They'd raided the tombs," Ebril said quietly. "See? There are lots of pieces of the bodies."

Now that he pointed it out, she saw them: the dirty gray-white of old bones breaking through a covering of leathery skin, clumps of matted hair like dried brown grass, a grinning, toothless skull.

"But why would they desecrate the tombs?" Prince Harkeld asked. "You said there was no treasure."

"There isn't," Tomas said. "Everyone knows that."

"Everyone in Lundegaard," Innis said. "But these men were from Osgaard. They may not have known."

Prince Harkeld glanced at her and gave a curt nod of agreement.

Tomas stepped forward, and then looked back at Dareus, his expression as baffled as his voice. "What happened here?"

Dareus joined the prince, his face grim as he surveyed the litter of body parts. "There's no blood on any of the swords."

A number of weapons lay on the ground: daggers, dirks, swords. The blades glinted in the sunlight, clean.

"They weren't attacked by men, then," Tomas said. "Or animals."

Someone muttered behind her. Innis caught the word faintly: witches.

She opened her mouth to refute the charge, and then closed it. She was Justen, not a mage. *If I knew nothing of magic, what would I think?* she asked herself, staring at the massacre. Her eyes fastened on a hand lying palm-up on the sand, the fingers curled slightly as if in supplication. The fingernails were ragged, bitten almost to the quick. Magic couldn't tear men limb from limb, but the soldiers didn't know that—and nor would Justen.

Innis waited for the soldier behind her to speak his accusation more loudly. He didn't.

Then I shall. "Witches?"

Dareus glanced at her, his gaze sharp. Tomas looked at her, too. He gave a small nod and turned to Dareus. "Did your witches do this?"

Gerit pushed forward, anger livid on his face. "You whoreson—"

Dareus held up his hand, silencing Gerit. "No," he told Tomas. "We did not do this." There was no bluster in his voice, just a calm matter-of-factness that made his words utterly believable.

Prince Harkeld stirred beside her. "What of other witches?"

Ebril shook his head. "The only scents here belong to the dead. No one else was here last night."

"But the tracks—" Tomas gestured to the sand surrounding them. It was churned as if a hundred men had fought here, tracks leading in all directions.

"Go only to the tombs."

Beside her, Prince Harkeld rubbed his face. She heard the rasp of stubble beneath his hand. "Could the ancient Massens have left spells?" he asked. "Could this be punishment for Ditmer pillaging the tombs?"

The question hung in the silence for a moment, before being swallowed by a low moaning wail.

"Is that possible?" Tomas asked Dareus.

"Magic can't do this to people."

"Then what killed them?"

Dareus shook his head. "I don't know."

Wind gusted up the canyon behind them, bringing with it a flurry of sand and a long, sobbing note.

"Is this all of them?" a soldier asked.

Tomas shrugged and turned to face the slaughter again. "How does one count—?"

"The heads," Cora said. "Count the heads."

Innis obeyed automatically, her eyes skipping from one head to the next—eyes closed, eyes open and staring up at the sky, eyes looking straight at her.

"Fourteen," someone said.

"That's all of them, then," Tomas said. "No survivors."

Innis looked down at the ground in front of her—
red sand, red pebbles, a spraying arc of dried blood.
Against the red of sand and stone, the blood looked
almost black.

"They were sleeping," Tomas said.

She looked up. He was walking among the dead,
placing his feet with care. "See?" He pointed. "Many
of them weren't fully clothed.'

A noise came from behind her. Innis jerked around,
reaching for her sword. The noise came a second
time: nothing but the wind stirring the dry branches
of a thorn bush.

Ditmer's supplies lay undisturbed, a neat cache in
a sandy hollow. Grimly, hastily, the soldiers gathered
Ditmer's horses and strapped on the new loads of
food and firewood, grain for the horses, bundles of
arrows.

"Do we bury them?" someone asked, when it was
done.

If they'd killed Ditmer's men themselves, they
wouldn't have buried them, but Innis understood
the question: the violated bodies seemed to deserve
some mark of respect.

Tomas shook his head. "I want to get as far away
from here as possible."

A final item lay half-buried in the sand. Innis
picked it up: a sack tied with a drawstring. The
weave was tight, the stitching sturdy. She opened
it. Inside was a second sack, folded, and an empty
silver flask. For a moment she stood staring at it,
her brow creased. An empty silver flask? What use—

Then she understood: one sack was for Prince
Harkeld's head, the other for his hands, the flask

for his blood. She grimaced, and glanced at the massacred soldiers. They had deserved to die.

But not like this, a voice inside her whispered. *Not ripped apart.*

She threw the sacks and flask aside.

"What was that?" Prince Harkeld asked.

"Nothing."

They mounted. "Stay alert," Tomas instructed his soldiers.

They departed at a hard canter, two hawks skimming ahead of them and another soaring in the sky. The red sandstone walls towered threateningly over them and the very air they breathed seemed filled with menace. The broken tombs were like eyes, staring at them.

After a quarter of a mile the damage to the tombs stopped. Innis should have felt easier, safer, but she didn't. What had killed Ditmer and his men? Where was it now?

CHAPTER FORTY-NINE

KAREL DIDN'T SLEEP well. He kept waking, kept worrying. He rolled out of his bunk not long after the first bell. All around him, armsmen slumbered. *How can you sleep?* he wanted to shout. *Don't you know that something momentous is happening?*

He busied himself sharpening his sword, mending his clothes, rubbing wax into his boots. Then he set himself to punching a horsehair-filled sack, slamming his fists into it until his knuckles were raw. When the third bell rang, he made his way to the mess hall, tense and exhausted.

Karel ate, not tasting the food. What was happening in the palace? Had Lundegaard's ambassador acted yet? Had Duke Rikard discovered his wife's perfidy?

His mind wasn't on his training that morning; he lost two sword-fighting bouts. "Getting soft, islander," the second victor sneered.

Not soft. Worried.

Karel washed the sweat from his skin, dressed in his armsman's uniform, and finally, *finally*, it was time to go on duty.

He strode through the marble corridors, past bondservants scurrying on errands and strolling nobles. The atmosphere was hushed, calm. No rumors echoed beneath the high ceilings, no soldiers hurried past with their hands on their sword hilts.

All was quiet when he reached Duke Rikard's rooms. The duke was visiting his wife; the door to the bedchamber was closed.

The armsman assigned to Princess Brigitta was in the salon. "You're late," he said, even though the fifth bell was still ringing.

Karel ignored the jibe.

"Stupid whoreson," the armsman muttered under his breath, and left.

Karel took his place in the salon: shoulders back, feet twelve inches apart, staring straight ahead.

THE DAY PROCEEDED on its course. Duke Rikard left. Yasma checked on the sleeping princess. Karel paced the salon, too tense to stand still. Outside, clouds darkened the sky. The room didn't glitter today; the gilt seemed dull, the crimson upholstery as dark as dried blood. He felt a sense of building doom. The princess's head was in a noose, and they all waited for the rope to jerk tight.

He swung around at the sound of a door opening.

Yasma exited the bedchamber. She looked as weary as he felt. She smiled at him briefly and walked into the formal dining room. After a moment, Karel followed.

Yasma sat at the long table, several large sheets of parchment in front of her. As he watched, she dipped a quill in ink and leaned over the parchment.

Does the duke suspect anything? he wanted to ask. Instead, he said, "What are you doing?"

The maid glanced up. "Drawing pictures." She yawned and rubbed her face. "Britta wants to visit her brothers, but she says she has to draw them pictures first. I thought I'd do one for her."

Karel strolled across to the table, trying to look relaxed. "What's that? A dog?"

Yasma looked down at the drawing. "A horse."

Karel reached across and took the quill from her fingers. "Here. Let me." It would give him something to do other than stand and worry.

"But—"

"Lie down," he told her firmly. "Rest."

BRITTA WOKE TO the sound of someone moving in the bedchamber. The noises were too quiet for the duke. She opened her eyes. Yasma stood beside the bed.

"I have a drawing for you to take to your brothers."

Britta bathed quickly, washing the duke off her skin, and then dressed. She knew she should be worried, but it was impossible when serenity cloaked her.

"The drawing, princess."

She unrolled the sheet of parchment and blinked. Her mouth fell open. "Oh..."

Soldiers rode on horseback through a forest. Hidden among the trees, watching, were archers. In the sky above, a bird with a curved beak and outspread wings flew. Other animals roamed in the forest. She saw long-tailed monkeys swinging between the branches, a huge serpent slithering up the trunk of a tree, a wolf with its head raised to howl. Stalking the wolf, axe raised, was a burly woodsman. Her eyes skimmed the drawing, noting the details: the feathers on the bird's wings, the diamond pattern on the serpent's skin. The animals almost seemed to move. Wasn't that the flick of a monkey's tail? The blink of a bird's eye?

"Yasma, this is marvelous!"

"Karel did it."

Her serenity faltered. Britta looked up, her fingers tightening on the parchment. "Karel?"

"I'm not very good at drawing."

Britta looked at the picture again, but the spell was broken. She saw black ink on white parchment—trees, soldiers, horses. Nothing moved.

Slowly, she rolled up the sheet of parchment. Why had the armsman drawn it? "Do you talk with Karel?"

"Sometimes. He's my friend."

Friend. A harmless word. And yet...

"What do you talk with him about?"

Yasma blinked, looking confused. "Things."

"About me?"

The maid flushed. "Sometimes."

Britta stared at her, feeling suddenly afraid. "Does he know?"

"Know?" Yasma blinked again, and then understanding dawned on her face. "Of course not, princess! I swore never to tell anyone." She took the roll of parchment from Britta, hesitated, and then said: "But he's guessed that something's happening."

The room seemed to lurch slightly, and then steady again. "He's what?"

Yasma twisted the roll between her hands, anxiety creasing her brow. "He could see that you were different. He... he asked me if you were planning something."

Fear clenched in Britta's throat. It was suddenly difficult to breathe. "What did you say?"

"I didn't tell him."

But he suspects. Britta tried to swallow, but fear was too tight in her throat. She turned away from the maid.

Yasma came after her, clutching the roll of parchment. "Princess, you can trust Karel. He won't betray you."

"He's an armsman, Yasma." Her voice sounded harsh. "He's sworn allegiance to Osgaard's crown. His loyalty is to my father, not me."

"When you taught me to read, you did it in front of Karel! You trusted him not to betray us!"

Britta closed her eyes, trying to think past the haze of fear and poppy juice. "I trusted him not to betray *you*. Because he's an islander."

"He would never betray you either," Yasma said. "I know he wouldn't!"

WHEN SHE EMERGED from her bedchamber, the armsman was standing at parade rest on the other side of the salon. The scarlet and gold uniform was the first thing she saw, then his brown skin and black hair, his hawk-like features and expressionless face.

Britta crossed the room slowly. She halted in front of the armsman, holding the roll of parchment. "You drew this for my brothers, Karel?"

"Yes, princess." His voice was as impassive as his face.

"Thank you," Britta said. "The children will love it."

He dipped his head slightly in acknowledgement, and opened the door for her.

Britta gripped the roll of parchment more tightly. Three years, he'd been assigned to her. Three years. And yet she had no idea who he really was. He was simply her armsman.

He's Yasma's friend. She trusts him.

Britta walked through into the antechamber. Karel passed her and opened the far door. The white marble corridors of the palace loomed on the other side.

Her gaze fastened on the armsman as he stood to attention, on the Osgaardan crest stamped into the gleaming metal. He looked dangerous: the hard muscles beneath his skin, the sword belted at his hip, the dark eyes.

What was he thinking as he watched her?

CHAPTER FIFTY

THEY REACHED THE top of the pass not long before dusk. The miller halted. It had taken them two days to reach this point, the road winding its way along the flanks of the hills, through fir forest, past farms and one half-empty village. Jaumé had learned that the family was from Andín and that the man was a miller. He learned the boys names were Luc and Gerrey. Luc was the same age Rosa had been: five. Gerrey was three.

"There you are, lad." The miller pointed. "The sea."

They ate while the sun set. The miller and his wife shared their food with him: bread, cheese, cured meat.

The world was spread before them. A plain stretched north, south, west. It looked like a quilt, a patchwork of fields and villages. In the distance, the dark blue of the sea blended into the paler sky. "Are we safe now?" Jaumé asked.

The miller shook his head. "We won't be safe until we're on the other side of the sea."

"Where's the other side?" Jaumé asked.

"Lundegaard," the miller said. "Or Osgaard. But the curse will reach there in time. To be truly safe, we need to get to the Allied Kingdoms, up over the equator."

Jaumé stored the names carefully in his memory. Lundegaard. Osgaard. The Allied Kingdoms.

THEY SLEPT UNDER the wagon. In the middle of the night, Jaumé woke. The miller and his wife were arguing in quiet voices.

"—only eight years old," the miller said.

"We'll run out of food."

"But—"

"You must think of your sons!"

IN THE MORNING, the miller said, "We'll part ways with you here, lad."

Jaumé hugged his blanket more tightly around him and nodded.

"Just follow this road," the miller said. "When you reach Cornas, find a ship that will take you away from here."

Jaumé nodded again. Lundegaard. Osgaard. The Allied Kingdoms. The names were engraved in his memory.

He watched the miller harness the horses and attach them to the shaft. The children scrambled into the wagon. The miller climbed up on the driver's seat. At the last moment, the miller's wife thrust half a loaf of bread at him. "Here," she said, and then she bundled her skirts in one hand and clambered up alongside her husband.

The miller looked down at him. "Be careful, lad. It's every man for himself."

Jaumé nodded, clutching the bread.

The wagon started forward. The children waved at him.

Jaumé lifted a hand in farewell. He watched the wagon until it was out of sight.

CHAPTER FIFTY-ONE

THEY COVERED MORE than ten leagues, pushing
the horses to their limits, before stopping for the
day. Tomas chose a defensive position: a low, rocky
mound beneath an overhang of sandstone. Nothing
could surprise them from behind.

Petrus changed places with Innis and ate his
dinner alongside the princes, Justen's amulet warm
and smooth against his breastbone.

It was a tense, silent meal. Petrus didn't lay aside
his weapons to eat. The baldric was tight across his
chest, the sword a comforting weight against his
back.

Gerit circled down as daylight faded from the sky.
Wind gusted fitfully, producing deep moaning notes,
and above them, one shriek.

"Anything?" Tomas asked, once Gerit had shifted
into human form.

Gerit shook his head. "No one and nothing. We're
alone." Cora handed him his clothes. He pulled
them on.

Prince Tomas nodded. He stood and raised his
voice: "Tonight we'll have double sentries. If we're
attacked, don't panic. We have advantages Captain

Ditmer didn't have." Tomas looked around the circle of soldiers, meeting each man's eyes. "There are more of us. We're prepared. And we have the witches to fight with us."

Petrus glanced at Innis. She was watching Prince Tomas, her face grave.

"Remember: nothing is more important than Harkeld's life. He *must* survive. Lundegaard dies if he dies."

Petrus glanced at Prince Harkeld. The prince was staring at the ground. His mouth was tight.

He found himself unexpectedly sorry for the man. *Poor sod*.

Tomas turned to Prince Harkeld. "If we're attacked, I want you back there." He pointed at the overhang of rock.

The prince looked up. His mouth tightened still further, but he nodded.

Tomas turned back to his soldiers. "You heard what Gerit said. There's nothing out there. The only things disturbing your sleep will be the man next to you farting." The joke garnered a burst of loud, nervous laughter. "First sentries on duty now." Tomas nodded at his sergeant. "Be extra vigilant." The directive was unnecessary. Memory of what they'd seen must be as vivid for the soldiers as it was for him. Petrus could still see it if he closed his eyes.

Prince Tomas sat. His sergeant began to give orders, directing the sentries to their posts.

"Justen."

Petrus looked across at Tomas. "Yes, sire?"

"If we're attacked, stay back with Harkeld."

Petrus nodded, relieved by the order. If whatever

had attacked Ditmer attacked them, he didn't want Innis anywhere near the fighting.

"You're the last barrier between him and whatever is out there."

Petrus nodded again.

"What about you?" Prince Harkeld asked. His tone was sour. "Where will you be? At the back, too?"

Tomas grinned. "Is that self-pity I hear?"

Prince Harkeld grunted.

The color drained from the sandstone cliffs as darkness gathered in the canyon. The wind fell and the wailing died away to a faint moan.

Petrus yawned, and listened idly to the princes talk. He glanced around, noting the sentries. Six men, facing out into the canyon.

He frowned. The curse shadows had darkened with the setting of the sun.

Something moved near his foot. He caught a glimpse of a small shape scuttling on the sand and jerked his boot aside.

"Scorpion." Tomas shied a stone at the creature. "Time to put out the fire." He stood and kicked sand into the fire pit, smothering the flames.

Petrus stood. "Won't be a minute," he said to Prince Harkeld.

He made his way away from the smoking fire pit. It was fully dark now. As he passed the mages, he nodded to Innis. *Time to swap.*

In the deep shadow of the overhang Petrus removed the baldric. He felt naked without it, vulnerable. He shivered, and shrugged off Justen's woolen cloak.

"You must be exhausted," Innis said, kicking off

her boots. "You've been shifted most of the day."

He was, but he wasn't going to admit it to her. He ignored the comment. "Tomas said that if we're attacked, Justen is to stay with the prince."

Innis stilled. He dimly saw her face, a pale blur in the darkness. "Do you think—"

"We'll be fine," Petrus said confidently. But privately, he wasn't so sure. The heaviness of the curse shadows made him uneasy.

Across the canyon, the silence of night was broken by the clatter of falling stones. Petrus froze, listening. The sound was loud. It echoed for a long time, bouncing off the sandstone walls.

"Sentry," he said, not believing it.

"That came from the other side of the river," Innis said.

"Rockfall, then." Another clattering cascade of sound swallowed his words. This time it was closer to them, on this side of the river. Petrus turned his head, trying to pinpoint the source.

Around the smothered fire came a stir of voices, of alarm.

Someone ran towards them with sharp, gritty footfalls. "Innis!" It was Dareus. "There's something out there. See what it is. Owl."

She obeyed instantly. Petrus heard the whisper of her clothes falling to the ground as she shifted, felt the rush of air as she took off.

"I'll go too—"

"No." Dareus's fingers closed around his wrist, hard. "Be Justen. Stay with the prince."

*　　*　　*

INNIS FLEW SWIFTLY. The clatter of falling rock was loud. She swooped low, heading for the nearest source. Her owl's eyes saw clearly: it was one of the tombs. The stone and mortar buckled, as if something inside tried to batter its way out. Rock showered down, bouncing and skittering across the canyon floor.

A cadaverous body hauled itself out of the tomb.

Innis shied in the air. Her eyes refused to believe what she saw.

The thing stood, lurching. It wasn't a skeleton; the bones were clothed in leathery skin, the domed skull surmounted by a thatch of withered hair. It was cloaked in curse shadows, so darkly shrouded that she could scarcely make out the empty eye sockets. The blind head turned as if seeking something.

Shouts rose behind her. Innis wheeled and headed back to the campsite, flying as fast as she could. The canyon was alive with movement. Stones sprayed down as more tombs burst open. Dark figures stumbled free of their resting places, too many to count.

A shrill neigh of panic captured her attention. She saw the horses rearing, kicking, tearing loose from their tethers. The thunder of their hooves echoed deafeningly as they galloped down the canyon, trampling everything in their path.

Fire flared in the firepit. She saw the soldiers in a ring facing outward, their bared swords glinting, saw Prince Harkeld and Justen behind them, swords raised, saw Ebril and Gerit pacing in front, snarling lions. Advancing on them were scores of warriors. They had arms and legs, heads, but those dark, lurching shapes had been dead for more than a thousand years.

Dareus cast a fire ball. Two of the corpses flared alight, but there was no faltering in the shuffling advance. *They have no fear.*

She arrowed downward, changing to a lioness as her feet touched the ground. Smells invaded her nose: the scent of ancient decay, the sharp odor of fear coming from the soldiers behind her.

Gerit opened his mouth in a roar. He charged at the advancing figures, scattering them, bowling them over.

Innis echoed the roar. She launched herself at the nearest warrior. It collapsed beneath her weight. She swiped with a sharp-clawed paw, snapping its neck, fastened her gaze upon the next corpse and leapt at it, snarling. Bones broke beneath her weight as the corpse tumbled to the ground. The skull separated from the neck and rolled, bouncing, beneath the feet of its comrades.

Innis leapt at the next corpse, knocking it down. She sank her teeth into its neck and ripped the head off. Bone and leathery skin disintegrated in her mouth. She spat, gagging, and looked for her next prey, launching herself forward.

A corpse blazed alight to her right, burning like a torch.

Innis glanced back. The corpses she'd beheaded were on their feet, shuffling towards the fire.

More gouts of flame erupted; more ancient warriors flared alight. They burned silently, their mouths open in soundless screams, crackling fiercely as fire consumed them.

A lion roared. Ebril. She couldn't see him. A jostling wall of corpses surrounded her.

Innis leapt at the nearest one, knocking it down. Dry, sinewy arms reached for her. Dozens of hands clawed at her. She roared and bit, struggling. The arms tightened around her neck, surprisingly strong, as if Ivek's curse had regenerated ancient tendons and muscles. Panic surged inside her. She shifted—a mouse, tiny, running between bony feet, then an owl, flapping swiftly up into the sky.

The canyon floor seethed with movement. Hundreds of corpses were converging on the campsite. Those behind marched relentlessly over the bodies of the fallen. Armless, they came. Headless, they came. Those who'd lost their legs dragged themselves with their hands.

Panic swelled inside her. *Nothing will stop them.*

The soldiers fought fiercely, swinging their blades, severing arms and legs, heads—but the creatures didn't falter in their advance. As Innis watched, one soldier disappeared beneath a swarming tangle of corpses. His scream rose in the air.

Innis dove and launched herself into the battle again. A lion was no good. She needed to be *big*.

CHAPTER FIFTY-TWO

HARKELD GRIPPED HIS sword and watched the soldiers struggle to hold back the tide of corpses. The creatures' silent ferocity was as terrifying as their sightless faces. The lions roared and fought, the fire witches cast balls of flame, but for every corpse that flared alight, every corpse the lions tore apart and the soldiers hacked to pieces, a dozen more stepped forward. The sheer number was overwhelming. They stretched as far into the darkness as his eyes could see, an endless, jostling mass of bodies. *We're all going to die.*

Movement on the ground caught his eye—a severed arm, fingers working like spider's legs, scrabbled over the sand towards him. Harkeld raised his sword and slashed at it, cutting it at the elbow.

The fingers kept moving, surprisingly fast, scrambling towards him.

Harkeld swung again, slashed again, cutting the arm off at the wrist. The hand still scuttled forward, like an immense, grotesque spider, the fingers finding purchase on his boot, scrambling up over the toe.

He kicked, trying to shake the thing off. The hand gripped his ankle with tight, bony fingers and hung on.

Harkeld threw down his sword. He tore the hand off, snapping the brittle fingers, throwing them away. The palm fell to the ground—gray bone, leathery skin—where it lay twitching.

Harkeld snatched up his sword again. His heart was beating too fast.

"Sire?"

"I'm fine." He jerked around as a panicked scream rose in the air. Another soldier was dragged off his feet. The man's cry cut off as he vanished beneath a seething mass of corpses.

Harkeld gripped his sword more tightly and started forward. If he was going to die, he'd die fighting.

Dareus thrust him back. "No."

Flames crackled from the witch's outstretched hand. Two corpses flared alight. Fire seemed to lick across Harkeld's skin, sizzling. He jerked away from Dareus's grip, stumbling back, falling to one knee. It felt as if a bonfire had ignited in his chest.

Justen hauled him to his feet. "Behind me, sire!"

A brassy, trumpeting cry rang over the battle, echoing off the canyon walls. Justen's head jerked around. He uttered a hoarse, disbelieving laugh. "An oliphant!"

Harkeld followed his armsman's gaze. There was indeed an oliphant. The creature towered over the milling corpses. Each of its legs was the size of a tree trunk. As he watched, open-mouthed, it charged, cutting a wide swath in the horde of dead, crushing them underfoot, the wicked tusks spearing the desiccated husks that had once been men.

The oliphant tossed its head. Skewered bodies smashed to the ground.

"Who is it?" he asked, but the creature screamed its brassy battle cry again, swallowing the sound of his voice. It charged once more, impaling the dead on its tusks, trampling them beneath its great feet. The huge gray trunk unfurled. It plucked a corpse from those pressing the soldiers and tossed it aside, smashing it against the canyon wall, plucked again and tossed again.

Another trumpeting cry rang out. There were two oliphants now, charging among the corpses. No, three of the creatures.

We may actually survive this.

But even as Harkeld thought the words, one of the soldiers stumbled and fell. A severed hand gripped the man's ankle, the leathery arm trailing in the sand. The corpses surged forward. The fallen soldier gave a shout and struck out with his sword, swinging upward, burying the blade deep in a bony ribcage. Gnarled hands grabbed the sword, yanking it from his grasp, grabbed at the soldier, fastening on his arms, on his legs. The man screamed and disappeared into the teeming corpses. They surged over him, like ants engulfing a piece of food. A high shriek of agony ended as abruptly as it started.

Flames roared up, consuming the corpses. They fell back from the fallen soldier, charred.

Harkeld clenched his jaw and looked away from what was left of the man.

THE NIGHT SEEMED endless, as if the sun would never rise again. They fought grimly—soldiers, mages—the darkness punctuated by bursts of fire.

Petrus stayed where he'd been ordered, guarding Prince Harkeld. It took every ounce of willpower he possessed. He watched with gritted teeth, every muscle in his body tense with the need to join in, to fight.

He concentrated on what little he could do, watching the corpses' amputated hands and arms, shouting warnings to the desperately fighting soldiers, hacking into pieces those crawling limbs that were within reach of his sword.

Some time after midnight a subtle change occurred. The corpses still came relentlessly, but the sheer weight of their numbers was no longer overwhelming. They arrived in twos and threes, not in their dozens, marching over the trampled fragments and charred remains of their comrades. Petrus knew that if they could just keep on their feet, they'd make it to dawn.

Prince Harkeld pushed forward again.

"No—" he started to say.

"There's no danger now," the prince said roughly. "We've won this battle."

Petrus took his place at Prince Harkeld's side, hacking and slashing, butchering men who'd been dead for centuries. After an hour his arm began to ache, after two, it was trembling, after three, the muscles began to cramp—yet still the corpses came, trudging across the sandy floor of the canyon to their second deaths.

Ebril and Gerit fought in human form now, wielding swords, not tusks. Only one oliphant patrolled the darkness, crushing the dead beneath its feet—Innis. She had to be as tired as them all, yet she still had the strength to maintain the shift.

Fewer and fewer corpses arrived at the firepit. "Rest your men," Prince Harkeld told Tomas. "Justen and I can deal with this."

Tomas didn't argue. He stepped back. Petrus was aware of soldiers slumping wearily to the ground behind him. It sounded as if someone were weeping.

Petrus raised his sword as another of the creatures lurched into the firelight, and lowered it as Prince Harkeld stepped forward. He watched the prince grimly and methodically dismember the corpse, taking off its head, its arms and legs, and then hacking each limb into pieces. In the darkened canyon Innis trumpeted again. He heard the stomp of her feet as she trampled more corpses.

Hour after interminable hour passed and then, gradually, almost imperceptibly, the sky lightened into the gray of pre-dawn. The corpses stopped advancing. Petrus stood, his sword half-raised, watching as dark, shadowy shapes stumbled back towards the tombs in the cliffs.

The sky became lighter. The last corpse scrambled into a gaping tomb on the far side of the canyon. The only thing moving on the battlefield now was the oliphant.

Petrus sheathed his sword. He flexed his cramped fingers. His hands shook. No, all of him shook— with exhaustion, with relief. It seemed impossible that he'd survived the night, impossible that any of them had lived through that nightmarish battle. He glanced behind him. Soldiers lay exhausted on the ground.

"Twelve dead," Prince Harkeld said. "Including one of the witches."

"What?" Petrus swung around to look at him. "Who?"

"Either the girl or Petrus," the prince said. He gestured at the oliphant. "Whoever that isn't."

"Uh..." Petrus blinked, and then squinted up at the sky, shading his eyes with one hand. "I saw a hawk up there a couple of minutes ago. Had a pale breast. Petrus, I reckon."

Prince Harkeld grunted. He sheathed his blade—a slow movement, as if his muscles ached—and lowered himself down to sit.

Petrus glanced behind him again, counting the survivors. Eleven soldiers were missing. His eyes skipped from person to person—Cora, Ebril, Gerit lying stretched out on the sand. Tomas sat beside Gerit, his head hanging, clearly exhausted. Dareus still stood, but as Petrus watched, he sank down on the sand, his face soot-stained and drawn, haggard.

Petrus sat down stiffly. He felt as aching and weary as an old man. He wiped his face. His skin was sweaty, sooty. Pieces of corpse littered the ground around him. Fingers, mostly, the dirty white of bone showing through the leathery skin. All he could taste, all he could smell, was burnt corpse.

He lifted his head wearily and watched as the oliphant lumbered towards them. One large, gray ear was ripped almost in half and caked with dried blood.

The oliphant shrank as it walked, becoming a black dog. Its ear was still torn. The dog picked its way carefully through the carnage, between the piles of broken corpses, past the smoldering fires. It panted, its tongue hanging from its mouth.

"Is there any water?" someone asked hoarsely, behind him.

Petrus was abruptly thirsty. His throat burned with thirst, hurt with it.

Tomas pushed to his feet with a groan. "We'll drink and eat," he said. "And then we'll bury the dead. And find the horses."

Petrus closed his eyes for a moment. All those tasks required more energy than he possessed. He touched the Grooten disc beneath his shirt—*Give me strength, All-Mother*—then opened his eyes and stood.

"Justen..." Someone spoke in a low voice, barely audible above the sound of soldiers clambering to their feet.

He looked around. Dareus beckoned, a tiny gesture.

Petrus walked across to him.

"Ah, Justen," Dareus said more loudly, as if he'd only just noticed him. "Would you be so kind as to help me to stand?"

"Of course." He held out his hand.

Dareus gripped it. "How are you?" he asked in a low voice. "Can you continue as Justen? I need Innis for something else."

Petrus nodded. "The prince has noticed I'm missing," he said in a whisper. "I said I'd seen a hawk flying."

Dareus nodded. "Thank you for your assistance," he said loudly.

INNIS COULDN'T FIND the clothes she'd been wearing; they lay somewhere beneath a smoking pile of corpses. She wrapped a blanket around herself instead. Right now, she didn't care what the soldiers or Prince Harkeld thought of her. In fact—she glanced at the filthy, weary faces—she doubted they noticed, let alone cared, that she wasn't clothed.

They ate in silence. Everything tasted of soot, of death.

When they'd finished, no one made a move to stand. Innis touched her ripped ear. Blood caked it. She should wash it, heal it; instead she ran a fingertip along the edges, sealing them. Small magic. The rest could wait. Exhaustion dragged at her, weighing down her limbs. She looked across the canyon. The red sand was hidden beneath a carpet of brown, gray-white, and black. Brown limbs lay strewn, graying ribcages gaped upward to the sky, charred bodies lay where they'd fallen. And buried beneath those things were eleven of Lundegaard's soldiers.

A breeze stirred along the canyon, bending the sluggish columns of smoke, coaxing a faint wail from the sandstone walls.

Prince Tomas stood. "We need to find our men. Bury them." His mouth tightened. "They died well. It was a terrible battle."

"It's a battle we'll have to fight again tonight," Dareus said.

Tomas's face blanched beneath the soot. "What?"

"This—" Dareus gestured to the carnage, "is the result of Ivek's curse, something he's done to guard the anchor stone."

"But I've been up here before," Tomas objected. "We've never encountered—"

"You haven't been here since the curse came into its power," Dareus said. "This is why the curse shadows became darker yesterday: we crossed a boundary. From now on, we'll face this each night."

"Is there another route?" Prince Harkeld asked. "Do we have to stay in the canyon?"

"We'd never get the horses out." Tomas gestured at the sheer cliffs. "And the only water's here."

"How many days is it to Ner?"

"Four, maybe five."

"We can do it," Dareus said. "Innis, are you up to another shift? I want you to fly ahead. Find somewhere we can camp tonight. Something we can fortify."

Another shift. So soon. Her weariness was bone-deep—but of all of them, she was the one most able to do it. She nodded.

"No more than six or seven leagues," Dareus said.

Innis nodded again.

"The first oliphant—that was you, wasn't it?"

"Yes."

"You did well, Innis."

A flush heated her cheeks. She was aware of others looking at her—Prince Tomas, Prince Harkeld, Justen.

"Yes," Tomas said, his face sooty and sincere. "Thank you."

Beside him, Prince Harkeld nodded.

Dareus turned away from her. "Ebril, are you up to a shift? We need to find the horses. Petrus is already looking for them. See if you can find him."

Innis fingered her ear again, checking the wound. Then she gathered her magic and shifted. The blanket slid from her back, pooling around her. Prince Harkeld was still watching her. His expression was indecipherable.

Innis stepped free of the blanket. She extended her wings, allowing a sense of her new form to fill her for a few seconds—the clarity of vision, the lightness of her bones—then she launched herself up into the sky. Even tired, the pleasure of flying caught her, as her wings caught the breeze.

PETRUS WORKED ALONGSIDE Prince Harkeld, heaving aside desiccated limbs and hollow heads, crumbling torsos, searching for the fallen soldiers. Guilt rode him, a heavy weight on his shoulders. Such a gruesome death. If he and Prince Harkeld had fought with the soldiers from the beginning, would some of these men have lived?

He pushed a smoking carcass out of the way, uncovering the body of another soldier. The man's back was charred. Carefully he rolled the soldier over. His face was unburned. Tomas's sergeant. The man's teeth were bared in a grimace of agony. The half-open eyes seemed to stare at him accusingly.

Petrus looked away. He wiped his face with a forearm, smearing soot and sweat. "Here's another one."

Tomas came to stand beside him. He looked down at his sergeant for a long moment and then sighed. "He's the last."

Petrus helped dig shallow graves. They were interring the last body when hoof beats echoed up the canyon. He leaned on his shovel, panting, and watched as three soldiers cantered up, leading the horses Ebril had found.

"That's not all of them," Tomas said.

"Lots of leg injuries," a soldier said, sliding from a horse's back. "Not fit to ride. Some we killed. Others..." He grimaced and shrugged. "We didn't have time to hunt them all down."

They loaded the horses once the final grave was filled and the words committing the men to the All-Mother's care had been spoken. The corpses had been single-minded in their purpose; the neatly stacked sacks and saddlebags, the bundles of firewood and arrows, had been left untouched. Petrus was strapping the last of the wood on a weary mare when Innis glided down from the sky.

He watched her land. Dareus held out a blanket, shielding her as she shifted, a small privacy.

Petrus fastened the last strap and followed Tomas and Prince Harkeld to where Innis stood. She was talking to Dareus, the blanket hugged around her shoulders. "...about five leagues," he heard her say as they approached.

"And it's big enough for us all?" Dareus asked.

Innis nodded.

"Then we'll camp there tonight," Dareus said. He turned to Tomas. "An outcrop of rock, large enough for us all. We can rest once we're there."

Tomas nodded.

"Innis, keep watch. If you see any movement at all—ahead or behind us—check it out. We can't afford more surprises."

Innis nodded. "I will."

Petrus opened his mouth to protest. Dareus caught his eye and gave an almost imperceptible shake of his head.

Petrus closed his mouth. He waited until Tomas

and Prince Harkeld had headed back to the horses, then spoke in a fierce whisper: "Innis has been shifted too long! She needs to be herself."

"She can't," Dareus said. "We need someone up there." He pointed at the broad ribbon of sky above them. "Neither Ebril nor Gerit have the strength, they're exhausted. Which leaves you." He pinned Petrus with his gaze. "Can you do it?"

Petrus gritted his teeth. Exhaustion trembled in his muscles, but more than that, it trembled in his blood, in the very core of him. He only had the strength for one more shift: back into himself. "No," he admitted.

"Then it must be Innis."

He looked at her, seeing the fatigue, the smears of soot, the dried blood on her neck. "Innis—"

"If I feel I'm near my limit, I'll change back into myself. I promise, Petrus."

Petrus gave a short nod, and turned away.

CHAPTER FIFTY-THREE

WHEN BRITTA WOKE, gray daylight filled the bedchamber. It was raining outside. She heard light footsteps and turned her head. Yasma stood on the other side of the bed. "Any news?"

The maid shook her head.

Britta climbed out of bed slowly. She was stiff this morning. Fresh bruises marked her skin, the color of half-ripe plums.

Yasma fussed over her, leading her to the bathtub. Britta lowered herself into the steaming water and began to wash. She paused. "What's that sound?"

The noise came again: a faint crash.

Yasma hurried out into the bedchamber. A moment later, she was back. Her eyes were wide with fear. "The duke's in his study. He's looking for something."

It's starting.

Britta pushed to her feet. Water cascaded over the side of the golden bathtub. "Quickly. I need to dress."

She toweled herself roughly dry, dragged on a linen shift, and then stood still while Yasma laced her into an undergown. The cream-white silk covered her from throat to wrist to ankle, hiding the marks Duke Rikard had left on her skin.

"The tunic, princess." Yasma held out rose-pink silk stitched with silver thread. Behind her, the door jerked open. Duke Rikard stood on the threshold.

Britta's breath stuck in her throat. She couldn't move, could only stand and stare at him.

The duke advanced into the bathing chamber. His face was flushed. With anger this time, not lust.

Britta swallowed. "My lord?" Her voice trembled slightly. "You're back early."

Duke Rikard pushed Yasma out of his way. He grabbed Britta's shoulder, pulled her towards him, shook her. "Have you been in my study?"

This close she could smell him, smell his sweat, his anger.

"*Have you?*" he yelled, shaking her again.

"Of course not," Britta said, but her voice was breathless and afraid, not firm. "Why would I?"

His grip tightened on her shoulder. "To betray Osgaard."

Britta's heart beat too loudly in her chest, too fast. *He knows.* Behind him, she saw Yasma. The maid's face was terrified.

The girl's terror steadied her. *Be strong.* Too much was at stake here: her own life, Yasma's life.

Britta took a deep breath and wrenched free from the duke's grip. She lifted her chin. "Have you forgotten that I am your king's daughter? How dare you accuse me of betraying my country!" Her voice rang in the bathing chamber.

"You spoke with the ambassador's wife."

"Which ambassador's wife?"

"Lundegaard." Duke Rikard spat out the word, as if it tasted foul in his mouth. "You spoke with her!"

"Of course I did. She was my guest." Britta turned to Yasma. "The tunic, girl."

Yasma stepped forward. She lifted the tunic and placed it carefully over Britta's head, twitching the seams into place across her shoulders, smoothing the silk. Her hands trembled as she worked.

"I spoke to the ambassadors' wives from Ankeny and Sault," Britta said coolly. "And Roubos. Is that also a crime of treason?" She walked into the bedchamber and sat down in front of the mirror. Her crown rested on the gilded table top, gleaming.

Duke Rikard followed her.

Britta picked up the crown. The gold was cool beneath her fingers. *See, I am a royal princess. I would never betray Osgaard.* She placed it on her head.

Usually the crown felt like a shackle, something that kept her imprisoned, like the iron band Yasma wore around her arm. This morning it felt like a soldier's helm, protecting her. Britta watched in the mirror as the duke came to stand behind her. "What has happened, my lord, that you speak of treason?"

Duke Rikard's face stiffened. She saw anger, and beneath that, something else: fear.

His fear gave her courage. "Well, my lord?"

"Ambassador Alrik departed the palace overnight, taking his wife and staff."

And the invasion plans. A quicksilver gleam of emotion stirred in her chest: relief, hope. "I fail to see that this is reason to accuse anyone of treason."

In the mirror, she saw Duke Rikard clench his hands. "Someone must have told him."

"Told him what?" Britta looked over her shoulder. "Yasma," she said, an edge of impatience in her voice. "Hurry along, girl. I'm waiting."

The duke stepped back a pace as Yasma scurried forward.

"Told him what?" Britta repeated, as the maid began to dress her hair. The overt terror was gone from Yasma's face, but her fingers weren't as deft as usual.

"Told him about... information in my study."

"I assure you, my lord, I haven't entered your study. Why should I?" She tried to sound bored, disinterested.

"Someone has." The duke's gaze turned to Yasma. "This bondservant, perhaps."

Yasma fumbled as she wove the crown into place.

For a moment Britta sat frozen, unable to think past panic, and then she uttered a shaky laugh. "My maid? A slow-witted islander who can neither read nor write?" Her voice was scornful.

The duke flushed. "She has reason to wish us ill, like all her kin."

"And reason to be very conscientious in her service to us! Her family's freedom rests on her shoulders, their very lives. What bondservant would risk such a thing?" As Britta spoke the words, she realized what she'd asked of Yasma. She glanced at her maid in the mirror. *I'm sorry, Yasma. I was thinking only of myself.*

Rage built on the duke's face. "Someone has been in my study—"

"Are you so certain?" Britta said. "Surely you're not the only person who was party to this information?"

The question hung in the air. She saw the duke's

eyes narrow, saw his brow furrow slightly, saw doubt cross his face.

"Look elsewhere for your traitor, my lord." Her tone was almost an order. "You will not find him here."

Duke Rikard's lips compressed. He looked at her face in the mirror, at the golden crown, and then turned on his heel and strode out of the bedchamber. The door slammed shut behind him.

Silence rang in her ears. She met Yasma's eyes in the mirror, saw the fear in them.

What have I done?

"I'm sorry," Britta whispered. "I didn't mean to place you in such danger. I didn't think—" She turned to face Yasma. "Remember: you're illiterate! You had no contact with the ambassador's wife."

Yasma nodded, her face pale.

Britta reached out and took her maid's hands, gripping them tightly. "It will be all right." Her mouth spoke the words, but her heart didn't believe them. *Were my wits so fuddled by the poppy juice that I didn't see these consequences?* Treason had been done, and someone must be blamed for it.

SHE WAS AFRAID to take the poppy juice, and afraid not to. What if the duke returned to question her again? She might say the wrong thing, might betray herself and Yasma. But what if he returned at noon to bed her, as was his habit?

Britta discovered she was twisting her hands together, as Yasma was wont to do. She stilled the movement. *Think.* There must be somewhere she could go, somewhere she'd be safe—

The nursery.

Yasma finished anchoring the crown in place. "Would you like the poppy juice now?"

"I think... today it wouldn't be wise."

Britta crossed to the door and opened it, trying not to look agitated as she entered the salon, aware that the armsman was one of the duke's men. Outside, the fourth bell tolled. What could she draw? Something that wouldn't take long.

Britta stepped into the dining room. She hurried to where the sheets of parchment, the ink flask, the quill, lay on the table—and halted.

The topmost sheet had a picture on it. Her eyes took in the details: a flock of geese arrowing across the sky, a jagged range of mountains, a vast cavern in which a giant winged lizard crouched atop a pile of treasure—tumbled coins and necklaces, jeweled goblets and kings' crowns. Cowering from the creature was a pretty peasant girl with braided hair and a scattering of freckles across her nose. And climbing the mountainside to rescue her, an axe strapped across his back, was a young woodcutter.

Britta closed her eyes briefly. *Thank you, Karel.*

She rolled up the parchment and returned to the salon. "Yasma," she called.

The maid emerged from the bedchamber. "Yes, mistress?"

"I shall have lunch with my brothers. Carry this for me."

And then, with Duke Rikard's armsman trailing behind them, she took Yasma and herself to the nursery.

CHAPTER FIFTY-FOUR

THEY LEFT THE destruction of the battle behind in a matter of minutes, but the broken-open tombs extended for several miles, lining the base of the cliffs on either side. Innis flew above them in wide circles, a speck in the sky. Petrus lifted his eyes to her often.

Their pace slowed with each mile that they rode. It wasn't just the horses that were tired; the soldiers sagged in their saddles, their faces dark with soot, with stubble, with exhaustion. "How much further?" Tomas asked Dareus, as the sun shone overhead, at its zenith. "We need to rest."

"We should be there soon."

The canyon narrowed, swung north a few degrees, widened again—and there on the other side of the river was an outcrop of rock. It pushed out of the sand like the prow of a ship, sheer-sided, its flat crest several yards above the canyon floor.

They dismounted at the riverbed and led the horses across the jumble of boulders. Petrus stumbled as he walked, holding on to the horse to steady himself. His eyes were gritty with tiredness.

He watched as Innis swooped low. She hovered

above the ground, some two hundred yards distant. Petrus squinted. What had she seen?

Innis landed. She shifted into the shape of a dog, sniffed the ground, and began to dig. Clouds of red sand rose behind her.

"What the...?" Petrus pushed away from his horse. "The mage has found something!"

He covered the distance at a half-run, scrambling over boulders, jogging across sand. He heard others following him.

Innis appeared to be digging a trench. It was already a foot deep when he reached her. "What is it?" he asked, crouching.

Innis paused and looked at him. Sand cascaded gently into the hole. She uttered a short, yipping bark.

"What—?" said Prince Tomas behind them, and then, peering more closely into the hole: "Is that a hand?"

IT TOOK SEVERAL more minutes to fully uncover the shallow grave. Innis sat down, panting. Her tongue hung from her mouth.

They stared down at what was exposed. Petrus silently counted the body parts. Like Captain Ditmer's men, these men had been torn limb from limb.

"How many—?" someone asked.

"Three heads."

Three heads, and a tangle of limbs.

"Fresh," one of the soldiers said. "About a week, I'd say."

Petrus turned away from the grave. He examined the canyon walls. Holes gaped in the nearest tombs.

"Who do you think they are?" Tomas said, crouching. "And where are their companions?"

"They must be heading towards Ner," Dareus said. "Or we'd have crossed paths with them."

A terrible thought seized him. Petrus narrowed his eyes, examining what was left of the bodies. The only skin he could see was covered by sand and dried blood.

With a muttered expletive, he reached down and hauled one of the arms from the grave. He stripped off the torn shirtsleeve and began to examine the skin. It was deeply bruised.

"What are you looking for?" Tomas asked.

"A tattoo."

Tomas understood. He turned and uttered a curt order. Within less than a minute the body parts were laid out on the sand. Tomas knelt at one of the torsos and tore off the clothing.

It was Prince Harkeld who first found what they were looking for. "Here." He held up an arm. A tattoo of a five-bladed throwing star showed on the pallid skin of the bicep.

Petrus released his breath with a hiss.

"Fithian assassin," someone said behind him.

A second throwing star was found on the shoulder blade of one of the dead men, and marching across the nape of the man's neck was a row of tiny daggers.

"How many?" Prince Tomas asked.

The soldier who'd found it bent his head and counted. "Fifteen, sire."

"Fifteen kills!" Tomas muttered a curse. "They're not beginners." He stood and looked down at the scattered body parts, at the shallow grave already filling with sand. "What do you think happened?"

Dareus looked back at the outcrop. "At a guess, they camped here for the night. They were attacked—as we were, as Captain Ditmer was. Some of them managed to climb to safety. Some didn't." He nudged a leg with the toe of his boot. "Someone buried them, so there's at least one assassin still alive. Possibly more. Innis—" he jerked his thumb upward. "Get up there. Keep watch."

Innis obeyed, shifting from dog to hawk, sweeping up into the sky again.

Dareus turned to Gerit. "Change into a wolf, see what you can smell. We need to know how many of them there are."

Gerit undressed. He shifted into the form of a wolf, broad-chested, its brown fur brindled with gray, and sniffed the remains of the three assassins, inhaling their scents.

The soldiers stood back, watching.

Gerit padded across to the outcrop. He circled it twice, sometimes with his nose close to the ground, sometimes standing up on his hind legs to sniff the sides. After the second circuit he dropped to his haunches and shifted into a hawk. He flew up on to the outcrop and became a wolf again. He spent several minutes up there, sniffing thoroughly, then changed into a hawk again and glided back towards them. Before he reached them, though, he circled to the left and landed.

Gerit changed into a wolf and sniffed the sand before trotting back to where they waited. He shifted. "The scent's very faint. As far as I can tell, there were about ten assassins, including these three."

"Ten?" Prince Tomas said, his voice sharp.

"Or so. It's hard to tell. The scent's too old." Gerit began to dress.

"Ten," Tomas repeated.

Petrus understood his dismay. Fithian assassins had a fearsome reputation. One assassin was more than a match for two soldiers. Three, if he was particularly well-trained.

"There's another grave over there." Gerit jerked his head to the left. "You can see it from the air. Corpses."

"Another?" Tomas swung round to look. "How do you know it's corpses and not more—"

"It smells of corpse. This one smells of men." Gerit pulled on his shirt.

Tomas surveyed the canyon floor. Sand grains scurried before a rising breeze. "They're trying to hide the fact they were here. They don't want us to know they're ahead of us."

"Obviously."

"When were they here?" Dareus asked.

Gerit shrugged into his jerkin. "About a week ago. Could be longer."

Petrus glanced at Prince Harkeld. He hadn't said anything since finding the first tattoo. His face was dirty, tired, grim. Was the prince afraid? *He has to be.* The assassins could only have one reason to be in Masse.

Poor sod, he found himself thinking, for the second time in two days.

THEY ATE LUNCH in the shade cast by the outcrop. Innis joined them; Ebril took her place in the sky.

Once they'd eaten, Dareus caught Petrus's eye. *Change with Innis*, he mouthed.

Petrus glanced at Innis. She was already standing. As he watched, she walked away, vanishing around the curve of the rock, a blanket hugged tightly around her shoulders.

Petrus had stiffened while sitting; his bones seemed to creak as he stood. "Need to take a piss," he told Prince Harkeld, and trudged around to the other side of the outcrop.

Innis was waiting. Her torn ear was healed, the soot and blood washed from her skin. Exhaustion still marked her face, though. The shadows beneath her eyes were as dark as bruises.

"Are you sure you're up to this?" Petrus asked in a low voice.

She nodded.

"But Innis—"

"You've been Justen all night and more than half the day. You need to be yourself."

"And you don't?"

"Not as much as you."

Petrus pressed his lips together, wishing he could refute her words. Small tremors ran beneath his skin and his heart was beating too loudly in his ears. He was close to the limit of his endurance. If he held the shift much longer, he wouldn't be able to change back into himself.

Innis took his silence for assent. She shifted into Justen's shape. Her hair became shorter, fairer. Stubble bristled on her face. "Hurry," she said, her voice deep. "Someone might come."

Petrus shifted. His body seemed to sigh with

relief. *I'm me again.* Quickly, silently, he stripped off Justen's clothes—soot-stained, sweat-stained—and gave them to Innis. "I'm sorry about the smell."

"Don't be."

The amulet was last. The ivory was gray with soot. Innis placed the cord around her neck and tucked the amulet beneath the shirt. "Is there anything I should know? Anything the prince has said?"

"One of the soldiers asked why only three oliphants fought last night, not four."

Her eyebrows lifted. "What did Dareus say?"

"That it's a hard shape, and I'm not strong enough to do it." Petrus pulled a face. "He said I was a lion, but I was fighting further back, where the oliphants couldn't trample me."

"Not strong enough?" Innis smiled faintly. "Poor Petrus."

He shrugged, too exhausted to care about his pride, and picked up the blanket.

She turned to go.

"Innis."

She looked back at him.

"The oliphant was brilliant. Absolutely brilliant."

Innis smiled, flushing slightly beneath the stubble. "Thank you."

"You saved us, Innis."

She ducked her head, the flush deepening.

Justen wouldn't do that. Petrus bit back the words. "Go," he said, gently.

After a few minutes, he went back around the outcrop to where the others sat.

*   *   *

"I DON'T UNDERSTAND why there would be one assassin in Lundegaard," Harkeld said. "Let alone ten."

Tomas opened his mouth, and shut it again. He shifted uncomfortably. "I don't wish to give offense..."

"About what?" Harkeld said, scarcely noticing as his armsman rejoined them.

Tomas grimaced. "If there are Fithian assassins in Lundegaard, I think... it's because of your father."

"My father? Why?"

Tomas shrugged. "Osgaard has a history of rather aggressive expansion."

Harkeld frowned. "So?"

"So Osgaard has expanded as far north, south, and west as it can. If it's to expand further, it must look east. To Lundegaard."

Harkeld looked away from his friend's steady gaze. "I hardly think we're going to invade—"

"That's why my father offered to foster you. He hoped to strengthen the ties between us. It's why he gave my sister to your father as a bride. Sigren didn't want to, but she understood the necessity."

Sigren. Harkeld rubbed his brow with hard fingers, remembering his father's fourth wife, remembering the night she had died.

"On the map, we're almost as large as mainland Osgaard—but half of our territory is this." Tomas opened his hand, gesturing at the rock and the sand. "Empty. If you measure us by our population, we're much smaller than Osgaard. If you chose to invade, you'd probably win."

"And every other kingdom on this continent would come to arms against us!" Harkeld said. "We'd hardly win *that* war!"

"You think they would? No one came to Esfaban's aid. Or Meren's or Lomaly's. We sat back and let you take them."

Harkeld looked down at his boots. *That was long before I was born.* "If we took you, we'd be as big as Ankeny. A threat to the other kingdoms. They wouldn't let it happen."

"Perhaps." Tomas shrugged. "It's a risk your father might be prepared to take."

Harkeld shook his head.

"But supposing our royal family died?" Tomas said. "What if the closest living heirs to Lundegaard's throne were Sigren's sons, *your* half-brothers."

Harkeld frowned at him. "What?"

"My uncle and his sons died last year in a fire," Tomas said. "There were indications it wasn't an accident."

Harkeld shook his head. "No."

"Six months ago, my other cousin died of a fever. That just leaves us—my father, my brothers. Erik has only daughters so far."

"But—"

"If my father was to die, if *we* were to die—your father could claim Lundegaard in his sons' names."

Harkeld stared at him.

"An accident. Another fire. A poison that looks like a fever. Something that seems natural, but isn't." Tomas shrugged. "Easy enough to arrange... for an assassin."

"You have no proof of this. This is just... just supposition!"

"In the past year we've found three assassins within Lundegaard's borders. Unfortunately we couldn't question any of them." Tomas grimaced. "A Fithian would rather die than be caught."

"You think they were sent by my father?"

"Do you?"

Harkeld was silent. His father had planned to use the Ivek Curse to Osgaard's gain. If he was capable of that, what else was he capable of?

He stared down at the ground and turned Tomas's words over in his head. A couple of sentences caught, repeating themselves in a loop. *That's why my father offered to foster you as a boy. He hoped to strengthen the ties between us.*

Had it all been false, then? King Magnas's many kindnesses, the princes' friendship?

He looked at Tomas. "Your father offered me sanctuary in Lundegaard, after the curse is broken."

Tomas nodded.

"Why?"

Tomas blinked. "Because you've been banished. Where else will you go?"

"Does your father think to use me against Osgaard?"

Tomas blinked again. His forehead creased. "What?"

"Does he think to use me against Osgaard?" Harkeld repeated in a hard voice. *I was a pawn in my father's game. Am I now to be King Magnas's pawn?*

"Of course not! He offered you a home because you need one!"

Harkeld studied Tomas's face. His indignation seemed sincere. "I apologize," he said.

For a moment, he thought Tomas would push to

his feet and storm off, then his friend's face relaxed. "You are an ass sometimes, Harkeld."

"I know. I'm sorry." He rubbed his face. His skin was gritty beneath his fingers, greasy. He was abruptly aware of how filthy he was. The stink of last night's battle was ingrained in his skin: smoke, blood, and the dry, dusty smell of the corpses. He climbed to his feet. "I need to wash."

THEY STACKED MOST of their supplies against the side of the canyon, where the bundles wouldn't be trampled by the corpses. A tomb was burrowed into the sandstone only a few yards from the cache. Its shape was only partly natural; the ancient Massens had clearly enlarged a cavity to suit their purpose. Harkeld eyed the hole warily. The blocks of stone that had once sealed it lay crumbling on the ground. "Why don't they come out in daylight?"

Dareus paused, and wiped his brow. "Don't know," he said. "Something to do with the way Ivek set up the curse, I guess."

Once the stores were stacked, they debated the horses. "If we tether them, they'll panic once the corpses start moving," Tomas said. "Hurt themselves breaking free."

"How many did we lose to injury last night?" Harkeld asked.

"Upwards of two dozen."

"We could leave them free," a soldier suggested.

Tomas laced his hands together behind his neck and stared down the canyon. After a moment, he gave a short nod. "We'll tether them. Round that bend. It's a good half mile away. Maybe they won't panic so much."

WITH THE HORSES dealt with, they could rest. Harkeld trudged back to the outcrop. It was fully twice the height of a man, the sandstone rough, pock-marked with small holes. He made it to the top with the loss of some skin and hauled himself, panting, over the lip of stone.

He pushed to his knees and gazed down at the canyon floor. The climb was difficult for a man; impossible for a thousand-year-old corpse.

The outcrop was flat on top, and roughly triangle-shaped. The things they'd need—food, water, firewood, blankets—were stacked in the middle. Around him, men stretched out wearily on the stone. Harkeld counted them silently. Nine soldiers, and Tomas. Was that enough to fight six or seven Fithian assassins, and win?

No.

He glanced at the witches: Dareus, Cora, Petrus, Gerit. The girl Innis and Ebril must be up in the sky.

If a Fithian assassin was the equal of two soldiers, how many witches did one assassin equal?

"Blanket?" Justen asked.

Harkeld took the blanket his armsman offered and spread it on the rock. He unslung his baldric, kicked off his boots, and lay down. Weariness seemed to push him into the stone. Wind sighed up the canyon, drawing wails from the cliffs. He barely noticed the sound. Somehow, in the past day, he'd grown used to it.

Harkeld closed his eyes and slept.

* * *

JUSTEN ROUSED HIM, shaking his shoulder. "Sire. It'll soon be dusk."

Harkeld pushed up on an elbow, yawning.

They ate a hurried meal. "We shouldn't have any problems," Tomas said once they'd eaten. "But for the first couple of hours I want every man ready. After that, we can take it in shifts."

Harkeld looked out over the canyon. Dusk was rapidly falling, the shadows deepening, spreading. Broken-open tombs stretched as far as he could see along the base of the cliffs. The holes looked like dark mouths.

He narrowed his eyes. Was that movement?

"I want three fires," Tomas said, pointing. "There, there, and there. Now move; we haven't much time."

They built a fire at each of the three points where the outcrop jutted, prow-like, into the canyon. The light they cast illuminated the entire outcrop. Harkeld stood at the edge and looked down. Nothing would be able to climb up without being seen.

Night slowly enveloped the canyon. The shapeshifters became owls and swept up into the sky. Harkeld stood, listening, his sword clenched in his hand, his ears straining for the first sound—

A stone rattled in the distance.

"Harkeld, get back," Tomas said, from his position by one of the fires.

"But—"

"Back!" His voice was hard. "You too, Justen."

Muttering, Harkeld obeyed.

He stood in the middle of the outcrop, sword in

hand, ready. All around him, men faced outward. Firelight turned their faces ruddy. The sword blades gleamed red-gold. From above came the whisper of wings as the shapeshifters kept watch.

A minute passed, and then another. Nothing changed. Several more minutes passed. Harkeld's arm began to grow tired, holding the sword aloft. "Well?" he asked.

"Come and have a look," Tomas said.

Harkeld lowered his sword. He walked across to Tomas and looked down.

The firelight cast its illumination over a mass of corpses. He saw gaunt, hollow-eyed faces, brittle thatches of hair, leathery skin stretched tight over bones. The creatures were in constant movement, jostling one another. Those in front scrabbled at the outcrop, plucking at the rock with bony fingers, trying in vain to haul themselves up.

"They can't climb," Tomas said.

THE ONLY EXCITEMENT during the first hour was an unattached hand groping its way up the side of the outcrop. The soldiers watched as it climbed and chopped it to pieces once it reached the top.

Tomas turned away from the edge, sheathing his sword. "We'll take it in shifts, six at a time, half the night each. Who wants to go first?"

Harkeld raised his hand.

"You don't have to," Tomas said. "We have enough—"

"I want to." Last night, men had died for him; tonight, he would pull his weight.

"It'll be boring," Tomas said. "Cold—"

"Tomas, go to sleep."

His friend grinned. "Yes, sire."

TOMAS HAD BEEN correct: it was boring and, as the night progressed, increasingly cold. Harkeld alternated standing by the fire with Justen. Even so, he was shivering by the time the second shift relieved them. His fingers were numb. He almost dropped his sword, sheathing it.

Rolled in his blanket, the sandstone cold and hard beneath him, the shivering gradually eased. Justen was warm on his right.

Despite the constant, dry susurration of movement from the canyon floor, despite the cold, Harkeld slid into sleep.

"STILL COLD?" A *voice whispered. Arms came around him. A body pressed against his back.*

"That feels good," Harkeld murmured, turning, taking her in his arms. He didn't open his eyes, but the scent of her black hair was familiar, the slenderness of her body.

She nestled close, soft and warm.

Contented, Harkeld slid into sleep again.

INNIS WOKE AT dawn. She sat up, rubbing her face, feeling Justen's stubble on her cheeks. Prince Harkeld still slept. His face was relaxed, the grimness gone; he merely looked exhausted.

She looked out across the canyon. The sand churned with thousands of footprints. Even as she watched, a breeze began to smooth the tracks. A low wail rose from the walls.

Innis pushed aside the blanket and walked to the edge of the outcrop. A few fragments littered the sand: a skull, its eye sockets staring up at the sky, a bony leg. "Any trouble?" she asked the closest soldier.

He shook his head.

CHAPTER FIFTY-FIVE

THEY ATE BREAKFAST on top of the outcrop and then lowered everything to the ground. Prince Harkeld scrambled down. Innis was crouching on the edge, ready to jump, when she felt a light touch on her elbow. It was Dareus.

"Change with Petrus once you're down."

She nodded.

It wasn't easy to swap places without being seen. One of the soldiers, coming around the outcrop to empty his bladder in private, almost interrupted them. Innis shrank to a lizard, hiding against the sandstone, while Petrus fumbled to pull his trews up.

She waited for the soldier to leave, then shifted into a bird. Dareus was waiting on the other side of the outcrop, gazing at the sky, a blanket over his arm.

Innis landed at his feet. He held the blanket out, shielding her as she changed. She wrapped the blanket around her shoulders and listened to her instructions: "Innis, you're to look for the assassins. I want you to fly to Ner."

She nodded.

"If you haven't seen anything by the time you

reach Ner, assume they survived—and be careful. Don't let them see you."

Innis nodded again.

"I want numbers. We need to know what we're up against."

"Gerit," she heard Dareus say as she shifted into a hawk again. "I want you to fly ahead and search for a safe place for tonight." His voice faded as she swept up into the air.

INNIS FLEW FOR several hours with the sandstone cliffs towering on either side. At one point the canyon narrowed into a boulder-choked gorge— ancient rapids. Then it widened again.

For long stretches, the tombs were broken open. Innis knew what it meant: the Fithian assassins had passed through.

She looked for other signs of their passage, but found only two piles of horse manure, almost obscured by drifts of sand. Both were on the far side of the river, the side their own party hadn't traveled on. Another few days and even those telltale piles would be buried by the sand. Of tracks, there was no sign. The assassins had taken care to hide them, and what they'd not hidden, the wind and the blowing sand had erased.

Mid-morning, the canyon began to change. Fingers of rock split from the canyon walls and others rose from the sand, long spines like the fins of gigantic, buried sea creatures. And then she burst out of the canyon. Sand stretched ahead of her—and the ruins of the city Ner.

Innis circled, climbing high into the sky. Below her, rock fins stretched out into the desert like the fingers of a delta.

The desert they'd passed through before had been almost blood red; this desert was the color of rusting iron. It stretched as far as she could see, a broad bowl surrounded by arid mountains.

Innis swooped low, until she skimmed above the sandstone fins. Some extended for furlongs; others speared up like gigantic orange-red tree trunks. It was a forest of stone planted in sand, a jungle of rocky fins and spires reaching hundreds of feet into the air.

Ahead, pillowed in sand, were the ruins of Ner. Several thousand people had lived there when the Massen Empire was at its height, a dozen or more centuries ago, but little remained of the city now—a line of columns, most of which were broken stumps; a flight of stone steps in a patch of rippled sand; a roofless tower, with one window like a staring eye. The desert had almost swallowed the ancient city.

Crouching to the east of the ruins, like a beast ready to pounce, was a massive hump of rust-orange rock. It towered out of the desert, easily the size of a palace. A slit of darkness showed at its base.

The city lay ahead, but the hulking lump of rock drew her attention. Innis altered course, arrowing towards it. The slit grew rapidly in size until it was a gash the height of a man. The darkness inside was absolute.

She knew what that darkness hid: the city's graveyard. The catacombs of Ner, where the first anchor stone was concealed.

Innis circled in front of the opening, undecided. Should she look inside?

Oh, for pity's sake, stop hesitating, she told herself crossly. Justen wouldn't vacillate; he'd *do*.

She glided inside, changing form—from hawk to owl—dropping a couple of feet in the air as she shifted.

Sandstone pressed heavily down on her for a moment, and then the low ceiling of rock was gone and a cave opened out, vast and echoing.

Innis circled higher. The daylight didn't penetrate far, but the sparse light was enough for her owl's eyes. She'd expected something crude, simple; instead the catacombs were laid out like the spokes of a wheel. High sandstone walls radiated from the center of the cavern with deep avenues between them.

She swooped low, skimming along the top of one wall, and realized that the walls hadn't been built *up* from the floor of the cavern; the avenues had been carved down into the bedrock.

Innis glided down into one of the avenues, until she was a mere yard above the floor. It was like flying along a canyon. Sandstone reached high on either side, burrowed with niches in which corpses had been interred.

The niches had once been sealed, but now rubble littered the sandy floor—chunks of stone, drifts of crumbling mortar. Her keen owl ears caught faint rustlings of sound, no louder than the furtive scurrying of mice—the corpses were stirring in their graves. And tonight, once the sun set, they'd do more than stir; they'd walk abroad.

The passage narrowed until her wings almost

brushed either side, and then she burst out into a circular open space. Precisely at its center, a squat lump of rock stood like an altar. It was basalt, black, thickly draped with curse shadows.

Innis veered away from the anchor stone. She circled upward until she saw the avenues radiating in all directions beneath her. A faint slit of daylight marked the cavern entrance.

She arrowed towards it and burst out into almost-blinding sunlight, soaring up into the sky. Masse spread itself out beneath her in dull, muted colors and shades of gray, stretching as far as she could see—desert, rock, barren mountains. To the south, the canyon meandered like a river. Below her, the ruins of Ner slumbered beneath a thousand years' worth of sand.

Innis hung in the air and shifted from owl into hawk, barely dropping a few inches in height. The colors became vivid again, the desert rust-orange, the sky blue, the sandstone red.

She circled, examining the ruined city. If the assassins were here, they'd have found a hiding place safe from the corpses.

The only possibility was the ruined tower, sticking up out of the sand like a finger, its truncated shadow telling her it was nearly noon—but the tower, when she flew low to inspect it, was empty. The sole occupant was a lizard, sunning itself on a lip of rock.

Innis flew up into the sky again, widening her circles. If not the city, then where?

Her interest sharpened on the mouth of the canyon, where the forest of sandstone fins and spires thrust up into the sky. Where the prince had to pass on his way to the anchor stone. Where there was concealment from searching eyes—and safety from the corpses.

She found the horses first, hidden behind a long, sloping spine of sandstone. After that, it was easy. It would have been easier if she'd dared take the form of a wolf or dog and use her nose, but in the guise of a sky lark, flitting from one upthrust of rock to the next, she found the assassins eventually. They were in a cave halfway up a thick fin of sandstone. Six men. One slept, his weapons close to hand, three silently played a complicated game with small stones, another was sharpening his knives, and the sixth man sat guard, a sword laid across his knees, alert.

Two hundred yards distant, on another sandstone fin, in a hole barely large enough for a man, a seventh assassin crouched, utterly still, watching the river and the path to Ner.

Innis spent an hour looking for further sentries, but found none. She flew back to the first cave and shifted into the shape of a lizard and crept as close as she dared. She stared at the six men. Fithian assassins. Killers, with a harsh and legendary code of honor.

They looked disappointingly ordinary: tired, dirty, with unshaven faces and stained, rumpled clothing. And yet, for all their ordinariness, they were terrifying. The sentry didn't fidget, didn't yawn. His stillness, his focus on his task, was absolute. He was waiting. Waiting for his shift to end. Waiting for another night, with corpses prowling the canyon floor. *Waiting for us to arrive, so that he may kill the prince.*

*   *   *

IT WAS LATE afternoon when Innis reached the others. They were setting up camp in a cave on the eastern side of the canyon, hauling blankets, food and water up by rope.

"Did you find them?" Dareus asked, once she'd dressed.

"Yes."

Prince Tomas looked up from his task: lashing waterskins to the rope dangling from the cave. "How many?"

Innis was aware of men pausing, turning to look at her. "Seven. They're hiding at the mouth of the canyon."

"Seven." Tomas glanced at his soldiers, as if counting them.

"We can handle 'em," Gerit said. He cleared his throat and spat into the sand. "Bastards won't know what hit 'em."

THEY PASSED THE night with no more disturbance than the occasional detached hand creeping up from the canyon floor. In the morning, Harkeld stood in the cave mouth and looked out. Dawn flushed the sky. The sand was empty apart from the churned tracks of hundreds of feet and the odd, abandoned limb.

"Once the anchor stone is destroyed, will the corpses stop coming out?" Tomas asked.

"I don't know," Dareus said. "But my guess would be yes."

* * *

By mid-morning they'd gathered the horses—eleven had broken free, two needed to be killed—loaded their supplies and were on their way: another ordinary day. The disembodied wailing, the stark landscape, the broken tombs, had become familiar, almost normal.

At noon, they came to a place where the canyon was no wider than the ancient riverbed. They dismounted and led the horses, picking their way over the tumbled boulders.

"Rapids," Justen said.

Harkeld nodded.

The canyon grew narrower. They were climbing now, scrambling. Water must have once spewed through here with extraordinary force—the canyon was choked with boulders of all sizes, some larger than houses, and the cliffs were deeply scored and gouged. No water gushed through here now: the River Ner trickled deep below the jumble of rock.

The canyon walls seemed to lean over them, almost touching. The rock was veined with white, like fat marbling a slice of beef. There were no tombs, although the occasional cave still pocked the sandstone.

Harkeld halted to drink from his waterskin. His horse blew in his ear. He glanced at the men and horses strung out ahead of him, clambering upward, then turned and looked back down the rubble-choked gorge. The canyon echoed with sound—the clatter of hooves on rock, the scrape of hobnailed boots, the sound of men panting and grunting as they climbed.

Justen looked up from several yards below. "Over half way up, I reckon."

Harkeld nodded. He slung the waterskin over his shoulder. Several things happened simultaneously: something whistled past his cheek, hot liquid sprayed across his face, filling his eyes, and his horse stumbled into him and collapsed, knocking him to the ground.

A second object hurtled past his face, striking rock with a fierce *clang*.

"Sire?" he heard Justen call out. "What's wrong with your horse?"

The horse lay heavy and unmoving, pinning the lower half of his body. Harkeld struggled to push it aside, struggled to wipe his eyes, struggled to reach for his sword. The smell of fresh blood filled his nose.

His vision cleared. He saw a stranger crouched a few yards in front of him. The man's face was stubbled, grim. He detached something from his belt: a five-bladed throwing star.

Everything in Harkeld's body seemed to stand still: his heart didn't beat, his blood didn't flow, no breath filled his lungs. *Fithian assassin!*

A hawk dropped screaming from the sky.

"Sire! What's wrong?" Justen's voice was closer.

The assassin paid no attention to the hawk, no attention to Tomas now shouting and running back towards them. His eyes were fixed on Harkeld with fierce intensity. He raised his arm to throw. The blades of the throwing star gleamed in his hand.

Something ignited in Harkeld's chest—anger, fear, panic—burning as hotly as flames inside him. He thrust his hand towards the man, a futile gesture, as if that lethal weapon could be warded off with mere flesh and bone.

The assassin erupted into flames. Not just his clothes, but his hair, his skin, his screaming mouth. An answering fire crackled over Harkeld's skin with a *hiss* he felt deep inside him.

Justen scrambled over the horse and halted, his sword outstretched.

The assassin burned, writhing in agony, his skin crisping and blackening, turning to ash. The flames were intensely hot, almost roaring as they consumed him. In a matter of seconds the man was dead. On the rock lay a charred, smoking husk that had once been human.

Justen resheathed his sword. He turned to Harkeld, his face pale. "Sire, let me help you."

With Justen's assistance he was able to push aside the horse and scramble to his feet. Harkeld stood, trembling. Horror reverberated inside him. "Are you hurt?" Tomas asked, breathless, as he reached them.

Harkeld shook his head, unable to tear his gaze from the black, twisted corpse.

"There's blood on your face."

The horse's. His tongue couldn't form the words. He wiped his face with his sleeve.

Dareus pushed through the soldiers. "Are you all right?"

Harkeld turned to him. His horror found an outlet. "How could you do that?" His voice was hoarse. He swallowed and spoke more strongly, almost shouting, hurling the words at the witch: "How could you do something so monstrous!"

"We didn't." Dareus was looking at him as

intensely as the assassin had. "You did."

Harkeld stepped away from the witch, away from the smoking corpse, shaking his head. "You're lying." But even as he spoke, he felt the truth of Dareus's words: the remembered sensation of fire igniting in his chest, the sting of flames running under his skin. "You did it!"

"We were too far away."

"No!" Harkeld shook his head again. "I'm not a witch." He looked at Justen, at Tomas. Justen met his gaze squarely, with no hint of condemnation on his face; Tomas wouldn't meet his eyes. "I am not a witch!" The shout reverberated in the gorge, echoing off the towering cliffs. *Witch witch witch.*

CHAPTER FIFTY-SIX

THE ASSASSIN HAD been hiding in a cave, a dark hole a few yards from where his body lay. Inside were blankets, food and water, and bandages caked with dried blood.

"He was injured," Gerit said. "Left behind—or chose to stay behind." He backed out of the cave. "Decided he wanted to take the prince with him when he died."

And almost succeeded. Innis looked down at the blackened corpse. It had been reduced mostly to ash, although one charred hand reached out, claw-like, as if in supplication.

"Injured? How?" Tomas asked, not looking at Prince Harkeld.

"His arm," Innis said, remembering what she'd seen as she'd scrambled over the dead horse: a man crouching, reaching awkwardly for a throwing star. "That's why he missed."

Gerit grunted. "Likely," he said. "Fithians don't usually miss." He dropped down on one knee and stirred the ashes with the tip of his dagger.

Innis shuddered and looked up the gorge. Movement caught her eye: a large wolf with a silvery ruff, leaping lightly from boulder to boulder towards them. Petrus.

"How did he know which was Harkeld?" Prince Tomas asked.

"He was in the middle. The rest of you were in uniform. Easy." Gerit didn't bother to look up as he spoke.

Tomas bridled. "Justen was also—"

"Prince Harkeld is dark," Dareus said. "They'd have that much of a description."

The wolf jumped the last few boulders, padded over to Dareus, and sat on its haunches. "Any more of them?" Dareus asked.

The wolf shook its head.

"Stay in that form," Dareus ordered. "There could be others."

"Others?" Tomas said. "How can there be?" He turned to Gerit. "You said there were ten of them—"

"Or thereabouts." Gerit looked up at him. "The scent was old. Hard to tell."

"We made a mistake, thinking there were only seven survivors." Dareus rubbed his face. "And thinking they would stay together. This time, we were lucky. Next time, we may not be."

Gerit flipped the throwing star free of the ashes. It skittered several feet, coming to rest against a boulder with a dull *clang*. The steel was stained black with soot, the blades sharp, deadly.

PETRUS LOPED AHEAD of them for the rest of the afternoon, while Ebril flew above. Prince Harkeld was silent. He didn't speak while they rode or while they prepared for the night: tethering the horses a mile up the canyon, hauling blankets and water up to the cave Gerit had found, stacking the rest of their supplies where the corpses wouldn't trample them.

He sat alongside her now, chewing his food, sunk so deeply in his thoughts that she doubted he knew where he was. It was as if he'd erected a barrier around himself. The way he sat, the set of his shoulders, the set of his face, said as loudly as words could: *Leave me alone.*

No one spoke much. Tomas was almost as silent as his friend.

Friend? Innis doubted the word could be applied to the two princes now. Tomas's eyes held fear when he looked at Prince Harkeld.

The soldiers, too, eyed the prince warily. *As if he's one of us.*

Wasn't he?

Innis glanced at Prince Harkeld again. She'd never seen anyone look so grim, so bleak.

She curled her fingers into her palm, clenching them, and looked at Dareus. *Do something. Speak to him.* But Dareus didn't notice. He ate, talking with Cora as if nothing untoward had happened.

Innis looked down at her bowl. Beans and flakes of dried fish floated in a greasy soup. If she'd been closer to the prince, at his side as she was meant to be, he wouldn't have had to use his magic.

She stirred with her spoon, watching as the beans floated, bumping against one another. *I am not a witch!* the prince had shouted. It hadn't been anger that had made his voice so loud; it had been fear.

*   *   *

SOMEONE HELD HIM. Harkeld felt the soft warmth of a woman's body along his back, felt her arms encircling him.

He laid his hands over hers. His mind replayed the moment in the gorge: the assassin flaring alight, flames bursting from his hair, from his open, screaming mouth. *No. It wasn't me. I didn't do that.* Did she feel how he shook? Did she feel the tremors?

"It's all right," she whispered.

Harkeld shook his head. "It's not all right." *It will never be all right again.*

She sighed softly against his back. Her arms tightened around him. "Would it be so terrible to be a witch?"

Terrible?

He remembered how it had felt. Bones, blood, everything in his body on fire, as if he were burning alive.

Panic rose in him, squeezing in his chest, choking his throat. Harkeld wrenched free of her embrace. "I won't be a witch! I won't be a monster!"

Her skin was luminously pale, her eyes as dark as night. "We're not monsters."

"You are!" he yelled, shouting the words, screaming them at her. "I won't be one of you! *I won't!*"

She retreated, withdrawing from him, vanishing into the darkness.

Harkeld stayed where he was, half-sitting, panting, shaking, almost sobbing. *It's too late*, a voice inside him said. *You're already one of them. You are a monster.*

CHAPTER FIFTY-SEVEN

TWO DAYS AFTER Ambassador Alrik's departure from the palace, Lundegaard closed its border with Osgaard. The following day three squadrons of Osgaardan soldiers were ejected from Lundegaard. None were in uniform.

The palace boiled with rumors, with supposition and conjecture, with wild flights of fancy: the squadrons had deserted and tried to take Lundegaard's goldfields for themselves; no, Duke Rikard had been trying to invade Lundegaard without King Esger's knowledge; no, it was an authorized invasion and the plans had been stolen from Duke Rikard's study by Lundegaardan agents.

Karel listened to it all and kept his mouth shut. He watched the princess, he watched Yasma, and, most intently, he watched Duke Rikard.

The duke was rarely in his rooms. When he was, he brought with him the smell of rage, of desperation. His reputation, his future, his very life, were in the balance—and he knew it.

Investigators commissioned by the king roamed the palace, interviewing anyone with a connection to Duke Rikard or the Lundgaardan delegation—

armsmen, bondservants, nobles, army officers.

One of the first people they spoke to was the princess.

Karel answered the knock on the door to Duke Rikard's rooms just after noon, the day after the border closed.

"Announce me to your mistress," the royal investigator said. He was a burly man with graying hair, shrewd blue eyes, and a military stance.

Karel read the letter of appointment with its royal seal, and admitted the man into the salon. At that moment Princess Brigitta emerged from her bedchamber. She halted. "Armsman? Who is this?"

"A royal investigator," he said, scrutinizing her face for signs that she'd been drinking poppy juice. *Be extremely careful, princess.* "I have seen his letter of appointment."

The investigator bowed. "Your highness, I've been instructed to ask questions regarding the matter of military information being leaked to Lundegaard."

Princess Brigitta's chin came up. "Questions of *me*? Don't be absurd. I'm the king's daughter." Her tone was perfect: regal, affronted.

Karel relaxed fractionally. She hadn't been drinking the juice.

The investigator looked at her through narrowed eyes, and then nodded. "I meant no offense, highness." His gaze fastened on Yasma, standing behind the princess. "Your maid, then. She had the opportunity—"

"My maid can neither read nor write," Princess Brigitta said. She didn't say *Don't be absurd* again, but it was clearly implied. "Yasma, fetch my cloak. Hurry, girl."

Yasma obediently scurried back into the bedchamber. A moment later she emerged, a sable-trimmed cloak over her arm.

"Not that one," Princess Brigitta said, her tone impatient. "The one with the *white* trim. How many times do I have to tell you, girl?"

Yasma flushed and vanished back into the bedchamber.

"My maid is somewhat slow-witted," the princess told the royal investigator.

The man looked at her, as if assessing the truth of her words.

"Too many beatings," Princess Brigitta said, with a careless shrug. "I have to tell her most things twice. It's rather aggravating."

Leave it at that, princess, Karel told her silently.

She did. She returned the royal investigator's gaze, her expression guileless.

"Even so, your highness," the investigator said politely, "there are questions I must ask her."

Yasma returned, a second cloak in her arms, this one trimmed with white fox fur. The princess turned to her. "Girl, this man has questions for you. Answer them."

Yasma swallowed and clutched the cloak tightly. "Yes, sir?"

The investigator hesitated. He flicked a glance at the princess. Karel read annoyance on the man's face. He'd wanted to interview Yasma privately.

Karel held his breath. Would the investigator press the issue? *Please, All-Mother, let him not insist on—*

"Have you ever been in the duke's study?" the royal investigator asked.

Karel released his breath.

Yasma shook her head, her eyes wide and frightened. "No."

"Have you ever seen anyone other than the duke enter it?"

"No." Not by so much as the flicker of an eyelid did she show that she was lying.

"Another bondservant? An armsman?"

"No one."

"Have you ever had contact with anyone from Lundegaard?"

"No."

"At the garden party?"

"No."

"Is that all?" Princess Brigitta's tone was bored, impatient.

The investigator studied Yasma's face and gave that curt nod again. He turned his head and looked at Karel. "Your armsman, highness. May I speak with him? With your permission, of course."

"Certainly, but I require him now. You may wait until he's off duty."

The royal investigator bowed politely. "Of course, your highness."

KAREL ANSWERED THE man's questions after midnight, in a dark, candle-lit room not far from the armsmen's barracks. No, he'd never been in the duke's study. No, he'd not seen anyone but Duke Rikard enter it. No, he'd had no contact with any of Lundegaard's ambassadorial delegation.

The royal investigator rephrased the questions

and asked them again, and again, and again, while the candles in the sconces burned low and Karel's eyes grew gritty with tiredness. Finally he said, a bite of frustration in his voice: "I'm never alone in the duke's rooms. The princess is always present. I have no opportunity to enter the study."

"While she's asleep," the investigator said, his gaze intent on Karel's face.

Karel snorted. "With the duke asleep on the other side of the door? A man would have to be insane to take such a risk."

"You're from Esfaban. You have reason to hate Osgaard. Reason to take such a risk."

Fear tightened in Karel's chest. *They're going to pin it on me.* "I have a duty to my family, to prove that we're loyal and worthy of freedom. I wouldn't jeopardize that for anything."

Except that he *had* jeopardized it. He was complicit in an act of treason.

All-Mother, what have I done?

The investigator stared at him for a long moment and then pursed his lips and nodded curtly. He made a note on the sheet of parchment in front of him. "What about the maid?"

Karel blinked. "The maid?" He forced his thoughts to follow this new direction. "She's timid and not very bright."

The man gazed at him, clearly wanting more.

"She can't read or write," Karel said.

"She could have given someone access—"

"No, she couldn't. For the same reasons as me. Her family."

The investigator made another note on the

parchment. "And Duke Rikard's bondservant? What of him?"

"I've never seen the man. But he wouldn't have done it, for the precisely the same—"

"Yes. His family." The royal investigator pursed his lips and studied Karel's face for a long minute, before giving another brusque nod. "You may go, armsman."

CHAPTER FIFTY-EIGHT

FIVE HORSES HAD torn free of their tethers overnight; two had broken legs. The rest stood where they'd been picketed, a mile from the cave, sweating, trembling.

By the time the packhorses were loaded, the sun had risen above the canyon rim. They set off in a slow cavalcade, Innis in her place at Prince Harkeld's side. Ebril rode the thermals above them and Petrus loped a furlong ahead.

At noon, they halted for lunch. Innis loosened her horse's girth and turned to lead the weary beast down to the river. Dareus caught her eye. She walked slowly, lagging behind Prince Harkeld.

"How is he?" Dareus asked as he caught up with her.

"He hasn't spoken a word." Innis glanced at the prince, and away. "Yesterday was my fault. I should have been closer to him."

"You were as close as you could be, under the circumstances."

"But—"

"It's as well that we know what he's capable of. That *he* knows."

Innis walked for a moment in silence. She remembered the dream she'd had last night, the way the prince had trembled as she held him. She'd felt his fear, quite literally. *He's lost the person he thought he was. He's terrified of what he's become.*

She lifted her gaze to Prince Harkeld. She hadn't been imagining his emotions in the dream; she'd *felt* them with her magic, just as she did when she healed. "Dareus? Have you ever heard of mages sharing dreams?"

His eyebrows rose sharply. "Sharing dreams?"

Innis nodded.

"What sort of dreams?"

"Dreams when you're with someone. When you talk with them."

"Intimate dreams?"

"Sometimes." She felt a flush rise in her cheeks. "I've never had dreams like this before. They feel *real*."

Dareus nodded. "I've heard of it happening between healers. It's rare."

"Healers?" Her gaze jerked, startled, to Prince Harkeld.

They reached the edge of the riverbed and the clutter of dry boulders. Dareus halted. "When you heal, what happens?"

Innis looked at him, confused. "What do you mean?"

"Do you read people's thoughts when you heal them?"

"Of course not!"

"But... you feel more than just tissue and bone?"

"Yes."

"What do you feel?" he asked.

"Emotions," she said. But it was more than just that. Innis frowned, struggling to find the words to express it. She stared at Prince Harkeld, remembering the strong sense of honor she'd felt when she'd healed him, the stubbornness, the courage—and the loss, the despair, the rage. "It's like knowing someone really well. Knowing who they are as a person."

"For me it's just tissues and bones."

Innis turned her head and stared at him.

"Strong healers, healers like you who *feel*, sometimes have dreams like you describe."

"With their patients?"

"With each other." Dareus frowned. "It is Petrus you're talking about, isn't it?"

"No. It's the prince."

Dareus's eyebrows rose. "Prince Harkeld?"

She nodded.

"How unusual." He studied the prince, now halted in the middle of the riverbed. "I've only ever heard of it happening between healers who share a strong bond."

"A strong bond?"

"They're usually lovers."

Innis felt herself flush. She remembered the prince's hands sliding over her skin, remembered the taste of his mouth as he kissed her. "I have no bond with him. He hates us."

"Hate us, he might. But he's one of us. He's a fire mage—and a healer, if he's sharing dreams with you." Dareus glanced sideways at her. "Did you dream last night?"

She nodded.

"What did it tell you?"

Innis looked at Prince Harkeld, at his dark close-cropped hair, at his stubbled face, his grim profile. "He's terrified."

*   *   *

MID-AFTERNOON THE canyon swung north. Gerit was waiting for them. Behind him, an outcrop of sandstone sat squarely in the middle of the canyon, broad and squat. Petrus, loping ahead of them in wolf form, reached Gerit first. He sat down on the sand, stretched his jaws wide in a yawn, and began to scratch vigorously beneath his chin. Innis repressed the urge to scratch her own chin. Justen's whiskers were itchy, uncomfortable.

"It looks like a giant cowpat," one of the soldiers said, as they reined in.

Gerit ignored the comment. "This is the best defensive position I can find," he told Dareus.

"It's too low," Tomas protested.

"There's nothing higher until we reach the end of the canyon."

Petrus stopped scratching. He shifted from wolf to man and studied the outcrop, unselfconscious in his nudity. "If we ring it with fire—"

"We don't have enough wood," Tomas said.

"Corpses, then. We pile them up and set them alight. That way, anything that gets past the oliphants burns."

There was a moment of silence. Tomas looked at Dareus. "Could it work?"

Dareus nodded. "Yes."

THEY TOILED FOR the better part of an hour, dragging corpses from their tombs, hauling them to the outcrop, stacking them, while Ebril circled overhead, keeping watch. "That should be enough," Prince Tomas said, panting.

Petrus stood back, wiping sweat from his face. His hands smelled of tombs, of dust and crumbling bones and skin so old it had turned to brittle leather. The scent seemed to waft from his clothes, to trickle down from his hair.

"Let's rest. We've a few hours before nightfall," Dareus said. "Gerit, Petrus, stay behind. I need to speak with you." He caught Justen's eye, and then lifted his arm to beckon Ebril down.

Petrus lowered himself to sit on the sand. He rubbed his face and yawned as the soldiers and the princes and Justen clambered up onto the outcrop. Ebril glided down to land.

Half a minute later, Innis returned. She crouched. "I can't stay long."

"Change with Petrus," Dareus said.

She began to strip off Justen's clothes.

"Tonight we'll start with three oliphants, thin their numbers, then drop back to two."

Petrus listened as he undressed. He took the trews Innis tossed him—smelling of sweat and soot and corpses—and pulled them on.

"Innis, you'll be shifted all night," Dareus said. "Gerit and Ebril will do as much as they can."

Petrus paused in the act of buttoning Justen's shirt. "What about me?"

"You'll be Justen all night."

"But—"

"The outcrop will be brightly lit. No cover. You won't be able to swap with anyone."

Petrus pulled the shirt off again. "Then let Ebril be Justen. Or Gerit."

"You've been a wolf all day," Dareus said, a note of impatience in his voice. "Running. You need to rest."

"I want to fight."

"It's not a sinecure," Dareus said sharply. "If the corpses break through, you'll have to keep the prince alive."

"You think it could be that bad?" Ebril asked.

"They'll be coming at us from all sides," Dareus said. "If we can't hold them off, then yes, it will be that bad."

Silence followed these words. Petrus looked down at the shirt in his hand. Slowly, he began to put it on again.

Gerit surveyed the outcrop, the corpses piled high. "Do you have the strength to keep them burning all night?" he asked Dareus.

"We'll have to."

"Get the prince to help you. He's a fire mage. A strong one, by the look of it."

Innis looked up, a frown furrowing her brow.

"No," Dareus said.

"But—"

"He hasn't the faintest idea how to use his magic," Dareus said.

Gerit scowled, and spat into the sand.

PETRUS SLEPT ALONGSIDE the prince, awakening as the afternoon slid towards evening.

They ate silently, quickly, and readied their weapons.

As the sky began to darken, Cora set the ring of corpses alight. The bodies burned, crackling and hissing, flames leaping high.

Petrus tested the edge of Justen's Grooten sword with his thumb and watched as Innis unbuttoned her shirt and kicked off her boots. He understood how Prince Harkeld felt. *I want to fight, too.*

Innis shifted into an owl, settled her feathers with a brisk shake of her wings, and swept up into the air, leaving her clothes puddled on the ground. He followed her with his eyes: gliding over the soldiers' heads, over the ring of leaping flames.

"Justen."

He turned his head. Dareus beckoned.

Petrus slid the sword back into its scabbard and walked across to him. "Stay with Prince Harkeld," Dareus said loudly. "Remember: your role is to protect him, not join in the battle." Then he lowered his voice. "If the worst happens, shift into an oliphant and take him on your back. Get out of here."

Petrus nodded. Oliphants paced the sand beyond the burning pyres.

"If you have to deal with the assassins on your own—"

"It won't come to that, sir."

An oliphant bellowed. The sound echoed, reverberating off the cliffs. Dareus drew in a deep breath. "Here come the corpses."

CHAPTER FIFTY-NINE

TWO DAYS AFTER the border closed, another squadron was expelled from Lundegaard. The officer commanding the squadron arrived at the palace late in the evening, bearing a message from King Magnas of Lundegaard: any further Osgaardan soldiers found within Lundegaard's borders would be sentenced to death.

"Screamed with rage when he heard it," one of the king's armsmen said, in the mess hall that night.

"Sounded like a stuck pig," another armsman said, through a mouthful of food. "I just about wet myself."

Karel listened to the laughter, chewing slowly.

"Then what?" someone asked.

"He threw a vase at the officer. Smashed into a thousand pieces. And then he sent for Duke Rikard."

"What happened then?"

Karel looked up to hear the answer.

The man shrugged. "Bell tolled midnight. We'll find out tomorrow."

The armsman alongside him grunted and speared a piece of mutton on his fork. "I wouldn't want to be Duke Rikard, right now."

"Nor I."

Karel's hands clenched around his knife and fork. He wanted to push to his feet, to belt on his sword again and hurry to the princess's side. He couldn't. It was past midnight; one of the duke's armsmen had the duty of guarding her now.

He looked down at his plate. There was nothing he could do but wait.

CHAPTER SIXTY

THE BATTLE BEGAN well. The oliphants crushed most of the corpses before they reached the flaming pyres. Those that reached the fires burned, their hair and skin shriveling alight, their bones snapping and cracking.

As the hours passed, Gerit and Ebril took turns resting, and more corpses reached the blazing fires. The soldiers stood facing outwards, their swords drawn, the firelight playing across their faces, but no corpses came within reach of their blades; Cora and Dareus kept the flames roaring high.

Things began to change as night dragged towards dawn. At first it was nothing to worry about: a corpse broke through where the fire had momentarily dropped to a low smolder, but soldiers hacked with their swords, cutting off its arms, its head, and the body fell backwards and Cora was suddenly there, coaxing the flames up again.

Half an hour later it happened a second time. Then a third time. And each time it seemed to take more effort for the fire mages to raise the flames again. Cora and Dareus were pale, sweating. Each burst of fire took visible effort.

Petrus looked up at the sky. It was still pitch black, but dawn couldn't be far off. *All-Mother, send us the sun, please.*

The press of corpses beyond the flames grew greater. There were hundreds of them, pushing forward, smothering the fires with the weight of their bodies.

Petrus turned to where Gerit rested on his knees. The mage was half-clothed, a sword gripped in his hand. "They need another oliphant!"

"I can't," Gerit said, panting. "I can't shift again." He lurched to his feet, using his sword for balance, and grabbed Prince Harkeld's arm. "You have fire magic. Use it!"

The prince wrenched free, shoving Gerit away.

Behind them, someone shouted in a voice high with fear. Petrus spun around.

A section of the fire was dead. Corpses surged across it.

Soldiers converged on the spot, slashing with their swords, hacking. One man stumbled as a desiccated hand gripped his ankle. More of the creatures reached for him, groping blindly. The soldier disappeared into the crowd of corpses, and his cries were quickly silenced.

Prince Harkeld pushed past Petrus, his sword drawn.

"No!" Petrus grabbed his arm and hauled him back.

The prince rounded on him, his teeth showing in a snarl. "Release me, armsman!"

"No." Petrus tightened his grip. "I have my orders, sire."

Behind the prince, more corpses surged across the extinguished section of the fire. Dareus stood with the soldiers, a grimace on his face, small flames sputtering at the ends of his fingers.

Prince Harkeld cuffed Petrus across the face. "Armsman! Release me!"

Dareus swayed and fell to his knees. Gnarled hands reached for him. A blink of an eye, and he was gone, hauled into the seething mass of corpses.

Petrus released the prince, shoving him back. He drew his sword, running. "Dareus!"

He launched himself at the corpses, chopping with his sword. Arms as brittle as dry sticks wrapped around him. His sword was wrenched from his grasp. Petrus fought desperately, kicking, punching, biting. His hair was being ripped from his scalp, his throat crushed, the breath squeezed from his body. *Shift!* a voice screamed in his mind. He grabbed his magic—

An oliphant trumpeted. Something wrapped around his waist, jerking him free of the corpses.

Petrus managed—just—to keep his magic from spilling over, to avoid shifting. The oliphant tossed him onto the outcrop. He rolled, pushing to hands and knees. "Dareus!" he cried. "He's—"

But the oliphant had already turned. It waded through the corpses to where Dareus had vanished, tossing the creatures aside, squealing with urgency.

Around him, corpses began to heave clumsily up onto the outcrop. Petrus scrambled backwards on hands and knees, reaching for his dagger. Someone hauled him to his feet. Prince Harkeld.

Petrus stood, swaying dizzily. Hot liquid trickled down his brow. To his right, a man screamed.

Dareus's voice rang in his ears: *If the worst happens, get him out of here.*

Petrus turned to the prince, gathering his magic. "Sire."

Prince Harkeld didn't hear him. He swung his sword. The blade whistled through the air, shearing a hollow-eyed head from its body.

The ancient warriors seemed to hesitate, to falter in their advance.

Petrus looked up. The sky was no longer utterly black.

Prince Harkeld swung his sword again, splitting a brittle skull in two, sending a withered arm spinning.

"Wait." Petrus laid his hand on the prince's shoulder.

The prince shrugged him off.

"No." Petrus tightened his grip, halting him. "It's dawn."

Prince Harkeld paused, his sword half-raised.

Grayness seeped into the canyon. Petrus dimly saw towering cliffs, gaping tombs. The canyon floor seethed with movement—not towards them, but away. The creatures were retreating.

Petrus released the prince. He jumped down from the outcrop, brushing aside the last, laggard corpses. "Dareus!"

The oliphant who'd saved him was there, heaving aside corpses. Innis or Ebril, he couldn't tell, didn't care. He waded into the carnage. Blood trickled down his face and dripped from his chin.

The sun wasn't fully risen; the creatures still stirred feebly. Fingers grabbed at him, fastening weakly on his arms, his legs. Petrus ignored them.

He dug deeper, to where the corpses were charred. Others were alongside him, hauling bodies aside—

Prince Harkeld, Gerit, a soldier. Petrus heaved a headless corpse out of the way, and there, sprawled amid a tangle of wizened limbs, was Dareus.

The mage was dead. His neck was bent at an impossible angle, his eyes half-open, his mouth wide as if expressing his surprise.

Petrus sank down on his heels. He wiped the blood from his face.

Somebody exhaled, a quiet, regretful sound.

"Can they heal him?" a voice asked.

"He's dead," Gerit said. "No one can heal that."

Petrus raised his head. He saw drifting smoke, sand strewn with bodies, dawn breaking over sandstone cliffs. The oliphant stood silently, its gray hide streaked with soot. Now that the sky was lighter he could see who it was: Innis.

He stood wearily. Five more minutes. That was all they'd needed. Five more minutes and the sun would have risen, the corpses would have retreated, and Dareus would still be alive.

He glanced at the grim faces surrounding him: Prince Harkeld, Tomas, two of the soldiers, Gerit and Cora.

"How many did we lose?" Cora asked. "Do we know yet?"

"Three of my men," Tomas said. "And him."

Gerit swung round to face Prince Harkeld. "This is your fault." His voice was low, hoarse, thick with emotion.

The prince's face tightened, as if he'd been struck.

Cora frowned. "Gerit—"

Gerit ignored her. He took a step towards the prince. "If you'd used your magic, you sniveling coward, he'd still be alive! He's dead because of you!"

"That's enough, Gerit," Cora said wearily.

Gerit swung towards her, bullish, his head lowered. "Don't you tell me what to do."

Petrus stepped up alongside Cora. *Now that Dareus is dead, she leads us.* He was Justen, so he couldn't utter the words aloud, but Gerit understood the message.

Gerit inhaled a hissing breath. His fists clenched.

"If you can't control yourself, then leave." Cora's voice held quiet authority.

For a moment it seemed that Gerit would contest her assumption of leadership. He stood, hands clenched, his face twisted with rage, while smoke drifted around them. Then he made an angry sound of disgust and pushed between the soldiers.

Petrus glanced at Prince Harkeld. He thought he'd see anger, matching Gerit's; instead, the prince's face was tight, bitter.

A low moaning note began to whisper from the canyon walls.

Petrus looked around for the óliphant. It was gone.

He pushed past the prince and heaved himself up on the outcrop. Innis was there, dressing. "You all right?" he asked.

She glanced at him, her face pale and soot-smeared, and nodded. Tears glistened in her eyes. She bent her head, buttoning her shirt.

Petrus walked across to her. "Come here," he said, pulling her close. She inhaled a sob-like breath and hugged him tightly.

Petrus rested his cheek on her hair. It smelled of smoke and charred corpses. They stood for a moment, holding each other. He could feel her trembling.

"You're still Justen," she whispered.

"I know." Petrus released her, stepping back. He smiled crookedly. "Justen would like to thank you for saving him."

Innis didn't return the smile. "I thought they were going to kill you." She reached up and touched his forehead. "You're bleeding." He felt her magic flow into him, light, brief, sealing the cut.

Petrus captured her hand as she lowered it. "I'm hard to kill," he said, wrapping his fingers around hers.

Hobnails scraped on sandstone as someone else clambered up on the outcrop. Petrus released Innis's hand and stepped away from her. He turned and looked down at the deep drifts of charred bodies. To the right, soldiers were searching for their fallen comrades. As he watched, another man was unearthed from the tangle of corpses. It was the soldier who'd been stung by the scorpion a week ago. A lifetime ago. He was missing both his arms.

Petrus turned his head and watched as Cora approached.

She halted beside him. "Thank you."

Petrus nodded and resumed his inspection of the battlefield. He counted the remaining soldiers: six. After a moment he asked, "Where's Gerit?"

"At the river, washing. Ebril's keeping an eye on him."

Petrus nodded again. He understood Gerit's rage. The death—all the deaths—had been so unnecessary. *Another five minutes.*

The fault hadn't been Prince Harkeld's, though. He sighed and rubbed his face. Stubble rasped beneath his hand, sticky with blood, greasy with soot.

"How are you?" Cora asked. Her graying sandy hair was dark with soot, her face drawn and gaunt. "Can you be Justen for a few more hours?"

"Yes." He looked to where Dareus's body lay. The only person still standing there was Prince Harkeld. It was impossible to tell what the prince was thinking. Rage? Regret? Indifference?

Petrus turned away. "I'll get the shovels."

THEY BURIED THE three dead soldiers on the southern side of the outcrop, and Dareus on the northern. Tomas had looked relieved at the suggestion. Innis understood why: he didn't want his men to share their resting place with a mage.

Cora spoke the words over Dareus's grave: "All-Mother, we give this man to your care, that he may rest peacefully."

Innis looked north towards Ner. Wind puffed along the canyon, setting the cliffs wailing, swirling the sand. Within a week or two, all traces of the battle would be gone, as if it had never happened. The discarded bodies, the churned tracks, the graves, would all be covered in sand.

"Would you prefer to rest your men now?" Cora asked Tomas. "Or move on?"

Tomas raked his hair with one hand, making it stick up stiffly. He looked haggard, middle-aged, nothing like the laughing young prince from Lundegaard's castle. "Go," he said. "Get away from here."

*　　*　　*

INNIS FLEW TO check on the horses, picketed nearly a mile from the outcrop. For once, none of them had broken loose overnight. They stood tethered, stained with sweat, quivering with exhaustion. The air stank with their fear.

When Innis returned, she found everyone dressed in the forest green of Lundegaard's army.

"What's this?" she asked, as three of Tomas's soldiers set off to retrieve the horses.

"Ebril's idea," Cora said. "In case there are any assassins." She'd washed her face. The smudges beneath her eyes were exhaustion, not soot. "With the prince dressed as a soldier, they won't know who to aim for. Should give us a few seconds' advantage."

"You think they'd try an ambush so close to the canyon mouth?"

"No. But I don't want to take the risk. No one's got the strength to be a wolf today, sniffing for them. This is the next best option."

Innis glanced at Prince Harkeld. His uniform was as filthy as the soldiers', his face as exhausted and stubbled and grim, but to her eyes something marked him as not one of them. It was in the way he held himself; withdrawn, alone.

She wanted to hug him, to tell him everything would be all right, that he wasn't alone.

She knew what his response would be.

Innis turned away from him. "I'll fly ahead, look for somewhere for tonight."

CHAPTER SIXTY-ONE

"I HOPE YOU enjoy the cold, islander."

Karel glanced up from his breakfast. The armsman seated opposite him was one of the king's.

"What?" the man said, grinning broadly. "Haven't you heard?"

Karel feigned disinterest and returned to eating.

"Stupid son of a whore," the armsman said to his neighbor. "I'll be glad when he's gone."

"Gone? Where?"

"Horst. Rikard's being sent into exile. Ship leaves tomorrow."

Karel stopped chewing. He stared down at his plate.

"Duke Rikard? Are you certain?"

"He's not a duke any more. Stripped of his title, stripped of command of the army."

"What?" someone said, across the table. "Rikard leaked the invasion plans?"

"Left them unlocked in his study, where Lundegaard's spies found them—or so the investigators tell it."

"Spies?"

"Dressed as bondservants, they reckon. Slipped into the duke's study and copied the plans. Stupid whoreson, leaving them lying around like that."

"Too busy rutting his new wife to think beyond his cock," an armsman said.

Someone else grunted agreement.

"Who'll command the army?"

"Count Frankl. Rikard's with him now, handing over."

Karel stopped listening. He forced himself to swallow the food in his mouth. It took all of his self control to stay seated on the bench. Rikard was going into exile tomorrow.

Does the princess have to go with him?

AFTER BREAKFAST CAME training. Impatience ate at him. The wrestling matches weren't a distraction; they were chores to get through before he could go on duty. Karel fought with single-minded purpose, winning each bout with brutal efficiency. "Whoreson," his last conquest gasped, spitting blood. "You nearly broke my rutting neck."

"Islander!" the training master bellowed. "Out of the arena. Now!"

Karel went.

CHAPTER SIXTY-TWO

INNIS FLEW NORTH. No, it was more than flying, it was running away from what had happened, from Dareus lying dead beneath a pile of sand.

Finally the canyon petered out in a forest of stone fins and spires. She dipped a wing and glided back down the canyon until she could no longer see the spines of rock. She circled. Here was where they needed to camp tonight—out of sight of the assassins, but within a few miles of the ruined city.

There were no caves large enough, no ledges of stone, no outcrops. She flew higher, breaking free of the canyon walls. A rocky plateau stretched south, east, west, like a rumpled orange-red blanket that had been cast down.

There was no shelter up here, no way the horses could be brought up, but with ropes the men could climb.

Innis circled thoughtfully. How safe would it be up here? Was it as empty as it looked, or did creatures roused by the curse hunt here at night?

She glided down again, letting the canyon swallow her, and landed beside the trickle of the River Ner. She shifted.

Innis had felt her weariness as a hawk, but in human form it pressed down heavily. Her knees buckled as dizziness washed over her. She fell, catching herself on hands and knees.

For a few seconds she knelt, head hanging, eyes squeezed shut, then she looked up. *You told Cora you could do this. So do it.*

Her knees were bloody, her palms skinned. The pain seemed to help. The dizziness eased slightly. Innis drank from the river, splashing cool water on her face. The dizziness retreated even further.

She crouched in the rivulet and washed away soot and blood and sweat, washed away the terrible memory of last night. Then she sat on one of the smooth, rounded boulders and let the breeze dry her skin. Tombs lined the canyon to the height of a man's head on either side. Some were natural, others looked as if they'd been cut into the rock by the ancient Massens. Above the tombs, the cliffs towered, red sandstone veined with orange and yellow, white and slate-gray, and riddled with holes—tiny cavities the size of her thumb, holes that were fist-sized, head-sized, the size of a man's torso, and, scattered here and there, caves large enough for a person to huddle in.

Large enough for a person.

Her weariness evaporated abruptly. She caught her breath and scanned the cliffs. One, two... four... seven... ten, twelve. There were more than enough caves for them all.

Relief surged through her. There was no need to fight tonight. They'd be safe.

On the heels of relief, came grief. These cliffs were

no different from those that had loomed over them last night. *If I'd thought of this yesterday, Dareus would still be alive.*

Tears stung her eyes. Innis blinked them back. *This is what being a Sentinel means: death. You knew that. Dareus knew it too. Don't let him down by blubbering.*

She'd heard Dareus speak twice at the Academy about being a Sentinel. He'd concluded both lectures by reading the names of Sentinels killed performing their duty. It was a long list. Both her parents' names were on it. Now Dareus's would be too.

Innis washed her face. Crouching, she drew a circle in water on a boulder with her fingertip. "All-Mother, take care of him," she whispered, holding Dareus's face in her mind.

The water evaporated slowly, the sandstone drying from red to dusky pink.

When the circle was no longer visible, Innis gathered her magic, holding the image of a hawk in her mind. Her skin prickled, a sensation close to pain. She closed her eyes for an instant; when she opened them she saw from a hawk's viewpoint: the sharpness of vision, the wider field of view. Her eyes caught movement on the far side of the canyon: a lizard scuttling.

Innis spread her wings and lifted into the air, heading back down the canyon.

CHAPTER SIXTY-THREE

KAREL STRODE THROUGH the marble corridors, dressed in the gold and scarlet uniform, his sword belted at his side and the armsman's torque around his throat. *Hurry. Hurry.*

But when he reached Duke Rikard's rooms, all was quiet. The duke must still be briefing the new commander. There was no bustle, no noise, no urgency. The door to the bedchamber was shut.

The armsman he replaced left without speaking a word.

Karel stood for a moment in the empty salon. Should he take his place against the wall like a good armsman and wait for whatever happened next?

No.

He strode across to the bedchamber and knocked. After a moment, Yasma opened the door. "Karel." Surprise crossed her face. "Is it noon already?"

"I'm early." Behind Yasma, he saw the princess seated before the mirror, the golden crown partly bound to her head. "Is the princess going into exile with Rikard?"

Princess Brigitta's head turned. She stared at him across the room.

"You didn't know?" Karel said, looking at the princess, not Yasma.

"No," Yasma said. "The duke left just after midnight. He hasn't been back since."

"Exile?" Princess Brigitta pushed to her feet and hurried across the bedchamber. "Rikard?"

"Your father's stripped him of his dukedom," Karel told her. "And command of the army. He's being exiled to Horst. Leaving tomorrow." He waited a heartbeat, and then asked directly, "Do you have to go with him?"

It was an impertinence to speak so to her, but the princess didn't appear to mind. "I don't know." Her brow furrowed, and then she blinked and purpose came into her face. "No. I won't go with him!" She turned and half-ran back to the mirror. "Quickly, Yasma! Finish my hair!"

KAREL WAITED TENSELY in the salon. *If Rikard comes now—*

He paced to one end of the room and back. The door to the bedchamber opened. Princess Brigitta emerged. She crossed the salon, then turned in a flurry of silk. "You must come too, Yasma! Bring my cloak. Quickly!"

They walked briskly—mistress, maid, armsman—through the corridors of the palace. At the king's antechamber, the princess demanded entrance. "I must speak with my father," she said imperiously.

They waited only a few minutes. Karel stood to attention, staring straight ahead. On the wall was a map of the Seven Kingdoms, lettered in gold leaf.

Osgaard looked like a bloated octopus, its tentacles reaching north, south, west. It had swallowed Meren and Brindesan, Horst, Karnveld, Lomaly, and the Esfaban islands.

His eyes traced the borders of the Seven Kingdoms. If Osgaard conquered Lundegaard, it would rival Ankeny in size. There would be only six kingdoms and the maps would have to be redrawn, yet again.

An armsman opened the door into the king's audience chamber. "You may enter, highness."

Princess Brigitta took a deep breath. "Wait for me here, Yasma, Karel." She pinched her cheeks to give them color and stepped through into the audience chamber.

BRITTA HADN'T SEEN her father since the day of her marriage. He seemed to have grown in size, in anger. He sat on his golden throne, his face florid, his anger palpable as he watched her approach.

Her heart began to beat even faster. Harkeld's voice whispered in her ear: *Don't let him see you're afraid.*

Jaegar stood at one of the windows, a faint smile on his lips. Anticipation seemed to glitter in his eyes.

"Did Rikard send you to beg for him?"

"No, Father." Britta took hold of her courage. "I've come to ask that my marriage be annulled."

Her father's brows lowered. Rage seemed to gather on his face.

Britta spoke quickly: "Rikard failed you, and you rightly punish him. Exile him, Father—but don't allow him to take me with him. Else you'll be seen as rewarding him."

There was silence in the chamber. She was aware of the armsmen standing motionless against the walls, aware of the harsh sound of her father's breathing. Jaegar stepped away from the window. He strolled across the marble floor and halted in front of her, studying her face.

Britta swallowed. Her heart seemed to be beating in her throat.

Jaegar reached out and lightly touched her chin, tilting her face upward. He turned to their father. "She's right," he said. "You strip Rikard of his title and his command of your army, you exile him—and yet you reward him with this. Your own daughter."

Britta held her breath.

"Beautiful, isn't she?" Jaegar caressed her cheek lightly with his thumb. "Such a shame to waste her."

The king stared at her from his throne, heavy-browed, his mouth pinched in anger.

Jaegar released her chin. "She could be the answer to our most pressing problem." He strolled over to the dais and bent to whisper in their father's ear. Britta caught the word *Harkeld*.

The king's eyes narrowed as he stared at her. For a long moment there was utter silence. She heard her father's breathing, heard the beating of her heart... and then the king spoke: "Very well. Annul it."

JAEGAR WROTE THE annulment on a sheet of parchment. The king signed it, the quill making brisk scratching sounds as he scrawled his name.

Her brother applied the royal seal: scarlet wax and gold leaf. "Done," he said, rolling the parchment up and handing it to her. His voice seemed to hold faint amusement.

Britta curtseyed towards the throne. "Thank you, Father."

Jaegar escorted her to the door. "I suppose you'd like your old rooms back."

"I don't mind." *I'll sleep anywhere, as long as Rikard isn't with me.*

"Take them. No one else is using them."

"Thank you." Britta gripped the annulment tightly. "What did you mean? About me being a solution to a problem?"

Jaegar's smile widened, sharpened, showing his teeth. "We know how fond Harkeld is of you."

An armsman opened the door for her. Britta found herself in the antechamber before her mind had sorted through the implications of the statement. Was she to be bait to catch Harkeld?

PRINCESS BRIGITTA RETURNED to Rikard's suite. "Take what we'll need overnight," she told Yasma. "We can come back for the rest once he's gone."

Yasma hurried into the bedchamber.

Karel followed the princess to the dining room and took up position just inside the door. The picture he'd drawn last night lay on the table: soldiers chasing a party of bandits into the mountains.

The princess laid down the annulment and put the drawing aside without looking at it. She uncapped the ink flask, dipped the quill in it, and began to write hurriedly on the next sheet of blank parchment.

Karel tried to read upside down. *Rikard, my*

father has annulled our marriage. I am no longer your wife.

His gaze lifted to Princess Brigitta's face, to the faintly furrowed brow, the golden crown. She was stronger than he'd realized—to confront her father, to demand an annulment. He'd underestimated her courage.

In the salon, a door opened. Heavy footsteps strode into the room.

"Princess," Karel said in a low voice.

The princess had heard the footsteps. She sat frozen for a moment, her face leached of all color, then she stood, reaching for the annulment.

Rikard flung open the door to the bedchamber. "Brigitta!"

The princess stepped into the salon. Karel heard her inhale, saw muscles work in her throat as she swallowed, saw her hand tighten around the roll of parchment. "I'm here," she said.

Rikard turned. "There you are." He strode towards her. "Pack your belongings, my lady. We're leaving."

"I am no longer your wife," Princess Brigitta said. She held out the roll of parchment. "The king has annulled our marriage."

Rikard halted. His face stiffened as if he'd been struck. "No," he said. "You're mine."

The princess shook her head. "No."

That word, quietly spoken, seemed to enrage Rikard. Rage blossomed red on his face. He took a step forward, one hand going to the hilt of his sword.

Karel stepped in front of the princess. "Dare you draw your blade in the presence of a royal princess?"

Rikard gripped his sword hilt. "She's my wife!"

"Not any more."

Movement in the doorway of the bedchamber caught Karel's eye. Yasma stood there, terror on her face.

"Ernst!" Rikard bellowed.

The door from the antechamber swung open. An armsman came into the salon at a run. He stopped short when he saw the tableau, his sword half-drawn.

"Dare you draw your blade in the presence of a royal princess?" Karel asked again. He held Rikard's eyes, and then the armsman's.

The armsman listened to the words. He slid the sword back into its scabbard and lifted both hands, holding them palm outward at his waist. He took a step back, distancing himself from his master.

Rikard didn't listen. He took another step forward. "Out of my way, you whoreson islander. She's *mine*."

Karel took a pace forward too. "No. The marriage has been annulled." And silently, he said, *Come on, try to take her.*

Rikard seemed to hear the unspoken challenge. Metal hissed as he drew his sword.

Everything slowed down, dream-like: Rikard charging with his sword raised, Yasma opening her mouth to scream.

It happened just as Karel had imagined: the weight of the sword in his hands, the flex of his muscles as he swung it. The sword blade caught Rikard solidly below his chin, shearing through flesh, through bone.

He'd seen it a thousand times in his imagination—Rikard's head spinning, blood spraying across the walls and ceiling. In reality it was faster, less messy.

The head struck the floor, bounced, rolled to a halt. The man's body followed with a meaty thud. Blood gushed across the rugs.

Karel lowered his sword. Exultation sang in his veins. He met the armsman's eyes. The man's face was pale with shock. "Fetch Prince Jaegar," he said.

The armsman obeyed at a run.

Karel turned. The princess crouched behind him, her face buried in her hands.

He dropped the sword and knelt alongside her. "Princess?" He hugged her to him without thinking. "He's dead. It's all right."

She was shuddering.

Karel tightened his grip. He smoothed his hand over the nape of her neck, over her upwoven hair. "He's dead," he whispered, pressing his lips to her temple. "Britta, he's dead." And then he heard what he'd said—Britta—and realized what he was doing.

He lifted his head and pulled away from her, and stopped when her hand clutched his breastplate. "Princess?"

"Dead?"

"Yes."

For a moment she clung to him, shaking, and then she turned her head and looked at the body. Outside, the fifth bell began to toll: noon.

Princess Brigitta inhaled a deep breath. He felt the shuddering stop. She released her grip on his breastplate and pushed away until she was kneeling. She looked at him, meeting his eyes. "Thank you," she whispered, and then she took another deep breath and her face became composed, regal. She stood.

It was my pleasure, princess. He stood too, reaching down to pick up his sword. Rikard's blood dripped from the blade.

Karel wiped his sword on a satin cushion stitched with gold thread and sheathed it.

CHAPTER SIXTY-FOUR

Jaumé had never seen so many people or buildings in his life. The crush of houses and shops and inns, the crush of carts and horses and dogs, of farmers and townsfolk, was too much to take in. He shrank back against a dirty white-washed wall, hugging the blanket and waterskin tightly. Noise and smells buffeted him. His ears were full of shouts, full of horses neighing and dogs barking and the rumble of wagon wheels on cobblestones. The smell of the town filled his mouth and nose: wood smoke, cooking smells, sewage and horse manure, and sweat and panic and fear. Everywhere he looked were more people, more horses, more wagons. Even the buildings seemed to be moving, shouldering each other.

Jaumé repeated the names the miller had told him—Lundegaard, Osgaard, the Allied Kingdoms. He took a deep breath and plunged into the crowded street, joining the stream of people.

THE BOAT WAS a hundred times bigger than the little wooden herring boats that fished out of Girond. The dark hull came up out of the water like a cliff and the lofty masts with sails furled to their spars looked tall enough to scratch open the sky. Jaumé stared at it. *Not a boat; a ship. Built to sail across the ocean.*

Great white gulls with black wings soared and swooped overhead, their cries as plaintive as mourners' wailing. Each breath Jaumé took tasted of the sea—tangy, salty—and tasted of sweat and fear, too. People stood shoulder to shoulder, jostling each other. Despite the sunshine and the blue sky, the air was heavy, charged with tension.

It's every man for himself. And he made himself as small as he could and began to work his way through the crowd, slipping between gaps like an eel, using his elbows, moving towards the ship.

HUNGER CRAMPED TIGHTLY in his stomach, but Jaumé scarcely noticed. He was in the shadow of the ship now. He could see the sea—sunlight sparkling on a vast stretch of water—but it was the ship that commanded his attention: the hull jutting out of the water, the faces of the passengers peering down.

There was a name on the ship's side. He couldn't read it, but a picture had been painted below: a dolphin riding the crest of a wave.

Jaumé stared at the dolphin, at the tall masts, at the rigging and the furled sails. Soon he'd be one of those people climbing the plank up to the deck.

The blanket was gone, ripped from his arms, but he still held the waterskin. It gurgled limply. Someone had trodden on his foot. His toenails were bleeding, but it didn't matter because now it was his turn. He was the one who stood at the foot of the plank. "I want to go to Lundegaard," he said. "Or Osgaard. Or the Allied Kingdoms."

"This ship's to Lundegaard," the man said. He stood with an armed guard either side of him, a doughy, slope-shouldered man. He held out his hand. "One silver groat."

"What?"

"One silver groat. Come on, lad. People are waiting."

"But... I don't have any money."

The man closed his hand. His mouth screwed up in a grimace. "Sorry, lad. Can't let you on without payment."

"But—"

The man's eyes slid away from his. "Next!" he said, and someone shouldered Jaumé aside.

JAUMÉ LIMPED BACK the way he'd come. A silver groat. Twelve copper pennies.

Despair enveloped him. Where would he find twelve copper pennies?

He remembered the pennies Mam had kept knotted in her kerchief. He remembered Mam lying dead on the floor. He remembered the smell of her blood, the slickness of it beneath his feet. Tears welled in his eyes. He pushed forward against the crowd, buffeted by elbows, by voices.

It was almost dusk by the time Jaumé reached the town gates. Outside the walls of Cornas, a vast encampment stretched. People clustered around fires. He saw horses and wagons, dogs, a bleating goat. The smell of food rose, mingling with the smells of wood smoke and raw sewage. His belly cramped in a painful knot of hunger.

Jaumé hugged the almost-empty waterskin to his chest, blinking back tears, and looked down at his feet. The toes of his left foot were bloody.

The blood made him remember Mam again. The knotted kerchief with the pennies had been lying on the bloody floor. If he'd thought to snatch it up—

But then he remembered the sound of hens squawking in the yard as they flapped out of Da's way. Terror lurched inside him. He clutched the waterskin more tightly.

If he didn't find twelve copper pennies, it would happen again: the blood and the terror, the screaming—

"Young Jaumé," a voice said behind him. "I'm glad to see you made it, lad."

He turned his head. It was the miller. The man's face creased into a friendly smile above his curling black beard. "Are you hungry, lad? Come share some food with us."

HE FOLLOWED THE miller through the mass of people, past fires and bedrolls and horses and squalling babies. The man's wife and sons sat beside a small fire. Around them were their belongings: blankets, a few clothes, waterskins, a stew pot, a bundle of firewood.

"Look who I found," the miller said.

His wife glanced at Jaumé. Her nod of greeting was perfunctory. The smallest boy smiled shyly at

Jaumé from the protective curve of her arm. "How much did you get?" she asked.

"Twenty-three pennies."

"Twenty-three pennies?" Her voice rose; in despair, not anger. "For two horses and a wagon? They were worth five times that!"

"I know." The miller rubbed his face and sighed. "There's no market for them here, Sara. I was lucky to get what I did." He sat, moving slowly, as if his bones ached with weariness. "Sit, lad."

Jaumé sat. His eyes were drawn to the stew pot. He saw food in it: lumps of meat, chunks of carrot. His mouth watered.

"It's better than nothing," he heard the miller say. "It'll feed us in Piestany. For a few days."

His attention jerked back to the miller. "Piestany?"

"In the Allied Kingdoms. We're sailing tomorrow." He nodded at his wife. "Feed the lad, Sara. He looks hungry."

The miller's wife silently reached for a bowl. She filled it from the stew pot.

Jaumé put down the waterskin. He took the bowl and spoon the miller's wife handed him. His stomach twisted in painful anticipation.

The miller unfastened a pouch from his belt and tipped the contents into his palm. Coins clinked against one another.

Jaumé paused with the spoon halfway to his mouth. A small pile of copper pennies sat on the miller's palm. In their midst was a silver groat. "Here, Sara." He held the coins out to his wife. "Put them with the others."

Time seemed to stand still. Jaumé heard his heart

beating loudly in his ears. The groat stared at him from the miller's palm, winking silver among the copper pennies.

A silver groat.

The miller's wife reached for the coins.

Jaumé dropped the bowl and spoon and snatched the groat from the miller's hand and ran as if the curse itself was at his heels. Behind him, the miller's wife's voice rose in a scream.

HE RAN, DODGING through the throng of people and animals, wagons and campfires. At the entrance to the town he pushed himself inside along with the last few stragglers and heard the *clang* of the gates closing behind him.

Safe.

Jaumé leaned against a wall, panting. Emotions churned inside him. Hope. Triumph. And a different kind of despair to what he'd felt earlier. The groat was clenched tightly in his fist. He remembered the miller's smiling face, his eyes crinkling above the curling beard. *Are you hungry, lad? Come share some food with us.*

Jaumé bent over, trying to catch his breath, trying not to vomit from exertion, from despair. When his breathing had steadied, he lifted his head. Night had fallen.

He had no food, no water, no blanket—but he had a silver groat.

He remembered the miller's face again, his kind voice. *Had some trouble, did you, son?*

But the miller had also said, *It's every man for himself.*

Jaumé clutched the groat more tightly. It was a small, hard disk in his palm. It was the price of passage to Lundegaard. The price of his life.

CHAPTER SIXTY-FIVE

THEY REACHED THE site the girl had chosen in the late afternoon. "How far to the assassins?" Tomas asked.

"A couple of miles. Once we're past that bend, they'll be able to see us."

Harkeld dismounted. He followed the direction of her pointing finger. The red cliffs bulged and curved gently northward. Beyond that bend, were Fithian assassins.

The skin on his back tightened in a shiver.

They washed in the river and then sat down to a meal of stew. Harkeld ate, listening as the witches and Tomas discussed the next day's strategy. "The assassins have a look-out," Petrus said. "We'll fly ahead and kill him."

"Are you sure there's only one look-out?" Tomas asked.

"Only one," Petrus said. "Only one direction Prince Harkeld can come from."

Tomas conceded this with a tilt of his chin.

Harkeld looked for the girl. She wasn't seated at the fire with them. He glanced up at the sky. The hawk circling there had a russet breast. Ebril.

The fourth shapeshifter, Gerit, made no sign that he was listening. He sat cloaked in a cloud of anger, stabbing at the stew with his spoon.

You have fire magic. Use it!

The stew abruptly tasted like ashes in Harkeld's mouth. He forced himself to swallow. The witch's voice rang in his ears: *If you'd used your magic, you sniveling coward, he'd still be alive!*

Harkeld put down his bowl. He pushed the witch's voice out of his head and made himself focus on something else. "Where's the girl?" he asked his armsman.

"Huh?" Justen said.

"The girl. Innis. Where is she?"

"Uh... I think she's asleep. In one of the caves." Justen pointed with his spoon.

Wind gusted up the canyon, setting the cliffs wailing. Sand grains stung Harkeld's face.

"And after you've killed the look-out, what then?" Tomas asked, cupping a protective hand over his bowl.

"Then we have a choice," Petrus said. "Either we try to kill the others immediately, or we wait until you've passed."

"Why would you wait?"

"Because once we attack, the assassins will know Prince Harkeld's here."

"You think you won't be able to kill them all?"

Petrus shook his head. "I doubt it. These men are professional killers. Magic can only help us so far."

Harkeld studied the witch's face. *Do you expect to die tomorrow?*

"If you wait, you don't think the assassins will notice us riding past?" Tomas's voice was skeptical.

"With the look-out dead, no," Petrus said. "Innis says the canyon mouth is a maze of rock. As long as you're quiet, the Fithians won't know you're there."

Tomas tugged at his lower lip. "I'd rather they're all dead before we bring Harkeld through."

"I don't think we can do it. Not seven of them. If we had another dozen soldiers or a few more mages, we could attack them, hope to kill them all. As it is…" Petrus shrugged. "There are too few of us."

Tomas acknowledged this with a grimace. "And once we're out of the canyon? What then?"

"We make for the catacombs," Cora said. "While the shapeshifters try to kill the rest of the Fithians."

Harkeld scuffed the sand with the toe of his boot. He'd had confidence in Dareus, witch or not— the same confidence he had in King Magnas. He didn't have that confidence in Cora. He glanced up at her, seeing a small, plain, middle-aged woman with her hair pulled back in a plait. She was utterly unremarkable. *I wish Dareus was still alive.*

Tomas grunted. He ate another mouthful of stew. "And once we reach the catacombs? What then?"

"We go in," Cora said. "If any assassins come after us, your task is to stop them following us inside. You have three archers left?"

Tomas looked alarmed. "Yes, but—"

"I'd take plenty of arrows, if I were you," Petrus said. "Because if you run out, you'll have to fight hand to hand."

"But—"

"Don't worry, prince. We'll thin their numbers. Shouldn't be more than one or two reach the catacombs."

Tomas didn't look reassured. He glanced at his men, as if silently counting them.

"Who goes in?" Justen asked.

"You and Prince Harkeld and me," Cora said.

Harkeld looked at the faces surrounding the fire: Tomas, Justen, Cora, Gerit, Petrus. And six exhausted soldiers. *How many of us will be alive this time tomorrow?*

Movement caught his eye. "Scorpion."

Tomas stood. He crushed the creature with his boot and flicked it away. "And afterwards?" he asked, sitting again. "Once this anchor stone is destroyed. What do we do then?"

"We head for Ankeny and the second anchor stone," Cora said. "On the old trading route. More mages will meet us in Stanic. You may choose to come with us or not."

Tomas hesitated. He didn't want to go with them— that was clear on his face—as was his reluctance to say so aloud.

Then I'll say it. "Go back to Lundegaard," Harkeld said. His voice came out rougher than he'd intended.

For a moment Tomas met his eyes—and then his gaze slid away. He nodded.

Harkeld looked down at his bowl. He'd lost more than Tomas's friendship in that moment in the gorge; he'd lost the home King Magnas had offered him. He could never go back to Lundegaard. Not now he was proven a witch.

THE WITCHES, GERIT and Petrus, changed into hawks and flapped up to the caves, ropes gripped in their talons. Back in human shape, they hauled up blankets and waterskins and weapons—and finally men.

"You don't have to share with me," Harkeld said, as he and Justen waited for their turn. Above them, the sky began shading from pale blue to gray. "I'll be perfectly safe on my own."

Justen knelt on the sand, tying blankets to the end of a rope. At his back was the walled-up entrance of a tomb. "I'm your armsman, sire."

"Yes, but if you'd prefer to sleep on your own tonight—"

"Why? Because you're a mage?" Justen glanced up at him. "I don't care whether you're a mage or not, sire. You're the one who cares." He tightened the knot and looked up at Petrus crouching in a cave several yards above their heads. "Ready!"

The blankets jerked into the air and began bouncing their way upward.

"And besides," Justen said, standing. "What if you roll over in your sleep? You could fall out."

"I won't fall out."

"No. Because I'll be blocking the opening."

Harkeld studied his armsman's face—the broad brow, the square jaw, the frank, open features. *Aren't you afraid of me?*

A scorpion scuttled across the sand towards them. "Ach." Justen tossed it aside with the toe of his boot. "Wretched creatures. We must be near a nest."

You should be afraid of me, Harkeld told the armsman silently. *I am.*

A rope slithered down the cliff face. It was knotted to assist climbing.

"Do you want to go first, sire, or shall I?"

* * *

THE CAVE WAS cramped; they could only crouch, not stand. Harkeld removed his boots and baldric. "I apologize for striking you this morning. It was wrong of me. You were obeying your orders."

Justen blinked. His expression was bemused, as if he'd forgotten the moment on the outcrop. Then he shrugged. "Forget it, sire."

Harkeld silently spread a blanket on the rough sandstone. "Justen... I'd like it if you called me Harkeld."

In the gloom of dusk he saw his armsman's head jerk around. "Sire?"

"When we're in private, you may call me Harkeld." *Please*.

Justen blinked. "Yes, sire—" He paused. "Yes, Harkeld."

CHAPTER SIXTY-SIX

THE WHARF WAS still busy, despite it being night. Jaumé worked his way through the crush until he was near the front. Here the crowd funneled into a line. He stood, waiting to move forward, the groat clenched in his hand. The ship's hull loomed above him. The picture on its side—the dolphin riding a wave—was dimly visible.

"You got enough money, boy?" someone asked alongside him.

Jaumé glanced up to his right. He dimly saw a face. The speaker was taller than him, but unbearded. A youth. He nodded.

"It's a whole silver groat," another voice said on his left.

Jaumé turned his head. Standing there was another youth, with a faint, straggling beard. "I know." He clutched the groat more tightly in his fist.

"I don't think he's got it, Peray," the first youth said.

"He shouldn't be in this line, then. Not if he doesn't have a groat."

"I have a groat," Jaumé said.

The line shuffled forward, towards the armed guards and the gangplank and the flare of torchlight.

The youths kept pace with him. "Show us."

Jaumé shook his head. He clenched his other hand around his fist and counted the people in front of him. Two families; ten people.

Someone took hold of his elbow.

Jaumé tried to wrench free. "No—" he started to say, but a knee buried itself in his stomach.

He doubled over, unable to breathe. Dimly, he heard a voice above his head. "Our brother's feeling faint." And then hands grabbed him and he was hauled out of the line.

The youths dragged him away from the flickering torchlight and dropped him on the ground. Jaumé tried to draw a breath, tried to shout, but only a faint croak came from his lips.

A voice hissed in his ear. "Give us the groat!"

Jaumé clutched the coin with every ounce of his strength. His breath was coming back. He opened his mouth to scream—

A foot caught him in the belly. Pain flooded through him. He lost his breath again.

His fingers were prized open. He heard someone grunt, a sound of satisfaction. He heard someone say, "Got it!" He heard running footsteps.

He heard the miller's voice in his ears: *It's every man for himself.*

JAUMÉ LIMPED DOWN the cobbled street. Ahead, a door swung open, spilling light and noise and the smell of food and ale into the street. He glimpsed a wooden sign above the doorway—a bunch of grapes—before the door swung shut. A tavern.

Jaumé halted, hugging his stomach. The door opened again. A man stumbled out. Lamplight was bright for an instant, the roar of voices loud, and then the door closed. All that was left was the tantalizing smell of food and the man staggering down the street.

Memory of the miller's wife filling a bowl with stew came—and memory of her voice raised in a shriek behind him as he ran with the groat clutched in his hand. Jaumé hugged his stomach more tightly. Tears of despair welled in his eyes.

"Out of the way, boy." Someone cuffed him aside and entered the tavern, letting out the roar, the lamplight, the smells, again.

Jaumé blinked back his tears and edged closer to the door. When it next opened, he peered inside. He saw people seated on benches at long wooden tables, he saw bowls of food and loaves of bread and tankards of ale.

The door closed. Jaumé leaned against the wall, waiting for it to open again. Slowly he became aware that he wasn't the only person standing in the darkness. He heard breathing, heard the rustle of fabric as someone shifted their weight.

Jaumé stiffened and slid his hand into his pocket. The knife blade was smooth beneath his fingers, sharp. When the door opened again, he looked to his right. Lamplight fell on a man's face—sandy beard, dark pits of eyes.

The man wasn't looking at him; he was staring hungrily into the tavern.

Jaumé released his grip on the knife.

The door closed again, opened again. People went

in. People came out. And each opening and closing of the door brought glimpses of food, brought smells that made his stomach cramp.

Next time, Jaumé told himself. *Next time someone goes in, so do I. I'll take the nearest loaf of bread and run.*

Footsteps came striding up the street. A man mounted the doorstep, opened the door, entered the tavern. Jaumé followed.

The door swung shut behind him. Jaumé stood for a moment, looking at the tables, at the bowls of stew and loaves of bread, the tankards of ale, the flagons of wine. A loaf of bread lay on the nearest table, cut in half.

He darted across, snatched up the closest half, and turned back to the door as a shout lifted into the air behind him.

The door opened. Two men stood on the threshold. Jaumé barreled past them, clutching the bread.

"Stop!" someone shouted behind him. "Thief!"

HE THOUGHT THERE was someone else running behind him, but perhaps it was the echo of his own bare feet slapping on the cobblestones. He ran, turning corners at random, until his lungs were burning, then he slowed to a trot. Ahead was a glow of firelight.

Jaumé looked behind him. The dark street seemed empty. But... wasn't that the sound of someone else's footfalls?

He hurried again and came out into what must be Cornas's market square. It was milling with people, lit by dozens of fires.

Jaumé hugged the bread to his chest and skirted

the square. This was like the encampment outside the walls; there were horses, wagons, people eating and sleeping. He felt again the tension in the air, smelled sweat and fear.

He walked three sides of the square before he found a place that felt safe. Here, in the corner, a band of men had set up camp. Like everyone else, they had horses, a fire, piles of equipment—but something marked them as different. Jaumé studied them for a moment, seeing the shapes of sleeping figures rolled in blankets and two men sitting watch, firelight reflecting in their eyes. There was a stillness in those seated figures, a watchfulness—but no fear, no desperation. These men weren't afraid. They seemed untouched by the tension surrounding them.

He wasn't the only one to notice there was something different about the men; a gap ringed them, as if no one wanted to get too close.

The men's strangeness didn't frighten him; it made him feel safer. Jaumé hunkered down on the ground and tore into the bread with his teeth.

A shadow fell over him. "Give me the bread, boy."

Jaumé looked up, his mouth full of bread. A man towered over him, firelight illuminating one side of his face. He had a sandy beard, dark pits of eyes. The man who'd stood outside the tavern.

"No," Jaumé said thickly, around the mouthful of bread. He clutched the half-loaf to his chest.

"It's not yours. I saw you steal it." The man made a snatch for the bread. "Give it to me."

Jaumé scuttled backwards on the cobblestones. His back came up against a wall.

The man followed him. "Give it to me."

Jaumé swallowed the bread in his mouth, almost choking. He looked to the band of men for help. The two on watch had their heads turned towards him. He saw firelight glitter in their eyes. They sat still, unmoving. They weren't going to help him.

Jaumé hugged the bread tightly with one arm. He fumbled in his pocket for the knife.

"Give it to me!" The man lunged forward, grabbing Jaumé's shoulder, reaching for the bread.

Something inside him seemed to burst open. Rage and despair spewed out. Jaumé ripped the knife from his pocket. "No!" he yelled, dropping the bread, stabbing at the man.

The man grunted and tried to fend him off.

Fury possessed Jaumé. It wasn't just the bread, it was the youths at the wharf, the man who'd stolen the gray gelding, the man who'd taken the half-leg of ham. It was Mam and Da and Rosa. He slashed and stabbed in a frenzy.

The man uttered a high yelp of pain. He turned and ran, stumbling in his haste to get away.

Jaumé lowered the knife. He was panting, shaking. Hs heartbeat thundered in his ears. He turned back to the bread. Several of the men rolled in blankets had woken. He saw firelight in their eyes as they looked at him. One of the men on watch rose to his feet and began to stroll towards him.

Jaumé tightened his grip on the knife and held it out towards the man. "It's my bread."

The man stopped. His hands were loose at his side, relaxed. He smiled, his teeth reflecting the firelight. "I don't want your bread. I have plenty of my own." His voice was calm and almost friendly. The vowels had a strange twist to them that marked him as not of Vaere. "Where's your family, lad? Dead?"

Jaumé nodded warily.

The man looked back at his companions. "What do you think, Nolt?"

One of the men shrugged off his blanket and stood. He was lean, with a neatly-trimmed beard. He walked across to the first man and stood, studying Jaumé. "How old are you, boy?"

"Eight," Jaumé said, clutching the knife tightly. The men's stillness, the intensity of their attention on him, was frightening.

Nolt looked him up and down and then nodded. "He has potential."

The first man winked at Jaumé. He had curling hair and a round, boyish face. "Grab your bread, lad. You can sleep with us tonight. You'll be safe."

Jaumé looked at the band of silent, watching men, at the dark eyes reflecting the firelight. He looked at the half-loaf of bread lying on the dirty cobblestones. He looked at the blood dripping from his knife blade.

He thrust the knife into his pocket, snatched up the bread, and followed Nolt and the curly-haired man back to their fire. Men shuffled sideways in their blankets to make room for him.

Jaumé sat warily on the cobblestones.

The man with curly hair tossed him a blanket. "Here."

Jaumé caught the blanket. He slung it around his shoulders and huddled into it.

"Want some cheese to go with that bread?"

Jaumé nodded.

CHAPTER SIXTY-SEVEN

CORPSES SWARMED OVER *him, tearing the hair from his scalp, wrenching his arms from their sockets. "Use your fire magic, you sniveling coward!" someone yelled.*

Harkeld woke to the sound of the shout echoing in his ears. He pushed away the blankets and sat up, gasping for air.

A hand touched his back. "Harkeld?"

That voice, that light touch, steadied him. His panic receded.

Harkeld wiped the sweat from his face. His breathing slowed. He lay back down and turned to her, gathering her close. He knew who she was without seeing her. The witch, Innis.

Even though she was a witch, he held her tightly. This wasn't real. It was a dream, too.

Her head rested against his shoulder. One of her hands lightly stroked his back. "It's all right," she said. "Everything's going to be all right."

Harkeld wanted to believe her.

He was aware of her breath against his skin, aware of her heart beating, aware of her emotions: grief, guilt—and he understood that she too felt responsible for Dareus's death.

"It wasn't your fault," he said. *It was mine. I could have saved him. And the three soldiers.*

The witch sighed. She turned her head slightly, pressed her cheek against his skin. "It wasn't your fault either."

Yes, it was.

Harkeld stared into the darkness. He remembered the sting of fire running over his skin, remembered the sensation of flames igniting in his chest. Terror rose inside him. His heart began to beat faster.

She stroked his shoulder blade, soothing. "Don't be afraid. Harkeld, everything will be all right."

He held her tightly and tried to believe it.

CHAPTER SIXTY-EIGHT

JAUMÉ ATE HIS breakfast, swallowing bread and cheese, gulping cider.

"Where are you from, boy?" Nolt asked. His vowels were as short and clipped as his beard.

"Girond," Jaumé said, aware of the other men watching him as they ate. Seven men. Eight, counting Nolt.

"Girond?"

"Two hundred leagues east of here," one of the men said. "On the coast."

"Two hundred leagues?" Nolt pursed his lips, nodded. In the daylight, his face was older than Jaumé had thought, the skin leathery, creased and tanned. "What happened to your family?"

Jaumé's throat closed. Tears came to his eyes. He forced himself to blink them back, to swallow. These were not men to cry in front of. "The curse got them."

"But not you."

He shook his head.

"How did you get here?" another of the men asked, the one with the curly red-blond hair who'd winked at him last night.

"I walked," Jaumé said.

"Alone?"

He nodded.

"Two hundred leagues." Nolt studied Jaumé's face a moment longer, and seemed to come to a decision. "You may come with us if you wish. Bennick, he's your charge." He stood. "Let's move out."

The men stood, except for the one with curling red-blond hair.

"Are you Bennick?" Jaumé asked him.

The man nodded. He had a young, cheerful face and blue eyes that twinkled in the sunshine. "You want to come with us?"

"Where are you going?"

"To Ankeny. We have business there."

"Ankeny?"

"It's north of here, lad. And west." Bennick winked. "Don't worry. The curse won't catch us."

Jaumé stuffed the last of the bread and cheese in his mouth. Around him, men were packing up the camp. They worked quickly, but without urgency. There was discipline in their movements, in the way they worked together.

"What kind of business?" he asked, once he'd swallowed.

"We're meeting a man."

"A merchant?"

Bennick laughed. "No. A prince. If he gets as far as Ankeny—which I doubt."

"I've never met a prince before."

"They're nothing special. They die just as easily as other men."

Jaumé drained the mug of cider. He saw bundles

of arrows being loaded on the pack horses, bows being strapped down. He saw men slinging baldrics over their shoulders, saw sword hilts protruding from scabbards. "Are you soldiers?"

"After a fashion," Bennick said. "We're Brothers."

Jaumé looked at the men. They were short and tall, dark and fair, lean, stocky. He saw skin of all shades and hair of all colors, from Bennick's red-blond to a dark-skinned man with hair so black it seemed to suck up the daylight. The only things they seemed to have in common were their efficiency of movement and their quiet, unhurried discipline. "Brothers?"

"Brothers of the sword." Bennick pushed to his feet and looked down at him. His eyes smiled, the way Da's eyes used to smile. "We were all like you once, lad. Orphans. You can be our Brother, too. If you have what we need."

Jaumé looked up at him. Hope clenched tightly in his chest. "What's that?"

"Courage. Quickness. Toughness. You have all those, lad. It just remains to be seen whether you have enough." Bennick crouched. His face lost its good-humor, became serious. "The training's hard, lad. Very hard. But I think you're strong enough. And so does Nolt. You're a survivor, else you wouldn't have made it this far."

Jaumé stared back at Bennick. His heart was beating loudly. He knew he was on the brink of something momentous. "Training?"

"In Fith. Our home. We'll be going there after Ankeny." Bennick's eyes held his, steady and serious, blue. "Journey home with us, lad. Undergo the training. Become our Brother."

Home. Brother. The words resonated inside him, in time with the beating of his heart.

Bennick straightened. "You coming, lad?"

Jaumé took a deep breath. "Yes," he said.

CHAPTER SIXTY-NINE

"CHANGE WITH EBRIL," Cora told her the next morning. "And show Petrus and Gerit where the assassins are."

Innis nodded. She glanced around. Three soldiers had gone to retrieve the horses. Everyone else was gathered at the fire, checking weapons.

She walked across to the stack of supplies, pretending to rummage among the sacks as she eased her feet out of Justen's boots. Ebril came up alongside her, whistling between his teeth. Innis handed him the amulet. "Here."

Ebril kicked off his boots. His features wavered, solidified again, he grew taller, his hair became light brown instead of red. He bent to pull on Justen's boots. Innis cast a glance at the fire. No one was watching them. She slipped the baldric over her head and laid it on the sacks, then let herself shift back into her own shape. The forest green uniform grew baggy. She had to hold on to the trews to stop them sliding off her hips. "He's asked Justen to call him Harkeld," she told Ebril as he picked up the baldric.

Ebril stopped whistling. His eyebrows rose.

"When you're in private."

Ebril nodded, and headed back to the fire and Prince Harkeld. Petrus was already shedding his clothes. "Once the look-out's dead, one of us will fly back," Innis heard him tell Prince Tomas as he peeled off his shirt. "Don't move until then."

Tomas looked up from the arrows he was checking. "How are you going to kill him?"

"Tip him out of the cave," Petrus said. "One of us will wait at the bottom, in case he survives the fall."

Tomas nodded, and went back to his task.

Innis shifted. She stood for a moment in the nest of her shirt and trews, letting the sense of *bird* sink into her bones, then stretched her wings and leapt into the air.

The canyon floor dropped away beneath her. When she was level with the top of the cliffs, she glanced down. Cora was collecting their piles of clothing. In the distance she saw the soldiers returning with the horses. Petrus soared on her right, his feathers gleaming with the sheen of magic. Gerit was on her left.

They skimmed across the rocky plateau, gliding down into the mouth of the canyon from the north-east, out of the assassins' line of sight. Innis landed on an upthrusting spire of orange-red sandstone and shifted into the shape of a skylark. Alongside her, Gerit and Petrus did the same.

They flew through the forest of rock, flitting from outcrop to outcrop. Innis landed again. She shifted into a lizard and scuttled up and over a lip of rock. Ahead, in their cave, were the six assassins. They were eating. She caught the scent of dried meat, of cheese.

She gave Gerit and Petrus a few minutes to examine the surroundings, then sidled back over the lip of rock and became a sky lark again. They followed as she flew, as she landed, as she shifted into a lizard. Her tiny claws scraped on the sandstone as she scuttled up to a shaded vantage point. There, tucked in his cave, staring south down the canyon, was the seventh assassin.

They watched in silence for several minutes. Innis felt a twinge of sorrow as she observed the man. Shortly, he'd be dead. His eyes would never blink again, he'd never rub his bearded face again, never breathe again.

She pushed the emotion aside, annoyed with herself. Sorrow, for a Fithian assassin? The man would kill her without a second's hesitation—and certainly no regret.

She looked at Petrus. *Be careful.* But the words went unuttered; her lizard's tongue wasn't shaped for speech. She touched her shoulder to his.

Petrus nudged her back. He closed one reptilian eye in a wink and flicked his tail at her, a silent *Be gone.*

Innis backed away, leaving them to their task.

HARKELD DIDN'T OFFER to help saddle the horses; neither Tomas nor his men were easy in his presence any more. *And yet, today, they'll risk their lives for me.*

No, it wasn't him they risked their lives for; it was Lundegaard.

He looked down at the sand, scuffed it with the toe of his boot. Today, Tomas would try to keep him alive. But once the Ivek Curse was broken, what would happen? If they met, would Tomas try to kill him?

He glanced at Tomas, saddling the last of the horses. *You were a good friend.*

Harkeld turned away. Cora was assembling a bundle. He saw clothes, boots, a baldric and sword.

"Ach!" Justen said. "Cursed things!"

"Put out the fire," Harkeld said, turning to see the armsman stamping at something on the sand.

Justen bent, scooping up a handful of sand. "No scorpions on the Groot Islands, the All-Mother be praised." He cast the sand on the fire and bent again. "Although we have this fly that bites—" He uttered a yelp of pain and jerked back, shaking his hand.

"Scorpion?" Harkeld half-ran to his armsman's side and grabbed his hand.

Justen's face was screwed up in a grimace. "Son of a whore."

Cora looked up. "What's wrong?"

"Scorpion." Harkeld examined Justen's hand. The puncture wound was small, but the skin around it was rapidly reddening, swelling. "Does it hurt?"

"Like you wouldn't believe," Justen said through clenched teeth.

One of the archers, checking his bow beside the still smoldering fire, uttered a choked cry. He jerked back, beating frantically at his leg.

"Everyone away from the fire," Harkeld snapped. "And someone put the cursed thing out!"

HARKELD CROUCHED BESIDE his armsman. Justen was shivering. "Blankets," he said curtly, to one of Tomas's soldiers. The man ran to obey.

The archer who'd been stung groaned. He

stretched his leg out in front of him, grimacing, massaging his calf.

Tomas strode up. "What's wrong?"

Harkeld glanced at him. "Two scorpion stings."

Tomas swore under his breath. He looked at Cora. "Is it too late to call the shapeshifters back?"

She nodded.

"One of them's coming now," a soldier said, pointing north.

Harkeld followed the direction of the man's finger. The hawk had dark plumage. "It's the girl. Innis."

INNIS LANDED BESIDE the neatly stacked supplies. Ten saddled horses stood waiting; the rest were picketed alongside the river. Everyone was clustered around something on the ground. Cora broke away from the group and hurried towards her.

Innis shifted, reaching for a blanket. "What's wrong?"

"Ebril's been stung by a scorpion." Cora had lost her calm. Her voice was terse, urgent. "And one of the archers. Fly back and see if you can stop them."

Innis didn't bother to reply. She dropped the blanket. Magic surged through her. She pushed up into the sky almost before the shift was complete.

The campsite shrank rapidly behind her. At the mouth of the canyon she changed in mid-air to a skylark, plummeting for a moment, clawing with her wings to stay aloft. She sped towards the cave where the look-out hid, swooping over a fin of rock—

The cave was empty. Beneath it, on the rust-orange sand, the assassin lay sprawled. His legs were twisted at an impossible angle: broken. His face was raked by claws and his throat ripped out. Blood soaked into the sand, dark.

Petrus and Gerit stood beside the body.

Innis glided down and shifted.

"What's wrong?" Petrus asked. He wiped a smear of blood from his face with one hand.

"Ebril's been stung by a scorpion. And one of the archers."

Her words hung in the air for a moment, and then Gerit swore: "Son of a whore."

Petrus looked down at the dead man. "It's too late to stop now. We have to go on."

HARKELD SWUNG UP into the saddle and settled his baldric more comfortably across his back.

"Ready?" Tomas asked.

He nodded and looked back at his armsman. Justen lay wrapped in blankets. His face was pallid, shiny with sweat, twisted in a grimace of pain.

"Then let's go."

They left at a slow trot—Tomas, five soldiers, Cora, himself—riding in silence towards Ner. The canyon curved, turning north. Harkeld glanced back once, and then kept his gaze grimly ahead. Justen had ridden at his side for the last month. Now Cora rode there. He felt unarmed, naked, exposed.

A low moan accompanied them, teased from the cliffs by the wind. Above, riding the currents effortlessly, was the dark hawk. Seeing her up there was oddly comforting. It made him feel marginally safer.

Outcrops of rock pushed up from the sand

ahead, pillars and walls of red-orange sandstone. They followed the hawk, making their way silently between the towering monoliths. A second hawk joined her. Petrus, his underwings and breast pale. All around them, the rock sang its eerie song.

Harkeld's skin prickled. Somewhere in this maze were six assassins. The sounds the horses made—the muffled *clop* of their hooves in the sand, the faint jingle of the harnesses—seemed to shout their presence.

They skirted a long ridge of rock, passed from shade into sunlight again, and suddenly the desert opened out before them, an undulating orange sea stretching east, north, west.

Directly ahead, perhaps half a mile distant, a broken tower jutted from the sand. The river curved away to the east, hugging the cliffs. North and east, several miles into the desert, a vast hump of orange rock squatted in the sand.

"The catacombs are inside that?" he asked Cora.

She nodded. "Yes. But don't worry; it's daylight. The corpses will be dormant."

The pale hawk peeled off, heading back into the maze of sandstone. Harkeld followed it with his eyes for a moment. *Be careful.*

GERIT WAS WHERE Petrus had left him: in lizard form, watching the six assassins in their cave.

Petrus glided past him—above the men's line of sight—and swooped down to land behind a fin of sandstone. A moment later, a skylark flitted down alongside him. The bird folded its wings and shifted. Gerit. "They've passed?"

"Halfway to the catacombs by now," Petrus said. "How shall we work this? Sneak into the cave and shift into lions—"

Gerit snorted. "You want to kill as many as possible, that's not the way to do it."

"But we'd have the element of surprise—"

"For all of one second. Fithians won't run screaming from lions, they'll attack. While you're ripping out one's throat, the others will be slicing you up for steak."

"Yes, but—"

"Less than a minute, we'd both be dead. And most of them would still be alive."

Petrus closed his mouth.

"We need to get them out of the cave. Split them up." Gerit crouched and began to draw in the sand with swift, jabbing strokes of his forefinger. "Here's where they are. And here—" he drew several shapes, "this is what they can see. I'll walk past, right here." He gouged deep into the sand, marking it. "Let them see me."

"But a throwing star—"

"It's too far. Out of range." His tone was curt, authoritative. Petrus heard the unspoken message: *I'm senior to you. Don't challenge my leadership in this.*

Petrus nodded, his face carefully neutral.

"They see me," Gerit said. "They rush down. But all they'll find are footprints. I reckon they'll split up to look for me."

"And we attack them."

"Once they've separated, yes. We can hunt them down one by one."

Petrus frowned down at the drawing in the sand. "What if they leave a guard in the cave?"

Gerit shrugged. "Throw him out, like we did the other one."

Petrus studied the marks in the sand. *We need more of us to make this work.* "We could thin their numbers first. Wait until one of them leaves to take a piss or—"

"You got water to drink while we wait?"

Petrus was silent. He was abruptly aware of how dry his throat was. Gerit was right; if they waited much longer, they'd need water.

"Our task is to kill as many of them as we can," Gerit said brusquely. "And this—" he jabbed his finger into the sand, "is the best way."

PETRUS WATCHED THE assassins from less than three yards away, his lizard's body pressed flat to the sandstone. One was on sentry duty, a sword laid over his knees, looking outwards. The others played a game with small pebbles.

The sentry stiffened. "Hsst!" He pointed west.

All six men watched intently as Gerit crossed a stretch of sand, perhaps a hundred yards distant. He was shading his eyes with his hand, stumbling as he walked.

"Shapeshifter?" one of them said, when Gerit had disappeared from sight. "He's naked."

No other words were spoken between the men. They seemed to understand each other by curt gestures. The five who'd been at ease snatched up their weapons and clambered out of the cave, passing within a few feet of Petrus, pulling themselves up onto the top of the outcrop and then running soundlessly in their soft leather boots down the long sloping ridge to the sand. The sentry remained behind, his attention fixed unwaveringly on the view of rock and sand in front of him.

Petrus waited until the five men had vanished from sight, then he scuttled up behind the lone assassin. He paused for a moment, filling his mind with what he had to do: toss the man out of the cave, fly down, shift into a lion and finish him off.

Easy, he told himself, trying to believe it.

He took a deep breath and gathered his magic. The cave shrank around him as he shifted.

The man must have sensed his presence. He half-turned, his mouth opening in surprise. Petrus tackled the assassin, grabbing him around the chest, heaving him out of the cave.

One moment he was teetering in the cave mouth, wrestling with the Fithian, the next he was falling. He grabbed for his magic, but before he could shift, he'd hit the ground. The assassin's weight drove him hard into the sand. Petrus distinctly felt his left thighbone snap.

The assassin rolled off him and sprang to his feet. A throwing star appeared in his hand.

Petrus shifted blindly, without any thought of what he'd become. The spinning blades sliced through the air a foot above him.

What am I?

The answer came as he huddled in the sand: a lizard.

The assassin towered above him. Petrus saw the man's foot lift, saw the sole of a boot stamping down on him.

Again, he shifted in panic, without thought,

swelling in size, knocking the man off his feet. Sharp, curving tusks thrust out on either side of his face, a long trunk hung where his nose had been.

An oliphant.

The assassin scrambled backwards, scuttling like a crab on the sand. Petrus lurched forward, raised his right foot and stamped down, crushing the man's ribcage. Bones splintered and snapped beneath his weight. The man's mouth opened. He uttered a sound of agony. With it came blood.

Petrus raised his foot again. The assassin didn't move. He lay crushed on the sand.

Petrus lowered his foot. He swayed, steadying himself with his trunk. Pain and dizziness washed over him. He sank down on the sand. For a moment he lay, panting, then he shifted back to his own shape.

By the All-Mother. His leg—

He gritted his teeth in agony and reached for his magic, placing his hands on his left thigh, letting the magic run from his fingers and burrow under his skin, through flesh and muscle, along bone and blood vessel.

There: a jagged break in his thighbone. The sharp edges of bone had speared deep into his muscles and sliced his artery. Blood spurted with each beat of his heart.

Petrus hastily pinched the artery closed with his magic. He glanced around. Nothing moved except sand blown in eddies by the wind. The only sound was a muted wailing coming from the rock.

Hurry!

It took magic to persuade the spasming muscles to

release their grip, and brute strength to pull the bone into place. Petrus was sweating, close to vomiting, by the time the edges of bone slid gratingly together. Panting, he glanced around again. No assassins, no Gerit.

With the bone back in place, he was able to patch the artery together more effectively. It was a crude repair, thick and clumsy, but it would keep him alive. His leg needed more—the bone was still broken, the muscles still deeply sliced—but there was no time.

He turned his head at the sound of running footsteps. A man burst around the end of an outcrop, some twenty yards distant. Not Gerit; one of the assassins.

The man skidded to a halt. He reached for something at his waist.

Petrus shifted into the shape of a hawk and lifted clumsily up from the sand. His left leg trailed, making him list. A throwing star whistled past, clanging as it struck sandstone, almost hitting him on its rebound.

He clawed at the air with his wings, hauling himself higher. Another throwing star sliced towards him. He veered—too slow—the whirling blades actually touched him, shearing feathers from his right wing—a puff of white—making him lurch in the air. And then he was out of range.

Five men stood on the sand looking up at him. His feathers drifted down towards them, spinning in the breeze.

HE FOUND GERIT lying on a ledge twenty yards up an outcrop of sandstone, a bloody slash down his hip, another across his chest.

Petrus landed awkwardly. He waited for a wave of pain to pass before he shifted. Something warm trickled down his right arm: blood. He had a shallow wound from shoulder to elbow where the throwing star had sheared the feathers from his wing.

He ignored it, leaning forward to examine Gerit's chest. The gash was so deep he could see white rib bones. "What happened?"

Gerit grunted. "I almost had one, *ouch*—"

"Sorry." He touched the edges of the wound again, exploring with his magic. It looked much worse than it was: messy, but not life-threatening.

"One of them must have doubled back. I only just got away. My hand..." Gerit grimaced. "If you could do something—"

Petrus turned his attention from the chest wound. Gerit's right arm lay at an awkward angle, his hand half-hidden in shadow. "What—?" And then he saw: a throwing star was embedded in Gerit's hand. "By the All-Mother, how did you fly with that?"

"Didn't," Gerit said, through gritted teeth. "Bastard got me when I was up here."

He'd heard Fithians could throw their stars around corners, that they could hit targets they couldn't even see—but he hadn't believed it until now. Petrus shuffled closer. The throwing star pinned Gerit's hand to the sandstone; one of the blades was buried in the rock.

A sound made him cock his head. Hoofbeats, echoing among the forest of sandstone. *We should have set loose their horses before we did anything else.*

"How many did you kill?" Gerit asked.

"One."

"Five left." Gerit pushed up on his left elbow. "Tomas's men haven't a chance! Get me loose. Hurry!"

Petrus took hold of the throwing star with one hand and Gerit's wrist with the other. A quick wrench and both blade and hand came free. Gerit grunted, his face twisting in pain.

Petrus examined the wound quickly. One blade of the throwing star was embedded to the hilt in Gerit's palm, the razor-sharp point protruding bloodily from the back of his hand. The other four blades fanned out like grotesque metal fingers.

"Take it out! Hurry! We have to—"

"It's not that simple." Bones and nerves and tendons were sheared, not just blood vessels.

"But—"

"You won't be able to fight. I doubt you'll be able to fly. Not unless I spend a lot of time fixing the damage."

Gerit stared at him grimly. "How much time?"

"Hours."

Gerit's jaw clenched, then he jerked his head north, towards the desert. "Leave it, then," he said. "Go!"

Petrus nodded. He released Gerit's hand. He reached for his magic again, not the gentle magic of healing, but the more vigorous magic he needed for shapeshifting. It came slowly, grudgingly.

"Hurry!" Gerit said.

Shifting was a strain. Everything went gray for a moment. Petrus blinked and shook his head, taking a moment to orient himself. Then he hopped awkwardly to the edge of the ledge and spread his wings.

"Be careful!"

Petrus launched himself from the ledge, catching the updraft. For a few seconds he glided, and then he began to flap his wings.

The broken leg, the missing feathers, made him list drunkenly. He headed for the desert, crawling through the air, barely making headway, his muscles straining. *I'm going to be too late.*

CHAPTER SEVENTY

BY THE TIME they were halfway across the desert, the wailing was no longer audible. Silence surrounded them. Silence, and the muffled sound of horses' hooves on sand. Harkeld watched the sandstone mount loom larger and larger. A strange sensation grew in his chest, as if he was holding his breath. *You're afraid*, he accused himself.

Ahead, the dark hawk reached the outcrop. He saw it soar up, a tiny shape outlined against the blue sky, and then swoop and vanish inside the dark gash of the cave.

Harkeld unslung his waterskin and gulped a mouthful of lukewarm water. What was there to fear? Nothing. All he had to do was place his hand on a stone, spill a little blood.

He glanced to his left, where Justen usually rode, recalling the armsman's words: *I don't care whether you're a mage or not, sire. You're the one who cares.*

Justen wouldn't be so imperturbable, so cheerfully indifferent, if *he* were found to be a witch.

The remembered sensation of flames licking over his skin, under his skin, made panic spurt inside him. *It will never happen again*, Harkeld vowed silently. *Ever*.

But it had happened once—fire bursting from him—and he'd had no control over it. No control at all.

Harkeld re-stoppered the waterskin. If he could cut out the part of him that was diseased with witchcraft, he would. Anything, to avoid the feeling that flames ate him from the inside out, that he was burning alive.

An idea burst into his mind, so bright, so dazzling, that he was momentarily blinded by it. He blinked. The desert came into focus again—the orange drifts of sand, the outcrop looming ahead, the slash of darkness at its base—but behind those things was memory: a campfire in the forest, rain dripping from trees. *We strip them of their magic*, Dareus had said. *It's one of the tasks we're charged with.*

The witches could remove the magic from his blood, the fire, the flames.

Relief surged inside him. It was suddenly easier to breathe.

Harkeld slung the waterskin over his shoulder and glanced back. He narrowed his eyes. "There's someone behind us."

Tomas turned in his saddle. "Who—"

Riding hard towards them, a couple of miles distant, were horsemen. Sand puffed up from the horses' hooves.

"Assassins," Cora snapped. "Gallop!"

THE CORPSES WERE resting uneasily in their niches. Innis heard them stir, heard little rustlings as she completed a circuit of the catacombs. But her owl's eyes saw no movement; the creatures weren't prowling the dark, narrow aisles of the catacombs. Satisfied, she began gliding back towards daylight.

Shouts drifted in from outside, faint and urgent.

Innis flew faster. She swept down one of the aisles, stone rising high on either side, and burst out into daylight.

She saw it as an owl does, in dull colors and shades of gray. Horses and men milled in front of the cavern as Tomas shouted orders. The two archers ran forward, readying their bows, quivers slung over their shoulders. A soldier followed, carrying an armful of arrows.

Riding across the desert, a low plume of sand billowing behind them, were five horsemen.

Cora crouched in the cave entrance, a litter of bundles around her. She looked up. "Innis! Come here!"

Innis swooped down to land, shifting into her own shape before her feet had fully touched the sand. The world suddenly became full of color. "What happened? Petrus—"

"We don't know," Cora said tersely. She thrust an armful of clothes at Innis. "Dress! You're to go with the prince."

Was Petrus dead? Innis scrambled into her underbreeches and trews. Distress tightened her throat, making it difficult to breathe. She pulled the shirt over her head. Her fingers fumbled with the buttons.

"Archers, ready your bows!" Tomas shouted.

She turned her head and watched as the archers nocked their first arrows. Spare arrows stood in the sand alongside them, thrusting up like the spines of a porcupine, ready to be snatched up and used once their quivers were empty. Behind the archers, the swordsmen waited with their blades bared.

Prince Harkeld stood in the shadow of the cavern mouth, watching the horsemen approach. His sword was unsheathed, clenched in his hand.

Innis shoved her feet into the boots. *He can't be dead. Not Petrus!* Tears filled her eyes. She blinked them back.

"Sword," Cora said curtly.

Innis took the baldric, settling it hastily across her back.

"You know what to do?" Cora peeled open a cloth-wrapped bundle. Her plait fell forward over her shoulder. She flicked it back impatiently. "His blood and his hand on the stone."

"Aren't you coming—"

"I'm needed here."

The noise of the horses was louder. Innis glanced up. The assassins would soon be within bow-shot.

"Torches," Cora said.

Her attention jerked back to the bundle Cora had unwrapped. Pieces of wood lay on the cloth, stout and strong, bound with pitch-soaked rags at one end. Cora lit two with a snap of her fingers. "Hurry!"

Innis snatched up the flaming torches. "Sire!"

Prince Harkeld thrust his sword into its scabbard and ran towards her. "One of the hawks is here."

Innis looked up. A pale-breasted hawk glided towards them, lopsided, trailing one leg.

"Go!" Cora said, pushing her.

Prince Harkeld grabbed one of the torches. He headed into the cave.

Innis followed at a run, passing under the broad overhang of sandstone. As darkness enveloped her, she glanced back. Petrus had landed. He half-lay on the sand, panting and naked. One of his legs was clearly broken. "Give me a bow," she heard him say. "And arrows."

"Where's the stone?" Harkeld asked. Everything beyond the flare of his torch was as black as ink.

"In the middle," the witch said, pushing ahead of him. "Follow me!"

They plunged into what seemed like a canyon, walls of sandstone towering on either side. The floor was littered with broken stone and mortar. Tombs surrounded them, tier upon tier, their occupants exposed—gray-white bone, parched-leather skin.

The witch stopped so suddenly that he ran into her.

Harkeld grabbed her shoulder to steady himself, and released it. "What?"

"Shh!"

He held his breath and listened. He heard his heartbeat, heard shouts echoing from outside, heard—

Furtive rustling sounds.

"Is that—" The words dried on his tongue as, ahead of them, something moved. A skeleton groped its way from a tomb and stood unsteadily, extending bony legs. Its head turned towards them, blind.

"They're waking up," Innis said. "They know you're here. Get back!" She turned, pushing him.

They ran, stumbling, back the way they'd come. Withered hands snatched at them as they passed.

The black became gray. They were almost at the entrance. "Stop!" The witch grabbed the back of his shirt.

"What—"

"We need to climb the wall. It's flat on top. We'll be safe up there."

He looked up. Sandstone loomed above him, more than twice his height. Three tiers of tombs were cut into it. Inside them, corpses stirred.

Shouted voices came from the entrance, and the thunder of hooves.

Harkeld hastily laid down his torch. He bent, cupping his hands. "Climb!"

"No, you first!"

They matched stares for a brief second.

"Sire, you're more important—"

"Fire when in range!" Tomas shouted outside.

The witch dropped her torch and crouched. "Hurry!"

Harkeld placed his foot in her cupped hands and allowed her to heave him up. His fingers scrabbled for purchase, catching on the lower lip of the topmost tomb. He found a foothold in the next tomb down and hauled himself up. Brittle bones crunched beneath his boots. He groped for the top of the wall, shoving his knee in the uppermost tomb. Movement skittered across his thigh as bony fingers plucked at his trews.

Harkeld hauled himself up on top of the wall. He looked over the edge. He saw Innis's pale face, her dark eyes. She held up one of the torches. "Your belt!"

He removed it hastily, threaded the tongue back through the buckle to make a loop, and dangled it down. Light bobbed and flared around him as he pulled the torch up. He could suddenly see the top of the wall—as wide and flat as a road, stretching into the darkness.

He thrust the torch aside and lowered the belt again. Innis reached up with the second torch flaming in her hand.

"Leave it!" he cried, seeing movement flickering at the edges of the ring of torchlight. "Climb!"

One of the corpses stumbled forward as he spoke, reaching for her. Innis turned and struck at it with the torch, slashing like a sword. In the flare of light he saw a gaping, gap-toothed mouth and leathery skin stretched over a gaunt skull. The corpse had been a woman; long, brittle hair hung down her back.

"Climb!" he shouted again.

Innis dropped the torch and grabbed the belt, heaving herself up, stretching to get her foot on the edge of the first tomb.

Harkeld helped as best he could, hauling on the belt as she climbed. More corpses lurched into the circle of light cast by the fallen torch. They reached gnarled hands after her.

When Innis was close enough, he grabbed her wrist and pulled her up. She lay for a moment on her belly, catching her breath, her legs dangling over the edge. "Thank you—" She uttered a choked cry and began to kick. The corpse in the topmost tomb clung to her legs. "Get it off me!"

He grabbed her around the waist and hauled her fully on top of the wall. The corpse came too, its arms clasped around her legs. Its teeth snapped savagely at him.

Harkeld kicked, breaking the creature's neck, sending the head ricocheting down to smash on the ground. He kicked again. The torso disintegrated in a cloud of dust and shards of bone. Only the arms clung to her now, the skeletal fingers digging into her trews.

He ripped them off, snapping the brittle bones, sending the pieces spinning down towards the torch burning on the floor.

"They're wearing mail," he heard one of the soldiers cry outside.

"Aim for the horses!" Tomas shouted.

The witch pushed to her feet. "We must hurry!"

INNIS LED, HALF-RUNNING, holding the torch aloft. Their footsteps echoed back from the cavern roof. Dark chasms yawned on either side, filled with the sound of corpses moving.

Urgency pushed her to run faster. Her thoughts were full of Petrus, Cora, the two archers standing bravely to confront the Fithians.

The canyons on either side became narrower. Innis slowed. "We must be near the end."

A dozen more paces and their path ended abruptly, dropping away like a cliff. In front of them, darkness swallowed the torchlight.

Innis crouched at the edge, holding the torch out. The space ahead was filled with milling corpses. In the dim corona of torchlight, it was a vast sea of gray and brown, surging, moving in eddies and currents, with the shadow of the Ivek Curse floating blackly on top.

Prince Harkeld crouched alongside her. "Where's the anchor stone?"

"In the middle."

The prince was silent for a moment, while the sea of corpses heaved and rustled below them, then he said: "How do we get there? Could an oliphant—"

"There are too many of them." Scores, she could cope with, perhaps even hundreds—but this cavern must hold thousands of tightly-packed corpses. They'd overwhelm her, as a swarm of ants overwhelmed a single beetle.

Innis chewed on her lower lip. A strong fire mage could clear a path to the stone.

She turned her head and looked at the prince. She knew what his reaction would be if she asked him to use his magic.

So, don't ask; tell him. You're a Sentinel. Act like one.

Innis took a deep breath and spoke: "Sire, you must use your magic."

HARKELD JERKED HIS head around. "No," he said flatly.

"You have to, sire. It's the only way."

Harkeld stood. "We'll get Cora."

"She's fighting." The witch scrambled to her feet. "She may even be dead by now!"

He turned back the way they'd come. Innis's hand gripped his forearm, halting him. "You need to burn a path."

"No."

"You're strong enough to do it." She gestured at the milling sea of corpses. "The way you burned that assassin, you're far stronger than Cora—"

"No!" It was a yell.

"You're afraid of it." She met his eyes, her gaze oddly compassionate.

Harkeld shook his head. It wasn't fear, it was terror. A cold sweat of panic broke out on his skin at the memory of fire bursting from him, coursing through his bones and arteries, hissing over his skin—

"You can do it, sire."

He shook his head again. *I can't.*

The compassion left her eyes. Her mouth became scornful. "I thought you were braver than this."

Harkeld inhaled sharply through his nose. "Are you calling me a coward?"

"Isn't that what you are?"

The words were like slaps across his face. Painful, because they were true. He inhaled again, clenching his hands more tightly, rage mingling with terror inside him. "I'm not a coward."

"Then do it!"

The rage flared more brightly inside him, and with it, the feeling of fire, igniting in his chest. Harkeld shoved her aside and stepped to the edge of the wall. The sight of the corpses seemed to fuel the fire gathering under his skin, as if the witchcraft inside him recognized what it had to do. His skin felt as if it were smoking, his ribcage as if it would burst from the heat and the fire contained inside him. In panic, in terror, he thrust his right hand outwards. He tried to visualize what he wanted: a path, burned through the corpses below. "Burn!"

Flame roared from his palm, incandescent, searing.

*   *   *

INNIS STUMBLED BACK, dropping the torch, falling to her knees, shielding her face with her arms. Her hair felt as if it were on fire, her clothes as though they were on the point of igniting. Roaring flames filled the space ahead of them, too bright to look at. She squeezed her eyes shut. Her exposed skin felt as if it was stretching, bursting, burning.

The roaring seemed to last forever, punctuated by sharp retorts as bones splintered in the fierce heat. When it died, silence rang in her ears, almost deafening. Cautiously she lowered her arms and opened her eyes. Prince Harkeld was also on his knees, looking outwards.

He'd done much, much more than clear a path. The sea of corpses was gone. The cavern was carpeted with their charred remains. Fires burned fitfully and greasy smoke rose up.

The prince turned his head and looked at her. His face was ashen.

Innis swallowed. *I'm sorry I made you do that.* She pushed to her feet, grabbing the torch. "Come! We must hurry!"

They scrambled down from the wall, dropping the last few feet to land in a hot pile of cinders and ashes. Innis ran, skirting the largest of the fires, plowing through the charred bodies. Heat burned through the soles of her boots, through her trews. "Here, sire! The anchor stone!"

A SMOKING SKELETON lay across the anchor stone. The witch tried to push it aside with the torch, but the skeleton disintegrated into ash and embers. She swept them away with her sleeve.

Harkeld stepped closer. He looked down at the stone. He was shaking, trembling. Panic sparked and twisted inside him. He tried to concentrate on what was in front of him—not the fires, not the smoke and the burning corpses, not the flames that had roared through him. This was the anchor stone? It looked so ordinary, a lump of black basalt, pitted with tiny holes.

The witch put down the torch. She drew her sword. The blade slid from the scabbard with a sleek, hissing sound. She took a pace away from the stone and stood facing outwards, guarding him.

Harkeld drew his dagger. Tiny spurts of flame still seemed to sizzle under his skin. His hands shook so violently that he couldn't hold the blade steady enough to cut. Memory of the rush and crackle of fire roaring through him, bursting from his skin, was vivid.

He inhaled a deep, shuddering breath, trying to push back the suffocating panic, trying to hold his hands steady, and sliced across his left palm. There was a sharp sting of pain, then blood welled from the cut.

The blood of a Rutersvard prince. The blood of a witch.

He laid his hand on the anchor stone. The basalt was hot to touch, almost scorching. "How long?" His voice was hoarse, as if he'd been screaming.

"I don't know. A minute?"

Harkeld flattened his hand against the basalt. He counted the seconds in his mind. His palm felt like it was burning, blistering.

"There are more coming." The witch was tense.

The stone radiated heat, but at the same time it

seemed to suck at his palm, as if the tiny pores in the basalt tried to inhale his blood.

Harkeld counted ten more seconds and lifted his hand. He had to wrench slightly, as if his skin had adhered to the stone.

"Sire?"

He looked at his palm. It was pink from the stone's heat, smeared with blood. "Done," he said.

A few drops of blood lay on the anchor stone. As he watched, they sank into the basalt. In a few seconds, the blood was gone.

Harkeld wiped the dagger on his shirt and sheathed it. He clenched his hand to stop the flow of blood and turned away from the stone. The witch was right: more corpses were emerging from the shadows. Not just one or two, but dozens, scores, stumbling through the smoldering remains of their fellows, converging on them.

Fear kicked in his chest. He stepped up alongside Innis and drew his own sword, gripping it with both hands. The flames engraved on the blade seemed to dance in the firelight.

"You must use your magic again, sire."

Harkeld gripped the sword more tightly. He felt blood leak from the cut on his hand. "No."

"Sire!" she said fiercely. "You must—"

He turned his head at sound behind him. A piece of basalt broke off the anchor stone and tumbled to the floor.

The witch stopped speaking.

Another piece broke off, and then with a faint, crumbling sigh the anchor stone disintegrated into dust and fragments of stone.

As the stone crumbled, so did the corpses, falling where they stood, disintegrating as the witchcraft that had animated them departed.

For a long moment he and the witch stood side by side in silence, then Innis resheathed her sword. She glanced at him, her dark eyes reflecting the firelight. "It's done," she said.

Harkeld didn't reply. He slid his sword into his scabbard and turned away from her.

"Your hand," she said, reaching to take it. "Let me heal—"

Harkeld snatched his hand from her grasp. "No." He bent and grabbed the torch and strode back the way they'd come—crushing embers and charred bones beneath his boots. He plunged into one of the aisles, his pace quickening as he scrambled over the rubble of rock and skeletons littering the ground. He had to get away from smoldering fires and the choking smell of smoke, away from the memory of burning alive.

"Let me go first," the witch said, as they approached the sliver of daylight.

Harkeld didn't look at her, didn't slow down, didn't acknowledge her words.

Hard fingers gripped his arm, halting him.

He swung around to face her, his hand clenching into a fist. His panic, his terror, transformed into fury. "Don't touch me!"

She pushed past him. "Let me go first. We don't know if the assassins are still there."

I hope they are, he thought savagely. *I hope they kill you.*

"Innis!" A female voice called from the entrance. "Prince Harkeld! Are you there?"

*   *   *

INNIS BLINKED AS they emerged into daylight. The sky was an unbearably bright blue, the sand a dazzling orange. Bodies lay sprawled on that orange sand: men, horses.

She saw one of the archers lying with his arms outstretched and a throwing star protruding from the top of his head in grotesque mimicry of a cockerel; she saw an assassin's body, scorched and smoking.

Where's Petrus?

"There you are, Innis!" Cora cried, her voice high with relief. "Over here! We need you!"

Innis hurried to where Cora knelt beside a soldier. His leg was laid open from hip to knee, exposing muscle and bone. Prince Tomas crouched on the man's other side. A cut slashed across his cheek and half his right ear was gone. Blood flowed from these wounds, but otherwise he seemed unharmed. Another assassin lay smoldering on the sand nearby.

Innis knelt hastily, placing her hands on either side of the gaping wound.

"Will he be all right?" Prince Tomas asked.

"Yes." She glanced up, seeking Petrus, her gaze jerking from one sprawled body to the next: soldier, assassin, soldier, soldier, assassin—

There.

Petrus sat with his back to the outcrop. He was healing himself, his hands gripping his left thigh, his face furrowed in concentration. The last assassin lay a few yards from him, an arrow jutting from his throat.

Petrus looked up and caught her gaze. "You all right?"

She nodded.

"The anchor stone?" Cora asked.

Innis glanced at the prince, remembering the roar of flames, remembering the expression on his face afterwards: a mingling of terror, panic and despair.

Prince Harkeld's mouth tightened. He turned away and looked out across the desert. His back was rigid, his hands clenched at his sides.

"The anchor stone is destroyed," Innis said. She looked down at the soldier's leg. She was aware of the man's fear—not of being touched by a witch, but of dying.

As if in response, fear kicked in her own chest. One anchor stone had crumbled into dust, but two more remained. *How many of us will die before Ivek's curse is broken?*

Foreboding prickled over her scalp. Her skin tightened in a shiver. "You'll be fine," Innis told the soldier, as she reached for her magic and began to heal him.

HERE ENDS BOOK ONE OF THE CURSED KINGDOMS TRILOGY

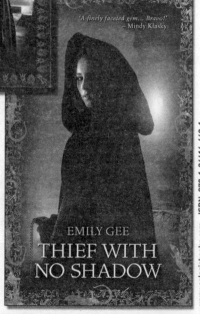